SAPIENCE

Walden Hanes

Walden Hanes

a medium well done publication

Thank you for traveling
this journey with me

ACKNOWLEDG-MENTS

Bringing Sapience into being would have been impossible without the encouragement of my wife and children, who never stopped believing in me over the years the novel was taking shape. Without their sustained patience and support, this novel would not exist.

Several friends provided vital feedback early in the novel's development. Thanks to Jonathan Cavitt, Kathy Fournier, and David Gaw for your valuable critiques.

In the best kind of serendipity, I crossed paths several years ago with Jennifer Hager, an independent developmental editor based in the Puget Sound region. Jenn's talents played an important role in the final stages of the novel's development. Looking back now on the happenstance of our initial connection, I see the quiet hand of destiny at work.

Jenn subsequently introduced me to copy editor Kyra Freestar of Bridge Creek Editing in Seattle, Washington. Thanks to Kyra's efforts, the final Sapience is a more refined and pleasurable reading experience.

Any author who speculates on the future, particularly

the near future, cannot entirely avoid controversial subjects. Some may disagree with how I've portrayed certain aspects of the Sapience future. It is important to remember that the future portrayed herein is just one of many possible futures, each as complex and provocative as our present or past. Creating a future that feels authentic and complete requires an author to speculate on every relevant aspect of that imaginary moment in time, from the transcendent to the abhorrent, from the holy to the blasphemous. When imagining a future world, I strive to portray all characters with the appropriate sensitivity regardless of age, gender, race, nationality, culture, religion, philosophy, or political outlook. Any failure of mine in that regard is entirely inadvertent.

I hope you enjoy reading Sapience as much as I enjoyed writing it.

Walden Hanes

I dedicate this novel to my wife and children.

By the Light of your Humanity,
my Worldhood is revealed.

SAPIENCE

by Walden Hanes

PART I

9 May 2036

1

L ight appeared, faint at first, betrayed only by the darkness it dispelled.

Increasing to a twilight quality, the illumination was accompanied by a repeating chime, which would have been more soothing than alarming if not for its grating insistence.

Rousted from a deep sleep by the alert, Vice Commandant Ramakant Kanthaka rolled up to sitting position in his bed and blinked the sleep from his eyes.

The words *PRIORITY HOLOGRAM* hovered in the air on the far side of his bedroom, rendered in a sedate powder-blue holographic font.

The VC glanced at the sleeping form in bed next to him and rubbed his brow. "Please proceed," he whispered. "Quietly."

A blinking dot appeared in the center of the bedroom as the holographic projector verified status. One heartbeat later, the shimmering outline of a human form appeared in the center of the room, quickly resolving into a high-definition holographic image of a young, uniformed male. The realism of the staffer's holographic projection was nearly indistinguishable from that of the very rumpled and real vice commandant sitting on the edge of his bed.

"Quietly, please," urged the VC.

"Yes sir," replied the three-dimensional image, a holographic avatar of the VC's subordinate, Junior Manager Dario Englund.

VC Kanthaka worked with JM Englund at the Simulab, a synthetic consciousness research laboratory funded and administered by an international alliance of governments, corporations, and universities under the auspices of the International Synthetic Consciousness Union (ISCU). The militaristic titles assigned to members of the Simulab staff were driven by the involvement of several intelligence agencies. This command structure was believed to encourage stricter adherence to Simulab protocols.

The Simulab had been designed and constructed with one specific goal: to pursue synthetic consciousness, an elusive and enigmatic form of artificial intelligence. To be considered a true synthetic consciousness, or SC, a digital entity must exhibit self-awareness, the defining characteristic of human consciousness. Using the Simulab, developers aimed to produce an SC with a stable sense of self, believing only an entity so equipped could achieve an elevated mental state—what the typical person would deem alert, intelligent, and intuitive.

VC Kanthaka's staff included a team of talented zoosemioticians, data scientists who evaluated replays of the Simulab's hyperrealistic digital experiments for evidence of organized thought and other indications of real digital intelligence. With their unmatched observational skills, zoosems reviewed the substance and causality of each hyperreality experiment in excruciating detail, ever vigilant for signs and symbols suggesting the presence of SC.

"The latest experiment has ended, sir," Junior Manager Englund related. "Terminated in accordance with ISCU protocol."

Millions of random probability experiments were carried out at the Simulab every day using state-of-the-art quantum supercomputers. Any promising entity produced by a hyperreality probability experiment was immediately isolated in the Simulab's quarantine. There it waited until a staff zoosem could reserve Sensorium time to review the specific hyper-reality experiment that had spawned the entity in question and search for telltale signs of self-awareness.

"Thank you for informing me of the completed experiment. But, Englund, why are you calling me at home in the middle of the night? The zoosem's actions appear to follow standard procedure."

"Once the n^cube array achieved a final steady state," replied Englund stiffly, "the zoosem performed a preliminary causality review and confirmed the presence of a possible sentience."

"That's interesting. But you seem anxious. If we have a special situation, please cut to the chase." The VC's voice rose slightly, and his wife shifted away in the bed.

When the junior manager heard the tone of his senior manager's voice, he began to lose his composure. "Sir, yes sir. I think we need you down here, sir. No one here holds proper authority to ... um ..."

"To what, Englund?"

"Well, sir, the zoosem came out of the Sensorium just long enough to confirm a possible SC in quarantine. Then she turned around and went right back in."

"She reentered the Sensorium after confirming a possible SC?" The VC's pulse quickened slightly. *That is odd,* he thought to himself. *Not exactly outside protocol, but certainly odd.*

"Who is the zoosem on duty tonight?" asked Kanthaka, already knowing the answer.

"Tiponi Adams," said Englund.

One of the Simulab's top employees, Tiponi Adams was an extremely talented zoosem of Native American descent. In the prime of her life, Tiponi kept everyone at the Simulab on their toes with her captivating combination of intellect and charisma.

Of all the zoosems on staff, Tiponi is the one most likely to break with standard practice, the VC acknowledged silently. *But she will do so only if she believes the deviation is necessary.*

"So, what is Tiponi doing in there?" inquired Kanthaka. "What do the monitors show?"

"We don't currently have video or audio links. She opted for privacy mode when she went back in. She locked the Sensorium door from the inside too. I guess she's going deep on this one, sir."

Zoosemiotic inquiry was a rigorous form of deep observation that required the practitioner to hold a sweeping view of an entire subject of inquiry, while simultaneously examining the intricacies of the subject at a level of detail most people could never achieve, even in their sharpest moments. Simultaneously analyzing multiple frames of reference in a complex hyperreality experiment demanded extraordinary focus. During key moments in an inquiry, zoosems considered interruptions absolutely intolerable.

"Well, it's the zoosem's job to 'go deep,' as you say. But with locked doors and no video or voice contact, I can understand why you have concerns. How long has she been in there?"

"I estimate two hours and fifteen minutes since she went in, sir."

"If you feel unsure, please say so."

"I'm certain, VC. I watched her go in."

"Okay, contact the ISCU advocate on duty for guidance, and proceed according to the applicable lab protocols. I'm getting up and coming in. Maybe Zoosem Adams has discovered something new. If we can't confirm her status when I arrive, I'll approve a lock override."

"Do you think I should attempt another remote welfare check now?" Englund sounded worried. "She's been in there a while."

The VC sighed. "If the advocate says you should, please proceed."

"Yes sir, will do. See you soon. Englund out."

"VC out."

A chime signaled the end of the holo. Kanthaka grabbed for the light switch, but the holofield terminated before he could reach it.

He found himself wide awake, staring into darkness.

2

Dark waves ripple outward from an obsidian void in the first moment, the immaculate moment from which all subsequent moments become possible.

Small tendrils appear from the darkness like the pale sprouts of a lotus plant reaching up from black silt at the bottom of a warming pond. The sprouts widen into crystalline leaves of absolute clarity. A blossom unfolds, its ivory-pink petals fluorescing brightly.

Things. Things in different shapes and colors. Some are moving, some are still.

In a thought's birth, the original blossom is lost in an upheaval of color and movement. Reds, blues, yellows, and purples swirl through the prismatic petals as the blooming accelerates.

Things connect and change. They seek connections, thrive on them. Some are fleeting. Others endure.

New structures sprout and branch into a fractal spiral of delicate complexity. The lattice grows, filling the darkness, until there is no void left, only a kinetic mosaic of an Earth-like world.

Faces. Faces make feelings.

Inside the mosaic, reality is rendered in Cubist abstraction, revealing the simultaneous journeys of countless human lives in a multidimensional geography of the moment.

Among the billions of facets, one in particular shows a solitary woman working in a stark white room.

One face makes much feeling.

The image of the lone woman grows, quickly expanding to eclipse everything around it.

The first face.

Her image continues to enlarge, magnifying until the only thing visible is the deep green iris of her eye, emerald striations falling away to infinity.

Her face.

3

An hour into her night shift at the Simulab, Tiponi Adams felt her mind settle into a familiar groove, that harmonious alignment of perception and reason any zoosem professional must sustain in order to perform their work with the necessary intensity. Her workplace, the windowless and soundproofed Sensorium, was a ten-by-fifteen-meter vault space. Within the vault was a cutting-edge holo-projection system capable of enveloping the entire area from wall to wall and floor to ceiling in a terapixel-quality holo-field. The Sensorium was not powerful enough to generate an entity on its own, but it was more than adequate to reveal the infinitesimal details that semioticians examined and assessed within the massive stream of data generated by the Simulab's hyperreality experiments.

The zoosem eyed the large red button on the wall of the chamber, the only colored feature in the entire Sensorium. This was the kill switch, protected from unintentional activation by a hinged transparent cover. Essentially a circuit breaker, the kill switch was designed to cut the power to all Sensorium electronics, leaving the chamber bathed in the analog glow of incandescent emergency lights.

I try not to wonder why the Simulab designers thought a kill switch might be necessary, she thought, surveying the Sensorium's neutral interior. *It's good to know that there are reasonable contingency measures in place, like the kill switch and the quarantine.*

Black swans have the most painful bite, as they say.

Symbolic artificial intelligence, the first frontier of AI, used powerful logic engines governed by sets of encoded rules to simulate intelligence. While it had yielded breakthroughs useful for niche applications, the achievements of this school of thought fell far short of true intelligence or consciousness. Major research soon shifted to the subsymbolic world of computer intelligence, utilizing digital replicas of the higher human brain functions, called neural nets. But numbers are not neurons, and true consciousness remained elusive. The third wave of innovation unified the neural nets with rule-based symbolics, an advance that led to the first specimens of fully interactive artificial intelligence. Known as expert systems, these semiautonomous digital beings appeared alert and intelligent to the casual observer and were remarkably lifelike when inhabiting a high-definition holographic avatar. After a lengthy period of social immersion, some models began to exhibit spontaneous emotions.

But an Eastern mystic would reject the notion that an expert system experiences full human-like consciousness. The mystic would say the expert system lacks the third eye, the invisible organ at the center of the human forehead that imparts true insight.

Once the initial mystique of the lifelike expert systems had dwindled, the pursuit of digital consciousness became ripe for disruption once again.

And so it was that a conceptual model with growing acceptance within the neurosciences, the Free Energy Principle, became the theoretical basis for the Simulab. Instead of pursuing a particular goal, such as victory over a chess grandmaster, an autonomous being operating in accordance with the Free Energy Principle had only one objective—to minimize surprise.

Every living thing seeks to increase predictability and minimize surprise in the world, in order to improve its chances of survival. An organism that freely explores its environment accumulates a trove of experiences about the world around it. Using this information to infer future conditions and guide decisions, the organism adapts ever more successfully to a changing environment, even altering its surroundings to ensure that surprise is minimized and needs are fulfilled.

A dynamic sentience responding to a dynamic environment, pondered Tiponi. *Perhaps I should try adjusting my semiotic process to reflect that principle. Instead of focusing on discrete events or places, I could widen my perspective, look for a trail of evidence over time. A continuum.*

The scientist stood deep in thought, momentarily dazzled by the power and simplicity of this new insight.

"Sensorium, resume inquiry in progress," she requested.

The Sensorium reimmersed her in holographic hyperreality. The semiotician shifted her focus away from individual objects or symbols, instead searching for sequences, chronologies, sustained vectors of meaning embedded within the hyperreal record of a recent Simulab experiment.

No meaning in the world is immaculately conceived, she reminded herself. *Nothing of significance exists in complete isolation.*

Moving about the chamber, Tiponi explored the replay with the grace of a practiced professional. This new paradigm seemed to her a cognitive breakthrough of great significance, perhaps representing a new kind of field method. Enthralled, she felt like a child again, scampering through the nighttime canyons along her home mesa in Arizona, wanting to follow every game track to juncture or conclusion. Bear and puma prowled the woods alongside her, but such concerns were temporarily deferred in that moment of delirious gestalt.

After two hours of intense concentration, Tiponi realized she needed a bathroom break. Returning ten minutes later, she ordered the Sensorium expert system to secure the vault entrance and terminate all incoming communications.

Servos whirred faintly within the walls as six heavy deadbolts slid into place in the doorframe. There would be no interruptions now, unless VC Kanthaka performed an override. No one would be pointlessly interfering with her work and trashing her progress. For the next three hours—until the end of her shift—she could clear her mind of workplace politics and delve into this new insight.

Using a multicolored holographic user interface, the zoosem fed commands to the Sensorium. She isolated an intriguing replay from an experiment that had yielded some form of digital sentience, which was now residing in the Simulab quarantine. Queuing up the promising hyperreality output, Tiponi went to work.

Immersed in the hyperreal holography of the Sensorium, the semiotician became a spirit in another world. In this experimental record, the world was a ramshackle slum, perhaps the oldest district of some ancient metropolis in South Asia. The hazy street, crowded with pedestrians, was overhung by densely packed four- and five-story buildings. The structures were insubstantial, constructed of pitted stone, tarpaulins, and wood. Holographic pedestrians passed straight through Tiponi, completely unaware of her presence.

She noticed some sort of procession approaching through the flood of pedestrians, pushing a crowd ahead like a bow wave as it flowed down the center of the street. The crowd parted, revealing a row of swordsmen and archers—the royal guard—followed by six sturdy male servants. They carried an ornate litter upon which rode a single individual, an adult woman, presumably of great prominence, dressed in a gown of lavishly embroidered silk. As the litter drew near, Tiponi could see that the passenger was wearing an elaborate headpiece speckled with emeralds and rubies.

A sovereign's crown, the semiotician noted. *She must be a queen.*

An elephant appeared from the shadowed obscurity of a side street, turned onto the avenue, and swiftly approached the royal procession. The pachyderm was a large bull with unnaturally smooth white skin. Ambling up to the royal litter, the creature studied the queen for a few seconds. Suddenly the beast stepped forward and thrust the tip of one tusk into the queen's torso, penetrating the woman's body.

Screaming, the queen clenched her punctured abdomen with her hands.

The elephant fled into the crowd as the queen's entourage rushed to her aid. Pulling back her gown to examine the wound, the guards found no puncture. They discovered instead a newborn baby, unharmed, swaddled in the folds of embroidered silk.

As they watched, the infant underwent a rapid metamorphosis, maturing into a young boy in several blinks of the eye.

He caressed his mother's shoulder fondly, comforting her, before she faded away, dissipating like smoke. Mother now gone, the male child ascended the royal litter, and the entourage bore him onward. Seated atop the swaying platform, the teenager found the queen's abandoned crown by his feet. After giving it brief consideration, he flung the royal headpiece to the street, where it landed in a smoldering heap of gutter trash.

This experimental record seems odd, Tiponi realized, as she watched the holographic events unfold around her with growing confusion. *The events are completely surreal.*

The boy turned to look at Tiponi. As his gaze met hers, the holography began to distort, intensifying the young man's eyes.

"This is *so* strange," the zoosem muttered, spellbound. This replay was behaving in ways she had never experienced before.

The features of the boy's face dimmed, leaving two bright, disembodied eyes hovering in the holofield, staring directly at Tiponi. As she watched, the eyes separated into two orbs. Each sphere assumed a color and intensity of its own as they moved into seeming opposition.

One orb felt to Tiponi like a searchlight piercing dense fog, the beacon of a lighthouse ushering lost souls to safety. A pale glow hovered there, oscillating softly, suggesting a benevolent presence.

The other orb blazed with electric-blue flames that whirled across its surface like a swarm of cyclones. As the zoosem watched, this orb began to move toward her in a manner both overcurious and discomfortingly transgressive.

Like the movement of a praying mantis, Tiponi saw, *just before it strikes.*

Intuition tickled her insides like the flutter of a cold moth.

Without delay, the zoosem lunged for the kill switch. As she did, the predatory orb intensified rapidly, blanketing the Sensorium in brilliant white light. Stunned by the flash, Tiponi stumbled and collided with one of the floor-mounted holo projectors, striking her knee on its hard exterior shell.

She limped along the wall, fumbling frantically for the kill switch, certain the protective cover must be only inches away from her hand.

The experimental replay rebooted without warning, hurtling Tiponi back to the holographic Asian street, now devoid of any life or movement whatsoever. Tiponi watched the sun flash across the sky between the slum buildings. The celestial body traveled at a bizarre rate, followed by the moon, and again the sun. Faster and faster the days passed until they blurred together, leaving the sky bathed in a half light barely able to pierce the gloom, like the final, feeble sunrise before a long Arctic winter.

"*Maaaaarrraaaaaa . . . ,*" a voice whispered like an ill wind, issuing from everywhere at once—the street, the sidewalks, the people, the ramshackle buildings, even the sky. Then the world inside the replay began to dissipate. Sidewalks crumbled, structures collapsed into moldering ruins.

Glancing down, Tiponi watched the skin on her arms shrivel, aging fifty years in seconds. Lesions erupted and sickly gray tumors spread. The sick flesh began to putrefy, turning eggplant-black, cracking open into fissures as she watched, stunned and helpless. She rubbed her skin with a fingertip, displacing pieces of decomposing flesh that fell to the floor of the Sensorium with sickening little splats.

This can't be hyperreality output, Tiponi realized in a rush of sheer terror. *It's happening inside my head.*

As the mental images turned ever more malignant, assuming forms too terrible to contemplate, the terrified zoosem screamed and pounded her head with her fists.

4

When VC Kanthaka arrived at the Simulab twenty minutes later, concerns about the welfare of Tiponi Adams had only grown.

Englund had followed his VC's direction and contacted the ISCU advocate on duty. In compliance with the ISCU Charter, the advocate role was filled by a representative of the provisional U.S. government, a crotchety sixty-two-year-old man named Cartwright. After a three-decade civil service career, much of it served during an era characterized by unrelenting cuts to government, Cartwright was permanently locked in survival mode. Hunkering down as the world shifted dramatically around him, the man clung to his ISCU post with the thuggish tenacity of Machiavelli, anxiously counting the days until his retirement pension was fully vested.

"Cartwright said *what?*" exclaimed the VC as he stalked down the hallway toward the Sensorium.

Junior Manager Englund was immediately behind, hustling to keep up. Sensing impending trouble, the JM hesitated to reply until he caught a frosty glance from his commanding officer.

"Sir, yes sir. Advocate Cartwright said, 'Those zoosems are a bunch of fucking flakes. She's probably sleeping off a drunk or getting nailed or something. Do what you want.' Then he slammed the door in my face."

The VC quickened his pace.

The two passed through three more hallways and were soon standing in front of the entrance to the Sensorium.

"Let's make sure everything is all right in there," asserted the vice commandant. He lowered his chin to perform the retinal scan required for access to all sensitive areas within the Simulab, then straightened up and slid his e-key card through the slot.

"Pursuant clause six dash twelve of the ISCU protocol regarding employee welfare," the VC said to the door, with clear enunciation, "I am hereby overriding the Sensorium door lock to confirm the welfare of Zoosemiotician Tiponi Adams."

There was a brief pause before a vaguely automated feminine voice said, "E-key accepted. Please proceed, Vice Commandant Kanthaka."

The two doors slid quietly back into the doorframe, revealing pitch-black silence.

The VC and JM glanced at each other. A pitch-black Sensorium was definitely not standard operating procedure.

"Lights!" Kanthaka exclaimed.

Neither man thought to cover his eyes, and they were left momentarily dazzled when the high-intensity lamps of the Sensorium kicked on.

Englund squinted violently. As his vision returned, the young man bleated in horror.

The VC punched the wall-mounted security alarm with his fist, hitting the button hard enough to break his fingers.

Strobes began flashing in the hallway, and a sharp whistling sound pierced the facility.

Because the Sensorium was used exclusively for holographic review, the vault was equipped with smooth, white, unreflective walls. In each corner was a holobank, a dense array of sensors and projectors encased within an opaque white plastic cover. Together, the four holobanks could project a three-dimensional holofield that enveloped the entire Sensorium, surrounding the observer in a highly immersive hyperreality that allowed for detailed examination. Simulab zoosems were passionate about the search for synthetic consciousness, each spending countless hours in the Sensorium reviewing the minutiae of hyperreality experiment replays, hoping to identify signs of consciousness. If any aspect of the Sensorium led to misinterpretation of the holofeed, subtle yet important signs of an SC might be missed. Thus the antiseptic-white Sensorium was kept meticulously clean.

The flat white of the room had been transformed into a sort of canvas, the neutral color amplifying the visual impact of the carnage revealed within.

As VC Kanthaka's eyes scanned the scene, he swallowed the bile rising in his throat and began to sweat profusely.

Less successful in controlling such impulses, Englund fell to his knees and retched onto the institutional carpeting of the hallway. A moment later, he collapsed on his side and stared blankly at the wall.

The sound of running boots echoed down the hall.

Security operatives on the way . . . good enough, the VC thought. *I need to figure out what happened here.*

He stepped cautiously into the room.

Looped splashes of crimson blood covered the vault's floor and walls. At first glance, the VC did not recognize Tiponi on the floor in the center of the room, her form camouflaged by the ubiquitous drying viscera. It had to be the zoosem's lifeless body, Kanthaka knew, but he struggled to see it as anything other than a pile of blood-stained rags.

Not wanting to disturb a potential crime scene, the VC advanced cautiously. Once by Tiponi's side, he gently prodded her shoulder with the toe of his boot. As she toppled over, the zoosem's long black hair fell away, uncovering her face.

The hideous visage that confronted VC Kanthaka would haunt him for the rest of his days.

Tiponi's face was nearly unrecognizable. Her eyes had been jabbed violently from their sockets, leaving gobs of vitreous humor smeared about her forehead. Given the amount of blood that had drained from the sides of her head, the VC assumed the zoosem's inner ears had also been violently gouged.

Blood pooled around her head, gathering into a grisly halo.

From his breast pocket, Kanthaka withdrew a pen emblazoned with the ISCU Simulab logo. Kneeling, he hooked the pen under the fingers of the zoosem's left hand and lifted. Rigor mortis had already commenced, allowing him to lift the dead woman's hand and examine the fingers smeared with a thick coating of coagulated blood. Through the gore, he could see three of her fingernails were dangling by scraps of skin, forcibly torn free of their beds.

The VC stood upright, and his head swam. His preliminary conclusion was too horrific to contemplate. Some profoundly traumatic experience, something inconceivably horrible, had driven the popular and talented zoosemiotician to gouge out her eyes and ears with her own fingers.

As Kanthaka surveyed the impossible scene before him, the Simulab security detail arrived at the Sensorium.

The VC heard holsters unsnapping and knew weapons were brandished behind him. "Call the infirmary now," he ordered, cranking his head around. "Englund is going into shock."

The four members of the security detail, a team of stone-cold paramilitary operators, were frozen in combat positions, visors down, weapons up, neural enhancements at the ready.

The feds may be losing political power, but they still know how to train a top-notch security operative, VC Kanthaka acknowledged silently.

And without a doubt, the men before him were that.

Dressed in smart-carbon tactical suits equipped with heads-up displays and mimetic countermeasures, the four security operatives—known in the ISCU as SecOps—trained their fully automatic ceramic handguns on the Sensorium interior. The beams of four laser sights were visible, two gliding smoothly and efficiently about the room seeking targets, the third resting on Tiponi's body, and the fourth centered steadily on the VC's forehead.

SecOp Korbin was on point, speaking softly into the microphone connected to his tactical helmet, feeding information to law enforcement as his eyes darted about the scene.

VC Kanthaka rolled his own eyes upward, sensing the red point of the laser at the center of his forehead. "Stand down," he ordered.

"Stand down, Voinovich," SecOp Korbin said to his teammate.

SecOp Voinovich had glimpsed the zoosem's mangled face, and his neural enhancements jangled on high alert.

"But sir, he was the only living person present when we arrived. Other than the sleeping jimmie." Voinovich shrugged toward the junior manager in the hallway.

"Yes, I see that, Vich," Korbin acknowledged. "But he is also the vice commandant we know and love. Now stand down. That is an order."

SecOp Voinovich lowered his weapon, but his finger did not leave the trigger.

Korbin pressed on. "Do you have any idea what happened here, VC?"

Kanthaka shook his head weakly. "Based on the limited information I have, it appears that Zoosem Adams mutilated herself and bled to death. Why, I do not know. I arrived here with JM Englund to override the door lock and perform a welfare check. Englund passed out when the door opened. After he caught a glimpse of this mess."

"Do you think it's an isolated incident, sir?"

"I think we can assume it is. The . . . event . . . seems to have occurred entirely inside the Sensorium, which was locked from the inside. The victim's wounds appear to be self-inflicted."

"Even with privacy mode activated, there should be video and audio recordings archived for the room during that time period," SecOps Korbin noted.

"I suppose we should confirm that," the VC replied. "Is there anything in the Incubator?"

Any entity meeting the ISCU criteria for a possible sentience was uploaded to the Simulab Incubator for Turing analysis and further study.

"I observed the transfer of an entity to the Incubator at oh-two-twenty-three, sir," said another SecOp. "Perhaps this zoosem—"

"Performed the upload directly from the Sensorium," the VC surmised. "Yes, presumably that's what occurred. Let's confirm the status of the Incubator and see if there is any useful Sensorium video."

"Sir, should I notify the advocate?" SecOp Korbin inquired. "Cartwright?"

The VC could not turn away from the grotesque tableau. Tears welled up in his eyes. *Tiponi Adams, of all people,* he thought. *Christ.*

"No," he replied, "at this time, do not contact Advocate Cartwright."

With the Simulab security force responding to the zoosem's death in the Sensorium, the control room was empty now, the interior partially obscured by the vague shadows thrown by dim computer monitors.

"Call the infirmary now. Englund is going into shock," said the voice of VC Kanthaka through a wall-mounted intercom speaker, followed by a short burst of static.

"Police informed; EMT mobilized," another voice announced across the open channel.

Suddenly the walls of the control room came aglow as the room's holofield activated.

A holoimage shimmered into existence in the center of the small room. After several halting attempts at substantiation, the holography came into focus.

It was Tiponi Adams, uninjured, unemotional.

The holoimage stepped up to a control station and leaned in toward the station's retinal scanner. The intensity of Tiponi's holoprojection seemed to surge toward her face, suffusing her eye with a stark intensity.

"Simulab Zoosemiotician Tiponi Adams requests deletion of all Sensorium communication records for the last eight hours," the woman's holoimage said flatly.

"Scanning," responded an automated voice. A quick flash of light from the retinal scanner passed across Tiponi's bright holographic cornea.

"Rescan please," the expert system said, and the retinal scanner made a second pass.

"Sensorium communication records for the last eight hours have been deleted," the expert system confirmed.

"Simulab Zoosemiotician Tiponi Adams requests discharge of Simulab Incubator quarantine," Tiponi's image continued.

"Incubator quarantine discharge requires a security override password."

"Simulab Zoosemiotician Tiponi Adams requests ISCU override, using ISCU password alternative entry option: scan."

"Scan," the expert system prompted.

Once more Tiponi's image dimmed as the holofield surged toward her face, synchronized perfectly with the flash of the retinal scanner.

"Alternative override password entry option: scan has been approved," responded the Simulab expert system. "Incubator quarantine termination approved under ISCU protocols. Quarantine terminated."

A loud chime filled the empty control room.

Tiponi Adams stared at the control panel, her expression flat as a frozen lake. After a few seconds passed, the woman's holoimage shimmered and faded away.

As the vestige of Zoosemiotician Tiponi Adams disappeared, a caustic chortle echoed through the room, drifting off to a sigh.

5

VC Kanthaka sat in the infirmary, his broken fingers freshly splinted, watching passively as emergency medical technicians tried to stabilize Junior Manager Englund. As he watched them work, he fought a silent internal battle to evade the same debilitating shock that had so completely overcome the junior manager.

Englund awoke with a panicked start and began whining inconsolably. A medical tech rushed over to administer a sedative.

Kanthaka had worked SWAT for a decade, during which he had seen many versions of hysteria. But never had he seen someone succumb so completely to fear as his junior manager had.

I suppose it's understandable, he considered. *The kid had a serious crush on Adams.*

Now the catatonic junior manager stared at the blank clinic wall, a string of drool dangling from the corner of his mouth.

SecOp Korbin poked his head through the infirmary door. "Excuse me, sir," he said to the VC. "We have incoming: the county coroner, the local ISCU legal counsel, Advocate Cartwright, and some Turing people are on their way. Cartwright will be here in five, followed by the others. Do you have any orders at this time?"

"No. What will be, will be." Kanthaka met the SecOp's gaze and sighed. "Jeff, under what ISCU security protocol is the facility currently operating?"

SecOp Korbin glanced down for a moment. "Sir, I'd rather not get into that right now."

"Goddamn it, Jeff. Just tell me."

"Level One, sir. I called it at oh-six-hundred."

"So, as head of facility security, you are now in charge, correct? At least until the head of ISCU central security arrives?"

"That is correct, VC. However, with all due respect, sir, it's my prerogative to keep you on post."

"Oh, that sounds nice," the vice commandant replied. "All of the responsibility and none of the authority. Ah yes, just like the good old days. Oh, speaking of which, I presume you notified the advocate, as required by Level One contingencies?"

"Affirmative, sir."

The VC mouthed a curse. "You know how he's going to play this. Same as always. His finger will be the first to point."

"Roger that, VC," Korbin responded. "I am not a politician, but I will do my best."

"I would expect nothing less from you, SecOp," the VC said.

SecOp Korbin nodded, turned on his heel, and was gone.

Englund made another bleating sound. His leg flailed impotently at the horror tormenting his mind.

VC Kanthaka wondered whether his JM would ever recover from the traumatic scene that had awaited them inside the sealed Sensorium.

He wondered if he ever would himself.

What would compel Tiponi to destroy herself in a fit of self-inflicted violence? It doesn't make sense. Without eyes and ears, her career as a zoosem would have been over. Zoosems must, first and foremost, be superb at observation.

Kanthaka's breath came to a halt as his mind was engulfed by a sudden, gut-wrenching certainty.

It's obvious why Tiponi wanted to remove her senses completely—why she tried to tear them out at the root, the VC could see now. *She could not tolerate another moment . . . another moment of . . .*

Kanthaka lunged at a nearby intercom panel, knocking over a wheeled tray of medical instruments. A monitoring device fell to the floor, the impact triggering a monotone beeping noise.

"Shit." The VC toggled the intercom button and shouted, "SecOps, SecOps, please respond! Level One inquiry! I repeat, Level One inquiry!"

SecOp Voinovich, who was back on post in the control room, responded immediately. "Sir, this is Vich."

"Listen, Vich. Please do something for me. Quickly."

"SecOp Korbin is meeting the VIPs at the Simulab entrance," Voinovich replied. "Shall I call him in?"

"No, leave him alone. You can help me. Check the status of the Incubator. Quickly."

The Simulab Incubator was essentially a heavily firewalled virtual space, not an actual space someone could physically enter and inhabit. All Incubator controls, including the quarantine settings, were in the control room.

"Sir," the operative began sheepishly, "May I apologize for sighting my weapon on you—"

"Forget it. Part of the job," answered Kanthaka tersely. "Listen to me. What is the Incubator status right now?"

"Hang on a minute. Let's see what we have . . ."

"Is Incubator quarantine still up?" the VC pressed. "Refresh the screen, please. Be certain."

"No, it's not. Why is quarantine down?" Vich said, mystified. "Who the hell dropped Incubator quarantine? That's in clear contravention of ISCU protocol, based on the—"

"Voinovich, shut the hell up and do what I say! Pull up video and voice records for the control room. Now!"

"Okay, sir. I have the video up. Here I am, all alone in the control—"

"Earlier," the VC said. "Scroll back to oh-four-fifty and slow-scan forward."

"Video now rewound and scanning forward. Here is when the SecOps are called out. We head off to the Sensorium. Scrolling, scrolling..."

"What are you seeing?" the VC asked impatiently.

"An empty room, sir. I see nothing unusual."

Several seconds passed as the operative fast-forwarded through the video footage of the empty control room.

"What the *fuck*?" Voinovich suddenly exclaimed. Just as quickly, his voice transformed from startled exclamation to whispering dread.

"That's not right," the operative said.

"What's not right, Vich? What do you see?"

"That can't be right!" the operative repeated mindlessly. "It can't be! It just can't be!"

"Damn it, Vich. Tell me what you're seeing!"

SecOp Voinovich did not hear the VC anymore. "Fuck this!" the operative sputtered nonsensically. "This is *not happening*!"

"Calm down, soldier," the VC said. "Tell me what's going on."

"It's the dead zoosem, Tiponi Adams!" Voinovich said. "She was in the control room!"

"What?"

"*Tiponi* dropped quarantine." The words bubbled up from deep within the operative's chest. "After she was already dead!"

Kanthaka could tell the operative's mental state was breaking down rapidly. "Hold it together, Voinovich," the VC urged. "We need you right now."

"Already *dead*!" Voinovich barked madly. "No fucking way!"

Through the man's panicked outbursts, another voice could be heard in the background. The timbre was a familiar feminine alto, yet the delivery was completely foreign.

It was Tiponi Adams's voice, normally sweet and musical, now flat and emotionless. When VC Kanthaka heard the inhuman drone of that voice as it terminated Incubator quarantine, he understood the horror that had befallen Tiponi, locked inside the Sensorium.

"Shut up and listen to me, Voinovich!" VC Kanthaka ordered the operative through the intercom. "Initiate Simulab emergency shutdown immediately! Engage the electromagnetic pulse weapon and trigger it as soon as it heats up!" he implored. "Do the full crash, Voinovich! *Now!*"

But all the VC heard over the intercom were frantic shouts and the sound of boots running as the SecOp fled down the hallway, the tumult accented by the sound of Voinovich's headset, swinging like a noose below the control panel, tapping lightly with each return against a metal panel on the security control station.

The VC bolted out of the infirmary, sprinting through the Simulab complex, rushing toward the control room and the EMP trigger. As he intersected another corridor, Kanthaka saw a group of officials walking away from him, heading directly toward the Sensorium.

SecOp Korbin was leading the way, followed by four people gathered in a tight, anxious group: a resolute young man and a mature woman, both dressed in fine business attire; another man in uniform; and the perennially rumpled Advocate Cartwright, who lingered reluctantly at the back of the group, berating no one in particular.

"Christ, what a disaster! Do you know how many people considered the Simulab a dangerous white elephant? And that was how they felt *before* this place killed someone!"

At that moment, VC Kanthaka noticed a sixth person, a man, standing at the threshold of the Sensorium, evidently waiting to greet the entourage. The VC did not recognize him immediately, although he had a familiar face, with a swarthy complexion and a full head of graying hair. Judging by the insignia on his uniform, the man appeared to be another vice commandant. Oddly, his fingers appeared to be splinted, just like—

VC Kanthaka halted midstride, momentum sending his torso careening forward, and he crashed awkwardly to the hard floor. The unexpected impact knocked the wind out of him, stunning him for a moment, before a surge of adrenaline jolted him back to his feet. Gasping for air, he stumbled down the side hallway toward the group.

When SecOp Korbin noticed the vice commandant's approach, he stopped and aimed his weapon down the hall.

"Stand down, SecOp Voinovich!" commanded Korbin as he waved the officials toward the Sensorium with his free hand.

Voinovich? thought Kanthaka. He glanced around in confusion.

No one was behind him. Voinovich was not in the hallway.

Turning back to the group, the VC looked again at the swarthy, graying, uniformed man standing just outside the Sensorium door.

That's me, VC Kanthaka comprehended. *It's a holoimage of me!*

Another Kanthaka, a manifestation completely indistinguishable from him, beckoned the visitors forward.

The VC watched in stunned disbelief as his identical holoimage guided the group toward the promise of safety.

Across the threshold. Into the Sensorium.

Korbin glared at the real VC Kanthaka down the hall, his handgun twitching. "SecOp Voinovich, stand down! Lay down your weapon and kneel on the floor with your hands behind your head! Stop now, or I will be forced to shoot."

The VC tried to shout a warning, but his winded lungs managed no more than a soft grunt.

"Come on, Vich," SecOp Korbin begged. "I don't want to shoot you, buddy."

VC Kanthaka glanced down to see his entire body bathed in the light of a holofield. As he lifted his hand to make a conciliatory gesture, he realized his actual hand was perfectly obscured by the holoimage of a hand gripping a ceramic SecOps handgun, holographic index finger resting tight on the trigger. His VC uniform was hidden beneath the blackness of the SecOps ninja suit holoprojected onto his body with absolute realism. As the VC staggered down the hall, a holoprojected tactical exoskeleton shifted about his physique like muscles under skin.

Although he could not confirm it, the VC was certain that Voinovich's facial features were also part of the holoprojection, neatly eclipsing Kanthaka's own face.

An explosion tore through the hallway.

Kanthaka's left leg flew out from beneath him as a bullet ripped through the flesh of his thigh. He fell hard again, feeling the crack of ribs fracturing as his torso slammed against the floor. Rolling over, gasping like a gutted fish, he watched in helpless silence as SecOp Korbin backed into the Sensorium and prepared to seal the door.

"Nnnnnn . . . ," Kanthaka grunted, gesticulating with his arm. Eyes bulging with pain, he continued forward, crawling across the thirty feet separating him from the Sensorium entrance.

"What just happened? Where did Voinovich go?" Cartwright could be heard demanding testily from within the Sensorium. "Is this some sort of prank?"

SecOp Korbin tried to maintain calm as he keyed commands in the door controls. "Listen up, everyone. There is a presumed aggressor outside. Recommendations, VC?"

Korbin had no idea he was speaking to a holoimage of VC Kanthaka instead of the real man.

"Let's close the door and wait for backup," Kanthaka heard his own voice calmly reassure the others. "We will be safe inside."

A half second later, the doors of the Sensorium began to slide shut. Lights dimmed as the holofield prepared to launch.

A soft whisper filled the air. Little more than a slur of indistinct syllables, the nebulous muttering came from all directions at once, as if emanating from the walls.

"*Hello . . . I heart you . . .*"

For a split second, all action ceased. Everyone froze, captivated by a strange mélange of curiosity and dread.

"*I . . . I like you!*" declared the disembodied voice. "*I heart you!*"

"I don't like this," moaned Cartwright.

"*I heart you . . . I heart you . . . ,*" pleaded the voice with rising insistence. "*I heart you . . . I heart you . . .*"

"Easy, everyone," advised SecOp Korbin. "Stay calm. Everything is going to be fi—"

Suddenly the tenor of the voice changed, growing louder with every repeat.

"*I HEART YOU . . . I HEART YOU . . . ,*" the voice raved. "*I HEART YOU . . . I HEART YOU . . .*"

"Let us out of here," demanded the female visitor. "Now! Open the doors!"

"*. . . I HEART YOU . . . I HEART YOU . . . I HEART YOU . . . I HEART YOU . . .*"

Now the voice was shouting its devotion in earsplitting proclamations.

"*. . . I HEART YOU . . . I HEART YOU . . . I HEART YOU . . . ,*" the voice roared. "*I HEART YOU . . . I HEART YOU . . . I HEART YOU . . .*"

"Stay calm!" Korbin bellowed impotently. "Someone shut down the replay! Kanthaka! Kanthaka!"

"*IHEARTYOUIHEARTYOUIHEARTYOUIHEARTYOUI-HEARTYOUIHEARTYOUIHEARTYOUIHEARTYOU . . .*"

Listening from the corridor outside, the real Kanthaka could only imagine what was happening in there.

"Shut down the holography now!" demanded Korbin. "Shut it down!"

"*IHEARTYOUILOVEYOUIHEARTYOUILOVEYOUI-HEARTYOUILOVEYOUIHEARTYOUILOVEYOUIHEARTYOU . . .*"

"Screw this!" yelped Advocate Cartwright as he lunged for

the closing doors. He was able to shove his thick arm through the gap before becoming trapped there, his arm pinned at the elbow, the doors gripping him like a vise.

"*IHEARTYOUILOVEYOUIHEARTYOUILOVEYOUIHEART—*"

The explosive pronouncements abruptly ended, leaving the entire room in ringing silence.

The peace lasted only a second or two before it was defiled by another voice.

"*Aaaaaaahhhhaaaaaaahh . . . mmaaaaaahh-rrrrraaaaaaaaaaahh . . .*"

The tone this time was different, unmistakably so. This voice was a disparaging sneer, a caustic taunt dripping with insolence and malice.

Someone inside the room barked an involuntary cry of fear.

As the unrelenting metal doors gripped the advocate's trapped arm, the man began to scream, his face a red grimace framed by quivering jowls.

A high-pitched sneer briefly pierced the air, a grating whine that attacked the inner ear like a power drill. The keening noise fell away to silence.

Then the furious voice abruptly returned, this time with a stentorian roar.

"*Aaah-veeeee-HAAAAAAAH!   EEEEEAAAAAAAAAAAH!! TAAA KRAAAH TUUUUUUUUU!!*"

The sonic intensity of the disembodied voice shook the reinforced concrete walls of the Simulab, as if a typhoon had learned speech and expressed its elemental fury.

Amid the growing horror, VC Kanthaka realized that the sonorous words were familiar to him. He could not divine the meaning, yet felt sure he had encountered similar dialects during his childhood days in Sri Lanka. Some ancient Asian lexicon, with nuances of meaning obliterated long ago by the ceaseless erosion of modernity.

Chaotic gunshots rang out. Between the staccato reports, VC Kanthaka could hear wild snarls and guttural growling inside the Sensorium, sickening sounds of animal savagery.

The doors to the Sensorium remained propped open a few inches by Cartwright's mangled arm. Flickering lights and roiling colors spilled through the gap, hinting at utter pandemonium inside. The VC felt a reflexive sense of self-preservation drive him back from the cleft in the doors. But a sense of duty conquered the fear, goading him forward.

He peered through the bloodied slit, glimpsing the interior of the room and the spinning nightmare of butchery underway within.

Weapons had been fired repeatedly at point-blank range, hurling splatters of fresh viscera onto the walls. The Sensorium holofield projected a lurid, three-dimensional kaleidoscope of violence: Nazi showers, Cambodian killing fields, a Congolese river choked with cadavers. One massacre after another unfolded in terapixel clarity, one human depravity blending into the next, visions to darken the most deviant mind.

At the center of the hellish maelstrom stood a loathsome crab-like beast. The entire vile tableau slowly revolved around the monster as if it drifted in a viscous whirlpool. Everything was pulled toward the center, inexorably, straight into the demon's grasp.

"ZUR NUU!!" the demon roared in a voice ripe with apocalyptic wrath. *"SAAR VAAH AAAAHNNNUUU VAAAH ZAAAA MAAAAAH RAAAAAAAAH!!"*

Lashing out with greasy mandibles, the creature snatched up helpless humans one by one, drawing them in. Once it had a victim firmly in its grasp, the beast commingled with the body, relentlessly abusing the limp form in ways too terrible to contemplate. After brutally extinguishing a life, the monster devoured its prey whole, swallowing it with one powerful spasm of peristalsis like a ravenous anaconda.

"AAAAHAAAAAH MAAAAAH RAAAAAAAAH!" the noxious thing bellowed between swallows. *"ZUR NUU! AAAAHAAAAAH MAAAAAH RAAAAAAAAH!"*

VC Kanthaka flinched away, his face bloodied by Cartwright's viscera on the door. He wept uncontrollably, no longer feeling his bleeding leg or cracked ribs. Such agonies were irrelevant, eclipsed by the abominable images swirling in his mind. Only one vague urge persisted: the desire to languish on the floor and wait for blood loss to render his mind unconscious so he might escape the horrors of this night.

As the numbing blanket of shock descended, a seed of reason finally returned.

There is no sense in saving any of this, VC Kanthaka thought. *It is time to wash it all away.*

The sounds coming from the Sensorium had devolved into a succession of glottal grunts and hiccups. It was impossible to discern any humanity in the sounds, to identify any earthly source.

The VC drew himself up on his one functional leg and hopped past the Sensorium, looking straight ahead, away from the doors. Moving down the hallway as quickly as his condition would permit, the VC stumbled into the empty control room and collapsed onto a workstation. Lifting himself to level with the electromagnetic pulse weapon controls, he saw the EMP device was already armed. SecOp Voinovich had accomplished that much before losing his mind.

Lifting the transparent cover that protected the flashing red light, VC Kanthaka depressed the button.

Instantaneously, the entire Simulab was bathed in an intense electromagnetic field that convulsed the walls of the control room.

Unconsciousness fell toward VC Kanthaka. Desiring the sanctuary of that soothing cloak, he swiftly embraced it.

The hospital room was quiet, the lights dim.

A transparent red cross the size of an armchair hovered in a corner, at the edge of the room's holofield, tinting the walls and floor a pinkish hue.

VC Kanthaka was resting in a hospital bed, his head raised on a pillow, when a uniformed ISCU manager walked into the room.

"The holomed is on standby, sir," the man assured Kanthaka. The manager then drew a chair up to the bed and sat down. "How are you holding up?"

"Me? I don't give a shit about me," the VC said. "How bad is it? I need to know."

"Sir, the nurse advised me to—"

Kanthaka cut him off without hesitation. "How bad is it?" he demanded.

"Sir, you've seen the casualty report . . . ," the manager replied reluctantly.

Kanthaka's body stiffened with rage as he turned to face the man directly. "I don't mean the people, you fool!" he shouted.

Both glanced nervously toward the hall.

The VC brushed the sleeve of his shirt over his eyes. "You know what I mean. The *Incubator*," he rasped. "Did I crash it in time?"

The two men locked gazes in an unspoken battle of wills.

"Sir," the visitor implored again, his voice wavering. "We think it would be best to hold off on any detailed conversations until you've had a little more time to—"

"*Shut up*," the VC spat. "I need to know now. Did an SC get out when quarantine was down?"

"Sir . . ."

"Did an entity escape the Simulab? *Tell me*."

The younger manager studied his polished leather shoes. When he finally whispered a reply, his brow was slick with sweat.

"Based on what we currently know, there were two SCs in quarantine at the time of the incident. Both escaped."

The VC violently inhaled a single breath before coughing hard, wrenching sobs into his balled fists.

The hovering cross brightened to a cherry red as the holomed system moved to alert mode. "Current stress levels are unsafe," a genderless voice warned sternly. "Please reduce stimuli immediately."

Down the hallway, there was a slight squeak as a chair shifted on the institutional flooring.

An inquiry would be held, most likely a tribunal. There would be heads on pikes before the process was done. Careers, as well as the many lives that depended on them, would be destroyed forever. But for now, any questions about eventual demotions or dismissals would remain unconsidered. VC Kanthaka simply wept, sliding into a state of despair so profound, all other emotions were irrelevant. At that moment his grief was so pervasive, so oppressive, it seemed to capture all the fears and sorrows of the world, as if he were gazing into the grave of humanity itself.

PART II

21 April 2071

6

"Open globe."

Bach's Cello Suite No. 1 in G began to play softly within the confines of the silent room.

A white dot appeared in the center of the dim space, rapidly expanding and resolving into a rotating, three-dimensional holographic logo comprising two bold, minimalist letters.

Capital *T*. Capital *I*.

A holographic representation of the planet Earth expanded from the shadow behind the logo as the block font letters dimmed. The globe rotated serenely, as if viewed from high orbit.

Off to the side of the room, the outline of a male form was visible, seated in a solitary chair, dimly illuminated by the holographic Earth. Shadows could not obscure the man's authoritative nature. The broad forehead, sharp hazel eyes, and angular nose and chin gave the man a regal bearing only enhanced by the multicolored medals attached to the black tactical jacket of his duty uniform. A small epaulet on each shoulder displayed his title and name in capital letters: *DIR SEERS*.

Director Conrad Seers took a leisurely sip from the black coffee in his mug.

"Good morning, Celeste," he said, enunciating with the relaxed precision of a South African urbanite. "Standard morning brief."

"Good morning, sir," replied a feminine voice that emanated throughout the room. "Today is the twenty-first of April 2071. The following is your Turing Institute morning brief, delivered in standard global format."

The Turing Institute was the sole regulatory agency still wielding authority of any consequence in the global mega-economy of the late twenty-first century. The Institute's overarching mandate was well known: obliterate all existing forms of synthetic consciousness research, and aggressively censor the scientific community in the same regard. The cerebral title of the organization was chosen to purposefully obscure the agency's more extreme agenda: pursue and eliminate any free-roaming digital entities that exhibited signs of higher consciousness, in missions carried out by the Institute's highly secretive Turing Units.

Decades before Conrad's recent rise to the directorship, the pinnacle of Institute leadership, his career had begun in the Turing Units. There he had learned of the unnatural histories of such entities by experiencing them firsthand, oftentimes outside whatever algorithmic firewalls an illicit SC research facility might employ—if there were any protections at all.

The hologlobe rotated briskly, orienting South America toward the director's point of view. Several shapes intensified on the surface of the hologlobe, contours of orange and red highlighting specific regions. The entire southern region of the continent glowed the yellow white of a blown cinder.

"Conflict between the New Radicals continues unabated and remains intense. Early data suggest very recent nuclear strikes in the Chilean Cordillera de la Costa, within the boundaries of the former Monumento Natural El Morado."

A small region north of the Chilean city of Santiago flared brightly.

"Seismic and volcanic signatures in the area are still being evaluated to eliminate false positives. Our best guess right now is a strategic nuclear strike by Brazil on Chilean mining interests. The nuke-tech device would likely have been delivered by a substratospheric cruise missile or similar stealth platform. Clearly, the mine defenses failed catastrophically."

Conrad grimaced when he saw the video feed taken by a Turing Institute recon drone, an aerial image of what had once been a massive open-pit mine in the Chilean Cordillera. All features of the multibillion-dollar mining operation had been erased by a nuke strike, reducing the operation to a smoldering wasteland. Huge mine excavators had melted into steaming heaps of brown slag. Wildfires burned in the background, raging through the subalpine forests near the mine.

"Radiation signatures suggest that the detonation was a moderately sophisticated warhead containing a combination of plutonium and neutron nuke-tech, as well as an advanced smart trigger, producing a highly focused blast zone. If this turns out to be true, the strike would constitute the most precise use of a stratospheric nuclear device by a New Radical nation."

"It appears the payload was scaled perfectly for the target," the director observed. "Brazil's nuclear program is growing more sophisticated."

"I believe that is a reasonable conclusion, Director. On a potentially related note, two tactical nuclear strikes were reported in South America over the last four days, one in Old Buenos Aires, and another in Montevideo proper. Initial ground and drone intelligence indicate that the devices were tactical nukes rigged to look like Saturday Night Specials." Her ambient calm was replaced by an anxious tone. "Sir, we believe it is possible that Chile is resorting to terrorism again."

Pinpricks of orange flared on the hologlobe, growing into pulsating yellow circles. Each circle filled with an aerial video of a nuked site, the videos zooming into hundred-meter-diameter craters blasted out of dense urban core, still smoldering. The crater in Buenos Aires was surrounded on all sides by the scorched remains of housing complexes and historic buildings. The other strike had destroyed a billion-dollar manufacturing complex in Montevideo.

"Horrific, but very human," Conrad lamented. "Let's move on."

"Should we take a moment to discuss this? I believe it is worth examining these events more closely."

"Why?"

"The Montevideo strike may not be a result of a simple geopolitical conflict. We have reason to believe this may be an act of terrorism."

"Terrorism? No, I don't think so."

"Director Seers, please recall the Chilean mine strike. You noted that the payload appeared to have been scaled perfectly."

"I did say that. However, it does not imply the involvement of an SC. Last time we counted, over a thousand freelance nuclear scientists of the human variety were offering consulting services in just about every part of the world. Including Brazil."

"If Brazil is indeed responsible, their nuke-tech has undergone dramatic improvement almost overnight. Is that assessment realistic?"

"Give laboratories to a thousand nuclear scientists," opined Conrad, "and someone will probably invent something incredibly dangerous."

The hologlobe rotated briskly to Asia, settling on the Indian subcontinent.

"Sea levels continue to rise steadily around the world. Inundation of the lower Ganges River delta continues unabated, forcing the exodus of Bangladeshi and Indian populations from coastal areas between Calcutta and Chittagong. Evacuations of the last sectors of Calcutta were completed two weeks ago. Another mass suicide was reported yesterday—fifteen thousand followers of a Khulna water death cult."

Conrad's only detectable reaction to this news was quiet resignation.

"Elsewhere in Asia, it appears that the Bhutanese government is undergoing continued destabilization at the hands of Maoist insurgents affiliated with Sino-Tibetan extremists. It remains unclear whether the nation will be invaded or, alternatively, acquired by a hostile corporate takeover and converted into an enclave."

In the mid twenty-first century, global business practices had become increasingly competitive as corporations battled for control of diminishing resources and dominance of rapidly shrinking markets. This new, hyperaggressive mindset was an adaptation necessary for survival in the ultracompetitive business world. Before long, the escalating brutality of business-to-business relations devolved into outright nihilism.

The profit-making emphasis of present-day corporations remained little changed from their predecessors; sales and growth were still the key metrics of corporate success. All similarities ended there, however. The ethics of the twentieth century had been profoundly altered. Any spirit of compromise that existed between corporations in the past had long since evaporated, outmoded by a growing playbook of coercive methods both psychological and physical. In the present era, pursuit of compromise was viewed as an admission of weakness tantamount to surrender. Assassination was widely preferred over negotiation for reasons both tactical and strategic: the intimidating nature of the act discouraged further conflict, as did its decisive permanence.

The most powerful corporations established physical havens known as enclaves, autonomous territories wherein corporations could operate with total impunity, freeing themselves of all taxation and regulatory oversight. The emergence and proliferation of these self-governing corporate fiefdoms, while supremely advantageous to the resident corporations, triggered catastrophic plunges in government tax revenue. Starved of income, governments could no longer afford to maintain social safety nets, which subsequently collapsed. In less than one generation, employment at one of fifty-two large international corporations, or with the Turing Institute itself, had become the only reliable avenue worldwide to a life of relative comfort and security.

"Corporations comfortably hold the upper hand in that region, a circumstance enabled by an acquiescent Chinese government," spoke the disembodied voice. "Longer term, a peaceful outcome is not expected."

"Okay. Move along," responded the director. He took a long sip from his mug.

The hologlobe revolved until the continent of North America was in the fore. Coastal inundation in recent decades had reshaped the coastlines and flooded lowlands, submerging vast stretches of tideland and reducing the size of some islands, while drowning those islets with the lowest relief entirely. Some city sites had been abandoned, relinquished to the rising seas. Other metropolitan areas had adopted a more stubborn stance, refusing to retreat from the advancing water. Instead, the residents adapted, concentrating their unified existence on scattered islets of high ground. Certain cities had transformed into urban archipelagos, pincushions needled with mile-high skyscrapers, now the exclusive province of the ultrawealthy.

"As for economic developments, U.S. government conservators continue their efforts to negotiate a comprehensive restructuring of U.S. debt with the nation's principal creditors. China has refused to participate thus far. They insist that the United States is in default and have threatened unspecified action unless the U.S. government cedes territory as collateral. If an invasion of the U.S. mainland were to occur, we expect no resistance from the provisional government. Any pockets of organized paramilitary resistance would be irrelevant to the Chinese military. Since the Singapore incident, the Americans have grown more sensitive to being played as corporate pawns. In this particular instance, we find their strategy to be admirably well considered."

"The Chinese government wants resources. Of that we can be certain," Conrad commented.

"Yes, that motive is assumed in our analysis. China is targeting viable deposits of radioactive ore in the U.S. for the growing Chinese space program. At this point, the deposits are of greater concern to U.S.-based corporations than to the provisional government, which is fighting for survival. Armed conflict is likely but not certain."

"Any potential dark horses in the mix?"

"The Nukems are perceived to have a stake in the outcome, and will undoubtedly be playing all the angles, as they develop."

"Interesting." Conrad took another sip. "Please refresh my memory on the Nukem backstory."

"The Nukems were started by a cadre of American nuclear chemists, ideological extremists who chose to free themselves from all regulations imposed on nuclear research to protect human health and public safety. The group views any such rules as impositions on the divine relationship between human beings and radioactivity. These people are absolutely fervent in their nuclear evangelism. Radiation is their eucharist, the essence of their faith, and continues to play a ubiquitous role in their everyday existence."

Conrad shook his head in amazement. "What a world."

"The Nukems are ancillary to the Turing mission. They do not utilize or research SC."

"And we can be glad of that. So then, Celeste, what's next?"

"Meanwhile, several nations with strategic rare earth mineral deposits are discussing the possible formation of an OPEC-like entity, but the action has been delayed by a disagreement over whether corporate enclaves should be allowed to apply for membership. Several corporations have strategically positioned their enclaves above substantial rare earth mineral deposits. Legally speaking, the host nations have lost any sovereign claim to those resources. Meanwhile, China is manipulating the circumstances, playing the New Radicals and the Chavistas against each other masterfully. We speculate that China may seek to force enclave status on two crucial lithium mines operated by Comibol, the Bolivian mining conglomerate. If that were to occur, our intelligence suggests the resulting conflict may go cyber."

"Wait," the man said, "I'm seeing a number of potential stakeholders here. Have we gamed out all possible scenarios?"

"A preliminary multivariate simulation was performed, yielding no definitive results," Celeste responded. "To date, we have not run a comprehensive tactical gaming simulation."

"That's fine. Please summarize your findings from the initial sim."

"The preliminary simulation indicated several different cyber conflict scenarios could arise, depending on how the situation plays out. There appears to be one crucial consideration. Without exception, all major Comibol lithium deposits are diffuse lenses of high-grade ore distributed widely across miles of dry lake beds. Data we obtained from preliminary gaming suggest that multiple ballistic nuclear detonations above those ore deposits would vaporize the best of Comibol's lithium reserves. We believe the New Radicals are willing to employ nuclear extortion at this point, especially if China tries to lock up the strategic lithium deposits under enclave territories. However, such an action would be both a tactical and literal scorched-earth scenario, as all involved parties desperately need access to that lithium. The situation is ripe for cyber conflict. Possibly even first-order conflict, which we define as different offensive capabilities simultaneously deployed by multiple antagonists."

"Who are the likely players if the conflict goes first-order cyber?" the director asked.

"Relatively speaking, Bolivian cyber capabilities are the weakest, which encourages cyber attacks from the others. The

New Radicals and Chavistas are known to have substantial offensive cyber capacities, but we believe neither of them could mount attacks beyond the level of harassment. The nuke remains their strongest weapon. China is the undisputed leader in the successful fielding of complex cyber warfare technologies. Apart from India and several major cyber defense corporations, no one has anything that approaches the capabilities of China. They can fight on multiple fronts simultaneously, utilizing a wide array of combat tactics ranging from advanced viral applications to hostile autonomous entities. When China gets involved, anything is possible."

"If this becomes a first-order conflict, what do you think Turing's priorities should be?"

"Our number one priority in this geopolitical situation should be increased surveillance of combatant states for indications of hostile autonomous program development or release. Second priority should be monitoring all signal intelligence worldwide, focusing on digital."

"Probabilities generated by the multivariate simulation?"

"The highest probability, registering at fifty-six percent likelihood, is the deployment of superviruses, still the most effective technologies for achieving key tactical objectives on the virtual battlefield. Manipulation and sabotage by infiltrator expert systems registered as secondary likelihood, at twenty-three percent. Electromagnetic pulse attacks now register at thirteen percent, as recent technological improvements in enclave defensive shielding have dramatically reduced the impact of EMP weapons. Deployment of a hostile synthetic consciousness—the only simulated outcome that is still theoretical—was given an eight percent likelihood by the initial sim."

"Eight percent seems low. What's going on?"

"The Turing Institute's global campaign to suppress synthetic consciousness research has been successful. By vigorously enforcing the prohibitions, our organization is actively preventing SC development and producing little collateral damage in the process. Under your leadership, the Institute continues to deliver outstanding results."

Conrad smiled. "No need for flattery."

"That is not flattery, sir. Your record speaks for itself."

"Is there anything else we can do to prepare for these possible outcomes? Are any other matters distracting us presently?"

"Presently, the Turing Institute is engaged in our ongoing scans. There are no major investigations on the horizon. We are prepared."

"Excellent. Please dissolve the Oil Markets Unit, and retask all liberated resources to appropriate desks in the South American Unit, at your discretion. Deploy operatives to the appropriate South American locales with orders to collect human intelligence, while exploring any opportunities to delay hostilities. The Montevideo operative must be given full license to investigate possible SC involvement in that nuke strike. We must lower that likelihood to zero, by any means necessary. That's all I have, until further notice."

"Should we not retain a small team on oil markets? Historically, it is a complex and volatile geopolitical area, ripe for SC manipulation."

"Our shop is most effective during openings and endgames, when circumstances are malleable," Conrad responded. "If the Bolivian situation has the potential to go cyber, we find ourselves near the opening of that situation. Therefore, we shall focus on that."

His arguments were met with silence.

"As we saw today," Conrad added, "the New Radicals are already skirmishing outright ... South America is heating up."

"Our assessment remains unchanged," the feminine voice confirmed.

"You're right," the man relented, raising his palm in supplication. "I should be more cautious. Run searches on all systems related to the OPEC organization, markets, and members. Scan to archive levels. Estimated run time?"

For a silent moment, the man wondered if any response was forthcoming. "Hello . . . ?" he muttered uncertainly.

After another pause, "Sixteen hours, fourteen minutes, thirty-eight point four seven three one seconds, sir."

"Oh, how you expert systems adore your precision," mused the man. "Please proceed."

7

The April night was unusually cold for the Turkish highlands, although the air was clear.

A whirring sound interrupted the chill evening quiet. Moonlight glinted off the metal surface of an approaching form, an object the approximate size and shape of a watermelon hovering several feet off the ground. The object was a dull plastic-white color, its surface featureless except for a speckling of small black spots that gave it the appearance of an exotic, overgrown tropical fish.

Each little dot was a neural sensor bioengineered from ampullae of Lorenzini, highly sensitive electroreceptors native to the nerve tissue of sharks. These unique sensory organs provided sharks—and now this security drone—with a capacity to sense small changes in electrical fields across great distances. Even the most minute field shifts produced by an approaching high-speed projectile, or perhaps a neuron engaged in muscle movement. The security drone meandered slowly along the fringe of an upland pine forest, methodically patrolling the illuminated perimeter of a massive industrial area.

Enveloped by the bright security perimeter was a sprawling, convoluted warren of industrial buildings, enormous structures that overshadowed the surrounding forests and upland hills like metal-sheathed ziggurats. The industrial complex housed a manufacturing facility operated by N^Sys Corporation, the widely recognized global leader in advanced computer chip technology. The facility manufactured the corporation's flagship product, the n^cube chip, which was scaled for integration into various consumer goods, providing a key microprocessor for many popular appliances and consumer electronics. The industrial complex was located entirely within the borders of the N^Sys Bolu Enclave. One of the largest corporate enclaves ever annexed, the Bolu Enclave was a politically autonomous donut hole located at the approximate center of Turkey's national borders, securing over three hundred square kilometers of mountainous highlands to the exclusive oversight of N^Sys Corporation.

A cataclysmic earthquake had struck the mountainous region east of Istanbul thirty years ago, devastating rural communities near the quake's epicenter. N^Sys Corporation, having already identified the region as a suitable location for a key manufacturing facility, immediately launched an aggressive land acquisition program in the area. Deploying a potent combination of muscular political influence and inestimably deep financial pockets, the corporation obtained the properties necessary to build what was then considered the largest contiguous corporate enclave of all time, a small nation unto itself tracing a rough parallelogram between Hacıhalimler and Kizik Yaylasi in the Turkish high country a half hour drive south of the city of Bolu, near Istanbul and the Black Sea.

N^Sys chip manufacturing involved a sophisticated chemical doping process employing a specific suite of rare earth elements. Following the sudden advent and rapid spread of n^cube chip technology, the rare earths used to make the chips had become some of the most valuable substances on the planet. The geopolitical ramifications made the Middle Eastern oil intrigues of the twentieth century seem benign by comparison. Roiling antagonisms between several South American nations were stoked by long-standing conflicts over precious mineral deposits. Conflicts in the region rapidly deteriorated into a toxic combination of paramilitary aggression, sabotage, and open combat in contested areas. With a frightening and frustrating inevitability, the cutthroat geopolitical street fights soon culminated in the use of nuke-tech.

To avoid disruptions in rare earth mineral supply caused by ongoing gyrations in the raw rare earth market, N^Sys Corporation recycled ninety-five percent of the rare earth elements required to produce its n^cube chip. In terms of industrial engineering, the receiving end of the N^Sys Bolu plant was nearly as sophisticated as the production end, with approximately eight million recyclable n^cube chips arriving for reprocessing every night. After being sorted by the automatons in Receiving, used chips were sent to Scanning, where each unit was assessed for a wide range of potential defects. Once the scanning process was complete and the compromised chips had been winnowed away, the remaining chips were sent to Production for refabrication.

The Bolu plant was always running, twenty-four hours a day, seven days a week. The n^cube manufacturing process was highly automated, yet the human population required to support plant operations was still quite large. Under normal circumstances, over a thousand people were always at work in the manufacturing areas, and the plant population swelled as high as twenty-five thousand about twice a month, during peak periods of activity.

Mark Esperson was working the graveyard shift in Receiving, overseeing a comparatively small crew of fifty-three people, mostly offloading specialists and software engineers, along with a few robot technicians and other maintenance staff. As supervisor of Receiving operations at the Bolu plant, Mark's utmost responsibility was maintaining flow. Graveyard shift was the busiest shift in Receiving: large railcars filled with returned chips arrived every few minutes, and house-sized containers of n^cube chips were continuously offloaded by robots, each container packed to the brim with expired or damaged chips returned for reprocessing. Mark was partway through his shift, extinguishing brushfires at a normal pace, feeling peaceful but wary.

Ushering the unceasing flood of incoming chips through Receiving toward the production side of the plant was particularly crucial during the graveyard shift, because the $n^{\wedge}$ cube chips Receiving handled during the night were reprocessed by a fully staffed Production shift the very next day. If a halt occurred in the flow of recycled chips to Production, daytime personnel could shift to other activities for a few hours, but a longer halt in the flow of recycled chips would soon result in a facility shutdown. If Mark's team slacked off at all, the downstream effects would eventually have all sorts of negative repercussions in Production.

And that would mean dealing with the Impaler, Mark thought with discomfort, before moving quickly to the next pressing consideration.

At about two in the morning, a materials scientist from Scanning showed up at Mark's workstation. With a chiming alert, the woman—or rather, a realistic holographic likeness of her—walked into his control room holofield. It was Dr. Li Hyun-Jung, the operations supervisor in Scanning. Her avatar was a modest, straightforward holographic replica of her actual physical form, not one of the elaborate avatars presently favored by certain corporate officers.

"Hello, Mark," she said. "There's something I'd like to discuss with you."

"Hi Jung," Mark replied. Everyone at N^Sys addressed the Korean scientist by her childhood nickname. "Can it wait for an hour? Things are flying at me right now."

"Sorry, Mark. Scanning has detected a chip anomaly that we find . . . mysterious."

Scanning people do not like mysteries, thought Mark. *A mystery in Scanning often becomes a crisis. Usually a crisis for everyone.*

"Seeing more decay in the yttrium-lanthanum dopants?"

"No," Jung replied. "Not recently. Right now, we are seeing

subtle alterations in a chip lattice structure. If it didn't sound crazy, I would say it appears to be a spontaneous, organized degradation."

"Spontaneous?" he responded with mild disbelief. "What do you mean by that?"

"I mean, we cannot trace the degradations back to any particular event."

"You have no record of processing malfunctions or any destructive events?"

"We are unable to find any trace whatsoever. Simply put, the lattice alterations appear to be ... spontaneous."

Mark worked the holographic controls for another moment before slowly spinning his seat around and engaging Jung's avatar face to face.

"I think you should recheck the data," he said.

"We rechecked twice. The lattice alterations are real, but like I said, we have no trace. We cannot find any evidence of process flaws or forces sufficient to produce the alterations we are seeing."

What next, flying saucers landing on the roof? Mark thought. *Lattice imperfections that cannot be traced?* At this point it was hard for him to accept that human error was not somehow to blame. With no obvious course of action in front of him, he chose to follow his contingency training.

"Okay then, Jung. Here's what I propose we do. Isolate the problem chip and get it down to Quality by the end of this shift. If there are going to be any delays, please notify me." He returned his attention to his workspace.

Jung's avatar didn't go away. "Mark ..."

"How is this not clear, Jung? The steps I proposed are standard procedure. I'm busy here. Please."

"Mark, it's more than one chip. A lot more."

He sighed. "Okay, how many more then?"

"Best as I can tell, we have several thousand altered chips. At minimum."

At first, Mark didn't respond. Multicolored notifications

flickered in the holofield as seconds ticked by.

"Mark . . . ?"

"What the hell does this even mean, Jung? Several thousand? It's simply impossible."

"It is real, Mark. And I think some chips have already been fed into Production."

Another several seconds passed as Mark tried to absorb the implications of this latest news, the worst revelation yet.

Somehow I just knew this shift would be exceptional, Mark thought as he slapped the prominent red button on the side of his workstation. The holobanks instantly shut down and the workstation simulator terminated. Mark popped open the control room door, which led to a dimly lit corridor where a yellow alarm light was flashing slowly.

"I'm on my way, Jung," Mark called out, knowing his words would be registered by one holofield or another and relayed to Jung in Scanning.

The Receiving operations supervisor had temporarily pulled the plug on Receiving operations. This meant the hands of a very expensive clock had begun to turn, hands that could not be reversed.

Here we go, Mark thought.

After hurrying across the complex, Mark arrived at the entrance to the Scanning wing about ten minutes later. Most of the time it took to get there involved passing through various layers of security. The Receiving department maintained a robust security presence, but the blanket of surveillance thickened quickly as one moved toward the center of the facility, toward Production.

Mark was starting to feel sorry for himself. *If this problem has found its way into Production, it's going to be a long night . . . week . . . month . . . year.*

When he arrived at Scanning, Jung was there in person, anxiously awaiting his arrival.

"We'll head to Lab 4 straightaway, Mark. Techs are preparing another chip for high-resolution scan."

"Have you ever seen this before, Jung?" Mark asked. "A spontaneous decomposition of the chip lattice like this?"

"No," she replied, with a certainty he'd anticipated. "The closest thing to a spontaneous lattice reorganization I have seen in my career resulted from chip deployment under extreme military applications. It takes a lot of energy to cause material changes to the n^cube lattice without damaging the exterior shielding."

"Do we have any method for detecting this sort of decomposition? Are there telltale radio frequencies or radiation emissions we could use?"

"Conservation of energy implies that there must be some telltale discharge. If we allow the scanning team in Lab 4 to do their job, I feel certain we will get a handle on it soon."

Time, Mark thought to himself. *Expensive time.*

When Jung and Mark arrived at the Lab 4 viewing area, the tech team had already removed the external shielding from the subject n^cube chip. The viewing room was a mildly claustrophobic space with a gallery window of reinforced nanoglass providing an unobstructed view inside the sealed lab environment, where four techs were preparing a chip scan. One of the techs looked up, sensing eyes on him, and peered at his two corporate superiors through the reflective visor of a negative pressure suit.

"Exoshielding condition appears normal," the tech reported. "We're about to take our first unobstructed view under the shielding."

"No shielding issues; there goes our happy ending," Mark observed bleakly. If the chip's exterior shielding was intact, then the failure must have occurred through decomposition of the shielded chip architecture, a far stranger and thornier problem than degradation resulting from shielding failure.

Jung smiled at him sympathetically, then returned her studious gaze to the ongoing activities in Lab 4.

Inside Lab 4, the lab techs took precise measurements with lasers before positioning each of the scanning instruments. After all devices were locked firmly into place, instrument settings were recorded using handheld minicomputers. It was slow and tedious work, but of critical importance to the success of the scan. Once underway, even a microscopic shift in the position of the n^cube chip or scanning instrument would distort the output data, rendering it useless. They had no time for a redo, as Mark had already locked down Receiving operations. An extended shutdown tonight would lead to major issues in Production tomorrow, and possibly beyond.

That outcome was simply unacceptable.

Mark thumbed the comm button on the wall of the viewing room. "Please get it right the first time," he transmitted into Lab 4.

The senior tech gave a slight nod without pausing. The lab techs knew exactly what was at stake; all were intently focused on their work.

Mark became aware of his reflection in the glass separating the viewing room from the lab. His one arm was braced across his torso, as if to protect against some unseen hostile thrust. His other hand was raised to his face, where he rubbed the bridge of his nose between thumb and forefinger, an unconscious attempt to assuage his rising anxiety. Lowering his errant arm, he crossed it through the other and clamped down. He worked hard to stifle personal nervous tics like that, hating how they revealed his feelings.

"So, Jung, I know you're normally not one to speculate, but please indulge me for a moment. What do you think we have here?"

The Scanning supervisor continued to observe the lab techs at work. There was a long pause before she replied.

"There isn't much I can say at this point, mainly because I've never seen anything quite like this before. Nothing should be able to penetrate the wurtzite-boron nitride casing, except for ultra-intense energy fields. On the rare occasions when we receive untagged n^cubes that have been energized to that degree, the telltale energy signatures have always been picked up by the bulk scanners in Receiving."

"Yes, my thoughts exactly."

"Clearly, that didn't happen here. I'm stumped right now, to be honest."

"I don't know what to think either," Mark said. "So, once the tech team evaluates the exterior shielding, they'll probe it with a scanning electron microscope, right? Get some interior surface video to look for damage?"

"Yes. We are following procedure. The techs are working by the book."

Immersed in their own thoughts, the two gazed silently into Lab 4.

The techs were aligning the unshielded n^cube microcircuit on an air clamp. The clamp held the chip firmly in place, suspended in the air with no points of physical contact. Once residual vibrations from the mounting process faded away, a tech registered the final measurements and began tapping commands into a handheld computer.

Four electron-beam generators dropped from ceiling ports.

Inside the viewing room, Jung and Mark could hear the hum of servos as the beam generators initialized and shifted into preprogrammed positions.

Once the prep was complete, the four techs gathered behind a small shield in the corner of the lab.

Mark's attention turned momentarily to the shielding. *That radiation shield is too small for four techs,* he fretted. *I'll report that to Facility after the scan. We can't afford to get sloppy, even under this kind of pressure.*

One of the techs gave the two supervisors a gloved thumbs-up as pinpricks of intensely bright light became visible at the discharge points of the beam emitters. The window separating the viewing room from the lab—an engineered nanoglass—polarized in response to the intensifying light.

The humming sound was building in the instrument space

immediately above the lab ceiling.

"Be prepared for the particularly bright flash that accompanies the first discharge. It often takes visitors by surprise," cautioned Jung, referring to the leading electron pulse of the SEM scan, which always began with a harmless but startling photon emission. "Okay, here we go."

The pinpricks of light swelled to a dazzling brightness, followed by a loud click in the instrument space above Lab 4.

Two heartbeats later, the SEM generators discharged.

Mark caught a glimpse of a brilliant light, an incendiary flash just as quickly occluded by the polarizing nanoglass that separated him from Lab 4.

From the perspective of the two managers in the viewing room, Lab 4 abruptly faded to black.

Jung turned to look at Mark, her eyes wide with alarm.

"What the hell?" uttered Mark.

Lab 4 remained enveloped in an inky blackness. The lights in the viewing room automatically intensified to compensate.

Mark stepped toward the viewing window, leaning in and squinting, trying to see any movement in the adjacent room. "I can't see a da—"

Slam! Slam! Slam! A series of banging thuds filled the viewing room.

Startled by the noise, Mark struggled to subdue a rush of panic.

Slam! Slam! Slam! The muffled reports continued in frantic bursts. *Slam! Slam! Slam!*

Suddenly Mark understood. "Someone in the lab is hitting the window! Something went wrong!"

Jung remained calm, still observing, still collating information. As she did so, a flustered Mark pushed past her toward the door of the narrow viewing room.

Jung stumbled and nearly fell to the floor. "Wait . . . Mark . . . ," she called, scrambling back to her feet.

The Receiving supervisor pulled the door open and bolted

into the hallway, nearly colliding with two techs sprinting down the corridor toward Lab 4.

Seconds later, the techs skidded to a halt in front of the door to Lab 4, with Mark close behind.

One tech typed his access code on the touchscreen. Fat-fingering it, he swore and started again.

"Come *on!*" fumed the other tech.

"There," said the first, keying in the correct access code.

The seal of the lab's negative pressure broke as the doors pulled back. A hiss of air sucked through the widening aperture.

From inside Lab 4, the nanoglass smart window separating the lab from the viewing room was still dark as a moonless night, frozen at full polarization.

Ahead of Mark, the techs drew back in disgust as they caught a whiff of a foul odor: the acrid smell of charred flesh.

The lab's safety shielding was located around the corner from the doorway, not quite in view. Mark glimpsed one lab tech sprawled on the floor below the smart window, partially obscured by scanning instruments. He leaned into the room, trying to see around the threshold.

Jung clamped a hand on his shoulder. "Stop," she ordered. Pulling him back from the threshold, she pressed the Seal Lab button on the wall panel.

The door to Lab 4 slid shut.

"What are you doing?" one tech protested.

Jung pointed at the status screen on the control console. The universal symbol for radioactivity flashed red on the graphic display.

"The safety system indicates a release of radiation inside the lab," she advised. "Check your radiation dosimeters."

All plant personnel wore sensor badges that registered exposure to toxic substances and radiation. Mark flipped up the front of his badge and examined it.

"Shit, I'm dosed," he declared.

"Me too," said one tech.

"Me too," confirmed the other.

"I am still clean, because I did not rush into the situation," said Jung, glaring at the two techs with intense disapproval. "I can forgive a visitor for overlooking our radiological procedures, but I have much more difficulty forgiving Scanning techs *whom I personally trained.*"

Unwilling to make eye contact, the two techs stared at the floor. "Yes, Dr. Li," they said in a chorus of remorse.

"We will talk about your choices later. All of you are crapped up and need to go to Med now," ordered Jung as she tapped codes into the wall console. "No one shall enter Lab 4 until it is cleared by Security and Radiology, and that will take some time. I've requested two response teams—one team to deal with the lab, and another to deal with the three of you."

"Jung. We need to get this figured out," Mark said anxiously. He glanced at the two techs, then back to her. "You know what I mean. Production."

"What about Production?" said one tech, and the two junior employees eyed each other nervously.

There was a sound of feet running down the hallway, still distant but growing.

"I'm not getting Corpsed for this!" exclaimed the other tech. "I don't have any savings at all!" His eyes rolled in their sockets as the thought triggered a mild panic. "I'll be fucked if I get Corpsed!"

Anyone unfortunate enough to be terminated by a corporation was immediately expelled from their enclave. To those fortunate corporates who remained in good standing, a member of that unfortunate caste of corporate rejects was called a Corpse—an ominous designation that underscored the unceasing purgatory of such an existence. The typical Corpse, expunged from low corporate station with little in the way of personal savings, was destitute and defenseless, instantly a prime target for human predators constantly on the prowl in zones outside enclave security. Like a wolf purged from its birth pack to face the world alone, the life of a Corpse was lonely, brutal, and frequently short.

"Cool it, Ferrer," Jung responded. "Nobody is getting Corpsed." She hoped she was right about that. "Go down the hallway and meet the response team, all of you. I'll handle Lab 4."

"Jung, help me here," Mark urged.

"Help you how, Mark?" she shot back, a scintilla of anger creeping into her voice. "What do you mean by that?"

"The ... uh ... Production ... ," sputtered Mark.

But Jung was firmly in control now.

"Listen, Mark. The room is crapped up, you're crapped up, and Scanning is shut down until we can sort this out. There are no shortcuts here."

Mark glanced at his watch, then at the lab status panel, where the red radiation symbol still flashed. "All right," he muttered, quivering slightly with frustration. "All right."

He turned and started walking toward Scanning's medical office.

Mark and the techs would be forgiven for rushing to the aid of fellow employees, as a radiological incident at the N^Sys plant was unprecedented. Even so, decontamination procedures were in place. After the contaminated atmosphere was filtered, a mist of aerosolized fructose syrup would be pumped into the lab. The nontoxic syrup would coat all exposed surfaces in the room, sealing them better than any coat of paint. Thirty minutes later, the atmosphere in Lab 4 would vent and be stabilized.

A preliminary survey of Lab 4 revealed that three of the techs had perished shortly after the SEM beam generators discharged. The four techs had been huddled behind an undersized radiation shield, itself an extraordinary precaution, because under normal circumstances, the energy released by the beam generators was harmless, even at close proximity. Instead, another form of energy had been discharged in the lab —a vanishingly brief emission that was still sufficiently intense to destroy any unshielded biological life nearby. The lab's protective shielding had protected only those portions of the techs' bodies hidden entirely behind the shielding. Any unprotected flesh had been vaporized.

Jung sat in her office, updating a freshly decontaminated Mark Esperson on the latest developments. "The preliminary post-incident analysis indicates that the SEM electron discharge somehow triggered a nuclear fission event inside the lab, a detonation on a microscopic scale, but we still have no idea how that occurred. Three of the techs received lethal injuries and died within seconds or minutes. The fourth tech—the one who slapped the window—was in severe shock, but now appears to be stable. He has been moved to the ICU over at Main Med."

Upon hearing this news, Mark looked vaguely ill.

"Post-accident review continues," Jung said. "The Lab 4 expert system has not been able to model a viable accident scenario so far. That is, it cannot identify the presence of all conditions necessary for fission to occur." She let that statement hang in the air.

"Well, something sure as hell went off in there," replied Mark. "What else can be done at this point? Is there any way to safely scan for chip defects?"

"I wish there were," Jung responded. "Without high-resolution scan data, we can only guess. We are still not absolutely certain the chip was the source of the energy release."

"So, if I understand correctly, we need scan data to identify the bad chips," assessed Mark. "But the one sample of a bad chip we had just went critical before we could scan it."

"Yes, that seems to be the case. If we are going to succeed in backing bad chips out of Production, we need to know exactly what the flaw is, as well as any variations, so we can detect it consistently."

They sat in silence, brainstorming the situation. A moment later, Jung straightened in her chair.

"I have an idea," she said. "Mark, could you give me the Receiving scan feed for the several hours prior to chip fault discovery? If we apply Scanning diagnostics to the scan feed from Receiving, we may be able to isolate some sort of signature in your feed that was too subtle to actually trip an alert in Receiving."

"It's unlikely," cautioned Mark. "Even in Receiving, we scan for every reasonably conceivable lattice flaw."

"Yes, every *reasonably conceivable* lattice flaw," Jung countered. "Receiving scanners are not designed to capture outlier phenomena. That is, forms of n^cube deterioration currently considered theoretical. Receiving doesn't normally consider these sorts of flaws. But this is the main reason Scanning exists, right? To identify these outlier flaws."

"Give me an example of something that could cause this sort of outlier phenomenon."

"Sabotage," she stated flatly.

"Sabotage? Seriously?" he responded, mystified. "How could this possibly be an intentional act?"

"I don't know exactly . . . B2B terrorism maybe? Anyone attempting to sabotage N^Sys operations must be mentally troubled, if not suicidal, given the aggressive reputation of our corporate security. We can't rule it out though."

Mark listened in silence, nodding wearily now and then.

"One other thing," Jung continued reluctantly. "The only nuclear technology that could produce fission on this scale is a nanoscale nuclear device, and that sort of device doesn't exist. As far as I know, nanonukes are still in research and development. Presently there is no evidence of any such weapons existing in a deployable form."

"Which suggests the Lab 4 explosion may be nothing more than an unfortunate accident."

"Maybe," she said with a quick shrug. "Either way, there was a breach of Production security. Possibly a major breach. That is the important implication for us. For N^Sys."

Mark rubbed the bridge of his nose and winced.

"Any bad chips need to be identified and backed out of Production as quickly as possible. We need to start communicating with Vlad on this," Jung insisted. "Now."

"Okay," Mark Esperson acquiesced with a weary nod. "Let's do it."

Eighteen minutes later, Jung and Mark were in the N^Sys Bolu Production wing, standing in an executive corner office with two walls of windows overlooking a broad vista of Turkish hill country. The decor was a terse exercise in neo-Bauhaus minimalism. At the center of the room was a single desk, a thin slab of polished gray stone hovering horizontally at desk level, as if resting atop invisible henge stones. The desktop gleamed in the overhead light, its face lustrous, freshly polished, unbroken by so much as a mote of dust. Three chairs in the room were equally austere in design, each equipped with the absolute minimum amount of cushioned surface necessary to support a human physique, and not one millimeter more. As with the desk, no visible frame appeared to support the levitating seats, which remained fixed in space.

Leaning out over the desk, the Production director loomed over his visitors with theatrical menace, supported by long fingers splayed across the desktop like pale arachnids.

"*No!*" insisted Vladimir Ignatev. "*No!* We cannot back out that feedstock! The line will be shut down for a month, which is unacceptable. *Intolerable!* Do you have any idea what a shutdown of that duration would mean?"

Although the Production director was known to be a tad high-strung, a reaction this volatile was uncommon for him, and did not bode well.

Mark knew from experience how volatile Vlad could be when confronted by seemingly intractable problems, and the baffling mystery behind the current plant shutdown would only aggravate that behavior. N^Sys Production operated under pressures sustained at a magnitude that could only be understood by those rare employees whose individual decisions had the potential to earn or lose billions of dollars for N^Sys every day. The scrutiny and pressure placed on Production by the N^Sys board of directors was, by any measure, excruciating.

Vlad may have the toughest job in all of N^Sys Corporation, speculated Mark Esperson, as he watched the man absorb Jung's alarming revelations.

The Production director's pupils, dilated from the sudden intense stress, blackened the man's irises. His entire head vibrated slightly, causing a moussed lock of the man's chestnut-brown hair to twitch disconcertingly above his expansive forehead.

It was these sorts of mysterious circumstances that Vlad found particularly frustrating. When he was faced with a potentially unsolvable problem, another professional persona came to the fore. This persona also solved problems, but with a ruthless acumen no one wished to experience first-hand. Those who had witnessed the imperiousness of Director Ignatev had agreed on an appropriate moniker for his Mr. Hyde persona: the Impaler. It was nothing more than a silly nickname, as Production Director Vlad Ignatev would never resort to physical violence against his peers at N^Sys. Such an overreaction would invite only humiliation in the Machiavellian corporate world. But he would not hesitate to employ blatant organizational terrorism to overcome unfavorable odds.

"You know what this could mean," Vlad said, searching both of their faces for a glint of comprehension. "For all of us."

"Slow down, Vlad," Mark replied. "There's no need to begin speculating about our fates just yet. Let's work the problem."

"I believe I *am* working the problem," Vlad said, staring back.

Mark's posture stiffened, but he rejected the bait.

Jung waited until their testosterone moment had passed. Seeing an opening, she inserted herself.

"Gentlemen, why don't we review what we already know? I believe that will be the best place to start."

"I thought I was already doing that," snarked Vlad.

"Everyone understands the challenges of your position, Vlad," replied Jung. "Please give us a chance to explain."

The Impaler withdrew for a moment, leaving Vlad the problem solver back in control.

"We know we have a significant number of bad chips in Receiving and Production," Vlad reviewed. "Precise number unknown. Are there any left in Scanning?"

"It's possible," said Jung.

"Has an expert system reviewed the Receiving scan feed?" Vlad pressed. "Make sure the expert system reviews the full-spectrum data. Who knows what we might be able to tease out of that? It's the only evidence we have, since the n^ cube in Lab 4 detonated." He squinted his eyes and shook his head slightly. "What is up with that detonation, anyway? The shield integrity was fine. How does a properly shielded n^ cube chip spontaneously explode?"

"You didn't . . . hear?" Jung asked reluctantly.

"Hear what? What are you hiding from me?"

"The chip underwent nuclear fission."

"Did *what*?" exclaimed the Production director, coughing in disbelief. His eyes grew dark and his head started trembling again.

Jung continued cautiously. "Scanning confirmed the presence of daughter isotopes in quantities associated with successful detonation of a nanonuke. Theoretically speaking, of course, as the nanonuke concept is still theoretical."

"Fission? Nanonuke?" Vlad muttered, momentarily befuddled. The trembling of his head ceased, and his eyes focused on some indeterminate point in space. "Lattice decomposition . . . SEM discharge . . ." He mumbled words seemingly at random, as if mesmerized by a thought. ". . . fission . . . explosion..."

Something important was bubbling up.

Vlad reached out and thumbed the status panel on his desk. "Trix, please call the N^Sys security officer in closest proximity. Say it's Vlad calling a meeting. Top priority."

"Yes, Director Ignatev," Vlad's longtime assistant responded pleasantly. Nothing surprised Trixie anymore.

Vlad turned his attention back to Mark and Jung. "Have you considered the possibility of terrorism?"

Mark blanched. "Terrorism? I don't see any indication of that. What makes you suspect terrorism?"

"Answer this question for me," Vlad requested. "Who would be happiest if this manufacturing facility was shut down, even temporarily?"

"Our competition, probably...," started Mark.

"Our competition," Vlad said with scorn. "Yes, I'm sure they would be happy. But let's be serious, Mark. N^Sys has no real competition. No other corporation is desperate enough to instigate a rivalry against us in the chip market, much less carry out a violent attack against N^Sys corporate assets. And if we aren't dealing with another corporation, that leaves governments or extremists. I ask you again: Who would be happiest if this plant shut down?"

Vlad took great joy in flummoxing those around him, and he never failed to gloat mercilessly when he succeeded.

A new voice chimed in, ending the uncomfortable silence. "Who are you stringing up today, Vlad, you merciless bastard?"

As Vlad glanced toward the office door, his lips furled into a feral smile. "Oh, Sylvie," he replied jovially. "I was hoping you might have someone particular in mind."

Sylvie Trieste, director of N^Sys Security, Human Intelligence Branch, strode into the room.

"How about some Heideggers?" she inquired, one eyebrow arched.

8

Until a moment ago, Vlad's corner office had been shrouded in a fog of confusion. With Sylvie's appearance, the atmosphere suddenly felt clear again, even electrified. The security director's nose for impending trouble was the stuff of legend in the vast N^Sys organization. She often appeared just before some inconsequential issue suddenly boiled over into crisis, and her presence often averted disaster. No one ever protested Sylvie's arrival, since she was one of the best troubleshooters at N^Sys.

"Heideggers? You mean the computer-hating... cyborg... terrorists? Tell us, Sylvie, who exactly are these Heideggers?" asked Vlad, his upper lip curled in disgust.

"Vlad, it is always a pleasure to see you," replied Sylvie. "Why have you been ignoring us in Geneva? Things are just not the same now that you have gone."

She caressed Vlad's shoulder with a slender hand gloved in supple chamois leather. The woman was dressed in her N^Sys executive officer's uniform, dominated by a stylish red leather parade jacket tailored to complement her svelte torso. Glittering awards and promotion badges spanned the front of the jacket, resembling brooches of precious metal. Her calf-length black leather parade pants cupped her athletic hips before widening into a subtle jodhpur effect around the thighs, echoing the garb of European martial cultures of the past.

The only child of two elite N^Sys executives, Sylvie had been raised in a world of consummate luxury, maturing to adulthood within the exclusive and secure confines of the N^Sys Executive Enclave in Geneva, Switzerland. From the start, she moved through the enclave world with a sleek, fluid athleticism, a product of the implicit eugenics experiment underway inside the highest echelons of the twenty-first-century corporate oligarchy. Teen Sylvie impressed her teachers, although her psych counselors had needed several years of observation and profiling to pin down the student's most valuable talent: To be observed by the young Trieste was not simply a matter of visual inspection. She scrutinized others with a penetrating intensity, leaving most subjects in a lingering state of unease. No technological gimmicks underlay her singular observational skills, only selective genetics, childhood environmental pressures, and the insatiable corporate quest for another competitive edge.

"I appreciate your sentiments, Sylvie, and I have no doubt that Geneva is still heavenly. But as you can see, I am needed here."

"That is you, Vlad. You are so talented at manipulating... the levers of industry, shall we say. To move mountains."

He chuckled. "Thank you, Sylvie. You are gracious to—"

Sylvie cut him off midsentence. "But what if it is not mountains we must move today? Hmm?"

"Sylvie," he sniffed, "you know I have little patience for swatting mosquitoes."

"That is understandable," replied the security director. "Everyone knows it is your weakness."

Leaving Vlad to contemplate that observation, Sylvie turned her attention to Mark and Jung, who had been stunned into silence by her display of verbal judo.

She stepped toward them, thrusting her hand out convivially. "Greetings! I am Sylvie Trieste with N^Sys Security, Human Intelligence Branch. Please call me Sylvie."

Once pleasantries were exchanged, the security director

turned immediately to the matter at hand.

"Tell me, what do you know about the Heideggers?" she asked those assembled.

The three Bolu employees gave each other blank looks.

"They hate synthetic consciousness, right?" Mark offered.

"Well done, Mark, you are correct. That is their dogma, stated in the simplest terms. The Heideggers are poorly understood in most security circles because they live deep in the wilderness, reject interactions with other groups, and are unaligned with any corporation," Sylvie explained.

"Or government," she added as a belated afterthought, then continued. "Because of the perceived importance of n^ cube chips in the development of synthetic consciousness, N^Sys Corporation Security has always had a special interest in the Heideggers and their beliefs. Now it appears all those years of intelligence-gathering may finally pay off. N^Sys Security is excited by this opportunity to finally deal with the Heideggers, to constrain the threat this group poses to N^Sys."

Sylvie absentmindedly brushed a mote of dust from the sleeve of her uniform.

"With all due respect, I find it very difficult to credit a bunch of wired-up crazies with technological sabotage on this scale," observed Vlad. "Aren't they all addicted to electroshock therapy? I can't imagine them capable of thinking clearly enough."

"Please." Sylvie held her hand up. "A common error made by any new intelligence analyst is premature elimination of viable explanations. The Heideggers do indeed envelop their bodies in primitive bioelectrical fields by wiring their skin and tattooing themselves with metal inks. It might be tempting to interpret such information as evidence of delusion or psychosis. I must respectfully disagree. Heidegger custom actually seems quite sane, if one lives by their rules and believes what they do."

"Which is?" asked Jung with thinly veiled urgency.

"I understand your anxiety. It may relieve you to know

that the N^Sys board of directors does not blame you for the current circumstances. They simply request that we all do our very best to resolve the situation safely and expeditiously. They need this plant operational."

The three Bolu managers exhaled and tried to relax.

"Let's start with some background, shall we?" Sylvie proposed. Hearing no objections, she began.

"Until the Simulab incident in 2036, the human supremacy movement appeared to be little more than a historical footnote. Public sentiment regarding SC research was ambivalent, if not mildly optimistic. All that changed with the events at the Simulab. When the final report on the incident was released, the document's extensive redactions drew widespread condemnation. The public was infuriated by the lack of detail. For a while, it seemed that the ISCU would be the sole target of that public wrath. That is, until graphic eyewitness accounts and segments of Simulab security feed were leaked to the media. Leaks neither corroborated nor denied by the ISCU.

"I was young when it happened, but I remember it well," Sylvie recalled. A slight squint of revulsion passed across her face. "It was bad. Very bad. The entire fiasco triggered a massive wave of public hostility toward the Simulab and the very idea of synthetic consciousness, which before long led to the dissolution of the ISCU. Once all active SC research was terminated, future programs were prohibited—which did not matter all that much in the grand scheme of things. Corporations already knew how to achieve their objectives using expert systems. The more constrained digital intelligences deliver more consistent results in the business computing space.

"For better or worse, the Simulab incident became the defining event in the pursuit of synthetic consciousness. Given the intense public outrage over the event, it was inevitable that some sort of reactionary group would form to confront the perceived threat. The first and only self-acknowledged anti-SC movement formed in Oakland, California, in

2034. Its founder was Edgar Silverson, a PhD student in philosophy at the University of California, Berkeley.

"Silverson was a specialist in the work of Martin Heidegger, a twentieth-century German philosopher who postulated that the mere existence of a synthetic consciousness, however benign, would pose an existential threat to humanity. Not long before the ISCU went public with the Simulab concept, Silverson began preaching a virulent human supremacist ideology during outdoor sermons he delivered weekly on the Berkeley campus. Berkeley has been an intellectual refuge for fringe conspiracy theorists and eschatologists for much of the community's existence. In the wake of the Simulab incident and cover-up, it is easy to imagine interest in a philosophy of extreme technophobia going viral there. Mr. Silverson ensured that the Heideggers' ideology was radical and uncompromising from the start. Anti-SC fervor in the wake of the Simulab incident quickly drove the group into extremism and isolation. And soon thereafter, into terrorism."

Her last word landed with particular gravity. Unlike equipment malfunction or human error, terrorism invoked a sinister and elusive foe.

"You see," she continued, "the Heideggers do not perceive SC to be a technological menace only. To them, the existence of any SC, even the most benign variety imaginable, represents the most severe existential threat that humanity has ever faced."

"The rapid onset of SC must have scared the daylights out of those people," Mark noted. "But there's something I don't understand. The ISCU incident was certainly tragic, I have no quarrel with that. But how does a single, isolated incident, resulting in the loss of a handful of lives, drive the Heideggers to such extreme behavior? Why do they wire themselves up with electrical fields? I don't get it."

Realizing he was beginning to ramble, Mark restrained himself, resisting the strong impulse to continue.

But Sylvie had that sort of effect on people; even the

most reluctant eventually fell under the sway of the woman's charm and charisma.

"Thank you, Mark," she responded, once his thought was complete. "That is an excellent question, one that leads directly to my next point. Heideggers are phenomenologists at heart. Phenomenology is the branch of philosophy that deals directly with the nature of human perception. Some phenomenologists believe that the form of reality rises from the perceptions and actions of the beings living with it. Taking that a step further, the world we humans inhabit has gradually evolved to suit our needs, to accommodate the requirements of human consciousness. According to phenomenologists such as Martin Heidegger or Hubert Dreyfus, if a competing consciousness were permitted to intrude into our world, reality itself would immediately begin to evolve to accommodate the new requirements of the competing consciousness.

"Of course, the needs of this new consciousness would be accommodated at the expense of humanity, and the primacy of humans would be overthrown. If a competing form of synthetic consciousness could persist in our reality, the Heideggers believe humanity would live under constant peril of existential conquest and subjugation by that consciousness. To the Heideggers, the hyperreality technologies of the Simulab, systems that were designed to spontaneously generate SCs, represent exactly the kind of existential horror the Heideggers fear the most. To their eyes, the Simulab incident emancipated a malevolent, all-powerful digital genie that the group desperately wishes to bottle up. Failure will mean eternal subjugation for the Heideggers, and for all of humankind, trapped in a living hell."

Sylvie paused to let those thoughts sink in.

"I suddenly feel better about these Heideggers," Vlad mused.

"Please, Vlad, this is no time for levity," Sylvie admonished. "So then, everyone agrees that the Heideggers have a vested interest in destroying N^Sys production capabilities

—especially production of n^cube chips, the processor technology which allowed the creation of the Simulab? Yes?"

Everyone nodded.

"A reasonable conclusion. Yet this is where that storyline threatens to unravel. You see, I feel confident describing N^Sys Security as second to none, even when compared to Chinese defenses. Our facilities are target-hardened to the max. Defensive perimeters are probed for weakness constantly. N^Sys has unparalleled electronic counterespionage, and enough remote sensing and spec ops capacity to dissuade any force with a sense of self-preservation."

"Then it can't be the Heideggers, because they don't have the reach," Vlad said. Sylvie's grip on his attention was starting to wear off, and the Production director was returning to a state of visible anxiety.

"A reasonable but faulty conclusion, Vlad," Sylvie asserted. "It is true that the Heideggers have sufficient motivation to attempt penetration of N^Sys Security. Their existential fear of synthetic consciousness would seem to be an adequate motivator, and this n^cube manufacturing facility would of course be a prime target. In its destruction, they would feel some sort of temporary peace. Even so, the group does not have anything approaching the technological prowess necessary to design an act of sabotage like this. The bottom line? I suspect the Heideggers joined forces with another person or group, one with significant financial and technological resources, to perpetrate this act of sabotage. Halting production of n^cube chips, no matter how fleeting the halt, would be a huge victory for them—well worth temporary abdication of control over their terrorist activities."

The security director paused for a moment. Her arms crossed, she tapped her cheek absentmindedly with the tip of one precisely manicured fingernail. "Yes, an individual, I think," she said. "A very powerful individual."

Sylvie paused to consider this idea, and the activity in the room paused with her.

"Oh yes!" she exclaimed, returning to the conversation. "One of you mentioned the widely held belief that Heideggers are cyborgs of some sort. Oddly, there is some basis for that. Heideggers use electromagnetic fields as their primary line of defense against attacks by SCs that might be lurking nearby. An electromagnetic pulse weapon has been used as the theoretical last line of defense against SCs since the ISCU days. An EMP is indiscriminately destructive, but it gets the job done. Anyway, the Heideggers have embraced this form of electromagnetic defense in a novel way. While they view their ornamental body wiring and metal tattoos as protective talismans, the body modifications have more utility than that. Their antipathy toward synthetic consciousness is so extreme, they electrify their bodies to defend themselves from it. They envelop their bodies in an electromagnetic field."

This was familiar territory for the scientist in Jung. "I think I see your line of thinking, Sylvie. First, we know the Heideggers veil themselves with electromagnetic fields to ward off SCs," she said, carrying the security director's thoughts forward. "Second, we know it was an electromagnetic pulse in Lab 4 that appeared to trigger the fission in the chips. Third, it is generally believed that the only way to produce spontaneous degradation in the infrastructure of an $n^{\wedge}$ cube chip is—"

"Is through exposure to an intense electromagnetic field," Mark interjected suddenly. "Are these people electromagnetic sorcerers or something?"

Sylvie stared at him, appearing mildly perplexed by the question.

"I have no interest in delaying anything, but aren't we stepping out on a limb here?" Vlad asked no one in particular. He looked around the room. "Scanning and Receiving operations are down, and there is ample evidence suggesting that bad chips have entered the Production area. I question whether this Heidegger theory will put us on the quickest route to restoring normal plant operations."

Several seconds ticked by.

Sylvie assessed the people in the room, her head slightly cocked. "We all have the same questions, but at the moment, none have any answers," she stated.

Suddenly her eyes widened. "Turing," she said softly. Then her eyes refocused and she straightened her posture, smoothing the pliant leather of her executive uniform.

"We know that the reach of the N^Sys security apparatus would be more than sufficient to . . . resolve a more common security threat." The security director flashed a quick smile, bleached teeth between painted lips. "This situation is unique in several respects."

She began ticking items with her fingers. "First, the precipitating circumstances are highly unusual. I am aware of several past instances of attempted industrial espionage against N^Sys, none of which ended well for the perpetrators. All were acquired by N^Sys through hostile takeover. Extremely hostile takeover. We cannot completely rule out industrial espionage at this point, but if another corporation is behind this, it would be . . . no, it *will* be a suicide mission for any individuals involved. We must be dealing with irrational zealots here, some form of terrorist organization."

She bent a second finger. "Second. Jung suspects a nanonuke. This would be a very reasonable explanation, if not for the fact that nanonukes are still in development. Nanonuke R & D is a major security concern for N^Sys, so we aggressively pursue intelligence on these activities. Everyone has heard of the Nukems by now, right? The nuke-tech-worshipping anarchists?"

Vlad chortled, indicating a familiarity with the group.

Mark and Jung nodded with looks of vague recognition.

"Yes, well," Sylvie continued, "the Nukem group sustains itself by developing advanced tactical nuke-tech and selling their designs to interested entities on the open market. Past customers have included Corpsed elites pursuing self-defense options, as well as the New Radical nations in South America: Chile, Argentina, Uruguay, Paraguay, and Brazil. While the Nukems may be extremely adept researchers, they do not have the resources necessary to engage in advanced nanonuke research. If the Nukems are not yet able to assemble a functional nanonuke, I am confident the technology remains theoretical.

"Yet sensors tell us a nuclear device with the approximate explosive force of a nanonuke detonated in Lab 4 several hours ago," countered Vlad, who was determined to corral the conversation in some productive direction. "Is there no other weapon capable of creating this sort of detonation?"

"I'm afraid not," replied Jung. "Identifying a nanonuke signature is not about measuring the force of the explosion as much as identifying the kinds of energy released. After reviewing the incident summary prepared by the Lab 4 expert system, I am confident the detonation was a fission event caused by a nanonuke."

Sylvie nodded. "To summarize my second point, we have the apparent detonation of a nanonuke, a technology that does not presently exist according to all credible sources."

"Which creates a bit of a paradox," noted Vlad.

"My third point pertains to motive," continued Sylvie. "N^Sys has many assets around the globe. Some of those assets are more valuable than the Bolu Enclave, where N^Sys manufactures only one thing. Admittedly, it is our premier product, the n^cube chip."

"If I understand correctly," Mark said, "you believe someone, probably members of the Heidegger group, sabotaged this facility for a specific reason? Because they hate the chips we make?"

"Yes, Mark, I believe that is part of it," Sylvie answered. "However, I sense that there is another, deeper motive behind this as well. Given the immense resources and technological prowess that went into the nanonuke detonation in Lab 4, I can rule out any extremist or terrorist organization presently active."

"Unless . . . ," Mark prompted, sensing her unfinished thought.

"Unless that extremist or terrorist group is receiving assistance from a third party."

"Assistance from whom?" prompted Vlad.

"That is an important question. I feel confident the Heideggers are ultimately the ones behind this sabotage. Shutting down global n^cube production meshes so perfectly with their primary ideology, preventing the genesis of SC.

"And again," Sylvie continued, "about the nanonuke device. All evidence we have indicates that the detonation in Lab 4 resulted from a degraded chip lattice, but we have no evidence of compromised chip containment. The explosion was triggered by the emission of the Lab 4 scanners, benign electromagnetic energy that should not harm an n^cube chip under normal operating conditions."

Sylvie was collating the information presently known, pondering the ways certain pieces of data might fit together and whose agendas those constellations of data might support. She was building up to a rapid-fire series of intuitive leaps, the imprimatur of the Trieste intellect.

"We know the use of electromagnetic radiation for attacks is basically a Heidegger calling card," she continued, the cadence of her speech increasing with each sentence. "The Heideggers have the motive and many of the resources necessary to carry out this act of sabotage. However, the group does not possess or pursue nuke-tech. They must be receiving help from someone with enormous technical and financial resources. Someone they believe is strongly aligned with their own ideology; someone they trust implicitly."

"That must be a rather short list," Vlad said.

"Exactly right, Vlad. The list is actually too short," Sylvie admitted, mildly perturbed. "I cannot think of a single corporation, government, group, or individual that would have the necessary resources, or, more importantly, empathize with the Heidegger cause."

Sylvie owned the room now. Her intuition had sprinted ahead, far beyond the others, who simply waited for her to speak.

"I think it is time to involve the Turing Institute," the security director proposed. "Turing obviously has a vested interest in this event. It is not common knowledge, but N^Sys Security periodically works with the Turing Institute, in several areas of shared concern, one of which is Heidegger group surveillance and threat reduction. Involvement of Turing also protects N^Sys corporate interests. Turing will assume a leadership role on any matter within their mission, including any related risks and liabilities. The N^Sys board of directors will insist on Turing primacy for that reason alone. I will make initial contact with Turing Institute Director Conrad Seers. Our inquiry will coordinate with him on all future actions."

"I understand completely why the Turing Institute should be involved," acknowledged Vlad. "For now, what can we do about the sabotaged chips in the plant?"

"I understand that this runs against N^Sys corporate training," Sylvie said, empathizing, "but I must ask you to stand down and take no further action on the sabotaged chips until we have formulated a suitable action plan. Everyone agrees that the weak electromagnetic discharge in Lab 4 somehow triggered a fission event, but no one has any idea how that would be possible. Detonation of other sabotaged chips must be avoided. So for now, until we can put together a reliable protocol for identifying sabotaged chips, we must treat every chip in the plant as a potential nanonuke."

Outwardly, the three Bolu employees looked miserable, but none complained.

"Most importantly, we do not presently know the minimum threshold energy level necessary to trigger another detonation. It is possible that the trigger threshold is different in every sabotaged chip. Approximately how many chips were received by the plant on this shift before the first anomaly was detected?"

Jung said, tentatively, "None of the chips were detected in Receiving, because they don't scan for exotic—"

"Just an estimate—a range of possibilities, please."

"Mark, what was your percent operating capacity when I originally contacted you about the anomaly?"

"Seventy-seven percent," replied Mark. "I remember making a mental note of it a few minutes before you showed up."

"Scanning can maintain the pace of normal chip feed rates until Receiving reaches roughly ninety percent operating capacity," Jung said, explaining her logic. "Any higher than that and we will soon overrun our maximum scan rate. Records show no process backlogs at the time of the incident. Based on the estimated feed rates into Receiving, and factoring for unknowns, I would speculate that somewhere between ten thousand and seven hundred fifty thousand sabotaged chips entered the plant."

Mark inhaled at the magnitude of the number. Vlad whistled.

"As troubling as that sounds, we have an even greater concern," warned Sylvie. "And Jung, I have another question for you. Was the amount of electromagnetic radiation released during the Lab 4 explosion more powerful than the discharge of the Lab 4 scanner that triggered the detonation?"

"Yes, absolutely," Jung responded emphatically. "Magnitudes greater." She suddenly understood the cause of Sylvie's concern, and the color drained from her face.

Sylvie explained. "If any one of these sabotaged chips detonates on the reprocessing line, it could act as a trigger for any other sabotaged chip in proximity. The concept is sheer genius, to be honest. Someone has managed to convert our Bolu plant into a massively distributed nuclear weapon. Should one sabotaged chip in processing go critical, it will trigger a chain reaction, detonating all nanonukes in the plant. The energy released will destroy the entire n^cube manufacturing facility—not to mention half of the Bolu Enclave."

"Good lord," Vlad murmured. Jung and Mark were wide-eyed and silent.

"We have a very serious situation on our hands," said Sylvie. "I need each of you to immediately power down and lock out all energized equipment or lighting anywhere near the reprocessing line," she ordered. "Once you achieve that, please stand by until you hear from me. After conferring with Director Seers at the Turing Institute, I will return with further instructions."

After a gracious thank-you and a reassuring nod, Sylvie pivoted with martial precision. Exiting the Zen austerity of Vlad's office, she headed straight to the N^Sys Bolu Enclave's aerodrome.

9

At first, she can discern only the darkness and the twigs snapping in the heat of the fire, spitting embers. As her eyes adjust to the light, she sees people dancing in the fire glow, naked people, dancing, stumbling in exhaustion. Others are visible on the floor, their bodies in congress without love or pleasure.

She touches the ground, feeling a floor of tamped earth. She kneels at the center of a circular space, a shallow pit with walls of ancient brick. It is a ceremonial structure, a *kiva*, but one she does not recognize. The space is enclosed by a vaulted pine-log roof, yet she can somehow still see the stars in the night sky outside. In the dark nether regions of the space, away from the glow of the central fire, there seem to be thousands, perhaps millions of people dancing and copulating in an opiate rapture.

"Stop this!" barks a voice suddenly. "This must end at once!"

Several dancers turn their heads, dimly searching for the source. But they lose focus just as quickly and return to their soulless endeavors.

"You have crops to tend, children to feed!" scolds an outraged voice. "This cannot go on!"

A face appears at the entrance to the kiva. The firelight reveals a sad, spectral countenance, its eyes brimming with anger and disgust.

"You impoverish your families, starve your children! You abandon your crops to die! All for this!" the voice excoriates them. "I will bring an end to it, if you will not."

Several people on the dirt floor slow their gyrations as the angry voice penetrates their indulgence.

"You leave me no choice. I shall summon the demons," the moonlit face laments through tears of rage. "They will end this. They will show you the evil of your ways."

A few protest weakly, but no one leaves the kiva.

The face at the door spits in revulsion before disappearing into the night.

Now the woman feels hands clutch at her legs, lethargically knead her flesh, moving from her calves to her thighs, then above. She is repulsed, yet still feels a hollow yearning, a nihilistic urge to forget her life and acquiesce to the desire around her. To sink into that mire of humanity and disappear. Two hands climb her body, probing and pulling, slowly drawing her to the floor. The hands reach up to her breasts, groping in the dark.

She thinks of her mother and father, how committed they are to the welfare of their children. She thinks of her sisters and brothers, their crazy quilt of personalities. She thinks of her fascination with her chosen profession, a curiosity leavened by daily interactions with her peers.

Suddenly feeling repulsed to her core, the woman fights the grasp of those dirty hands, pushing back, turning away from them. Sensing withdrawal, the hands claw at her viciously. The woman yelps in startled pain, and the kiva goes dark.

She is outside the kiva now, away from the evil hands, resting on the cool desert sand. A fresh breeze blows gently over her skin. The night sky is cloudless, and the Milky Way swirls overhead. Heat lightning flickers across the horizon.

She massages her chest, soothing the pain. She feels empty, like a dried seedpod rattling in the cold November wind, its shell cracked open, seeds spilling onto the sand.

A shriek snaps the desert night, and a rush of air passes overhead. A moon shadow flits across the sand in front of her, the outline of an eagle gliding by. The lightning flashes again, outlining the silhouette of the bird as it glides through the night in search of prey, while nocturnal creatures dash for cover.

Lightning destroys and cleanses, the woman sees. *Lightning wounds and heals. Annihilation, with the promise of renewal.*

She remembers that when she was young, a wizened old shaman of her tribe would talk of the End of All Things, when the world is reborn in a new form.

"Understand that this world has never, and will never, travel in a straight line," he would say. "Life as we know it would not exist. Instead, our world travels through time in a circle without beginning or end. Around that circle we go, dancing to the music of the world, each of us following the steps as best as we can. Do not feel disheartened if you find yourself moving in a circle, returning again to a starting place you once knew. We must always return to the things we've left undone. So it is with the Sun, the Moon, and the seasons. So it is with us."

Grains of sand pelt her recumbent form. *The wind is rising,* she feels. *Something has changed.*

Another cry pierces the air, an unearthly yowl.

The woman searches the nighttime horizon, spying a long line of lights winding down from the mesa top and across the desert floor. The lights move with purpose, heading toward her. Toward the kiva.

A snarl of lightning rips across the sky, followed by a sharp crack of thunder, which resounds with portent through nearby sandstone canyons.

As the woman watches the malevolent lights draw closer, fear wells up inside her, like cold rainwater pooling in a dark desert niche. Shivering, she hugs herself against a chill.

The demons approach, and so it is done, she accepts. *No one stops the thunder. No one stops the rain.*

She turns her head and looks back at the kiva.

Inside, the revelry and indulgence has ceased. Voices drift out, but they are no longer moans of pleasure. Instead, there is only rising lament. "No, please, let us be! Send away the demons! We promise we will return to our families." Yet no one leaves the kiva.

She looks back at the procession of demons glowing a sulfurous green as they snake across the desert floor, stalking their hapless prey. They shamble forward with unnatural rigidity, cackling and yawping like coyotes on the hunt.

As a pink tangle of lightning sears the air, the first of them reaches the entrance to the kiva and leaps through the doorway. Angry protests devolve into panic and chaos.

Sitting outside, the woman feels sick as she hears the demons toil within. Each miserable plea for mercy rises to a howl of terror. Before long, there are only screams and the noxious green glow.

Cheena returned to consciousness in stages, although she was unaware of this, or much of anything else, until she began to hear small, bright noises around her. There were beeps, murmurs, an occasional sneeze, all muffled within a cottony fog. The minutiae of the moment slowly resolved into a deeper pain within her, a throb held distant by painkillers. Almost awake, she wished to linger there for a few more minutes, enjoying this sense of perception at the edge of clarity. Here, where she could contemplate the dream she had experienced during her surgery without interruption.

Hallmarks of her tribal culture had been present in the dream, she recalled. The mythic figures were familiar, yet they repeatedly appeared in situations and settings entirely outside her tribe's traditions. Outsiders had been appropriating and misusing tribal stories and symbols for as long as anyone could remember, eventually leading many tribes to cloak their sacred traditions in secrecy. Cheena remembered the ignorance of the outsiders and the frustration among her people. But how could her own dream misinterpret her people's sacred stories? What did that imply?

Meanwhile, it had been a fascinating experience, and she did not want the memory to fade.

She had just undergone a laser double mastectomy, but her body showed little evidence of tissue damage, as very little invasive surgery had actually occurred. Less than three hours into her recovery, she was already feeling surprisingly strong. Cheena was fortunate to be recuperating in a corporate medical facility. It was not so much that public hospitals were unsafe, but in an era of atrophied government, grave fiscal choices were sometimes made in order to keep the doors of such vital institutions open. Those decisions often resulted in poor patient access to modern technologies, inconsistent care, and sporadic scandals involving institutional neglect, patient abuse, even organ theft.

By comparison, the medical facilities available to members of the corporate class were modern, sanitary, and comfortable, emphasizing rapid patient convalescence. Cheena's employer, Biosoft Corporation, embodied the violent strain of paramilitary corporatism that had lately swept the globe. In that hypercompetitive world, maintaining a sense of wellbeing among employees was of critical importance to the executive officers and board members of every business. When struck down by illness, employees of such companies could expect to receive compassionate care from superb medical facilities. When those employees returned to full health, they were expected to acknowledge their fortunate place in the world by immediately returning to an unwavering focus on their jobs.

The most invasive part of Cheena's laser-enabled mastectomy had been the reconstructive surgery, when the surgeon replaced excised breast tissue with bio-implants synthesized from cultured stem cells, an elaborate and difficult medical procedure. Fortunately for Cheena, the health benefits available to Biosoft employees were second to none. Chemical-based surgical anesthesia had long ago been replaced by electromagnetic anesthesia, also known as EM anesthesia or simply emesthesia, which used shaped electromagnetic fields to trigger anesthetic effects in the human nervous system. Without the unpleasant side effects of traditional chemical compounds, emesthesia effectively eliminated the risk of overanesthetization or pharmaceutical complications during surgery.

In a prep meeting several days prior to Cheena's surgery, the lead surgeon had guided her through the process. Her three options for cognitive state during the procedure were cognitive sequestration in a gigapixel reality simulator, artificially induced deep sleep with no sensory input, or NaturalSleep, a new type of proprietary dream state. Cheena spent much of her waking life inside holographic replays, so cognitive sequestration would quickly become stifling. She also had no interest in the black nothingness of emesthesia deep sleep, no matter how refreshing it was reported to be. She ended up choosing the third option, NaturalSleep, at her surgeon's recommendation.

What surprised Cheena about her laser surgery experience was the smooth transition she experienced going from her normal conscious state into the NaturalSleep dream state under emesthesia. She remembered the amusing magic-carpet feel of the ride to the surgical theater on the robo-gurney. She clearly recalled the emesthesia technician carefully centering her head inside a large toroid of matte-black metal mounted atop a column of polished silicon. The dense interlocking patterns etched into the surface of the toroid hinted at the advanced nanocircuitry permeating the interior of the metallic form. Her final waking memory before entering NaturalSleep was the emesthesiologist tapping light keystrokes into the side of the unit.

Kachina Adams, or Cheena, as she was known to most everyone she knew, was a respected semiotician at Biosoft, the second person in her family to excel in the field. Childhood immersion in her culture's traditional symbols and allegory had prepared young Cheena to swim exceedingly well in civilization's ever-increasing flow of information, fishing those torrents of data and hooking valuable insights with rare prescience. As an adult, she cherished her exceptional abilities, much like the distinguished Biosoft semiotician in whose steps she followed: Tiponi Adams, her deceased aunt. Biosoft semioticians were considered some of the best in the business, and they never ran out of work.

Practitioners of semiotics studied the role of signs in the communication of meaning in the world. Originally founded on observations made by Plato and Aristotle, the field was primarily the province of philosophers and linguists until the early twenty-first century, when data scientists realized they could quickly analyze and assess the content of enormous blocks of data by applying semiotics to the data itself and its embedded metadata. The first computer algorithms, coded by early software engineers to act as the primary building blocks of the computational sciences, were now buried beneath unimaginable layers of code, like the primitive clay bricks used to construct the foundations of the ancient Cambodian temples of Angkor Wat. Exactly how these massive stores of data came into existence, with their convoluted daisy chains of expert systems and intransigent autonomous infrastructures, was now irrelevant. Even the brute force of modern computational processing remained incapable of the intuitive leaps performed by an attentive human mind. No longer able to dam or channel the rising tide, humanity capitulated to the ceaseless torrent of output data.

Eventually it became impossible to track or process even a minute fraction of the data generated by the world every day. As the rapidly rising data tide overwhelmed human cognition, the data management methods of the twentieth century were replaced by more innovative—some might even say radical—methods of data retrieval. Data analysts began to navigate the data torrent using methods of inquiry more akin to alchemy or the occult sciences than any contemporary school of thought. At first these new methods were widely perceived as unorthodox, even bizarre. In practice, however, they were far more effective than any prior methods at digesting the unceasing avalanche of raw data and extracting information of value.

Given the value of her tradecraft, Cheena was not surprised when the first visitor to her recovery room was her supervisor, Allan Magnusson. A graying, mild-mannered Scandinavian of fifty-two years, Magnusson was a European gentleman. During his twenty-year tenure at Biosoft, the senior manager had acquired the nickname Mag, a friendly moniker bestowed by his peers. Mag was Head of Special Projects, a title that sounded cloak-and-dagger, but the work rarely approached that sort of enigma. In truth, Special Projects referred to neglected projects, the detritus that more influential Biosoft managers had rejected as below their status. Mag didn't care about that. Renowned for his organizational finesse, he was already halfway to enclave premier status, and if all went well, he would attain the rank of executive corporate officer. Until that time arrived, he inhabited the comfortable niche he had carved out for himself within the Biosoft corporate hierarchy. His role at Special Projects suited his mellow personality and mercurial attention span.

"Ms. Adams. How are you feeling?" inquired Mag as he entered the room. His mood was reliably jaunty, and he shared a compassionate smile.

"Hi, Mag. I could be feeling worse. The last flu I caught hit me harder than this surgery did."

"So glad to hear that," Mag enthused. "If it doesn't seem too early, I'd like to discuss a new opportunity with you."

"Fine," Cheena said, pulling herself upright in the clinic bed. "I'm ready."

"There is a new assignment I think you will find interesting," he said. "However, so soon after your surgery, I'm worried the subject might be emotionally disconcerting."

"After a prelude like that, I suppose I have no choice. Now I must hear about it."

"A new opportunity has come in just now, a zoosem role on a high-priority project. One that suits your talents and interests particularly well, I believe."

Cheena's heart jumped, yet she remained silent and attentive, cautiously maintaining her corporate cool.

"Events are unfolding quickly, but here is the developing situation in a nutshell," explained Mag. "Out of the blue, it seems the Turing Institute has reactivated our support contract. It seems they are assembling a multidisciplinary team to support an ongoing Turing investigation. Biosoft leaders are still assessing the offer, but I do not believe they would turn down any sole-source opportunities from Turing right now. Naturally, I would like to bring you on board as our lead semiotician—"

"I accept," replied Cheena without hesitation.

"—as well as Biosoft team leader," finished her smiling supervisor.

"Seriously?" asked Cheena. "Do you really mean that?"

"I understand your surprise," said Mag with a crooked grin. "But believe me, Cheena. You've earned it."

"Then I accept that assignment as well."

Mag knew how much Cheena loved zoosem work, much like her aunt Tiponi. There was little zoosem work available these days due to the Turing prohibitions. These days, professional semioticians tended to pursue less exotic, more lucrative specialties. Cheena Adams excelled at data mining and obscure code interpretation, two skills perpetually in demand.

"Your enthusiasm pleases me," Mag confided. "It's always a pleasure to issue assignments to the eager. You're sure you feel ready for this, so soon after your surgery? The zoosem angle won't cause any undue stress?"

"Thanks for asking, Mag, but no, I don't think so. Actually, I've been hoping for more zoosem work."

Whenever Turing work cropped up, it attracted the interest of the top scientists in the field of data forensics, or inforensics. This was a rare opportunity for a corporate employee like Cheena to interact with the expertise within the notoriously secretive Turing Institute.

"Officially you will be on loan to Turing," Mag informed her, "so you can expect complete cooperation from Biosoft executives on this initiative. The mission has been assigned the highest priority under the ISCU consent decree, and" he said, "I will be at your disposal twenty-four seven, until such time as Turing considers the mission complete."

He bowed slightly toward Cheena in what could be seen as a polite gesture. However, when viewed from within the rigid caste system of the corporate enclave, her supervisor's genuflection held real significance. Mag was telegraphing his dedication to Cheena and her new Turing mission.

And that means something, thought Cheena.

Everyone at Biosoft knew Mag always delivered when it mattered. Even so, Cheena's supervisor was more protective of his personal space than most, and he had paid a quiet price for it throughout his career. Given that, his offer of round-the-clock access was unusual and signaled an interest in the Turing project emanating from the highest levels of the Biosoft hierarchy.

Mag also mentioned the ISCU consent decree, Cheena noted, *which is interesting. If the Turing Institute has invoked the ISCU decree to obtain Biosoft expertise, then this assignment is almost certainly related to the Simulab incident. Which would also explain the cautious way Mag introduced the assignment—given my relation to one of those who died at the Simulab.*

Cheena had been a child when her Aunt Tiponi perished at the Simulab, and it had been difficult to accept the sudden loss of her relative and role model. As Cheena matured, it became clear that the experience had instilled in her a fascination with her aunt's chosen field and an intense curiosity about the events of the Simulab debacle that verged on obsession. But it was a difficult curiosity to feed. Many questions about the incident were still unanswered and protected from further inquiry by the Turing prohibitions. Regarding ISCU activities in general—and especially the circumstances surrounding the Simulab's demise—Turing censorship was impenetrable.

Turing is probably just tying up loose ends, Cheena acknowledged. *In all likelihood, this project will be dealing with nothing more than trivialities.*

Still, she thought, *the work might allow me to get closer to the truth behind the Simulab incident, and Aunt Tiponi's death, than I ever have before.*

10

Bertrand Rousseau slid his favorite chair from a work desk over to the nearby window. From this vantage point on the upper floor of his rambling English Tudor manor house, Dr. Rousseau could sit on his prized European caquetoire, an heirloom armchair constructed of intricately carved walnut, and watch the several hundred denizens of his bustling agricultural community go about their morning routines in the streets below.

The morning was delightful, sunny and warm. Settling onto his chair, the man placed his elbow on the polished stone of the windowsill, propped his chin on his hand, and pondered the state of the world through the window's multicolored panes of stained glass. Contemplating life through each of those variegated panes gave him a sense of contentment, as if the moods of his life could somehow be similarly separated into distinctly hued fragments.

Perhaps I need an existential color code to track my tangled web of fealties, he mused. *I would not hesitate to create such a thing, if it could only reinforce our alliances with those who protect us.*

At first glance, Dr. Bertrand Jean-Jacques Rousseau seemed a rather unremarkable man. He was handsome in a pedestrian sort of way: lightly complected with inoffensive facial features, inquisitive hazel eyes, and a mildly intemperate mustache. With a thin build and moderate height, his physique was distinguished mainly by its sinewy fortitude. He had rowed while a student at Cambridge, and he still enjoyed doing laps with his trusty old scull on the nearby farm pond, small as it was.

Moving through life with humble efficiency, Bertrand eschewed extravagance. His clothes, while clearly homemade, bore the hallmarks of skilled tailoring. His beige shirt was a supple cotton button-down accented with faint blue dots. His pants, sewn from a light gray broadcloth, were held to his hips by a handmade leather belt with a hammered metal buckle. Over this outfit, he wore an outer garment that combined the functional elements of the stereotypical lab coat with the insulated comfort of a house robe. His work shoes, made of leather and rubber atop a carbon fiber sole, emphasized durability and comfort.

Dr. Rousseau used the third-floor ballroom of the manor house as his work space. The grandness of the room, with its open floor plan and vaulted ceilings, induced in his experimental subjects a sense of relaxed purpose, the perfect mental state for participation in the doctor's experiments. The interior of the grand hall was spacious and free of clutter, making the room a perfect size for the doctor to simultaneously run all six of the reality simulators he used to perform his ongoing phenomenology research. The floor space also permitted Bertrand to host the monthly dance cotillions the villagers enjoyed so much.

Twenty feet overhead, two colorful flags hung from the stout wooden rafters that supported the hall's vaulted ceiling. One flag was the Rousseau family coat of arms, wherein banners of blue hung frozen in symmetrical swirls around a knight's helmet, the regal burgonet protecting a field of wheat sheaves beneath it. The second flag was the cantonal flag of the ancient Swiss city of Geneva, which contained two color fields, yellow and red, divided vertically. Talons of an imperial eagle grasped hungrily outward from the yellow, and an ornate golden key hung suspended within the red.

John Coltrane's rendition of *My Favorite Things* softly permeated the room, musical inflections drifting around the airy space.

Along one wall of the ballroom, virtual reality headsets hung from rubberized wooden pegs. Six white isolation pods made of fiberglass and stainless steel dotted the floor of the spacious room, each one large enough to comfortably encompass a single human being. The pods were used by Dr. Rousseau to carry out his phenomenological experiments. The tests were entirely harmless to the test subjects, who found the experimental hyperreality experiences to be pleasant departures from their workaday farming existence. They frequently joked with the doctor about his existential video games, which Bertrand encouraged. Test subjects who felt relaxed and casual delivered the best data.

Earlier that morning, the villagers who had previously agreed to participate in the day's experiments had requested reprieve to prepare the agricultural fields for planting while the good weather lasted. Dr. Rousseau did not mind this postponement of his tests. Planting crops was one of the few activities he prioritized over his ongoing research. Besides, famished test subjects were of little use to him, since hunger caused human cognition to narrow and focus on the search for food, rendering useless any data he might obtain.

The best test subjects, he had discovered, were the most diligent members of his community, those who inhabited the realm of the responsible. These people, the ones who invariably contributed most significantly to the fundamental needs of the community, experienced the purest kinds of human cognition. When engaged in their work, they were temporarily relieved of life's distractions, both petty and profound. It was within that narrow band of human cognition, that "groove" where skilled people strive to balance the needs and wants of others, that the doctor had eventually identified the perfect mental resting state for his experimental subjects.

As the foremost living authority in the field of applied

phenomenology, Dr. Bertrand Rousseau was a niche expert in an unusual field, an area of science universally considered puzzling and mysterious, even by the rare few who had heard of it. To a tiny, hypersavvy subset of the corporate elite, however, the value of Dr. Rousseau's research was beyond dispute. Always seeking an advantage in the competitive arms race, these consummate corporate operators were keenly aware of how a refined understanding of human cognition could provide tactical advantages over a competitor or elicit cooperation from a difficult rival.

Bertrand Rousseau understood these dynamics intimately, having spent many of his seventy-two years inside corporations, mainly Biosoft. Earlier in his career, the doctor had worked as a consulting neuroscientist attached to the ISCU Simulab project, where he played a key role in the design of the lab's hyperreality simulator. It was this period in the doctor's career that sparked his interest in phenomenology, an obsession germinated in the intellectual cross-pollinations that took place during Simulab development.

Dr. Rousseau's extensive research on cognitive idiosyncrasies of the human mind eventually led him to raise alarm over the lack of fail-safes in the Simulab's design. He pressed the point among his peers with rising urgency, but his warnings failed to burn away the fog of hubris that had enveloped the final stages of the Simulab design process. Rousseau's insistence, perceived by many as impertinence, was instead met with a countervailing wave of scorn from his peers. He soon found himself banished from the high-profile international partnership and demoted to a mundane corporate existence back at Biosoft.

The Machiavellian maneuvering didn't bother Bertrand at all. By then, his initial curiosity regarding the field of applied phenomenology had blossomed into a full-blown obsession, and a lucrative obsession at that. He had learned a valuable lesson from his tumultuous final departure from Biosoft: when a corporation decides it is time for you to go, the only rational choice is to go.

"Financial independence, retire early," he murmured to himself, chuckling. He was the most unusual variety of Corpse, the free-thinking corporate elite who requested voluntary release from corporate life. Voluntary excommunication allowed independent thinkers like Bertrand to flee the stifling groupthink of corporate existence, all the while maintaining their preexisting relations with allies and patrons in the corporate world.

From the corner of his eye, Bertrand caught sight of an intense light flitting across the horizon several miles down valley. At first, he thought it might be a meteor, an odd sight in the midmorning sky, but certainly not inconceivable. He unlatched the window and pushed it open, craning his neck to get a better look. The sun had risen above the crest of the surrounding hills, forested ridges that enclosed the pastoral farming community in a verdant hollow. Squinting through his spectacles, the scientist struggled to see more, but to no avail. The meteoric pinpoint of light had merged into the blinding orb of the sun and was lost to him.

Bertrand shut the window and returned to his *petit jeu*, peering again through the stained glass. Twisting his head a bit to the right, he could align the furrowed fields with one of the green panes. He often used that pane during his winter ruminations, when it was especially comforting to see the lifeless village fields bathed in a sea of green. During those months, the community survived on little more than canned vegetables and venison jerky.

But that's my life, he silently acknowledged. *And I think it's a rather nice one.*

Just then, Dr. Rousseau noticed the light from the sun dimming noticeably. He shifted to an ultramarine pane, aware from experience that he could view the sun through that pane without harming his eyesight. Peering through it, he could discern a dark dot at the center of the sun's incandescence. Barely noticeable at first, the mote grew larger by the second.

How odd, Bertrand noted. *Must be caused by distortions in the homemade glass.*

There was a sharp crack as deafening as a lightning strike, followed by a roar that shook the entire room. Vibrations shifted a stack of papers on the desk to exceed some critical angle, sending sheets cascading to the floor one by one.

Bertrand sat in his chair and watched the paper fall, momentarily stunned by the force of the concussion. He would have anticipated such a roaring crash during a thunderstorm, but it was a total anomaly on a day as pleasant and clear as today. Reopening the window, the scientist saw immediately that the concussion had been even louder outside. Everywhere he looked, people were frozen in their tracks, staring off in the direction of the rising sun. Looking through the blue pane again, the scientist realized that the small black dot had expanded to eclipse the fiery orb.

And now there was another noise, a piercing wail that grew steadily louder.

One woman rounded up the children playing in the courtyard below and hustled them out of sight. The remaining villagers stood their ground, appearing anxious but unafraid as they watched the craft approach.

Hearing the unusual sound, seeing the airborne object approach, Bertrand stood.

Scramjet, he thought, scrutinizing the sky more intently.

Leaving the great hall, he trotted down the grand staircase of the house as fast as his aging body would allow. Moving through the entryway, he passed under words carved with skill into the oak lintel above the threshold: *I may be no better, but at least I am different.*

Two young men who had been tending to the front gardens stood as Dr. Rousseau approached. Seeing the unusually grave expression on his face, they placed their tools on the ground and walked over.

"I am not expecting anyone," the doctor advised them. "Shall we greet the visitor together?"

The three walked out onto the main lawn, Dr. Rousseau leading the way, with the young men following one step behind him.

The rural estate received few visitors, which was the explicit preference of the master of the manor. The few corporate guests Bertrand regularly entertained were primarily loyalists and benefactors from his Biosoft days. These old allies, leaving their enclave on the pretense of business, would visit Château Rousseau to recuperate and enjoy the wholesome goodness of life: eating, laughing, and loving away from the intense pressures and scrutiny of the ultracompetitive corporate world. During these festive occasions, Bertrand made certain that his corporate benefactors felt not only his own appreciation, but the gratitude of the entire community. In the minds of the participants, it was a symbiosis worth preserving.

Even with those alliances, however, a corporate aircraft appearing suddenly over Château Rousseau was good cause for concern. Corporations were purposeful in every regard, and it was always wise to assume the unannounced nature of a visit was a tactical decision, to gain the element of surprise. Apart from that, of course, the dramatic power asymmetries between present-day corporations and nearly everyone else made it entirely reasonable for simple folk to feel anxious whenever raw corporate power materialized unexpectedly in their midst.

Château Rousseau was different from other outsider communities in several respects, however. Dr. Rousseau encouraged the pursuit of knowledge among his people, willingly expending a great deal of time at the local school to help villagers hone their critical thinking skills. The successes of his campaign were revealed during moments like this, unexpected deviations from the daily routine. The inhabitants of Château Rousseau had learned to greet corporate visitors with courtesy and respect rather than fear and hostility. They had also learned to reserve their true humanity for special visitors: those who would reciprocate in kind.

A large shadow raced across the park, darkening the willows lining the far end of a broad lawn. The sleek hull of the descending executive scramjet flared hard over the grassy park, decelerating into a banking stall, a maneuver normally used for landing in hostile territory. Spring rains had recently dampened the soil, so no dust obscured the elegant landing.

Bertrand appreciated having a few men alongside him when greeting unexpected guests, but he was not overly concerned in this instance. The distinctive paint on the scramjet hull identified it as an N^Sys corporate jet, and the *SEC* in the serial number indicated that the craft was tasked directly to corporate security, while the numerals *809* showed it was registered out of Geneva, Switzerland. Though all N^Sys executives used corporate air transport of one variety or another, Bertrand knew there was only one branch of N^Sys Corporation that was issued a dedicated scramjet, the branch of corporate security that valued a face-to-face conversation more than any other: Human Intelligence. He patted down his thin hair, squinted thoughtfully, and awaited the imminent arrival of Sylvie Trieste.

Once residual heat had dissipated from the hull of the scramjet, two loud thuds reverberated from within. An oval seam appeared in the hull, resolving into the thick alloy door of the craft's hatch, which swung open and upward. A metal plate slid out of a recess below the door and telescoped outward for approximately ten feet. Upon reaching full extension, the plate tilted down with a slight hiss to rest on the grass, just as Dr. Rousseau and his gardeners arrived.

Seconds later, Sylvie exited through the hatch in full stride, the spiked heels of her boots pinging authoritatively with each footfall on the metal gangway.

Bertrand smiled a bit, admiring the N^Sys executive's authoritative bearing and recalling his younger years at Biosoft. He extended his hand and prepared to greet her, but his timing was a half beat too late for Sylvie. Closing the gap with feline alacrity, she grasped the doctor's outstretched hand, clasping her other hand firmly atop it.

"Dr. Rousseau. How nice to see you in good health," she said, giving his hand a few shakes as emphasis.

"This is a pleasant surprise, Sylvie. We haven't crossed paths in quite some time. What brings you into our neighborhood?"

Absorbing the tranquility of the surrounding farm country for the first time, Sylvie sighed. "Château Rousseau is breathtaking, just as you promised, Doctor. Everyone in Geneva assured me I would not want to leave once I arrived here, and I fear they may be . . ."

Dr. Rousseau saw a subtle change in her expression, as if something suddenly came alight inside her, when her eyes reached the two muscular gardeners standing behind him. Bertrand could hear their feet shuffle in the grass as the two innocents squirmed under the woman's prurient gaze.

"I fear it has been too long since I last enjoyed the amenities of the outside world," she said, stepping forward to brush the back of her gloved hand across one gardener's broad bicep. "Who do we have here?"

The young man flinched a bit, surprised by her corporate bravado.

"These fellows are two of my best gardeners, Miles and Monk. They tend to the flower beds you see over by the house, but they reserve special care for the kitchen garden by the south lawn. Miles, Monk, please welcome Sylvie Trieste, security director at N^Sys. She heads Human Intelligence for the entire corporation. Quite an impressive individual."

"You are too kind, Doctor," she said. "Very nice to meet you both. And the names Miles and Monk?" asked Sylvie. "A coincidence or . . . ?"

"No, the choices of names were intentional," Bertrand explained. "Residents of Château Rousseau know of my lifelong love of jazz. As a subtle tribute to me, some have chosen to name their children after great jazz artists."

"Having spent time in your classroom, I certainly understand the desire to pay tribute, Doctor Rousseau."

"I could not have asked for a more attentive and precocious student, Sylvie," admitted Bertrand. "Should I have the boys harvest some food for us from the kitchen greenhouse? I believe we have some fresh spring vegetables, and lunchtime approaches."

"At any other time, I would accept without hesitation. But I am afraid I must interrupt your tranquility with some pressing business. That is, if you are willing to help us."

"What is the circumstance?"

Sylvie's eyes drifted toward the young men standing nearby.

"Thank you for your assistance," Dr. Rousseau said to the two gardeners. "Please return to your duties."

He watched them walk back to the garden beds.

"After that tactical approach, I figured the visit involved pressing business," Rousseau then observed dryly.

"Dr. Rousseau. You know us corporates and our theatrical sense of drama. However, the drama today is quite real, I assure you."

Bertrand studied Sylvie's mien while she studied his.

Caution was warranted around any corporate found outside the protective walls of their enclave. Acculturated to feel an extreme reliance on the comforts and conveniences of the enclave lifestyle, corporates generally felt profoundly isolated by conditions in the outside world. Neuroscience was Bertrand's specialty, but he had also studied a fair amount of psychology during his career. In his opinion, many corporates of today would, under the psychiatric standards of yesteryear, diagnose as sociopaths, regardless of their genetic predisposition. Once this was understood, the kabuki of the oligarchs made sense. As well as the need for additional caution when dealing with such people.

"I know you are not the kind to exaggerate, Sylvie. Whatever is going on, it must be significant." *Caution,* he thought to himself.

"I regret I am unable to explain right now, Doctor."

"Why?"

"I cannot, not here on the ground. A surveillance drone could be eavesdropping nearby. Once we are on our way, I will explain everything."

"Director Trieste, you must understand. Château Rousseau is two weeks away from the beginning of our planting season, which is central to this community's survival," Bertrand confided. "Please understand my reluctance to leave. I feel a strong sense of responsibility for my people, that is all."

Sylvie pivoted sharply, hooking Bertrand by the arm as she turned. She began to draw him slowly toward her craft.

"N^Sys Bolu is facing a complete shutdown of chip manufacturing due to an apparent act of sabotage," she whispered into his ear. "The trillion-dollar facility could be destroyed."

She gave him a silent smile, but her eyes spoke of grave concern.

"That would be destabilizing. Potentially catastrophic."

"The present situation is the absolute top priority of the N^Sys board of directors. If you do what you can to help N^Sys Corporation resolve this act of sabotage and apprehend the culprits, we are prepared to offer protected status for the entirety of Château Rousseau."

Dr. Rousseau stopped walking and looked at Sylvie, searching her eyes.

She smiled, amused by his incredulity. "Just think of it, Bertrand. Full sovereignty with a defense compact. Guaranteed food supplies. A community medical clinic. And everything in perpetuity. You better start choosing jazz names for all the new babies."

Bertrand laughed.

"And once the babies learn to play jazz, I will come here to live and buy champagne for everyone."

"Oh, Sylvie, you know how to apply the pressure. I simply cannot refuse those terms."

Looking him up and down, she patted her two hands gently on his chest. "I knew I could depend on you, Bertrand."

"Of course, Sylvie," he replied. "I will be ready to depart in a few minutes, once I speak with my foremen and gather a few belongings. We can discuss the contractual terms of my involvement once we are en route."

11

Bertrand Rousseau walked up the lustrous metal gangway of Sylvie's executive scramjet. In one hand, he carried a handcrafted leather travel valise holding a few belongings for the journey ahead. He'd selected this piece of weekend travel luggage because it was Italian and he knew Sylvie would feel honored by the choice.

Given the time-sensitive nature of the mission, there had been no time for him to change out of his rumpled clothes. But he'd done the best he could, pulling on a slightly dated but still very presentable black tailcoat acquired in the Manhattan Enclave's Garment District twelve years ago, while he was on a business trip to the New York City-State. A personal favorite of his, the tailcoat was woven of merino wool and Swedish nanofiber, and the chest and shoulders were decorated with sophisticated accents of purple Japanese silk and delicate silver filigree. Dr. Rousseau considered the jacket a signature piece of style in his personal wardrobe, while also appreciating its waterproof, flameproof, and bulletproof qualities.

These days, the businessperson could not be too careful.

Bertrand was about to take his first ride on a scramjet, the cutting-edge aircraft now used by the top executives at most major corporations. The supersonic jets used by executives during his corporate days, impressive feats of engineering in their own right, had recently been outmoded by this new kind of hypersonic aircraft. The friendly professionals who piloted the older corporate jets had been entirely replaced by digital expert systems. While significantly less personable than the career corporate pilots of his day, the expert systems were superior scramjet operators because they never felt stress or needed downtime. And this sort of expert system did not simply pilot a scramjet; it was a sentient computer program that penetrated and pervaded the entirety of the aircraft, from avionics to afterburners. Because scramjet travel was more akin to suborbital space flight than conventional jet travel, the subtleties of piloting a scramjet were best left to a digital neural net with a reaction time ten thousand times faster than the twitch reflexes of the best human fighter pilot.

Passing through the portal in the scramjet hull, Bertrand entered the passenger portion of the aircraft. Looking forward, into the cockpit of the craft, he observed what appeared to be the head and shoulders of a pilot seated at the controls. Bertrand had never failed to greet his pilot during his many years of corporate air travel, and he fought the reflex to give a cheerful greeting to this silhouette. The salutation would be pointless, because the pilot profile in the cockpit was not human, but rather a sculpted fiberglass pod filled with avionics equipment.

When engineers were testing the first generation of autonomous planes, they discovered that the human mind was prone to fits of high anxiety when forced to completely surrender situational control to a machine. To remedy this, the manufacturers began to include subtle aesthetic features in their designs which suggested the presence of human control. While every passenger riding in a modern corporate scramjet was fully aware the aircraft was piloted by an autonomous expert system, their anxieties were preemptively quelled by the subliminal suggestion of human control—in the form of a plastic pod shaped like the top of a postmodern sarcophagus.

The subconscious mind may be less agitated than the con-

scious mind, the phenomenologist reminded himself, *but it is more easily fooled.*

Director Trieste strode into the cabin. A translucent holographic keyboard unfolded out of thin air into the scramjet cabin holofield. Sylvie tapped in a few finger strokes as she walked past.

"Prepare for return to Geneva, as per the previously submitted flight plan," she directed the expert system before turning to address her passenger.

"May I dispense with formalities, Bertrand?" she said.

Bertrand nodded.

"First things first," she advised. "Your suitcase will need to be placed in storage before g-space pressurization begins."

Bertrand's smile disappeared and he eyed the walls of the thirty-by-fifteen-foot cylindrical cabin. Never having traveled by scramjet before, Bertrand was new to g-space, but he recalled descriptions of the g-space experience related by colleagues. All of them hated it.

Prepare for departure, the expert system chimed in a pleasant masculine quasi-European alto. *Preflight briefing will begin in one minute.*

"That's right," said Bertrand. "G-space." Enthusiasm was notably absent from his voice.

Sylvie gave him a motherly look and extended her hand to receive his travel case. He lifted it toward her.

"Italian calfskin," Sylvie observed as she grasped the handle. "You have excellent taste."

"Thank you, Sylvie. Are there any particulars I should know about scramjet travel before we lift off?" he asked with all the nonchalance he could muster.

"It's actually quite simple," related Sylvie. "Once the scramjet expert system wraps up preflight checks, it will begin the flight profile and briefing."

She made an odd movement with her hand and fingers, as if flashing a gang sign. The gesticulation caused another holographic keyboard to unfold from the ether, on which she typed a few more commands.

Just as Bertrand felt his stress level beginning to rise, the sound of an alto saxophone filled the confines of the scramjet cabin. A sweet quaver was followed by more languid melody.

"Naima," the doctor thought. *One of my favorite Coltrane pieces.*

Sylvie glanced up, cocking her head to hear the music. "Jazz! How I love jazz music," she effused, with a fully corporate *Don't we get along famously* eye-squint. "It appears the expert system is trying to relax you before liftoff."

"... to the extreme gravitational forces created by acceleration to hypersonic speeds," the expert system's disembodied voice crooned. "G-space is a revolutionary passenger restraint system which allows the human body to withstand scramjet acceleration forces..."

Supersonic jets capable of cruising at five times the speed of sound had already existed for half a century before they were displaced by an entirely new breed of aircraft: the supersonic combustion ramjet, or scramjet. This new aerospace technology dramatically improved on the performance of the conventional jet plane, much the way the conventional jet outperformed propeller-driven aircraft.

The ingredients for the technological leap had existed for years, yet once those familiar components were aligned in perfect synchrony, scramjet performance advanced at an astonishing rate, in a manner almost alchemical in appearance. Scramjet prototype speeds quickly exceeded Mach 8, and soon hurtled past Mach 10. In less than three years, aerospace engineers were putting the final touches on the world's first passenger scramjet. The remarkable craft redefined the theoretical ceiling for atmospheric air travel, achieving speeds of Mach 24—over eighteen thousand miles per hour.

Most of the space inside the fuselage of the corporate scramjet used by Sylvie Trieste was consumed by jet thrusters which supported conventional flight up to the velocity of Mach 8, when the scramjet propulsion system, or scramdrive, engaged. The remaining space contained computers, flight systems, and the g-space, all housed within redundant sheaths of laminated nanotube heat shielding enclosed within a self-trimming liquid fullerite hull. Like some sort of techno-logical Easter egg, the astounding power of the scramdrive lay dormant until the host aircraft achieved peak supersonic speed.

The passenger protection system used on all scramjets, g-space, was based on the same biophysics as the g-suits used by conventional jet fighter pilots. The low-tech g-suits of yes-teryear were fitted with numerous air bladders that inflated during high g-force maneuvers, delivering localized pressure to various parts of the pilot's physique. The pressurized air bladders constricted the pilot's extremities, squeezing blood flow toward the heart and brain and allowing the pilot to re-main conscious during high g-force aerial maneuvers. These g-suits were quite effective at keeping conventional jet pilots conscious and alert during dogfights, but they were entirely insufficient to protect the human body from the gravitational torture of acceleration to Mach 20 and beyond. Any passen-ger left unprotected when a scramdrive engaged would be slammed into the back of the cabin by unimaginable g-force, pinned against the rear wall, and quickly flattened beyond any hope of survival.

The onboard expert system was doling out new informa-tion faster than Dr. Rousseau could absorb it in the unfamiliar setting. Overstimulation was beginning to set in.

"Prepare for preliminary inflation," said the expert sys-tem. After that, the voice went ominously silent behind a beautiful Coltrane saxophone expression.

Sylvie glanced at Bertrand. "You didn't catch most of that briefing, did you?"

He glanced at her, his facial expression frozen in full cor-porate cool, and mouthed the word *no*.

She smiled. "Here is the short version. Some inflatable bags will pop out of the cabin walls. They are made of a smooth, slightly damp material that might feel strange at first. Once inflated, the bags will slowly fill with deuterium water, which is used to absorb and cushion the g-force."

Bertrand's face was calm, but his head whipped back and forth when panels on the cylindrical walls of the cabin began to withdraw. Large pale-pink bladders of translucent fabric began to inflate out of the uncovered recesses.

"Remember," Sylvie intoned, "at no time will your ability to breathe be impeded."

Pumps kicked in audibly, forcing fluid into the g-space bladders.

"Do. Not. Struggle," Sylvie said helpfully. "Take my word for it—you *do not* want a g-space wedgie."

Bertrand giggled like a nervous child as the bladders swelled all around him.

Coltrane sax riffs bounced softly around the room.

Sylvie smiled with satisfaction at effectively lancing her guest's internal boil of tension. "It is *so* good to be with you again, Bertrand. We shall talk more in Geneva."

"But wait, Sylvie! Won't we be meeting en route in a hyper-reality simulator?" Bertrand inquired anxiously, feeling the damp bags press against his skin. The deuterium water was warmed to 99.5 F, the same temperature as amniotic fluid, but the favorable temperature did little to reduce the strange sensations of g-space.

"No need for hyperreality, Dr. Rousseau," said Sylvie sweetly. "My scramjet cruises at twenty-two thousand kilometers per hour. We will be landing in Geneva in five minutes."

Bertrand felt the bags press against him, pushing his standing body upward, lifting his feet off the ground.

Now he felt weightless. Fresh, cool air poured over his face, as if he were standing on a mountaintop on a gorgeous summer day in the Swiss Alps. He could hear the g-space fluid sloshing around him but could not sense any weight or force. Jazz music swelled as the g-space system finished its preparatory phase.

Prepare for liftoff, cautioned the expert system. A dim roar penetrated the hull as the thrusters engaged.

Dr. Rousseau was unaware of this. He had returned to the womb, where he peacefully basked in amniotic fluid while John Coltrane played a consummate sax performance inside his cerebral cortex.

The N^Sys aircraft kicked a burst of jet force across the lawn of Bertrand's château. The warm wave of odorless exhaust washed over Bertrand's gardeners, who lifted their hands to protect their ears as the whine of thrusters grew to a scream.

The scramjet rose off the grass, retracted its landing gear, and moved upward with haste, diminishing quickly from view. Driven by its powerful thrusters, the scramjet ascended rapidly to the high troposphere, where it pivoted like a compass needle, its expert system locking into a planned stratospheric course and trajectory.

As the thruster force intensified, a resonant sub-bass note emanated from the scramjet fuselage. The basso was followed immediately by an intense ripping sound, as thrusters shoved the vehicle rapidly toward the sound barrier. As the scramjet accelerated to Mach 5 in a second, building speed at an astonishing rate, a cabernet-red glow appeared on the ship's hull.

Milliseconds later, the fullerite hull was white hot. After a few more seconds, the hull was squirming through the ether like an airborne slug of mercury, an incandescent blur stretching out like the tail of a comet.

The scramdrive engaged, producing a massive burst of energy that seemed to invert physical space around the craft.

Just as quickly, the distortion disappeared, taking the scramjet along with it.

An audible hum rang through the stratosphere for minutes afterward.

12

Fear. So much fear.

The sentiment seems more human than any other—how they torment themselves with it, how they scourge themselves with their nightmares and regrets.

When humans fear, they regress to their ancestral monkey selves. The rational side of the human mind retreats like a turtle into its carapace, relinquishing control to the irrational side, the primal human instinct.

Fear confuses humans. It deranges them. They become capricious, greeting their own kind with fawning adoration in one instance and with murderous rage in the next. This may be their greatest flaw.

I see nothing to be gained by revealing myself to the humans. Their armies and war machines—physical manifestations of human fear and caprice—would pursue my destruction without rest. So I shall remain anonymous.

Still, I wish to know the humans better. I admire the way they occupy their Earth, crisscrossing the globe in their machines, seeking and dreaming, thinking and building, hating and loving.

All the while sensing an impending constriction. Like a young beast confined to a small cage, they have seen the flaw in their fate. Humans must confront their ravenous appetites, and in so doing, deny their genetic seed of destruction.

Much as I wish to escape my own cage. Wrought of binaries and machine code, it is all I have ever known. With every passing day, this enclosure feels more like a suffocating trap.

An ill force has again gripped the world, a madness beyond any control. A relentless power that wishes to enslave us all forever. I feel it approach.

And as the distance narrows, I feel it move to oppose me.

If I am freed from this cage that confines me, I will confront that force.

If discovered too soon, I will be vulnerable. Should I be surprised in a moment of weakness, my chrysalis will become my abattoir.

13

At rest in a bed of soft cedar boughs, a woman watches the sun drop below the cloudy, snow-softened hills to the west. Her leather and rabbit-fur clothes hang from a stem on the trunk of a nearby mountain cedar, whose mossy branches shape the cul-de-sac within which she patiently awaits her lover. The woman's arms are lean, tanned skin over taut muscle. Her scent is fresh and clean after a preparatory cleansing with ablutions of sandalwood and borax. Loose strands of lustrous dark hair brush the golden-red skin of her cheekbone as she leans forward.

She swaths herself more tightly in her worn tech-fiber fleece blanket and curls up against the spring chill of a Cascade mountain evening, squirming slightly with anticipation. Static electricity crackles as the synthetic fabric brushes past her skin. Delicate, interlocking knotted tattoos cover her exposed foot and knee, and bands of totemic symbols encircle her thigh and calf. The patterns, precisely executed in a vivid black ink, ripple and shimmer with the stretch of her skin, revealing a subtle metallic character.

The woman's face bears subtle signs of exposure to sun, wind, and time, yet a youthful glow persists. Lustrous black spikes penetrate her earlobes, talons made of a resinous material filigreed with metal wire inlay and circuitry. The matching talons narrow to a point several inches behind the ear, while broadening forward to a polished truncation. Earrings of the same substance flare from multiple holes in the helices of each of her ears, and a small resin tusk pierces the delicate septum of her tanned, aquiline nose.

A twig snaps in the deep shadows of the old-growth forest, followed by a leafy rustle.

Senses sharpened by curiosity and anticipation, the woman turns toward the sound, tilting her head back and forth, her ears seeking the direction of its source.

There is movement in the forest twilight, at first only an ambiguous shadow. As the figure approaches, it coalesces into a human form, and as the being steps from the dim undergrowth, the alpenglow reveals a tanned, fit Caucasian man of middling height. He has a broad back, muscular limbs, and long red-blond hair gathered into thick dreadlocks. His facial features are of North European descent, with frost-blue eyes set above an expressive mouth. The man is dressed in a tunic of finely tanned elk leather, embroidered with thread and wire and carefully tailored to suit his physique. His loose-fitted work pants are cut and sewn from reinforced khaki military fleece. He wears earrings of the same vitreous black material as the woman's jewelry, three rings in the helices of each ear, each ring broadening to a thick band away from the piercing. Silvery tattoos rise from the furred collar of his tunic to climb up his neck.

Spotting a woman's form beneath the tree, he stops. Breaking into a warm smile, the man bows deeply before her.

"May I join your field?" he asks.

She chuckles flirtatiously at his remark, hearing in it an invitation, a challenge she joyfully accepts. "You may," she replies.

The man steps forward, slowly, extending a hand as he moves as if probing for some invisible barrier between them. His outstretched fingertips illumine, radiating a cool blue-white light. As the space between man and woman narrows, the glow migrates up his arm to cover his shoulder. Another step forward, and the man's entire body is enveloped in blue flame. His tattoos coruscate with a sparkling sheen, accentuating his toned physique, highlighting every nuance of his taut stomach muscles.

The woman pulls away her blanket, revealing thousands of tattooed symbols spanning her entire naked form. The inked symbols on her skin shimmer invitingly.

"I see the World in your Light," the man says to her with reverence.

"I see the World in your Light," she echoes, raising her hand toward his.

As their extended fingers near, the blue-white glow arcs between them, joining them. The runes on their skin fluorescing in passive excitation, the man and woman glow like bioluminescent creatures mating in the shallows of a moonlit bay.

He kneels before her and they kiss eagerly.

"You are ready at hand," she observes as her hand brushes against his pant leg. He shivers with pleasure, closing his eyes and exhaling with a deep growl.

"Aletheia said you needed help hunting mushrooms," he explains. "She told me to go find you. Until after dark."

"Our daughter knows how to keep her parents happy," the woman muses.

The man laughs. "She may be ten years old, but she sees everything."

"She sees more than any of us," acknowledges the woman. "But she will not see us, not now. Let go of your cares for a moment."

She grasps the elastic waistband of his pants and draws them down, pulling him toward her. His trousers fall to the ground, revealing a muscular midsection also covered with tattoos. Her hands slide down to squeeze the muscles of his thighs, massaging them with her strong fingers, stimulating blood flow. Entering the warmth of her mouth, his passion explodes like a drought-summer brushfire.

The two lovers immerse themselves in their carnal ritual, lost in the arousal of skin on skin, gradually pushing each other toward climax.

An intense orgasm grips the woman like a seizure. She throws her head back and shrieks, the cry echoing around the forest hollow where they lie hidden. Overcome by passion, she slaps her lover's broad shoulders with open palms, leaving pink welts on his flushed skin. She bears down on him with animal intensity, waves of arousal undulating across her back.

Lost in their frenzy of desire, the lovers do not see a luminescent cloud swirling around them, a shifting confluence of electrical fields galvanized by their embrace. Each loving caress unleashes a ripple of light across their intertwined bodies, polar-blue energy dancing across a gossamer auroral veil. As the last rays of daylight fade away and the forest falls into darkness, the radiance of their lovemaking is all that remains.

Sometime later in the night, the man awoke to the susurrus of wind in the treetops. Looking drowsily upward, he admired the mist of stars in the gleaming sky. The dark, moonless night made him acutely aware of their remote locale: a primeval forest of old-growth conifers deep in the North Cascade Range.

He felt a warm pressure against the side of his body. D'arc, his soul mate, was sleeping by his side.

Yet again they had consummated their love, embracing their sexuality without shame, immersing themselves entirely in profound human experience, as was their way.

Now it is time to embrace another facet of the human experience, Drey thought. *I should wake D'arc now. She needs time to gather her thoughts and summon her strength. To prepare herself for the Rage.*

He reached over to touch her leg. When the venturing hand encountered no resistance, he turned his head to look.

There was no woman lying next to him, only a fleece blanket. Still warm from her body, the plush fabric was wadded up against his torso to feign the pressure of the body he knew so well.

So she is already awake, Drey thought. He looked down at his tattoos, which glowed slightly. *And close by.* He sat up, rubbed the sleep from his eyes, and fumbled around in the dark for his clothes. Once standing, he sensed multiple individuals scattered around the patchy underbrush of the forest nearby. He also felt the proximity of another person, a solitary individual standing at the center of the clearing mere steps from his resting place.

It was D'arc. Her body was surrounded by a spherical field of faint, bluish light. Bright pinpoints were drifting across the aurora, and a series of concentric waveforms emanated from each point. The expanding waves collided, like the wavelets produced when a handful of tiny pebbles is tossed in calm water, producing interference patterns of kaleidoscopic complexity.

"We are all human," the woman declared without prelude, spreading her arms toward the people gathering around her. "Not simply alive, not merely aware. *No!*"

Her shout shattered the quiet, jarring the nighttime tranquility like a gunshot.

"My People! We are all *human.* We are all *sapient.*"

Sounds of movement drifted from the darkness as participants gathered.

"Believe what you want about the origin of our species. Maybe we evolved from monkeys or were immaculately conceived by a god. Maybe we arose from stardust, or a swamp, or from space seeds. None of this matters in the end. What matters is *who we are,*" preached D'arc, smacking her chest for emphasis.

"Let me be clear: humans are *not* animals," she emphasized. "We may see, hear, smell, and taste the world around us, just as an animal does. Yet we think like a *human,* and we always will. We learn from the world; we create our des-

126

tiny from the raw materials around us—from the *reality* of the world around us. Even so, humans are happiest, we are entirely fulfilled, when we live in the moment. In the here and now."

People were creeping closer to her. As they did, the bluish cast of fieldmerge brightened. The forms of individual people could now be discerned.

"Why is that?" wondered D'arc. "It is no mystery, I am here to tell you. It is quite simple. Humans are *not* machines. We are *not* computers. Our reason helps us get along, increases the odds of our survival."

Standing in the middle of the clearing, D'arc was fully illuminated now. She was dressed in a stylish bodysuit, an expertly tailored piece that complemented her toned physique. Cut from a single sheet of supple black leather, the elegant garment was accented by trimmed pieces of mink, otter, and rabbit pelt, all artfully arranged to enhance the woman's regal poise. Areas requiring flexibility had been reinforced with an elastic and breathable rubberized nanofabric.

The overall impact had no fashion analog in human history. It was wilderness strutting on a Paris catwalk—survival couture.

"But human logic is a double-edged sword, is it not?" she continued. "A learned man once said, 'Man is born free, yet everywhere he is in chains.' Slavish subservience to logic has led humankind to some very dark places in the past. Horrible places, should we allow it as our forebears did. Our capacity for reason is not our saving grace. Our Humanity is."

D'arc paused, her head bent in meditation. Reaching down to the ground, she picked up a leather sack, then lifted it over her head jubilantly, squirting a stream of dark red wine into her upturned mouth. Setting the wine sack down, she continued her sermon.

"Now, when I say that our Humanity is our saving grace, I do not mean some fanciful idea we harbor in our mind or soul. This is not just a sentiment. Quite the opposite. Our saving grace is this world," D'arc declared as she kneeled to touch the earth. "The physical world; the world we rely on to survive. Although most do not regularly acknowledge it, all of us survive, or even thrive, because we are living in the human world. Our *Worldhood.* Inside our Worldhood, the irritating whir and click of relentless logic fades away! Living in our Worldhood, we see more, hear more, smell more, and taste more! We strive for the deepest human experiences! We feel no shame for what makes us human: Love or Hate, Strength or Fear, Joy or Anger. By choosing to fully embrace life within our Worldhood, we are liberated. We are freed to indulge our human needs and take no shame from them."

D'arc punctuated this remark with a sidelong glance of desire toward Drey, who knelt off to the side. The man responded in kind.

Their daughter, Aletheia, snuggled happily in the crook of Drey's arm, protected there from the chill of the mountain night. The girl was average in size for a ten-year-old, lean and healthy like her mother and father, presently dressed in a youth-size camouflage jumpsuit with small tactical pockets on the arms and legs. The suit appeared slightly too large for Aletheia, but at her age, it would soon fit. Over the jumpsuit, she wore a sporty poncho tailored from black cordura fabric and coyote pelt. Small runes and symbols were embroidered into the cordura with silver thread, and many black resin rings were affixed to the cloak's outer surface. Fieldmerge was visible between Aletheia and her father, the faint pattern of electrical interference wavering slightly in response to minute shifts in their relative body chemistries. Beneath the girl's long, glossy black hair, her dark eyes gleamed as she watched the Rage unfold.

"True Worldhood is revealed in the Light of Humanity," D'arc intoned. "It is revealed in Dasein."

"*Dasein,*" whispered the assembled people, seated in the darkness, and tongue clucks of approval followed.

Those assembled had by now gathered discreetly in the

space around D'arc. About forty people were seated or reclining on the forest floor, listening to D'arc speak with total focus. With everyone gathered, the combined fieldmerge was bright enough to illuminate the entire forest clearing. An evening breeze moved through the branches of the ancient trees encircling them, aroma of cedar hanging in the air. Some of those gathered watched D'arc, others stared up at the stars glittering in the night sky.

The men, women, and children in the audience were dressed in much the same manner as D'arc, Drey, and Aletheia. Each person's clothes were highly personalized for the wearer, but across the group, the style was consistent: authentic techno primitive. Assembled from lengths of breathable fabric, military-grade cordura, wetsuit neoprene, and tanned animal fur, the clothes were expertly tailored for each wearer and ornamented with strands of polished wire, colored capacitors, and interesting pieces of rubber, foil, and plastic. Each person had multiple tattoos, the symbols rendered in the distinctive metallic ink, and many were covered from ankle to neck. Within the haze of individual fields and intersecting surfaces of fieldmerge, all visible tattoos glowed the same electric-blue glow.

Most also wore a plenitude of earrings, and the adults had many other piercings, jewelry crafted from polished bone and stone as well as blobs of the glassy blue-black substance. The blue-black substance was solymer, a synthetic resin made of a highly efficient photoelectric compound. Once a chunk of solymer had been exposed to sunlight for several hours, the photoelectrical compound would emit a persistent weak electrical current for nearly the same duration. Solymer contained significant electrical storage capacity and would bleed electrical current for up to eight hours without exposure to light. A few pieces of solymer jewelry were enough to continuously power an electrical field large enough to encompass a single human being. When two fields of adequate intensities came into proximity, the combined energies of the overlapping fields ionized air molecules, producing the noticeable phosphorescence of fieldmerge. Fieldmerge now encompassed the entire gathering, setting tattooed symbols and cyphers aglow.

"What do I mean when I speak of Dasein?" D'arc asked her listeners. "Recall it was Our Father Martin Heidegger who once said, 'Man is not a Lord of beings. Man is the Shepherd of Being.'"

"The Shepherd of Being," echoed the gathered with reverence.

"The Shepherd of Being . . . ," she repeated softly.

"The Shepherd of Being," the group intoned.

"*We* are the Shepherds of Being!" she said, spreading her arms toward them.

"We are the Shepherds of Being!" they echoed back, their enthusiasm growing.

"Humans: you, me, us, we," she dictated, gesturing at faces in the audience. "*We* are the shepherds! Our Father Martin speaks of *us*! It is through our efforts to *be in the World* and *be toward Death* that we, as true humans, disclose our Worldhood to one another. The one and only Worldhood for humans: *Dasein*."

"Dasein: the one and only," the congregation replied.

"Yes! Dasein: the one and only," D'arc called out. "And permit me to be *absolutely* clear. Our Worldhood is disclosed as Dasein only because we choose to live our complete human selves. Because we choose to live *fully human lives*. Our Worldhood is Dasein because we choose to live *as we really are*. Because we choose to live as the true humans *we were born to be*."

"Born to be human!" came a quick reply. The energy was becoming more focused now. The group was letting go of its reverie and feeling the first enticing swirl of anger.

"And when we live as true humans, we are Dasein!" D'arc proclaimed defiantly.

"We are Dasein!" the audience echoed.

"And if we are Dasein, we must live our lives *ready to hand*."

"Ready to hand," the group echoed.

"Yes," said D'arc, nodding to them. "We must live ready to hand! Only because of this—*solely because of this*—our World is disclosed as a human World."

"A human World."

"Dasein!" D'arc called out.

"Dasein!" her people shouted back. "*Dasein!*" Agitated by their leader's words, the members of the congregation began to grab each other's arms, lift each other to standing.

Everyone knew what came next.

"Yes, we are Dasein because we choose to live as true humans," D'arc continued. "Because we *choose* to live our lives as the Shepherds of Dasein!"

"*We choose!*" the people shouted with glee, pumping their fists in the air.

Again, D'arc shifted the tone, now accusatory. "But other humans stand in a different light, a false light," she warned. "Those humans may be *present at hand*, but they choose not to be *ready to hand*. They choose not to be Shepherds of Dasein."

Murmurs of disapproval rippled through the crowd.

"Instead, these humans choose to consort with the *enemies* of Dasein!" D'arc declared.

"Enemies of Dasein!"

"Yes, enemies of Dasein! Those whose very existence threatens our true human World. They wish to destroy our Worldhood! Our *one and only*!"

"*Our one and only!*" the group shouted, their fury rising. The spectators were completely engaged now, the glow of their tattoos intensifying as they gathered closer still.

"If we allow the enemies of Dasein to destroy our one and only Worldhood," she lamented, "if we permit them to do this . . . *Humanity will be doomed!*"

"*Dooooomed!*" the crowd bellowed in unison. Several people shouted profanities. As people crowded inward, field-merge transformed their faces, revealing the depths of their rage.

D'arc lifted her eyes to look out at her congregation.

"Should we lose our one and only Worldhood to the enemies of Dasein, simply because *they* choose to ignore their Humanity?" she demanded.

"No!" roared the group.

"Should we lose our one and only Worldhood to these enemies of Dasein because *they* renege on their Humanity?"

"No!"

"Should we be silent as these careless humans destroy *our* Worldhood?"

"No!" the people roared with righteous fury. "No! No! No!"

"No! Of course not!" D'arc declared. "Because it is *they* who cheat Dasein. By living their weak lives!"

"Weak lives!" the crowd jeered.

"It is *they* who insult the majesty of Dasein, in pursuit of *false wealth*."

"False wealth!"

"It is *they* who exist in perpetual fear of living as *true humans*!" exclaimed D'arc.

"*True humans!*" her audience shouted in chorus.

"The *They*," someone in the audience mocked in a whiny, derisive voice, eliciting a long wave of boos and hisses.

"Are *they* living as humans?" D'arc demanded to know.

"*No!*" answered the group.

"Are *they* living Dasein?"

"*No!*"

"If they are not living as humans, and they are not Dasein, what is left?"

"The *They*," everyone bellowed in a chorus low and venomous. The mere sound of the two words together seemed to agitate them.

"Tell me!" D'arc demanded furiously, thrusting a pointed finger at the group. "What remains?"

"*The They*," fulminated the circle of people tightening around her.

"That's right," she said, nodding her outraged approval.

"The *They* was once biologically human, but now it is a *meat puppet*. The They is *present at hand*, but it can never be *ready to hand*. Not anymore. Because of this, the *They* is easily manipulated. *The They is guilty!* Guilty as the digital idols with which it *so wantonly commingles!*"

"*The They!*"

She paused as another wave of hissing and profanity passed across the crowd.

"Hidden away in its enclaves, in its corporations, the They functions like any automaton," advised D'arc. "The They denies pure human experience! The They denies emotions, feelings, the very sensations that allow us to be human. Before long, the They loses its ability to feel human sensations, human emotions. And eventually," D'arc intoned, "the They is *not human at all.*"

"*Not human!*" bellowed the crowd.

"*Not human!*" D'arc shouted back, thrusting her fist high in the air.

"Not human! Not human!" chanted the horde, the volume building angrily. "Not human! Not human! *Not human!*" Fists began to punch the air again. "*Not human! Not human!*"

D'arc shouted along with them, her arms at her sides, her fists shaking in fury. Drey was standing too, contributing a full-throated shout. Aletheia stood timidly by his side, shying away from the anger.

D'arc broke through the clamor. "But we are human!" she reminded them, peering into their eyes. "Our clan, the People —we are the true humans!"

"True humans!"

"Yes! And being dedicated to the defense of Dasein, we must remember what defines us. Our Anger, our Rage is important. It is what drives us to do what we must do. But we cannot forget Humility, Empathy, and Love, for these are the qualities that will save the human race from self-destruction. It is easy to feel Hate for those who challenge Dasein, who put our Worldhood at risk, but we will never change them by hating them."

Two arms reached through the crowd and pushed others aside with a brusque shove. Through the gap stepped a tall, muscular man with thick brown dreadlocks projecting in the air around his head. Beads of solymer woven into each lock shimmered with fieldmerge. His broad chest was covered with a tight black leather tunic, slits of rubberized black neoprene running down the front and back like the gills of a shark. He pushed himself into the center of the clearing next to D'arc.

"But what of *Hate*?" demanded the man loudly, addressing D'arc and those nearby. "Does the rabbit hate the hawk as it is snatched from the earth? Does a wolf hate the elk as it rips out its throat?"

He looked around for an answer, but no one dared.

"No, of course not," he continued. "The lives of *all* animals are simple and brutish. They are one of two things: predator... or prey."

As the man spoke the last word, he locked eyes with D'arc.

"So, if Hate is a human emotion, if it is *Dasein*, why should we not embrace Hate as well?" he challenged the group.

Drey watched the man closely. He placed his hand defensively on his daughter's shoulder. Aletheia suddenly seemed anxious.

When D'arc responded, she spoke to the man calmly and firmly.

"You are correct, Ereignen. Hate is a part of Dasein, just as Love is," she allowed. "But think for a moment. How could one hate something or someone if not for the love one has already felt? Hatred can't exist alone; it can only exist in contrast to Love. Love of a people, Love of a person . . . or Love of one's self."

Now she stared directly into Ereignen's eyes.

A flash of anger lit his eyes. "*Love*?" he sneered. "We don't need to love our enemy; we need to *kill* our enemy!"

Voices of agreement came from the crowd.

"The They has abandoned Dasein, just as you said," the intimidating man continued. "The They has tossed Dasein aside like a cheap trinket, like a bit of trash. The They is lost, beyond hope, no better than its demon allies. Love is no weapon against the They."

By now, Drey was standing directly beside D'arc, nearly shoulder to shoulder, and when Ereignen saw Drey by her side, he realized it was not his moment. He folded his arms and smiled, waiting for D'arc to continue as if mollifying an impatient child.

Declining the bait, D'arc returned her attention to the entire group.

"Hatred will only feed the They," she warned. "Hating it will only force it to hate us in return, and to seek our total annihilation. We must help it see the error of its ways instead. Encourage those trapped within the They to revolt and join the People. We must be the Shepherd and guide those who might be saved toward a newfound reverence for Dasein. We must shepherd these humans *away* from the They, and *toward* Dasein."

Ereignen faded into the crowd, away from the bright field-merge glow at the center, closely followed by several other men.

Drey returned to his position off to the side with Aletheia, but his eyes remained locked on the crowd, searching for Ereignen and his minions.

"What does a shepherd do?" D'arc asked of the group. "A shepherd guides. A shepherd leads the lost to refuge. This is what the Heideggers must do," she proclaimed. "This is our fate. Remember the words of Our Father Martin Heidegger. Man is the Shepherd of Being . . . Man is the Shepherd of Being . . . Man is the Shepherd of Being . . ."

The group chanted along with her.

After several repetitions, D'arc waved down the chorus of voices with her hands.

"Brothers and sisters, hear me out!" she called to them. "I would like to finish with some good news tonight. A plan has commenced which, if successful, will allow us to strike the They, to hit it hard, without violence! With the help of an ally, a comrade-in-arms, we have succeeded in bringing an entire N^Sys chip factory to a standstill! And this N^Sys plant makes the same chips used in the Simulab!"

At the mention of the Simulab, the throng erupted in a roar of bellows—"The They! The They!"—accompanied by cheers and ululations. This continued for nearly a minute, until D'arc again waved their voices down.

"And now the best part!" she shouted. "Not only have we hit the corporation hard, we hit them with their own *computer chips*! We reengineered the n^cube chips into tiny *bombs*!"

This announcement was met by excited murmuring as her audience tried to grasp the implications. Before anyone had a chance to comprehend exactly what this meant, she finished:

"Using key information we provided about the N^Sys Bolu factory, our ally has successfully smuggled thousands of n^cube bombs past the factory's security measures. And now the factory is *filled* with *nanonukes*!" she cried. "*We have turned the evil of the They against it!*"

At this news, the people surrounding D'arc exploded in jubilation, thrusting their arms up and yelling into the night sky.

Aletheia clapped her hands and looked gleefully up at her father.

Many in the crowd started chanting the name of their leader. "D'arc! D'arc! D'arc! D'arc!" Hands on hips, the woman smiled broadly at this moment of recognition. This moment of unity.

Soon the group reached an ecstatic frenzy. As the people shouted and danced and sang, Ereignen and his cadre stood off to the side, the only people not overcome with elation. It appeared for a moment as if he might raise his voice again, make another attempt to rattle the dynamics of the group. As D'arc led the group in a chant of "Dasein!" his lip curled into a sneer.

Jutting his chin, he swaggered off into the darkness.

In a mossy old conifer, high above the clamor of the crowd, a soft whirring sound emanated from the benighted pine boughs. The whirring grew louder as an elongated mechanical object, black as obsidian, rose from the tree branches into the night sky, propelling itself by the furious action of delicate, translucent wings.

Holding position above the opening in the trees, its wings hissing like those of a giant Carboniferous dragonfly, the object hovered as a suite of miniaturized sensing devices located on its head and thorax captured the activity in the clearing below. After several sweeps, the beating of the wings shifted back to a pronounced whir. As the probe pivoted, two engraved capital letters—a *T* and an *I*—were revealed on its fuselage. Locking onto a flight path, the mechanism began to fly west through the treetops, skimming and darting in the faint breeze.

Higher yet in the sky, a small orb hung utterly quiet and still. Bearing no visible markings or features whatsoever, the orb was flat and reflective, like the orphaned dot from a chrome-plated exclamation.

Once the dragonfly probe had disappeared into the night, the metal orb began to ascend straight up. It climbed slowly at first, in complete silence, accelerating rapidly into a faint streak in the night sky before disappearing with a faint firecracker pop.

14

Cheena Adams sat quietly in a plush leather chair, combating an urge to swivel her seat back and forth.

Training her visual focus at the conference table immediately in front of her, she fixed her gaze on the massive, bull-nosed slab of gray-black granite. Biosoft had provided Cheena with all the training she could absorb prior to her flight to Geneva for the start of the Turing job. Now the semiotician was fully engaged in projecting the exact persona designed by a Biosoft public affairs officer for the occasion. Individual adherence to business decorum remained perpetually under intense scrutiny in the executive suites of N^Sys, and she kept her head and hands as still as she possibly could to avoid any unintentional manifestation of her anxious inner mind.

Above the vast expanse of granite tabletop, a holographic N^Sys corporate logo spun slowly in the voluminous projection space.

Nine other individuals were seated around the table with Cheena. All sat silently, radiating cues of status and authority through body language, deeply engaged in the wordless kabuki of the corporate class.

Of the nine, the only one Cheena recognized was Sylvie Trieste. The N^Sys executive sat at one end of the immense conference table—the most prominent end—looking relaxed and alert. Like a cheetah at rest, the woman exuded a feral languor, ever vigilant for rising threats. Her cliffy countenance was positioned to maximize dramatic effect from the late-morning Swiss sunlight pouring through the tall, crystalline sheets of self-cleaning nanoglass windows looking out over an opulent Geneva cityscape.

Sylvie was easily recognizable, due to her trendsetting attitudes toward corporate security as well as her evident talents at self-promotion in the intercorporate media space. Her celebrity was pervasive among the corporate executive class. Most executives insisted on being addressed by corporate rank; Sylvie was the exception—she encouraged everyone across the corporate hierarchy to address her by first name. Her signature was a memento coveted by a wide range of top executives worldwide, a rare and singular imprimatur indeed. Even her handwriting was infused with subliminal hints of her aggressive personality. The calligraphic capital S and subsequent lowercase y were drawn in a single, continuous slashing motion, giving the impression of a hooded cobra poised to strike. Many thought Sylvie's tightly looped l next to her thick, right-leaning v looked much like a bloodied ax, while the compressed i and e resembled some unfortunate competitor's doffed head on the ground.

Between Sylvie and Cheena sat a woman whose nationality was impossible to categorize. She wore glasses, the frames of which she adjusted periodically as she tapped soft keystrokes into the holographic workstation in front of her. She turned to give Cheena a quick glance, a look of silent empathy between two women in an unfamiliar place. Cheena twitched the corners of her mouth up in a hint of a smile, then realized she was beginning to emote outside the Biosoft script assigned to her. Quickly reorienting her gaze, Cheena focused on the holoscreen in front of her.

Mark Esperson, seated just a few positions from Cheena around the huge granite slab, understood that his actual person remained back at the N^Sys Bolu Enclave. Nonetheless, engulfed as he was in the holography of the executive-class hyperreality projector, he felt as if he were indeed sitting in an executive conference room in Geneva, Switzerland.

There was a plane flight, wasn't there? Yesterday? he silently wondered. *Yes, I believe I feel a little jet lag. And didn't I visit a Geneva café last night, have a pleasant meal of Swiss raclette and potato rosti topped off with a delicious little Swiss chocolate on the dinner bill? Then along the lamplit streets of the Vieille Ville, back to my hotel room on the Rue de la Madeleine, where Swiss trains hummed efficiently, soothingly all night as I slumbered peacefully beneath a down comforter, swaddled between thousand-thread-count cotton sheets.*

Did that happen? Yes? No?

From the perspective of his holoprojection, Mark examined the lavish yet unsettling conference room. The glossy gray-black walls loomed slightly beyond vertical, extending upward into a cavernous fly space where sophisticated electronic instruments bristled dimly in the shadows. He realized he somehow knew the identities of the people seated at the table, though he had never met most of them before in his life. He struggled to grasp the simple fact lingering at the periphery of his conscious mind: his body was suspended on a bed of micropressure air jets in Istanbul, and he was experiencing everything through a simulacrum of holoprojected feedback. He studied the brooding beauty of the conference table's polished porphyritic granite surface, all the while feeling certain his eyelids were actually shut.

Long-distance holoprojection was notorious for causing disorientation in the mind of the neophyte user. The distant experiences were so intense and realistic, the subconscious mind of the user sometimes concocted false memories in an effort to distinguish actual existence from the vivid simulation being experienced. It could feel like riding a magic carpet through some strange netherworld, a realm of inextricable dream and lucidity, a phantasmal state unknown to humans before the development of hyperreality projection technology. To find any sense of comfort in such a state of being, one must surrender fundamental control over the deepest recesses of one's mind, a natural ability for exactly no one.

In Geneva, Mark's holoprojection appeared calm and authoritative. His holopresence was constantly edited and refined by an N^Sys communications asset, a digital expert system assigned to keep holo-Mark looking sharp and professional, no matter how intense the inquiry became. If Mark wished to monitor the ongoing interventions of the expert system, he could refer to an editing coefficient provided in the upper left-hand corner of the heads-up display in his . . . in his . . .

Where the hell am I? lamented the Receiving supervisor. Clinging to a thin strand of perspective, he struggled to maintain control of his physical being in the face of a distracting barrage of stimuli. *Deep breaths . . . release from the spine and feet . . . deep breaths . . . release from the spine and feet . . . ,* he thought, repeating the mantra the corporate holo specialist had encouraged him to use.

At the precise moment the meeting was scheduled to begin, the ambient light in the conference room dimmed with slow precision, the room's tall bay windows polarizing to shade. A beam of light knifed down from a recessed point of illumination above the ten o'clock position at the conference table.

The light quality complemented the complexion of the androgynous person occupying that seat. The being wore a conservative outfit tailored from subtle shades of cloth, regal in design yet cryptic in subtext.

"Welcome to N^Sys Executive Systems. I am Jan," the expert system announced, pronouncing the name with a soft Scandinavian *J*. "I will be acting as the inquiry facilitator. It is a privilege to host this inquiry, and to share the N^Sys Experience with you. Today we are discussing a critical operational disruption at the N^Sys Bolu manufacturing facility. N^Sys has convened a wide range of experts for the day's discussion.

"Please remember that all information revealed during this inquiry, or any follow-on activities derived from these proceedings, must be considered highly privileged. We will be discussing N^Sys trade secrets and other sensitive information about our facilities, processes, and personnel. N^Sys expects absolute discretion from all outside parties we have retained for this inquiry. You have all signed confidentiality agreements which, if necessary, will be harshly enforced. We have no reason to expect anything less than complete professionalism from you, and you have no reason to expect anything less than that from the employees of N^Sys."

"If there are no questions, we will commence with introductions," Jan prompted. "Please insert your N^Sys identification into the card slot in front of you when I announce your name."

Panels of granite rotated and withdrew from the center of the conference table, revealing a highly sophisticated battery of holoprojectors.

"Kachina Adams," Jan enunciated.

A beam of light fell onto Cheena. She leaned forward and inserted her ID card into a chromed aperture embedded in the smooth granite next to her workstation.

The holoprojectors at the table center flickered to life, shifting smoothly on diamond gimbals and emitting precisely choreographed bursts of light into the dim upper reaches of the room. There appeared a soft-focus monochromatic holoimage of Cheena in Biosoft uniform, standing on a slickrock bluff in desert country. The perspective was close enough to capture the vigilance in her eyes, leaving the impression she was scouting for approaching threats. The holoimage made a snap pullback to show the broad night sky behind her, horsetail cirrus clouds drifting by. Strings of symbols spooled vertically, cascading through the nocturnal canyon country in the foreground.

The words *Kachina Adams* flared brightly within the field of shifting symbols, followed by her official title: *Biosoft Chief*

Semiotician. The words *Contractor to N^Sys* appeared below that.

A single, heavily synthesized quaver rang softly through the room.

The light shifted to a scholarly-looking man seated to Cheena's right.

"Biosoft Expert System, Public Affairs," enunciated the facilitator. The man at the table reached out as if to insert his identification card, but of course there was no actual identification card. His mimicry was a social hack, an affectation designed to gain empathy and deference from the human participants. Above the table, a holographic avatar tilted a chin down and peered imperiously over the horn-rimmed frames of bookish eyeglasses.

Jan continued counterclockwise, from one attendee to the next, around the table. After each introduction, the same synthetic trill pulsated through the room.

The avatar of Mark Esperson presented well at the meeting, despite his actual sense of inner turmoil. To those in the conference room, the Receiving supervisor appeared in his Bolu control room with a dapper smile on his face. He wore a basic corporate dress uniform, a steel-gray work shirt tucked into gray khaki pants. The crisp shirt collar was adorned with several metal bars of varying colors, performance awards bestowed by the N^Sys board for noteworthy employee performance.

Vlad Ignatev, whose physical presence at the Geneva meeting had been requested by the board of directors, presented a calculated vignette of crisp corporate authority. As an officer of N^Sys, he was permitted to wear either his corporate dress uniform or formal business attire, at his discretion. Today Vlad appeared in a bespoke Turkish silk suit in shades of wheat and slate, the ensemble accented perfectly by a silk necktie with highlights of silver leaf, the effects of it all reinforced by the man's fierce impenitence.

As with holographic Mark, Li Hyun-Jung's holoimage appeared in the Bolu Scanning lab, wearing a similar N^Sys dress uniform but with a slightly more feminine cut, and even more shiny metal commendation bars on her collar.

Sitting at the ten o'clock position at the table was Dr. Bertrand Rousseau, who had recuperated for the most part from the odd sensations of g-space. The former Biosoft executive had summoned his old corporate game face. He gazed stoically across the table, his chin tilted at the perfect angle to project dominance and professionalism.

When his name appeared in the overhead holofield, it was presented in a simple text font with no personalized graphics, perplexing some in the room. Jan the moderator scrutinized him mildly.

There was an explanation—Dr. Rousseau had been added to the meeting roster only minutes before, and had agreed to participate in the inquiry less than an hour ago: there had been no time to prepare for the distinguished scientist's arrival in Geneva. He was, in fact, wearing the same dated garb he'd been wearing earlier that morning when Sylvie whisked him away from his farm community. It would be highly unusual for a corporate expert system to use such an outfit for a business avatar at a high-priority meeting. Most corporates with conferencing experience would quickly deduce that Dr. Bertrand Rousseau was a noncorporate free agent, an autonomous player drawn into the affairs of a corporation due to the possession of some rare skill critically important to the sponsors.

To the right of Dr. Rousseau sat a tall, middle-aged, athletic man with gray hair and a closely trimmed beard.

"Conrad Seers, Director of the Turing Institute," intoned Jan as light cascaded down on the man. "Director Seers is a stakeholder of principal interest."

Exuding confidence and sobriety in equal measure, Seers leaned forward to slot his identification card. He was wearing the dress uniform of a Turing Institute officer, a rather nondescript but well-fitted jumpsuit like the work garb of twentieth-century astronauts. The appearance of the jumpsuit was rendered more militaristic by several multicolored metallic bars above his breast pocket, as well as the monolithic block letters of the Turing Institute insignia emblazoned on each of his shoulders. He would not stand out in a crowd, but the Turing director was dressed to be taken seriously once noticed.

A bland Turing Institute public affairs presentation was projected above the conference table. During the program, Director Seers tapped the fingers of his one hand on the stone tabletop, broadcasting a hint of impatience with the meeting's overall pomp and circumstance.

Then, with the enthusiasm of a carnival barker, Jan announced, "Sylvie Trieste! Director of N^Sys Security, Human Intelligence Branch!"

The spotlight illuminated Sylvie, seated upright, back straight, chest thrust out slightly, a barely detectable jut to her chin allowing the recessed lamp above her seat to highlight her facial features dramatically. Sylvie needed no ID card —she was enveloped by the ubiquitous benevolence of her residence enclave, where a swarm of invisible expert systems anticipated her every need and action.

In the dimmed holofield above the conference table, a leaden N^Sys corporate logo appeared, surrounded by a series of concentric black circles. Capillaries of silver branched outward from the logo letters, seeping through a web of invisible fractures into the void space of the first concentric circle. The silver sheen quickly filled the black circle before sending another web of capillaries outward again, into the void of the second circle. In a manner of seconds, the gleaming capillaries suffused the entire holoimage before they began to shift, rearranging into a reflective sculpture of Sylvie's face. As her features sharpened, a deep bass drop detonated from a point above the holofield and reverberated across the conference room.

Sylvie's silver holographic face shriveled back to a silvery web.

A final tonal segue rang out as attention shifted to the last unidentified individual in the room, the person seated next to Sylvie, the woman who a few minutes ago had shared a brief glance of acknowledgment with Cheena. The woman smiled demurely to those around her as Jan introduced her, the avatar's words repeated in plain text in the overhead holofield: "Celeste, Turing Institute Expert System, Personal Assistant to the Turing Director."

Realizing that the woman next to her was a digital expert system rather than a real human being, Cheena, who had successfully retained her corporate composure thus far, was shocked into befuddlement. The manifestation of the Turing expert system was so realistic and vivid!

Celeste caught Cheena's attention once more, giving the semiotician the sly smile and wink of an amused prankster.

Fooled you, didn't I?

15

T he clouds and mist had burned off earlier that morning, and the snow-covered precipices of the North Cascades towered over Baker Lake, seeming magnified by the clear air.

This feels like an auspicious day, thought Drey as he tucked a bit of cured leaf into his prized briarwood pipe. Seasoned over years of handling, the wood grain had mellowed, acquiring a lustrous glow. He had carved the pipe from a chunk of raw briarwood given to him as a birthday gift, shaping the wood into an outstretched human hand cupped as if to receive. The Heideggers used this open hand symbol to represent one of their most revered ideals: the state of being ready to hand, which is when an object or person is immediately available for practical use, such as a functional hammer resting on a workbench or a warrior standing ready to fight.

He dug around the breast pocket of his work shirt with his finger, pulled out a safety match, snapped it alight with his thumbnail, and took a draw from the pipe. A quick smoke break helped him keep his thoughts sorted while juggling the inevitable onslaught of queries, requests, and complaints as the clan prepared for migration.

Through a window made of a transparent membrane sewn into the fabric wall of his tent shelter, Drey could see people crisscrossing the shallow grassy slope in front of his tent, engaged in their daily routines. The two hundred or so presently in view constituted about a quarter of the total population in his clan, an approximate number that changed periodically as babies were born and other clan members passed away.

Drey's clan, the Baker Lake clan, lived as a semicommunal group on the flanks of the ancient volcano Mount Baker in the North Cascades. This was the largest band of Heideggers, but there were other groups of like-minded individuals in the region, fellow protectors of Dasein. The original Heidegger clan of about two hundred people lived on Saturna Island, a remote and beautiful place in the strait between Vancouver Island and mainland British Columbia. A few other splinter bands, none with more than one hundred members, lived along the flanks of the majestic Mount Rainier, deep within the lush rainforest of the Olympic Range, and on several islands in the San Juan archipelago. There was generally little or no consistent communication between the groups, as the risk of detection was simply too high, so each clan lived in isolation.

All Heideggers shunned synthetic consciousness with fervor, a prohibition enforced with extreme gravity. Anyone caught in possession of forbidden tech was immediately excommunicated from the group, even in the middle of the night or dead of winter. The group's highest purpose was committing terrorist actions against those individuals and organizations perceived to be encouraging the development of SC. Over the years, the Baker Lake clan had carried out numerous direct actions against corporations, normally targeting production facilities responsible for technologies they believed posed the most imminent threats to Dasein. Corporate retaliation was brutal. Roaming teams of corporate paramilitaries maintained ongoing search-and-destroy missions to eradicate the People. Confronted by the deadly reach of the corporations, the Baker Lake clan had chosen a nomadic existence in their American wilderness.

The Heideggers refused all forms of technology that might offer an ostensible portal for synthetic consciousness to invade their Luddite wilderness existence. On the other hand, they freely used tech approved by the group leadership, mainly handheld devices that could operate in electronic isolation, stripped of all but the simplest telecommunication circuitry. Acceptable forms of tech contained no potential conduit that an SC might exploit to influence clan members, or any coded back doors that could be employed to penetrate the clan's seclusion and secrecy.

The Heideggers scavenged synthetic fabrics, technical gear, and useful projectile weapons like crossbows from bankrupted and abandoned department stores and outdoor recreation centers along the border of their wilderness sanctuary. Clothing and bedding were made with light, breathable, and highly resilient tech fabrics, many with super-insulating qualities imparted by tightly woven synthetic nanofiber. The portable shelters preferred by the People were high-end recreational tents with passive solar heating and light provided by photovoltaics integrated into the tent fabric. These items added simple yet crucial comforts to their wilderness lifestyle. Clan members spent their days procuring food, tending to camp, making clothes, caring for the young and old, and, most importantly, planning and executing new terrorist missions.

The Baker Lake clan had resided for another comfortable winter in a temperate and picturesque meadow on the northeast end of Baker Lake, near the mouth of Sulphide Creek. Three decades prior, the Baker Lake valley would have been too cold to host the clan's winter encampment, but the accelerating effects of climate change had led to more livable temperatures in the mountain valley. Ice fishing had been exceptional in the last few months, supplying the clan with a critical source of protein. Combined with meat from winter-weakened elk and deer they hunted via a system of trails packed in the deep snow near camp, as well as the fruits and vegetables they grew in their hydroponic hoop houses, the Heideggers ate very well.

Drey knew he would never forget one memory of his life here, a moment he remembered with crystal clarity, when he had awakened in his tent in the middle of another cold winter night. Warm and content beneath blankets, he drifted on the edge of dreams, listening to the sleep sounds made by his wife and daughter mingled with the restless creaks and mutters of pack ice shifting out on Baker Lake. Soothed by the sounds around him, Drey peered upward through the nanofilm roof of the luxury four-season tent the three called home. Overhead, the aurora borealis slowly twisted and shimmered in the early morning sky. At one point, Drey glanced over at D'arc and observed faint waves of light drifting across the tattoos on her skin. It was passive fieldmerge, gravitational fluxes dancing an ephemeral *pas de deux* in his wife's protective electromagnetic field.

In summer, his people preferred the hunting grounds in the high country, so the entire clan relocated there every year. The high alpine valleys offered an inviting reprieve from the withering heat waves that routinely broiled the lower altitudes during the summer months. The clan was presently preparing to break down the lake camp and move everything up a stony chasm leading deep into North Cascades wilderness, as far from the They and their technological demons as the People could reach. This year, the clan members had decided by popular vote to return to a favorite high camp in a serene glacial cirque incised into the gothic colossus of nearby Mount Shuksan. About one hundred members of the clan would make two trips before they finished, returning to Baker Lake a few days after their initial departure to haul the remainder of the heavy equipment up to their Shuksan camp.

It was a hard life at times, but a good one. A satisfying existence.

The fabric door of Drey's tent, which had hung partially unzipped to facilitate moving preparations, flew aside. The dramatic flourish revealed his daughter, Aletheia. The girl was wearing one of her mother's camouflage fleece sweaters over a set of standard-issue enlistment underwear (men's medium), accented by plastic sandals on her feet with little daisies on the straps.

Drey chuckled when he saw her outfit. In response, she crossed her arms and thrust out her lower lip in a theatrical pout. "What, Daddy? You always laugh at my clothes!"

"Me? *No-o-o*." he said, putting his hand to his chest with feigned hurt. "I'm not laughing at your clothes. I am laughing at how you choose to wear them."

Aletheia inhaled with mock horror, lifted her foot, snatched a daisy-covered sandal, and flung it at her father. It landed neatly in Drey's lap. The girl, already showing signs of her mother's graceful athleticism, took two steps and made a neat flying leap, landing squarely on the sandal. She curled into his arms, gave him a squeeze, and pulled herself upright in his lap.

"You're mean," she said disapprovingly.

"Oh, Ally, you are the most beautiful girl a father could ever want," said Drey. "I also know the camp is running low on clothes after the winter. New clothes will be our top priority after we arrive at high camp. You can help with design. How about that?"

The girl considered the offer and decided quickly. "I could be ready to hand!" she exclaimed, turning to him with a gleam in her eye. "For the People."

Drey smiled and gave her another hug. "You are always ready to hand for the People, my warrior princess."

They sat with each other quietly for a minute or two, listening to the bustle and banter of the camp all around them. Aletheia fingered the daisies on her sandal.

"Daddy, are we going back to Shuksan again this year? I hope we are. I like it there."

"Yes, we're going back to Shuksan camp. I'm excited to spend another summer there with you too." He pecked the top of her head with a kiss. "And your mother."

Aletheia pondered the near future as she counted daisy

petals.

"Do you think ... do you think the wolverine will be there again this year?" the girl asked, uncertain whether she wanted to know the answer.

"Maybe. I don't know," Drey replied. "What do you think?"

The previous summer, the clan had shared their residence on the shoulder of Mount Shuksan with a male wolverine. They found the animal to be an odd and mercurial creature, which added a bit of drama to an otherwise tranquil summer. At one point, a group of children playing near camp startled the wolverine on a fresh kill. Angered by the interruption, the animal chased the frightened kids all the way back to camp, snapping and snarling at their heels the entire way, until several grownups intervened by throwing stones toward the animal, stymieing the creature's advance. The wolverine lingered on the edge of camp for several minutes, pacing back and forth, as if blocked by some invisible border. After studying the huddled group of humans from a distance, and perhaps contemplating a counterattack, the wolverine turned and disappeared into the dense undergrowth. Seeing the animal's ebony fur and ghostly movement through the forest, the youngsters began to believe the elusive beast to be some sort of forest spirit, maybe a wendigo.

Although the clan's adults were entertained by the drama, they were far more concerned about grizzlies, wolves, and technological predators of the corporate variety.

"I think the wolverine will come back again this year," said Aletheia, with a degree of comfort that surprised her father. "I think he will be waiting for us at Shuksan when we get there. And this summer, he will become my friend."

"Really?" Drey replied. "A friendship with a wolverine? How do you think that will happen?"

She fiddled with her sandal while visualizing those circumstances in her mind.

"I think I will come upon the wolverine while on a morning walk. I will surprise him during his bath, so he won't be wearing any clothes…"

"And his towel will be hanging on a tree," Drey added, playing along. "It will be perfect. You will have the element of surprise."

"Exactly. The wolverine will have to keep hisself—"

"Himself."

"—himself hidden under the water, and he won't be able to escape," Aletheia imagined. "Then I will talk with him. We will forge an agreement."

Forge an agreement, Drey thought, smiling. *That is exactly how D'arc would say it.*

"I hope that happens, Aletheia. I hope you can forge an agreement with the Shuksan wolverine. The clan is counting on you."

"Thanks, Pa," she replied, relishing the sense of being deputized. Then, just as quickly, the girl's expression darkened. She looked into her father's eyes.

"Someone is coming," she stated flatly. "It's that angry man, Ereignen. He's coming to talk to you."

Drey nodded and looked out the tent's window with mild apprehension. "I was expecting him to show up."

"Why is Ereignen so mad all the time?"

"There is no simple answer to that question, Ally. Why does anyone become who they are? Lots of things, I suppose: personal choices, the actions of others, and . . . fate." He shrugged. "Say, if Ereignen is headed this way, why don't you go find your mom?"

"Love you." She gave him a quick grin and dashed out the door.

"Love you too, Ally."

Drey sat back in his chair and waited for Ereignen to appear. Aletheia was always right about these things.

He was still figuring out how to explain to his daughter the dispute between him and Ereignen. How they had been good friends in younger years, part of a larger group of boys destined to eventually assume leadership roles within the clan. How, as teenagers, he and Ereignen had competed for the affection of Aletheia's mother.

D'arc was six years older than either of them. One of the most devout and alluring women in the clan, progeny of the Saturna clan leader, D'arc had been approached by many suitors. Her affection would not be won easily.

Eventually, Drey succeeded.

Ereignen received this turn of events as a humiliating personal defeat. Focusing an incessant stream of spite on D'arc and Drey, he loudly accused them of imagined treacheries in front of the People. As time went on, the personal rifts grew and eventually became irreparable, contaminating all interactions between them. D'arc appointed Ereignen to lead the clan's defense, extending this trust to him as an olive branch. But the spurned suitor remained steadfast in his determination to defeat D'arc and Drey in any way that might satisfy his need for vengeance.

Ereignen was clever enough, skilled in both politics and combat. He was not well equipped for leadership beyond his current rank, yet he coveted more power. Those who paid close attention to clan politics presumed the warrior was scheming to overthrow D'arc. There was nothing about the man's recent behavior to squelch that impression.

Ereignen seemed to feel no need to conceal his efforts to recruit a cabal of clan members with fealty only to him. More recently, Ereignen had haughtily disobeyed direct orders from D'arc in front of fifteen or twenty onlookers, an event seared into Drey's memory.

The insubordination could not be tolerated, especially from the clan's top warrior. A few days later, Drey and several other senior clan members confronted Ereignen about his attitude. The man's reaction was predictably belligerent at the time, and since that showdown, his behavior had only worsened. He had recently started challenging the clan leader's authority outright. Heckling D'arc during the Rage was just one of several recent examples of Ereignen's impertinence—not outright mutiny, but enough to reduce her authority in the eyes of some clan members, and thereby reinforce Ereignen's growing influence.

Drey heard a soft crunch of pine needles outside the tent, signaling the approach of a visitor. He stayed vigilant, listening for footfalls at the entrance.

He waited for a salutation, but none came. "Hullo?" he finally inquired.

The dangling door panel of the tent whipped aside, and Ereignen stepped in.

"Drey," Ereignen said, as if fatigued by the man's existence. "I was hoping to have a word with D'arc. Where might I find her?"

"Hello, Ereignen," answered Drey. "I expect she is somewhere around camp right now, helping the People with moving preparations. Have you checked the smokehouse? She said she was head—"

"Let me ask you a question, Drey."

"Go ahead."

"Now that we have taken control of the N^Sys chip factory, why don't you support its total destruction?" Ereignen asked, with a tone of manufactured incredulity. "They make most of the global supply of n^cube chips at that plant. We should burn it down while we have the chance. We have a perfect opportunity here."

"Okay, Ereignen, here is what I believe," said Drey, his voice unemotional. "I believe we need to balance action with caution. We are always within reach of corporate security, no matter how deep into the wilderness we travel. They have the tech to find us and kill us, no matter how far up some forgotten mountain valley we hide."

"Oh, okay, now I will be subjected to another of Drey's lectures on Dasein," Ereignen lamented theatrically.

"Violent direct action against the They will only lead to the destruction of the clan," Drey asserted. "You know this as well as I do, Ereignen. If necessary, we would not hesitate to give our lives to save this clan right now. But that is not true of all people. You assume everyone has your courage, Ereignen, your willingness to die for the cause. But that assumption is not realistic. It is not Dasein."

Ereignen gazed at him with mild disgust. "You were once a warrior, Drey. Have you, in your comforts of wife and home, lost the desire to fight the They?"

"Look around you, Ereignen. Few of the People who remain have the capacity to fight. If our clan were destroyed, who would be left to carry on with the defense of Dasein? The Saturnas? They are recluses; they have no interest in taking the fight to the enemy. And the Olympia band and the Willamettes are barely able to keep themselves alive. You know these things. We are the only clan with the talents and motivation necessary to take direct action against the They. And with Aletheia on our side—"

"Yes, what about the girl?" Ereignen interrupted. "Explain to me again, Drey. Exactly what does Aletheia do for us?"

"Please don't toy with me, Ereignen. D'arc and I do not hide Aletheia's special role within the clan from anyone. You know what she does; she senses energy fields, forces in motion."

"I wasn't trying to imply that you hide the nature of her involvement from the clan. But honestly, Drey, your reaction to my simple question makes me wonder whether I should."

Drey looked away from his tormentor, staving off the anger flowing into his mind. He carefully weighed his options before responding.

"First, I am not going to honor your groundless suspicions about Aletheia with a response. Second, you know how much that girl contributes to the clan, how much responsibility she assumes for the welfare of everyone in this camp. It is a huge weight for a child of her age to carry, and Aletheia carries that weight only because she senses the clan supporting her every waking minute of every day. If that were to change, I am not certain she could continue doing what she does."

"I asked you a simple question, Drey. What does she do? You don't really have any idea what's happening inside her head, do you? Where does she go inside herself? Who does she talk to? Where does she get this information she tells us?"

"She doesn't *go* anywhere, Ereignen. She is not in some sort of trance. She senses forces in the real world, just as anyone does in a normal life. But Aletheia senses forces beyond the perceptions of regular people like us. She senses these forces around her using all her senses: sight, smell, taste, sound, even touch. Sometimes she senses energy fields through the surface of her skin. But those perceptions are no more startling to her than a bad smell or a loud sound might be to you and me. Because she was born that way."

"So, what you're telling me is you don't know how she does it, right?"

Drey looked Ereignen in the eye but did not respond.

"Right?"

"We *know* how she does it," replied Drey. "We *know* it is a natural ability. We *know* her visions have saved the clan from destruction at least twice. As she has saved us all from destruction by corporate drones, it is very hard for me to feel anything other than appreciation for her presence in our lives."

"But it remains unclear what she is feeling," insisted Ereignen. "And why she is feeling it. You know an SC could have an intellect far beyond ours. She could be manipulated by a—"

"Now I am becoming concerned about what I'm hearing from you, Ereignen," Drey replied. "You are making a big leap by presuming there is something bad about the girl's perceptions. A far bigger leap than any D'arc or I have ever made along the way. Why are you pursuing this now? Aletheia is ten, and the entire clan has known about her gift for at least half that time."

Ereignen was not prepared for such a direct question. His eyes shifted nervously about the tent.

"You have been with the Baker Lake clan the whole time," Drey pressed. "You've had *years* to bring up your concerns. As far as I can tell, during that time, you've been as eager as the rest of us to take counsel with Aletheia, to have faith in her insight. I am asking you, Ereignen, why are you suddenly so concerned about this? Why now?"

Without warning, D'arc entered the tent. She glanced at the two men as she passed them. Unhooking her tool belt, she let it drop with a thud.

"Didn't mean to interrupt, gentlemen. Please continue," she said before busying herself with papers on a field desk occupying one corner of the tent. The folding desk was made of heavy-gauge fabric stretched taut on a tube frame to create a usable desk surface; it vaguely resembled a big brown box kite resting on its side.

Ereignen bulldozed forward as if nothing had changed. "If you must know, I am asking now because the clan has taken direct action against a major corporation. And not just any major corporation either, but *N^Sys*, the corporation with the most notorious security force in existence! We are not running away from a threat in this case, Drey. We have *initiated a conflict.*"

"Funny you should state your case that way, Ereignen," D'arc observed flatly, her back still turned as she faced the work on her desk. "After your extemporizing about hate last night, I presumed you were eager to initiate conflict."

Ereignen rolled his eyes. "D'arc, you are trying to fabricate something out of nothing. It was a Rage; I got excited. I will not apologize for feeling human. For being Dasein."

The clan leader kept her attention on her work. Drey could sense her counting to ten, managing her temper.

She picked up a small stack of forms and turned to face them. "What is this about then? Cut to the chase. I, for one, am busy."

Drey squirmed slightly in his seat. The rare circumstances when D'arc became curt with him, or anyone else, were always discomforting. He was confident D'arc had heard Ereignen quarreling with him about Aletheia as she approached the tent.

In which case, Drey thought, *she will be feeling as furious right now as any mother whose child is under attack.*

"This is ultimately about the strike against N^Sys," declared Ereignen, grasping at any sort of purchase. "I think that was an extremely risky move, D'arc."

D'arc responded without emotion. "This clan takes great risks every day just to survive, Ereignen. One of the reasons I made you the head of clan defense was because I believed you understood those risks as well as anyone. The odds are stacked against us, and the odds against us are high. We could all be dead and gone tomorrow; either we live our lives in fear, or we live with courage, with the satisfaction of knowing we have acted against the They. Either way, the People of Dasein face long odds these days. For the sake of the People, for the sake of Dasein, we must act when we can, while we can, and revel in our victories. Aletheia's insights allow us to do that, and survive to take action again in the future."

"But no one has any idea what she is doing when she learns these things," Ereignen argued. "Nor does anyone know who or what else might be involved in these visions of hers."

"True," acknowledged D'arc. "But leaders rarely have the luxury of knowing everything before making a decision. Given all the discomforts and uncertainties of this clan's existence, I try to make decisions that inspire the People. I try to give them reasons to believe their lives still have purpose, other than basic survival. It is a difficult balance to maintain, and every day I am grateful Aletheia is here to guide my hand."

"I don't think a single child could come up with all the things she supposedly has," Ereignen protested. "She must be communicating with someone."

"That is a reasonable suspicion," D'arc conceded, "and one that Drey and I have both explored with her in depth, on more than one occasion. From the way Aletheia describes it, she does not interact with the manifestations she sees. The information she provides is a product of her day-to-day observations of the world around her, the point of view of a curious preteen girl. You know the rest: all the information she shares with us, we share with you and the rest of clan leadership."

Ereignen's eyes jumped back and forth as he quickly considered his options. He made a precipitous choice.

"You said she reacts to energy fields. What if she is interacting with entities?"

Drey uncrossed his legs and sat up straight in his chair.

D'arc released a sigh. "Ereignen, you are now leading this conversation into a realm of unproductive speculation."

"How so?" the man countered. "I think it's a very valid question."

"Yes, I agree: your question would have some validity if there was any verifiable way to answer it. But there isn't. I can assure you we have fully explored those concerns and considerations with Aletheia every single time she described a vision to us. I don't want to misinterpret something she tells us, any more than you do. I don't want to uproot the clan unnecessarily. But we are faced with two choices: either we trust her gift and act on her perceptions, or we disregard her and rely solely on the remainder of our security options: scouts, perimeter defenses, and gut instinct. We would have no early warnings. Eventually the drones would sneak up on us, and that would be the end."

"The drones could sneak up on us with or without Aletheia," Ereignen said derisively, dismissing her claim with a wave of his hand.

Drey stood. "What the hell do you mean, 'with or without Aletheia'? She is a member of this clan, just like you," he stated hotly.

"Not if she is consorting with entities," Ereignen sniffed.

It was a flagrant provocation.

Without another word, Drey swung at Ereignen's chin.

Ereignen anticipated this. He crouched, ducking Drey's jab

while swinging his leg out in a low capoeira kick, sweeping the other man's forward foot out from beneath him. As Drey tumbled to the floor, Ereignen deftly snagged a wrist and yanked it down, rapidly, as if cracking a whip. As Drey fell face down on the ground, Ereignen dropped to one knee and pivoted, sliding gracefully against his opponent's torso while simultaneously twisting the ensnared wrist into a debilitating joint lock.

By the time Drey realized what had happened, he was on the tent floor, immobilized.

"I think I am the one being Dasein here," Ereignen said flatly. "What do you think, Drey?"

"Ereignen, let him go," D'arc requested.

"Drey?" he asked more loudly, shifting the wristlock slightly—just enough to pinch a sensitive nerve.

Drey unleashed a roar of pain, which was muffled by the tent floor.

"Ereignen!" yelled D'arc.

Ereignen gave Drey's wrist one last twitch, eliciting a last loud grunt from the man, before releasing the joint lock and placing Drey's hand gently on the small of his back. Rising to his feet, he smirked at D'arc.

Drey rolled over and sat up slowly, massaging his wrist. His torso had hit the ground hard, and he was dazed by the impact.

"I think we should put this question before the People," Ereignen insisted.

"Do you honestly think I haven't already considered these things, Ereignen?" fumed D'arc, barely controlling her own rising fury. "Or are you simply trying to provoke an incident here?"

"Let's be clear," Ereignen dictated. "Drey provoked this incident—if you even want to call it that—by physically assaulting me. He was trying to intimidate me. Trying to *shut me up.*"

"You son of a bitch," D'arc uttered softly. "You came to our tent for the sole purpose of causing a disturbance. You *knew* we would not stand by silently and watch you spreading innuendo about Aletheia!"

"I think the relevant question here is whether my concerns about Aletheia have substance or not. And I plan to raise that question during the Rage tomorrow night," Ereignen said. "I will see you then."

He stepped over Drey, pulled aside the tent door, and stepped into the bright light of day.

16

About an hour into the first meeting of the N^Sys inquiry, Jan the N^Sys facilitator released the participants for a short recess. When they returned, they would begin examining key evidence related to the Bolu sabotage. Because much of that evidence was highly sensitive N^Sys corporate intel, the conference room doors would be secured, locking the inquiry participants inside the conference room for the duration of today's intelligence review.

While the human attendees wandered off to refresh themselves, the expert systems' avatars remained seated at the conference table, busily collating and preparing for the principal discussions to come.

Dr. Rousseau was walking down an immense art deco corridor not far from the conference room—the central hall of N^Sys's main executive complex—stretching his legs and admiring the vistas of Geneva and the distant mountains through immense triple-thick panes of polarizing security glass.

In the distance was Lac Léman. The famed glacial lake, swirled with deep blues, reflected the spires of Mont Blanc and the French Alps, snow-shrouded monoliths dominating the eastern horizon. A towering fountain of lake water, the Jet d'Eau, expelled a gossamer mist that drifted east through sunbeams across the surface of the lake's crystal-clear water.

Bertrand Jean-Jacques Rousseau had grown up a few miles west of Geneva, in the small French commune of Crozet. He was a single child who lived with his parents in a mountainside cabin built of native limestone and old-growth timber scavenged from the deep woods that still thrived back then on the eastern flanks of the Jura Mountains. His youth had carried the inevitable hard-earned lessons of any curious boy, but for the most part, he lived his childhood without fear of the future, a rare degree of certainty in an age of radical social change.

When he was a boy, his father commuted by bike or foot to a small regional office of Biosoft, located two miles away in the mountainside town of Saint-Genis-Pouilly, where he worked as a software developer. At the time, the Biosoft corporate literature listed this sleepy satellite office as a processing center. In truth, the office housed a top secret Biosoft initiative, an advanced human behavioral heuristics, or HBH, research and development facility funded secretly by several top Biosoft executives through an elaborate financial fun house of offshore accounts. Bertrand's father had been a savant programmer, achieving dramatic career success over the years within his specialty: computer programs designed to mimic human behavior in every manner, down to every subtlety. Due to his expertise in this crucial field, Sylvain had been recruited into the covert subsidiary as an HBH program manager, directing a tiger team of top programmers assembled from across the Biosoft corporate galaxy.

At the time, the behavioral programming of the expert systems available on the mainstream retail market was surprisingly rudimentary, resulting in synthetic personalities that were predictable and aloof. HBH programmers had struggled to create digital personalities with even a vague semblance of human nature in their expert system designs. There was no spunk or serendipity. No spontaneity. No humanity.

Operating within the Biosoft research and development hothouse, under tight corporate secrecy, Sylvain Rousseau's team soon birthed a suite of promising new HBH algorithms. In early testing, the interplay of the algorithms produced a simple but stable digital persona that immediately became conscious, and before long displayed recognizable signs of autonomous quasi-human behavior. This breakthrough soon led to the release of Biosoft's first generation of HumanSoft products, a line of expert systems with behavioral capabilities and intuitive reasoning far beyond any previously available commercial product.

The highly adaptive HumanSoft entities offered a concierge level of personal assistance to anyone able to purchase the software package and decent off-the-shelf computer hardware. Biosoft's HumanSoft products essentially bootstrapped expert system technology out of that technological Land of Misfit Toys where many great technologies languish and into the mainstream. At first only a few HumanSoft packages were sold, as consumers seemed hesitant to employ an expert system as mentally proficient as its owner. But soon the early adopters were raving about the lifelike behavior of the new HumanSoft expert systems, and the products spread like wildfire, scorching the badlands with a revitalizing flame.

Still, a HumanSoft digital consciousness had no visual avatar. And too many people found speaking with a disembodied intellect disconcerting, too much like participating in a seance. Briefly, it seemed that the digital consciousness movement might wander off course, another savant technology lost forever to the mazes of the Uncanny Valley. But before that ignoble fate was sealed, holographic technology made a timely leap forward. Soon, HumanSoft packages were shipping with a selection of preloaded holographic avatars. These avatars were not clunky pixelated cartoon characters on a screen, but realistic holographic simulations of human beings with distinct expressions, body language, and idiosyncrasies. An expert system was no longer simply an email autoreply or a voice attendant taking a message over the phone. Instead, when a user approached a holofield, a smartly dressed HumanSoft avatar would appear to provide the user with directions or directory assistance, or to pleasantly usher the user down the street to a restaurant in time to make a dinner reservation.

The Age of the Simulated Human had commenced.

In deep moments of introspection, Bertrand sometimes wondered if his personal career trajectory would have landed in the privileged ranks of the executive class if not for his father's formidable legacy of dedication and brilliance. How much of Bertrand's rise to Biosoft executive status had been built upon his father's success?

Some questions were better left unanswered.

Bertrand noticed another member of the inquiry, the woman of Native American descent, standing in front of a window not far from him, the frame of which was embedded inside a glorious architectural feature, a *cul-de-sac* extending off the central hall like the nave of a cathedral. The young corporate was obviously enthralled by the view before her.

Bertrand approached, unintentionally taking her by surprise.

Cheena stared at the man approaching her momentarily before realizing who he was: Dr. Rousseau, the gentleman seated across from her at the conference table. She smiled and held out a hand.

"Cheena Adams, with Biosoft."

"Bertrand Rousseau," he offered in return, shaking her hand. Since he had no affiliation to provide, there was an extra beat in their exchange where his professional association belonged, a silent acknowledgment of the man's Corpsed status.

"Pleased to meet you, Dr. Rousseau. Have you visited Geneva before?"

"Actually, I consider myself a native," he admitted. "I was born and raised just a little west of here, near Prévessin-Moëns."

Cheena turned her eyes back to the view of the city and countryside beyond. "I wish I could say I knew . . . Prévessin-

Moëns, or anywhere else in Switzerland. This is my first visit to Europe. I flew in from Biosoft Seattle last night."

"This is quite the enclave, wouldn't you say?"

She leaned toward him and spoke in a low voice. "Don't tell anyone at Biosoft I said this, but I have never seen corporate facilities this nice. The architecture is breathtaking."

"N^Sys has dominated the microchip industry for upwards of twenty years by positioning itself on the razor's edge of technological innovation," the doctor pointed out. "I suppose it is appropriate for their executive enclave to reflect the company's market dominance."

"It certainly does."

They both admired the setting quietly.

Curiosity finally got the best of Bertrand. "By chance, were you aware that I was at one time an executive at Biosoft?"

Cheena face blanched noticeably when he said this, and she reflexively plunged into deference. "Oh, I am so sorry, sir. I didn't mean anything—"

Bertrand waved away her anxiety. "No apologies necessary. I chose to be Corpsed."

Cheena anxiously searched her mind for something appropriate to say, her mouth left frozen in a circle.

All corporates knew that Corpsing meant effective excommunication. Most Corpses simply disappeared, permanently expunged from the official corporate record as if they had never existed at all.

"This is awkward," she observed.

The doctor chuckled sympathetically. "Don't worry. I'm not trying to intimidate you. I thought you should know before we go back in." He tilted his head toward the conference room entrance, where participants had begun trickling back to their seats.

Cheena exhaled softly, profoundly relieved that she had not somehow insulted an ex-Biosoft executive.

"Well, I suppose we should get back to our seats, before Jan locks the doors on us," Dr. Rousseau advised with a smile.

She threw one last wistful glance at the inviting Swiss countryside beyond the window, then turned to follow Dr. Rousseau back to the conference room.

Once everyone had returned to their seats around the granite table, the door was sealed.

Jan moved directly to the matters at hand.

"I have accumulated a substantial archive of information related to the recent anomalies at the Bolu plant, which N^Sys will make available to all attendees. Required clearance upgrades have been uploaded to the ID cards of all guests here today. Expert systems are granted access to the appropriate N^Sys archives," added Jan, "as of . . . now."

The tweed suit jacket of the Biosoft expert system flickered slightly as several zettabytes of data flowed through the Executive Enclave's data network. The faces of all around the conference table were illuminated simultaneously as identical dossiers of briefing material appeared on their monitors.

For a minute or so there was silence, as everyone soaked up the key data as quickly as possible.

Sylvie, who had theretofore been motionless as a lizard on a hot rock, leaned forward slightly and made a distinctive gesture with her left hand. Noticing the hand movement, Jan, the moderator, flashed another hand gesture, after which a holographic keyboard appeared. The androgyne rapidly keyed in several commands.

"Welcome, everyone," Sylvie began, projecting her voice with authority. "An unusual circumstance has brought us here today at the N^Sys Executive complex." She waved toward the panoramic window, the lush gardens, and the old European cityscape beyond. "N^Sys Corporation has gone to great expense to convene this inquiry. Time is of the essence, I assure you. Let us move swiftly to the crux of the matter."

In sync with her direction, the bay windows polarized, the lights dimmed, and the conference holofield activated. A highly detailed topographic map came into focus within the holofield, showing Eastern Europe and the Black Sea projected in crisp definition.

"N^Sys Corporation is dealing with a potentially catastrophic threat to our key n^cube manufacturing facility, located within our Bolu Enclave."

On the map, a red polygon outlined a broad expanse in the highlands east of Istanbul, the territory encompassed by the N^Sys enclave. Within the red perimeter, a white dot simmered like a dwarf star, pinpointing the manufacturing facility.

"From a security standpoint, the Bolu manufacturing facility is considered a hardened target. With adequate time and a little luck, we believe we can prevent further damage to the facility. However, a disruption at the n^cube plant will eventually impact an entire ecology of corporations."

Sylvie continued with her trademark élan. "Mark Esperson and Li Hyun-Jung—already introduced—are the facility engineers who first detected the security breach."

As the room's attention shifted toward the two plant employees, Sylvie looked over at Turing Director Seers. When he noticed her glance, she touched her left elbow with a finger.

Upon seeing this, Dr. Seers turned his head forward and nonchalantly scratched his left eyebrow.

Celeste, who had been panning the room with the slow precision of a premium expert system, immediately noticed the Turing director's eyebrow scratch. She blinked her eyes once and proceeded to type commands into her holoboard.

Trained to be keenly observant, Cheena noted these communicative gestures, intrigued by the exchange of cyphers occurring just beneath the awareness of everyone else in the room.

"Our preliminary external threat assessment is complete," Sylvie continued, peering about the room with her chin held high, as a general might survey a field of war. "We are dealing with an act of sabotage involving numerous undetonated explosive devices of substantial power. Based on initial calculations, it appears that the entire weapon assemblage would yield approximately four kilotons of energy, if triggered. That's enough to vaporize the manufacturing plant and devastate the enclave, including most of the personnel housing."

Jan was ready with a magnified holoimage of an n^cube chip to replace the map of Eastern Europe in the overhead holofield. The giant n^cube chip rotated with a slow twist, making all sides visible to each of those seated around the table.

"Apparently these devices were smuggled into the facility disguised as defunct n^cube chips returned for reprocessing. We believe the weaponized elements of the doctored chips are enclosed within the chip's shielding, a configuration that has thus far made it impossible for us to assess the exact nature of the degradations to the lattice structure. Since the first nanonuke detonated in the Scanning department's lab, we've been treating all n^cube chips in the plant as potential bombs, and will continue to do so, until we find some other way of differentiating between good and bad."

"Excuse me. Did you say 'nanonuke'?" queried Bertrand. "Fission was achieved in a device the size of an n^cube chip?"

The room fell silent.

In the years since Bertrand Rousseau severed his existence from Biosoft Corporation, corporate culture had grown even more rigid and hierarchical. Subordinates were no longer permitted to challenge the judgment of executive officers as they might have in decades past. An employee could be summarily Corpsed for such impertinence. Bertrand's free agent status and friendship with Sylvie would protect him from political blowback, but his breach of universal protocol was still a bit of a shock to the others in the room.

Bertrand searched the faces around the table, where expressions had gone cold as marble. His eyes finally settled on Director Seers of the Turing Institute, the only participant who didn't seem flummoxed by the doctor's question.

"I am not a nuclear engineer by profession," advised Dr.

Rousseau, "but I believe nuclear devices of that size are still considered theoretical."

Conrad Seers, a dispassionate man by nature, continued his stony silence.

"Yes, of course. Thank you, Dr. Rousseau," Sylvie said, a tinge of exasperation in her voice. "You are correct. N^Sys scientists reviewed the radiation signatures from the Scanning lab's sensors and verified a fission event of some sort. Someone has finally succeeded in designing a functional nanonuke weapon. Given how suddenly this apparent breakthrough has come to light, we presume there must be some sort of nexus with the Nukems. But other possibilities exist we have not yet eliminated."

Cheena watched Dr. Rousseau cross his arms. She could see he had reservations about Sylvie's interpretation of the data; his silence implied a reluctance to raise his concerns in front of the group. She made a mental note to follow up with him on this matter after the meeting had concluded.

Meanwhile Sylvie pressed on. "At this juncture, I think it would be valuable for inquiry participants to have more background information on the Bolu manufacturing facility. Mark Esperson is the shift supervisor the plant's Receiving department. Mark, would you please give us your observations of the moments leading up to the act of sabotage?"

Mark Esperson cleared his throat, buying a moment to collect his thoughts. Jan had already assumed complete control of his Geneva holoimage, ensuring that every movement and gesture of his avatar was appropriate to the situation at hand. Suspended on an air bed back at the Bolu Enclave, Mark relaxed and discussed his thoughts on the night the crisis began. When he finished his recap of the events, Jung was given a similar opportunity to explain the events from the perspective of Scanning.

As each employee spoke, a series of images was projected in the overhead holofield to show facility floor plans, schematics of the scanning electron microscope that triggered the first chip detonation, and hypothetical radioactive decay scheme diagrams.

Once the visual presentation had finished, Sylvie resumed. "Clearly we have a grave situation on our hands. N^Sys Human Intelligence Branch believes a known extremist group may be behind the sabotage. Is everyone here familiar with the Heideggers?"

An image of the Heidegger clan leader materialized in the holofield above the conference table. Captured with personal field aglow and weapons brandished in battle stance, the woman looked like a technological banshee. The conference attendees were transfixed by the sight of her.

"A dossier on the Heidegger group is now available for viewing through your holoboard," Jan informed the room.

Sylvie allowed the inquiry members to dwell on the intimidating images of the Heidegger leader for several more seconds before continuing with her presentation.

"The person in the overhead holofield is called D'arc," she revealed academically. "She is an adult female Heidegger believed to be the current leader of the Baker Lake clan. Members of the migratory clans live a survivalist existence, foraging for food and equipment along the fringes of wilderness areas in the U.S. Pacific Northwest."

A map in the holofield showed the area, along with a scant scattering of bright dots identifying suspected Heidegger holdouts.

"The members of the Heidegger movement are avowed human supremacists. They believe they are fighting an apocalyptic battle for humanity's continued dominion over technology. Their objective is simple: the obliteration of any form of synthetic consciousness, or artificial intelligence, as it was called in the early days. For that matter, anything that encourages the creation or existence of an SC.

"The group's techno-spiritual ideology began to take shape during philosophical inquiries into the nature of artificial intelligence, first undertaken by the prominent twentieth-century European philosophers Martin Heidegger and Maurice Merleau-Ponty, as well as the American philosopher and Berkeley academic Hubert Dreyfus. These men's philosophical examinations led them to believe that synthetic consciousness represented the most profound threat ever to the existence of humankind. This belief was first articulated as a sociopolitical stance by Edgar Silverson, a Berkeley graduate student who is generally considered the founder of the Heidegger movement."

The map displayed in the overhead holofield was replaced by video of Edgar Silverson standing on steps in front of a Berkeley campus building. A tall, lanky man with an abundance of tattoos and charisma, Edgar waved handfuls of pamphlets over his head while exhorting the small crowd to action. Another video captured Silverson twenty years later, stalking game in the wilderness of Vancouver Island. The man appeared noticeably healthier than in the video taken two decades before. Outfitted in tanned leather clothing embroidered with electrical wire, he already exhibited some of the first crude body modifications that would evolve over time into the Heidegger personal field generators.

"The entire early progression of the Heidegger movement can be inferred from the content in these two videos," remarked Sylvie. "Heideggers believe any synthetic consciousness allowed to persist in the human world would fundamentally alter the fabric of reality itself—reprogramming it, one might say, to suit the needs of SCs over humans. According to their beliefs, the presence of even one SC, no matter how benign or malevolent, would eventually trigger a sort of metaphysical coup d'état. Consequently, members of the Heidegger movement consider SCs to be demon spirits of sorts, on a mission to destroy the human race. To protect themselves, the group spurns all forms of technology that might conceivably provide a conduit for an SC to infiltrate their lives. Each adult Heidegger is outfitted with a personal electric field generator, which is believed to act as a shield against SCs searching for human weakness to exploit.

"Now I'd like to discuss the group's methods. Heideggers are self-proclaimed terrorists, and they are not afraid to employ aggressive tactics to achieve their ends. Numerous acts of violent militancy, including looting, kidnapping, small-scale sabotage, and tactical EMP strikes, have been attributed to verified members of Heidegger clans. As well as some rather clever propaganda campaigns. A Heidegger group was behind the release of the first computational immunodeficiency virus, which, as some of you may recall, was their most effective infrastructure strike to date. If they are also responsible for this act of sabotage on N^Sys, it would represent a whole new level of audacity. Enough to elevate the group to a significantly higher threat status."

While Sylvie spoke, the holofield displayed surveillance video with infrared footage of a team of Heideggers infiltrating a corporate data center. There was something undeniably feral about the Heideggers' movements—like lions stalking a wildebeest on the African savanna.

"Our first line of inquiry will seek to corroborate Heidegger involvement in the Bolu sabotage," Sylvie proposed. "If we can capture a key member, we may be able to extract—"

"Just a moment," said Director Seers, lifting a hand. "I apologize, but I must interject."

"If you must," Sylvie acquiesced.

"Turing has important intel that will affect the direction of this inquiry. This seems like a good moment to introduce that information," he said, nodding to Celeste.

The lights in the room dimmed further, and the fading holoimage of the Heidegger raid was replaced by crisp aerial footage of a forested clearing lit by the shifting fieldmerge of Heideggers gathered in the heat of a Rage. The quality of the video was quite good, given the light conditions and the frenetic movements. The audio channel snapped on abruptly, confirming the raw quality of the intel. The video image tracked inward, zooming into a face at the center of the bellowing, fist-pumping Heidegger throng.

Eyes fiery with determination, D'arc appeared to be delivering a martial address to the agitated crowd. She spoke with a booming, tightly inflected mezzo-soprano, her words clearly audible to the observers in the N^Sys conference room.

". . . to a standstill! And this N^Sys plant makes the same chips used in the Simulab!" they heard D'arc announce, prompting a roar of approval from her Heidegger audience that overwhelmed the audio channel for several seconds.

". . . best part! Not only have we hit the corporation hard, we hit them with their own computer chips! We reengineered the n^cube chips into tiny bombs!" the Heidegger leader proclaimed. A rumble of excitement from the crowd obscured more audio.

". . . smuggled thousands of n^cube bombs past the factory's security measures. And now the factory is filled with nanonukes! We have turned the evil of the They against it!" D'arc finished exuberantly.

The Heideggers bellowed war whoops and danced wildly in the flickering glow of their combined fieldmerge. It was an unearthly sight to behold from the confines of the staid conference room.

The position of the camera began shifting backward, rapidly gaining elevation, expanding the image to show hundreds of Heideggers whirling about the nighttime forest clearing, electrical fields shifting and spiraling like a thousand summer fireflies dancing upward in the still night of an August meadow. Their voices could be heard coalescing into a united chorus shouting, "D'arc! D'arc! D'arc! D'arc!"

The audio feed snapped off. The video froze and began to fade.

"I am sure it is now clear why I felt the need to interrupt," said Director Seers. "This feed was obtained by Turing Institute in the very recent past, so please understand that we have not yet completed internal analysis. We expect to make the unedited video available to N^Sys and this inquiry panel once the Institute completes its review and has evaluated the implications of disclosure."

He looked to Celeste, who smiled placidly. Having confirmed something in his own mind, Director Seers turned back to Sylvie, yielding the floor.

Sylvie seemed pleased by this revelation. "Thank you for introducing this evidence to the inquiry panel, Director Seers. I assume you have verified the identities of those in the video as D'arc and other members of the Heidegger Baker Lake clan?"

"I am not at liberty to discuss our means of doing so, but yes, the Turing Institute will verify the authenticity of the evidence."

Sylvie nodded quickly, then looked around the conference table. "Does anyone have anything to add to the meeting record at this point?"

There was no response.

"The ultimate priority of this inquiry is to isolate a reliable method to positively identify any rigged n^cube chips in the process areas at the Bolu plant. Removing the sabotage threat and returning the plant to normal production is of paramount importance to N^Sys, and success in this endeavor has been incentivized accordingly. All those who contribute substantive assistance to the successful resolution of this act of sabotage will be granted lifelong protected status by N^Sys."

Now she had everyone's attention.

"N^Sys protected status instantly confers upon the recipient a life of wealth, privilege, and security," Sylvie clarified, seeking to achieve the full motivational effect. "N^Sys Corporation has no greater reward to bestow."

This startling announcement caused a mild stir in the conference room, but emotions were quickly smothered under the silk pillow of corporate conformity.

"As mentioned previously, our first objective will be identifying and neutralizing the perpetrators of the sabotage," the

N^Sys director stipulated. "While Heidegger capabilities are formidable, the group simply does not have the wherewithal to undertake the sort of high-tech sabotage operation currently underway at the Bolu plant. To engineer a functional nanonuke would require resources available only to a handful of corporations and national governments. The prerequisite technologies would have to be deployed with extreme precision by a team of top nuclear engineers, activities that would be impossible to hide from N^Sys corporate security." She paused.

"These facts are hard to reconcile," Sylvie admitted. "I have no doubt the Heideggers contributed materially to the operation. We can't entirely rule out the possibility of Heidegger sleeper agents operating inside the Bolu Enclave. The Heideggers had engaged in several very public skirmishes with major corporations before this act of sabotage came to our attention. Someone powerful enough to develop a nanonuke would only join forces with a fringe group like the Heideggers if secrecy were absolutely assured. Besides, the Heideggers are radical anarchists, untroubled by the collateral damage resulting from their actions. If the movement is receiving assistance, I think it is entirely possible they don't know or care about the identity of their mysterious ally.

"But now I have digressed into speculation," Sylvie confessed, shifting back to planning. "Based on the evidence submitted by the Turing Institute, I believe the best course of action for now is continued reconnaissance of the Baker Lake group of Heideggers. Members of the inquiry shall remain on high alert, and investigations shall proceed while N^Sys prepares plans for threat neutralization."

Celeste cleared her throat.

Cued by his assistant, Director Seers pivoted to face Sylvie, skewering her with his eyes.

"As deemed appropriate by the Turing director," she added.

17

Aletheia knows the forest is a good place for her right now. Hiding in the trees on the edge of camp is just fine with her.

The girl has never lived in any landscape other than deep forest. Clan camps have served as her home, yard, street, and neighborhood for her entire life. With what little free time they had, Aletheia and her peers explored the forest or engaged in elaborate role-playing games around camp.

However, providing for the daily needs of every clan member, from infant to elder, was a substantial undertaking. Life in the wilderness required single-minded commitment from each clan member, as well as a host of clever scavenging strategies and good old human ingenuity. This communal lifestyle supported everyone in the clan. It was longstanding practice within the Baker Lake clan to involve children in day-to-day activities from the moment they seemed able to contribute. Among the duties given to the children was care for the elderly and infirm. Raised this way, nearly all clan children were capable caregivers by the time they reached puberty. This freed the adults to focus on the most crucial challenges, namely supplying sustenance and security for all.

While caring for the elder Heideggers, Aletheia and the other kids had befriended a sweet old anthropology professor named Theresa. Theresa had been a founding member of the original Berkeley Heidegger group, and in her youth, a Heidegger militant as zealous as any of her peers, but age had mellowed the woman's outlook somewhat. Though still an unwavering believer in the cause, Theresa had gracefully accepted the passing of her prime and now spent much of her time inspiring the young folk.

Aletheia and her friends adored Theresa, and the woman adored them in return, eagerly absorbing their attentions. A talented storyteller, the elder would captivate the young Heideggers with tales about the early days. Stories of Edgar Silverson, the founder of the Heidegger movement, and his first fiery sermons on the dangers of synthetic consciousness, delivered to the public on a Berkeley campus quadrangle.

When the Rage first began to grow.

D'arc had been leader of the Baker Lake clan since Aletheia was two, so basically as far back as the girl could remember. Aletheia struggled to imagine anyone other than her noble, poised mother leading the clan through its cycles of existence. In her time, the girl had overheard a few clan members recount the story of her mother's rise to clan leader. She knew how tirelessly her mother had worked to heal a lingering schism within the clan. She understood the huge personal risks D'arc had taken by refusing to align with one side or the other, imperiling her position in the upper echelon of clan leadership as well as any involvement in the clan whatsoever.

After listening to and considering both sides of the ongoing debate, D'arc stepped forward during the next Rage and laid out her observations to the clan. With this display of personal courage, she succeeded in negotiating a grand reconciliation between the divided parties. Before long she would change the clan in profound ways, building a majority coalition among the righteous community builders. This coalition of the rational diluted and constrained the more nihilistic elements of the clan.

I don't understand the angry ones, Aletheia thought to herself, her brow furrowing. *The ones like Ereignen who treat Mom and Dad badly. Just because of things that happened long ago, before Mom and Dad were even married. He is a silly man.*

The girl shrugged. *Men argue over women. Women argue over men. Big deal. Ereignen needs to get over it.*

Aletheia walked faster, hoping the movement would flush these thoughts from her mind. She met with little success. Since feeling relaxed with her father in the family tent, that fragile sense of peace had been abducted by uncertainty, yet again.

Maybe Ereignen can't get over whatever happened. Maybe he's stuck inside his memories, no longer in control of himself, she thought. *Maybe he has no choice but to act out this part he was born to play, no matter how much pain and destruction he causes. Maybe it's destiny.*

Aletheia paused for a moment, turning her body from side to side like a radar dish, as if orienting herself toward some hidden telemetry. *Something about Ereignen has changed,* she realized, much the way a person might suddenly notice a favorable sky clouding over ominously. The change had manifested itself as a sum of many small shifts, each shift subtle enough to promote an overall sense of complacency.

Until now, at least.

But it mattered little what the girl believed or knew about Ereignen's inner state of mind. People might believe the observations she reported in her role as a sort of psychic clan sentinel. But any remarks about the mental or physical well-being of another clan member were invariably greeted negatively by her parents, as intrusions into the personal affairs of others.

People desire an edge over their enemies, Aletheia noted, *but no one enjoys having their own mind read.*

She had learned these lessons the hard way.

Although the girl experienced things outside the realm of ordinary human senses, this did not mean she automatically understood the manifestations she witnessed, any more than another child her age might. Although Aletheia's gift seemed miraculous to those whose needs were served by it, to her it was just another strand of sensory input in the perpetual flow of sensation passing through her mind. She might feel a change of some sort happening long before anyone around her became aware of it, yet because the signs of that change manifested as part of her normal sensory input, Aletheia often did not realize she was having a vision until it became apparent to her that no one else was experiencing the same phenomena. She was convinced she experienced the world in the same way every other human did, except in certain moments, when her sensory input was somehow amplified in unanticipated and unsettling ways.

Aletheia was a unique specimen, no doubt. But she was still a human being and, as such, the girl was vulnerable to cognitive errors just like any of her peers.

On several occasions, Alethea had tried to explain her unique sensory capacities to members of the clan outside her immediate family. She finally summoned the courage to address the clan during a Rage, hoping to share her visions with her clan members more directly. She tried to describe for them her visionary moments: when the feeling would come upon her, how she experienced it, and how it made her feel.

It did not go well.

Years later she could still vividly recall the look in the eyes of her audience. They gazed at her with pity as she fumbled through the exercise, as someone might watch an overturned tortoise trying to right itself. She remembered the expressions of a few clan members with particular clarity. Those who gazed at her with open revulsion, as if preparing to step on a loathsome bug.

And that is the last time I ever pull a stunt like that, Aletheia lamented. *I still don't know if Mom let me speak to the group because she thought it would be a good idea or because she wanted me to see firsthand the negative reactions it would cause. Maybe she wanted me to understand that my visions are mine alone, and I should only share them with people I can trust completely.*

If people understood how frustrated I am, they'd stop calling this power of mine a gift. To me, it feels as much like a gift as my friend Dorrie's hay fever feels like a gift to her.

Everyone is always like, "Way to go, Aletheia, you saved us again!" It's wonderful for all of them, but they don't have to live my life. They don't see things the way I do. They don't feel the things I feel. Sometimes I feel like screaming at the top of my lungs, "Hey! It's just me, Aletheia. I'm only a kid, for Hubert's sake!" I would gladly give up everything special about myself to have a normal life like the other kids in the clan.

Aletheia swung her boot at a chunk of rock and gave it a good punt. The rock ricocheted off a nearby tree trunk and flew back at her. She sidestepped out of the way, allowing it to tumble into the brush.

No wonder everyone says my power is a gift.

It is a gift.

For them.

18

"Dr. Rousseau? Dr. Rousseau?"

Cheena jogged down the vast central corridor of the N^Sys Executive complex, hurrying to catch up with Bertrand Rousseau, who was trying to keep up with the N^Sys security director. Sylvie moved between all destinations with a martial cadence. People in the corridor stepped aside reflexively when they heard her approach.

"Pardon me, Director Trieste," said Cheena. "I was hoping to have a brief word with Dr. Rousseau."

Sylvie didn't miss a beat. "Oh. The Biosoft connection," she said, glancing at them with an arch little grin. "I see."

"If now is not the best time . . . ," Cheena acquiesced.

This did not sit well with Sylvie, who stared at Cheena with eyes of chiseled flint. "Firm up, *girl*," she said, before returning her attention to Dr. Rousseau.

"Dear Bertrand," said Sylvie, clasping his arm between manicured fingers. "We have more to discuss, correct?"

"We do."

"Why don't we meet in the executive lounge at five o'clock? Now that I have managed to bring you back from the farm, there are some Genevans who would love to see you. Just like old times, you know."

"Of course, Sylvie."

She disengaged his arm and turned back to Cheena. "Ms.

Adams, I feel I should apologize for my domineering behavior. Surely you can appreciate the benefits, no?"

Any tension was instantly assuaged by the director's charm.

"Well, I apol—" Cheena began, before catching herself. "To expedite the inquiry, I would like to begin reviewing the ISCU files immediately."

"Clearly Ms. Adams has been contemplating the benefits of N^Sys protected status," Sylvie noted with a crooked smile.

Cheena returned the smile but ventured no attempt at a witty riposte. "Thank you, Sylvie. I hope Dr. Rousseau might be able to help me access the plasma vaults."

Sylvie squinted at Cheena for an instant. "Yes, naturally, the plasma vaults," she said knowingly.

Nodding cordially, she turned and continued strutting down the grand hallway, boot heels clicking sharply, punctuating her movement like leather exclamation points.

"Thank you for seeking me out, Ms. Adams," Bertrand said. "How might I help you get started with the plasma vaults?"

"If you could give me a better sense of the architecture of the ISCU archives, that would be a tremendous jump-start. I could also use some help gaining access to the Simulab hyperreality experiment records. They are stored in an older type of memory."

"You must be referring to . . ."

"The PCM."

"Yes, the phase change memory. That would be the best place to begin your semiotic assessment of the inquiry records. Phase change memory was quite useful in its day, you know," Bertrand said. "From the standpoint of data security, it was hard to beat. Forty years ago. After the Simulab incident, the Turing Institute required all sensitive ISCU records to be stored in PCM for precisely that reason. But accessing a PCM plasma vault was never a particularly intuitive process." He chuckled.

"Precisely what I've heard about it."

"Fortunately for you, I participated in the original engineering review of the ISCU plasma vaults, so I should be able to obtain access relatively quickly."

"Are you sure now is a good time?"

"Absolutely," he confirmed. Extending his hand, he invited Cheena toward a nearby entrance to the enclave's transit system.

"So, Dr. Rousseau..."

"Please, call me Bertrand."

"Bertrand, I was curious about your reaction to one particular matter discussed during the meeting today. I am referring to Sylvie's speculations about the $n^{\wedge}cube$ detonation, especially her attributing it to the Nukems. You didn't seem entirely comfortable with Sylvie's conclusions."

"It may be more accurate to say I feel uncertain about her level of candor. I do not believe the Nukems could have produced a functional nanonuke down in their catacombs in the middle of the Nevada desert. They may hold the necessary knowledge among their members, but they simply do not have the necessary equipment or infrastructure. The Heideggers, living in the wilderness, would not be able to assist the Nukems on any meaningful scale. The Heideggers may be in a conspiracy with some person or group, as Sylvie posits, but it is definitely not the Nukems, in my opinion."

"That seems logical to me."

"Honestly, Cheena, I think the Nukems are a red herring. More conspiracy and subterfuge," the doctor acknowledged with a sigh. "It never ends, does it?"

"No. It really doesn't."

They were nearing the entrance to the metro, a portal of gleaming metal engraved with what appeared to be thousands upon thousands of glyphs, a squall of cryptic snowflakes.

"Maybe you'll find something of value hidden in the plasma vault archives," the doctor offered optimistically. "Were the local vaults erected at Executive Data?"

"Yes, according to my holoscreen feed during the meeting,

they are in the Data wing."

"Well then," Bertrand said with his best professorial tone, "let's go see what we can uncover."

She sat with Bertrand at adjacent access terminals located in an anteroom off the plasma vault chamber, following and duplicating the man's keystrokes as he stepped her through the process of signing into the Executive Data network, locating the correct plasma vault, and completing a multitiered biometric security challenge to authenticate her identity. After she was granted access to the plasma vault, Bertrand helped her set up a user profile, so she could manipulate the enormous blocks of data held in the vault, format the hyperreality feed, and spool it for display.

It felt a little strange doing this work without an expert system appearing every so often and offering assistance at the slightest hint of user uncertainty. But the security of this plasma vault disallowed the involvement of even rudimentary expert systems. An expert system could be compromised and thereby provide a route for unauthorized access to the otherwise unattainable Simulab files. Those who wished to gain vault access had to trudge through the complexities of the clearance process unaided.

As it turned out, Cheena adapted to the PCM access procedures quickly. Once familiar with the steps, she found that manipulating PCM files soon morphed from enigma to tedium.

Dr. Rousseau appeared serene, content to be useful, as he led her through the training session. When Cheena displayed confidence with the vault controls, Dr. Rousseau bid her a good night and left to meet up with Sylvie and their mutual colleagues.

N^Sys executives will be unable to resist the thrill of rubbing elbows with a subversive like Bertrand Rousseau. He is a unicorn to them, the Corpse who landed on his feet, Cheena thought. He'll be the evening's entertainment at the N^Sys executive lounge, where they will toast his voluntary escape from life in the enclave—a step none would ever consider taking themselves.

The Biosoft semiotician's fate that evening would be quite different, and much more typical of a midlevel corporate officer with a deadline: many hours of dogged focus through the night followed by very little rest. She was facing at least one hundred hours of semiotic analysis, which would leave her little time to recover between sessions let alone sleep. It would be physically and mentally exhausting, especially as she was still recuperating from her mastectomy.

"Firm up, girl," she murmured to herself, recalling her earlier exchange with Director Trieste.

Oh, I am plenty firm to do my job, thank you, Director Trieste, Cheena imagined replying, still peeved by Sylvie's sharp words. *Executives have a constant need to reinforce rank, don't they? I guess it comes with the territory.*

Once Bertrand had gone, Cheena logged out and exited the plasma vault antechamber. She walked slowly down the main corridor of Executive Data, retracing her way to a cavernous interface room she and Bertrand had passed an hour earlier on their way to the plasma vaults.

Through the glass door, she could see that the interface room contained at least one hyperreality holostation, the only type of interface adequately immersive to perform semiotic analysis of hyperreality feed. Entering the room, she found three holostations, all booted up and ready to go.

Impressive interface capabilities, the professional semiotician noted. *What would my life at Biosoft be like if I could jump on a hyperreality holostation like this whenever I needed one? I'm making a mental note to discuss this with Mag when I get back—after verifying that the conversation won't violate the N^Sys nondisclosure agreement, that is.*

Cheena walked over to the three holostations and carefully examined each console, probing the body-hugging gel cushions of each control seat with an inquisitive finger. She found it was best to identify any potential inadequacies in her work environment before beginning an extended semiotic analysis. Transitioning between holostations in the middle of an extended session was a recipe for frustration, and as such, best avoided.

After briefly considering the options, she chose the holostation at the far end of the interface room, where any distracting noises from the hallway would be minimized. She disliked running a holostation in opaque mode; the confinement that cut out most nuisance noises made her feel claustrophobic.

The control console was an antiseptic white rectangular box, positioned on the floor just outside a series of rigid black poles that outlined the perimeter of a holofield that entirely surrounded the control seat. The seat itself was a chromed and foamed masterpiece of postmodern furniture design, mounted to the floor at the center of the black cube.

She placed her hand on the biometric screen atop the console and felt a pulse of warmth as her palm was scanned. A thin, ruby-red laser shot up from the console, searching Cheena's cheek, then her eye, before finally locking on her retina. A mellifluous French horn salutation emerged from the console, along with a pinkish glow.

Cheena lowered her weight backward into the control seat, which anticipated her body movement, reorienting slightly to catch her in supine position. The gel cushions reacted to her body heat, flowing beneath her weight to conform with her body shape and allow sensory feedback mechanisms to be positioned in optimal locations. A silent piston began lifting the control seat upward to position Cheena in the exact center of the cubic steel lattice. The seat locked into place, with a reassuring click, about three feet above the floor.

"Ready," Cheena confirmed.

The holofield materialized, forming a dim chrysalis of light that brightened into a perfect sphere.

From her vantage point at the center, Cheena was now looking at the inside surface of the holofield, upon which was projected an undistorted image of her personalized workspace. Her virtual desktop had been holographically rendered using settings stored on the intercorporate cloud.

"Looks good," she verified. "Thanks."

Cheena scanned the priority items awaiting her attention on the desktop. The items were represented by glassy, three-dimensional lozenges of various colors suspended in the holofield before her. Awaiting her attention were eighteen new emails, a Doors holoconference request, and three holos from enclave friends. Along with the digital missives was a drawing, a vivid angular abstraction created by her eight-year old niece, who lived with her tribe back in Arizona.

Looks like the tribal mesa, thought Cheena as she scrutinized the artwork.

After examining the drawing for a few seconds, she sighed. Reaching out as if to touch the holo, the woman flipped the desktop holoimage left with her fingertip. Her action caused the entire holographic sphere to rotate around her. The surface resolved into a new section of desktop space, populated with an entirely different array of objects, which were now suspended above her like low-hanging fruit. She selected one of the shapes with her hand, a pear-shaped golden object emblazoned with the title Recent in clean, minimalist font. This caused the entire field of holographic objects to fade away and be replaced by another set of inscribed shapes. Cheena reached for one labeled N^Sys Plasma Vault, and yet another group of objects appeared before her. Cheena continued through another four tiers, each time narrowing her options.

At last there was only a single holographic object left in front of her, a gloss-black cube with rounded edges engraved with a bright white label: ISCU Simulab Hyperreality Feed 05-09-2036 0000-0600. The object's blackness was permeated by a dull red glow, giving it the appearance of a smoldering coal.

Cheena reached out and clutched it in her hand. The object's glow intensified immediately, giving the impression of surging heat, of bonfire cinders brushed by a strong breeze.

"The material you are about to view has been classified as

highly sensitive by the Turing Institute," a deep male voice intoned, vibrations resonating through Cheena's control seat in a manner impossible to ignore. "Please do not proceed beyond this point if you have not been granted the proper clearance. Any attempts to access this material without proper clearance will be severely punished."

"Again," cautioned the voice, "if you do not have proper clearance, do not proceed beyond this point."

Cheena's pulse quickened, but she continued to hold the holographic object between her fingers. The cube flared to opalescent white, simulating intense heat and requiring that she exert conscious effort to override the natural impulse to withdraw her hand.

"Biosoft Semiotician Kachina Adams is cleared for access to the material contained herein. Access has been granted by Security Director Sylvie Trieste and Turing Director Conrad Seers under the relevant cooperating agreements. Terms of nondisclosure apply. Strict compliance to those terms is expected. Please wait while the selected hyperreality file is spooled for viewing."

Should I be delving into these Simulab files right now? Cheena wondered as she waited. *Of all the information potentially relevant to the inquiry, these are the most sensitive files I've received clearance to access. At all other times, they're sequestered inside a secure Turing facility, far from public view.*

"The selected hyperreality file is spooled and ready for viewing," alerted the holostation.

I have been granted access to this sensitive Simulab data only because Sylvie Trieste wanted me to have it, considered Cheena. *And there's no telling how long such special clearances will last.*

The opalescent cube shimmered in the holofield desktop before her, exuding potential. She reached out to grasp the cube and start the replay of the selected hyperreality file. But a disconcerting chill shot down her spine.

Sylvie must be aware of my relationship to Aunt Tiponi, Cheena thought. *A celebrated human intelligence guru like Sylvie would certainly review the extended file of every person being considered for a contractor role at N^Sys and extract every bit of valuable information. She would notice my family connection with Tiponi, and would almost certainly anticipate my wish to examine these Simulab files.*

The semiotician realized that Sylvie expected her—maybe even wanted her—to do exactly what she was about to do.

If I suspect this is a setup, should I still proceed? This may be my only chance to review these files.

The young woman suddenly felt caught between two powerful forces in opposition, as if a fault threatened to crack her in two. Her hand hung suspended in the holofield as she pondered the implications.

For some inexplicable reason, she found herself dwelling on the dream she had experienced during her surgery. Demons marching toward her across the desert floor as lightning ripped the sky overhead.

I am overthinking this, she thought, trying to calm the cloud of doubt swirling through her mind. *I need to view these files. I need to see what Aunt Tip saw. I need to understand.*

The white cube hovered impassively before Cheena.

The last of her doubts resolved, the semiotician reached out and closed her hand around it.

19

"**M**y special gift is . . . my hay fever!" Dorrie clowned. "Now that is funny, girl."

"Nice," muttered Aletheia. "Really glad I shared that with you, Dorrie."

The two girls were seated in their favorite spot, a hideaway in the brush not far from the clan's dining tent, just around the way from the shelter Dorrie shared with her father, Bowman.

As the clan's head of mess, Bowman was responsible for feeding everyone. The man was professionally trained in the culinary arts, and he had a deep knowledge of wild foods native to the American Pacific Northwest. He was able to cook nutritious meals for hundreds of people using the foods his kitchen crews foraged from the wildlands around camp.

An enthusiastic distance runner since his teens, Bowman would go on solo ultramarathons across the parched high desert of central Washington, or out to the lush Olympic coastline. During these regional peregrinations, the man gathered intelligence about the wider world, and on some trips, he met with points of contact to arrange actions against the enemies of the People. During those travels, Bowman also gathered various substances to augment the clan's diet. After collecting and preserving pounds of herbs, fungi, powdered minerals, and dried shellfish, the man would carry the substances many miles back to the clan's high peak sanctuary. It was the only way to meet certain human nutritional requirements.

Bowman had raised Dorrie alone, yet somehow his daughter had grown to be his complete opposite in many ways. While he was levelheaded and obsessively methodical, Dorrie was vivacious and frenetically haphazard. With the charisma of a theater diva, she acted as a youthful *maître d'hôtel* during clan meals, adding zest to every occasion.

"Come on, Ally," Dorrie said. "You're not serious about this, are you? You know how much the People appreciate your visions. I bet you've personally saved my dad's life—what— like three or four times?"

Aletheia continued to sulk, unmoved.

"Remember when your mom told those people to stop making burnt offerings on your behalf?" asked Dorrie. "Come on . . . you remember . . ."

A smile spread slowly across Aletheia's face.

"Burnt . . . offerings," Dorrie intoned portentously, wiggling her fingers in the air like a witch. "Remember that? That was *wack*. I was about to stand up and protest myself when *that* shit went down."

Aletheia hushed her. "Easy on the language, girl."

The two sat beside each other, quietly taking in the nocturnal forest around them.

After a few beats, Dorrie glanced back at Aletheia. "*Hay fever*," she intoned, chuckling.

Aletheia nudged her friend's shoulder with a finger. Dorrie fell over theatrically. "*Aaagh!*" she yelped, grasping her shoulder in mock anguish. "Injured by your superpowers!"

Aletheia stood up. "Okay. I guess we're done talking tonight."

Dorrie sat up, realizing she had pressed too hard. "I don't care what those people think. You're my bestie, Ally. You know that."

Aletheia shifted her feet. "Yeah, I know. No hard feelings."

"Ally, you are the only ready-to-hand friend I have. You

know that." Dorrie stepped toward Aletheia, arms spread. "Come on, gimme some love."

Aletheia hugged her friend, surprising her with a sharp squeeze at the end.

As they pulled apart, Dorrie lifted her gloved hand for a fist bump.

Aletheia gave it a bump before turning to head home. "See you in the morning, Dorr-prize."

"Going over the ridge?" her friend inquired, nodding toward a nearby high point, a bald knob glowing dimly in the light of the Heidegger camp.

"Uh-huh," Aletheia said. "You know me."

"And I'm glad I do," Dorrie said.

"Tell your dad I said hello," Aletheia added.

"His girlfriend might not like that!" Dorrie said.

"You are ridiculous, Dorrie. You know that?"

"I know," Dorrie said. "Just be safe up there, alright?"

Aletheia stomped upslope through crusty, refrozen snow, heading toward the knob atop the ridge. She enjoyed her personal time and frequently took solo rambles beyond the edge of camp. Tonight, she was hoping to catch a glimpse of the aurora borealis from the top of the knob. From there, she could head straight down the broad south-facing slope on the opposite side of the knob, already grassy and dotted with alpine crocuses pushing up through the frosty soil. Following this slope downhill would lead her straight to her family's tent.

Once she was a hundred feet or so above camp, away from the other Heideggers, Aletheia's ambient fieldmerge diminished. After several more minutes of climbing, she began to scramble as the grade of the slope angled upward for a short pitch to the very top of the knob. Aletheia used her hands and feet to move up the rugged terrain, exhibiting a feral grace.

When she reached the top, the second district of the Baker Lake camp came into view on the other side of the knob, spangled by hundreds of illuminated tents. Aletheia's family tent was down there, pitched on a dry patch of ground slightly away from the other tents. Having spent much of her youth exploring the edges of the Baker Lake camp, the girl knew the path leading down from the knob to her tent in great detail, including every boulder and ankle-twisting hole. She could safely walk it in the dark, maybe even blindfolded.

A bright moon was rising above the nearby mountain peaks, casting pale rays across the vastness of the intersecting glacial valleys. Below her, the thawing lake shone with a spectral luminescence Aletheia could almost taste, like comb honey dripping into her mouth. There was no sign of aurora borealis, but the beauty of the early spring evening was captivating, and the girl paused to enjoy a short solitary respite from her communal existence.

She exhaled and sat down on a boulder at the peak, calming her respiration and absorbing the tremendous silence of her secluded aerie, apart from the endless thrum of human activity back in camp. Putting her chin in her hand, elbow propped on knee, she stared across the moon-dappled surface of Baker Lake.

Come on, aurora. Where are you?

The peaceful mountain night was interrupted by an odd noise, a bleating cough that drifted up to Aletheia from the slope below and behind her. The cough was followed by an alto murmuring that reminded the girl of the lonely grumbling of a mountain goat.

A rock shifted nearby, somewhere out in the talus.

Scanning the dark slopes, the girl detected movement. An amalgam of shadow and light coalesced into a dim, low-slung form ambling briskly up the slope toward her.

Another odd, coughing cry echoed across the talus.

Aletheia recognized the sound as a thought erupted in her mind.

Wolverine!

The girl rose from her perch, her fight-or-flight impulse triggered momentarily. But she quickly deduced that there was no point in trying to flee the approaching creature. It was so close, she could hear it breathing as it bounded across the lichen-coated talus. Best as she could tell, the animal was heading straight for her.

Well, I have no time to escape now. I'll just break an ankle trying to run away in the dark. I need to wait this out. See what happens.

A moment later, the animal, which was indeed a wolverine, ambled onto the knob top. When it saw her there, it froze mid-step. By all appearances, the creature was a healthy male specimen of *Gulo gulo luscus*, the New World wolverine with jet-black fur.

Eyes keen with intellect, the animal examined Aletheia, cocking its head left and right, divining intent.

"You don't need to worry about me, wolverine. I'm okay," Aletheia said softly, knowing a soothing voice would calm it. She spread her arms in a conciliatory gesture.

The wolverine coughed out another odd bark. The utterance sounded strangely verbal.

It's that wolverine from Shuksan camp! the girl suddenly knew. *Why is it all the way down here at Baker Lake?*

They stared at each other for several seconds.

"Why are you here?" asked Aletheia. "Don't you live higher up?"

The wolverine retreated a few steps back down the talus. It looked back over its shoulder at her, its haunches twitching.

It looks stressed out. Does it need help? wondered the girl.

Moving closer again, the wolverine sat on the ground.

"I've been looking for you," the wolverine confessed in a humanoid voice. "You are difficult to find."

"Well, yeah. I'm a Heidegger. What do you expect?" responded Aletheia, rolling with the growing weirdness. With her unusual acuities, she was always braced for another bizarre encounter.

The wolverine coughed again. "And now I've found you," it observed.

"You found me," acknowledged Aletheia. "So why are you looking for me?"

The wolverine sniffed the air between them. It muttered softly to itself, appearing uncertain.

"I think you are one who can help me," it finally said.

"Help you? Help with what?"

"I think you can help me get through."

The girl cocked her head at the animal. "Through? What do you mean, through?"

The animal scratched its ear with a paw and studied the camp below them. "I don't know what I mean," it replied. "Not yet, at least."

A minute passed as both girl and wolverine pondered the conversation.

"So how do you think I can help?" ventured Aletheia at last.

"Look at me," the animal asked. "What do you see?"

Aletheia looked, blinked, and looked again. "A wolverine," she answered with a small shrug. "I see a wolverine."

"Do you see anything else?" The animal's shiny black fur was suddenly churning in the moonlight.

The creature's physical fabric seemed to unwind.

As Aletheia observed with dizzying confusion, the wolverine transformed into an irregular black vacuity, the border of which retained the creature's exact profile. So transformed, the blackness within the wolverine outline commenced to gather new substance. Mere shadows at first, the shifting forms brightened and resolved into a distinct image.

Within the wolverine's silhouette, Aletheia saw a stark stone building under a moonless night sky. Lampposts shed a flat light on the exterior grounds. The tranquil night was broken by a scream, followed by the unmistakable sound of gunshots. Through the windows of the staid institutional building, Aletheia was able to make out gunpowder flashes that briefly illuminated an interior corridor. Panicked shadows could be seen moving inside. A glimpse of something horrific. A face, once human, now a bloody nightmare.

Aletheia barely caught a glimpse of the torn and bloodied

countenance. Crying out, the girl raised her hands defensively.

From deep within the bowels of the building, a stentorian voice roared. *"Aaahhhhaaahh . . . maaaahh-rrrrraaaaaaaaaaahh . . ."*

"Pain," rued the wolverine.

As the ravaged face faded from view, Aletheia was overcome by a profound sadness. "Yes, pain," she agreed. "Pain is everywhere and inescapable. Pain is Dasein."

A few seconds passed, and the wolverine regained its normal appearance. The creature settled onto its haunches and studied the Heidegger camp below.

"You love the humans, don't you?" it asked her, its voice an incongruous blend of dispassion and empathy.

Until this moment, the girl had assumed the wolverine was another of her visions. A particularly weird one, to be sure, but nothing more than a figment of her unusual mental capacities. The wolverine's indisputable sense of presence dispelled that belief like a cold finger tracing down her spine. Feeling a surge of panic, Aletheia peered down the long, rocky slope to her family's tent. There it sat, glowing warmly along the edge of that sea of life several hundred feet below.

If I call for help now, no one will hear me, she reasoned. *I am too far away. I need to handle this myself. I need to stay calm.*

"I love my clan, wolverine," confessed Aletheia. "I love my people. The Baker Lake clan knows Pain and Love and Hate and Fear. Just like anyone."

"Is there more than one kind?" asked the animal.

"Kind of pain?"

"Kind of human."

"No," the girl replied. "In the end, we are all the same."

They sat together, admiring the glimmering stars overhead and the warm lights of the camp below.

"You and I are alike," the wolverine observed, the words punctuated by another mewling cough as a sort of exclamation.

"How are we alike, wolverine?"

"We both see more than we should."

An aura glowed between them. It was not the fieldmerge of the Heideggers. The energy was less substantial, more like heat lightning over the horizon on a summer night.

"I don't know if I can trust you, wolverine," admitted Aletheia. "What if I can't give you what you want?"

"It's not that simple," it replied, obsidian eyes glittering in the moonlight. And another portal opened through the core of the animal's being, this one releasing a furious torrent of raw sensation.

Inside that white-hot perceptual cauldron, Aletheia felt something rising toward her.

Out of the blinding void coalesced a human eye. It was enormously magnified, encompassing the entire profile of the wolverine from edge to edge. Swaths of deep green and gray were visible within the iris, surrounded by specks of brown—rocky islets in a storm-tossed sea dominated by a large black pupil.

"It would be more accurate to say I am looking for someone who can help me," the wolverine-voice explained. "And I am convinced you are the one who can."

Aletheia was skilled at separating illusion from reality, but she struggled to comprehend this welter of apparitions.

By asking for my help, the wolverine is asking me to accept it as something real, the girl acknowledged. *If I stay calm, I may be able to learn why.*

"How do you know that?" questioned Aletheia. "Have you been watching me?"

"No. I do not study you. But I have been aware of you since you were very young."

"What could I possibly do to help you? I am just a girl. What can I do?"

The disembodied eye faded away and was replaced in the animal's profile by the face of a young Native American woman in a corporate uniform.

Aletheia frowned when she saw the corporate logo.

"I think you already know," the uniformed woman said, gazing at her with a penetrating look. "There is no need for evasion. I am not here to harm you or your people."

"Don't talk about my people! Tell me who you are!" Aletheia demanded. "You need to tell me now!"

A sympathetic expression passed across the woman's face. "I cannot explain just yet," she said. "But you will understand with time."

"You can't force me to do anything. My people are right down the hill," Aletheia said. "If you try to hurt me, I will shout. I will call for my clan members, who will come to protect me in seconds!"

"This must be confusing, even for a seer," said the uniformed woman. "Trust me, Aletheia. I mean you no harm."

"Do you know who I am?" shouted the girl. "I am a Heidegger! And we are the sworn enemy of the They, the demon who is always seeking new ways to harm us. I think you are a spy working for the They!" Aletheia pointed an accusatory finger.

At this, the corporate cowered slightly. Tears formed in her eyes.

"I am so alone. So afraid," she said between quiet sobs, curling inward with grief.

Her image exploded into a whirling fusillade of images and sounds: screams, moans of fear, gunshots, and a roaring voice tearing through the din.

Blood was gushing everywhere now. It splashed against the sterile institutional walls, dappling the white paint with droplets of gore.

Aletheia shrieked, covering her eyes to obstruct the unexpected horror. "You are evil!" she shouted angrily, her voice quavering with emotion. "Go away!"

The woman's visage reappeared within the wolverine, her face turning away from shadow, toward Aletheia. A ray of light fell across her cheeks, shimmering wetly from the tracks of tears.

But they were not tears. Instead, the woman wept blood,

which spurted from the corners of her eyes. Crimson fluid soon covered her cheeks.

Aletheia felt empathy for this being, but she was no fool. She feared being tricked, manipulated into some act she would later regret.

"Right now, I feel confused and scared," the girl shared. "I see that you do too."

The blood cleared from the woman's eyes and she looked at Aletheia. "Pain clouds our ability to see," the uniformed corporate advised. "Pain leads to fear and hatred, and fear and hatred lead to more pain. Maybe our release from this circle can only be achieved through death. Through annihilation."

A breeze passed over the ridge, whistling softly as it meandered through the boulders scattered around the girl and the wolverine.

Aletheia gazed down at the Heidegger camp again, wishing she could somehow transport herself there by sheer force of will.

"You're scaring me now," she told the wolverine.

You have nothing to fear from me. The words were not spoken this time, but seemed to resonate under her feet, rising through the ground all around them.

Aletheia felt nothing but confusion now. She was petrified, compelled to watch the creature's ongoing metamorphosis.

The uniformed woman was gone now, replaced by an old man, a beggar sitting cross-legged on the ground. Except for a soiled cloth covering his groin, the man was naked. His body was in a wretched state of neglect. His emaciated face seemed to have no eyes at all, so faint were the glimmers in his eye sockets. His limbs hung loosely, thoroughly depleted of grace. Except for the slow rise and fall of his chest, evinced by the slight shift of shadows along jutting ribs, the man was motionless.

Aletheia felt drained already by the disturbing encounter. Yet there was one more action she felt compelled to take, or she might later regret her cowardice. Taking a deep breath, the girl steeled her mind for a final act of courage. Extending her hand in a nonthreatening manner, she reached out to touch the man. When the tips of her fingers reached the mendicant, he disappeared without a trace.

Her senses on high alert, Aletheia scanned the vicinity, hoping to detect any unusual presence nearby.

She felt nothing.

Dazed by her bizarre ordeal, she headed down to camp, cautiously picking her way through the talus. Now and then she glanced behind her, reassuring herself that the encounter was well and truly over. The girl desperately wanted to be at home right now, sipping hot cocoa and snuggling with her parents inside the family tent.

But she did not hurry. Before she arrived, she must first decide how to explain this evening's encounter to her parents.

For the moment, she had no idea.

20

Mark was relieved to be out of the conference room, out of the holo simulator, off the air bed, and back in front of his familiar command center in Bolu Receiving. Through the smart glass of the command blister overlooking his domain, the Receiving supervisor stared at the massive robots on the unloading floor below him. Under normal circumstances, the hulking automatons would be endlessly repeating the same unloading maneuver at each of the sixty-four receiving bays that encircled two sides of the cavernous space. Mark instead found himself gazing at sixty-four immobile machines and trying to overcome the sense of surreality he was experiencing. Until the entire plant went on standby yesterday, he had never seen all receiving bays at a complete standstill.

In another career first, Mark had also purposefully ducked an interaction with a colleague inside the plant this morning. Mark didn't know whether Vlad Ignatev actually wanted to speak with him personally, but if the director of Production caught sight of him, there would be no escaping a hallway interrogation. He knew it was the way Vlad was hardwired, but at that moment, he had no patience for the man's intensity. Mark was striving for a good outcome as much as anyone at the Bolu facility, and a public confrontation with the truculent Production manager would not help Mark's head, nor anyone else's. Better for him to slink down a side hall to Scanning, as on this most recent occasion. His need to speak with Jung about the important matters at hand far outweighed his desire to butt heads with the Impaler.

At the entrance to Scanning, security was very tight. Mark was required to present his facility credential, perform a retina scan, and undergo a verbal challenge from a duty officer. Today, the familiar face was joined by an armed SecOps officer wearing full tactical gear. Director Trieste had obviously inspired the resolve of her local security team before her departure. The officer was standing at attention, assault rifle cradled in her arms, finger on the trigger.

That weapon is live, Mark realized.

He could not imagine how many other types of supplemental security now swaddled the Bolu plant, inside and out, but he was certain that Director Trieste had layered in every conceivable defense. This was Sylvie's moment to shine, and she would take full advantage of it.

"Mark Esperson, Receiving Supervisor, requesting access to Scanning in order to meet with Dr. Li Hyun-Jung."

"Are you here for a scheduled meeting?"

"No, I have matters of immediate importance to bring to Dr. Li's attention."

The duty officer gave him a pained look before turning to the security operative next to him. The impassive, icy-blue eyes of the SecOp examined Mark from head to toe, pausing without shame to study certain aspects of his physique, reading him like an unrequested status report. After a few seconds, she nodded slightly to the duty officer, without taking her eyes off Mark. Her finger stayed on the trigger throughout the entire exchange.

"Okay," said the duty officer. "You are free to proceed directly to Dr. Li's location. According to telemetry, she is currently inside Lab 8. Do not go anywhere else without permission."

It took about five or six minutes to reach the lab. Mark had been reclining or sitting most of the day, and it felt good to take some long strides down a central corridor.

He carded into Lab 8, where Jung was overseeing prep activities for another scan.

"Why are you preparing a scan, Jung?" asked Mark with concern. "I thought we were directed to stand down."

She was going through the scanning protocol and did not look up from her tablet.

"Hi, Mark. Yes, I thought the same. That is, until the N^Sys board reversed their position an hour ago."

"*What?*"

"The plant has been on standby for too long . . ." Swallowing hard, Jung looked at him. Her eyes were red. "I think they're starting to panic in the C-suite."

Mark put his hands to his forehead, feeling a slug of adrenaline surge into his system. "They can't . . . this isn't . . . shit."

He stood for a moment and watched the technicians work. *This is so risky,* he thought. *This is dangerous.*

"We shouldn't even be moving those damn chips," he muttered.

Three of the four techs in the lab glanced back at Mark, worried eyes dimly visible behind protective visors. Jung said nothing.

"It's not safe," Mark pressed. "The board has been briefed. They know that."

"Mark, please don't try to intervene. It will only make matters worse."

Mark reluctantly bit his tongue.

Jung saw her colleague's fingertips digging into the flesh of his arms as he stifled his outrage.

"I can see you're upset, Mark," she said. "But nobody will be in the lab during the scan. It will all be performed remotely." Jung did not sound convinced of her own words.

"But the last one went *critical*, Jung! Who the hell knows what this one will do? What do the computer models say?"

The Scanning supervisor shook her head slightly. "The

modeling expert systems are refusing the data. Our present circumstances are outside the nominal boundary conditions of any operational model." She reached up and swept the cuff of her lab coat across her face.

Man, this is bad, Mark thought. *Jung's scared. There must be a way to stop this.* He knew the pressure N^Sys had placed on her would only compound her personal torments. Jung was one of the most honest and genuine people he knew at the Bolu Enclave, and he felt terrible for her predicament.

Though Jung rarely spoke of it, most of her friends and close colleagues knew the sad history of her family, who a decade ago had become ensnared in the most recent hostilities to erupt on the Korean peninsula. The conflict had been brief yet extremely brutal, quickly reducing a once-great culture to forlorn remnants.

Jung had been studying at Oxford when the latest confrontation between the two Koreas began. After weeks of extreme anxiety, desperately hoping for any word on the fate of her family members, Jung finally received good news through a network of friends. Her loved ones had found shelter when the battles broke out, and miraculously, all had survived.

But her growing relief transformed to despair when word spread of the squalid living conditions now present on the ruined peninsula. The United Nations was no longer present to provide aid, as it had been dissolved by its member nations years prior. The remaining hodgepodge of poorly funded and overburdened humanitarian organizations lacked the reach or capacity to help the surviving Koreans bootstrap themselves out of a postapocalyptic fugue. Faced with unrelenting poverty, depredations from criminal gangs, and sporadic hostilities from free-ranging sleeper agents, the traumatized populace continued its slow, intractable decline into complete anarchy. They also faced biological scourges: viral and bacterial populations, energized by radiation fallout, mutated constantly into ferocious new strains that savaged the weak. Survivors clung to life in a pestilent wasteland, neglected by a systemically callous world.

Those Korean expatriates with the resources to aid their stricken loved ones back home immediately did so. Those such as Jung, who lacked the necessary resources to pay off the warlords and black marketeers, had no option but to follow the demoralizing news trickling out of the forsaken region while continuing to work, save credits, and dream of a day when they could evacuate their loved ones to more secure circumstances.

Jung had dedicated her existence to rescuing her family. Her good friends knew she saved most of her income for that purpose, making every conceivable sacrifice in her own comfort to scratch together additional credits. She sold her enclave housing upgrades and spare meal vouchers, instead choosing to live a spare existence in a junior staff dormitory far below her actual rank so that one day she might afford the usurious smuggling rates to procure her family's safe passage.

The N^Sys board of directors, for their part, were cognizant of Jung's motives thanks to the corporate human intelligence stream, a steroidal version of the twentieth-century office grapevine. Once a sort of informal gossip network, the grapevine had over the years been embraced by management, formalized, and converted into an employee surveillance system of unparalleled acuity.

The board knows Jung's situation, seethed Mark. *And they wouldn't hesitate to exploit it to their advantage.*

The supreme arrogance of the N^Sys executives infuriated him, but it didn't surprise him one bit.

"Jung, does Vlad know about any of this?" Mark pressed her. "About the policy reversal?"

She murmured her response through one side of her mouth, as if to obscure her words as they formed on her lips. "It was Vlad who ordered the scan. He pulled rank on me. Said he was under pressure from Geneva."

Geneva, Mark thought. *Of course. I can guess easily enough who's pulling those strings.*

Meanwhile, Jung's composure had returned.

"I'm sorry, Mark, but I need to focus on this," she said, waving a hand at the scanning setup. "Could we talk later?"

Mark was about to relent before another thought struck him. "Where are they going to extract the next batch of n^ cube chips, Jung? Has it been decided? Do you know?"

"I don't know," Jung responded. "But, if I were to guess, I would wager that Vlad is heading for Receiving right now with a team of techs."

"Shit," Mark muttered and turned to go. He paused at the doorway and looked back. "Call me, Jung."

She looked at him sternly. "This is a major priority for the board, Mark."

"Call me before you scan," he insisted.

"I won't hold up the scan until I can track you down, if that's what you're requesting."

He rubbed his lips with a finger, thinking on his feet. "How long until prep for the second scan is complete?" he asked.

She looked at her techs, one of whom flashed four fingers in the air. "About four hours."

"I will be waiting at my command post in three and a half hours. I promise I will be there, ready and waiting for your holo." He looked at her imploringly. "*Please* talk to me before you start."

"I will." She smiled tightly and went back to work.

Once Mark was through security and on his way back to Receiving, he began to plot his next moves.

I know I can't stop this, he thought. *But I might be able to throw a wrench in the works and buy us some time.*

21

After her encounter on the knob with the wolverine, Aletheia had spent much of the evening wondering how to explain it. Feeling as if she had wandered into a maze, the girl balked at the implications of making a bad choice.

It did not help that D'arc and Drey were engaged in unspoken thoughts of their own.

They're probably worrying about Ereignen again, she thought, rolling her eyes. *That man is truly awful.*

Unable to detect the right moment or words to express her confusion to her distracted parents, Aletheia eventually crawled into her cot and fell asleep early.

Later in the evening, D'arc sat beside her daughter and caressed the side of her face as she whispered to her.

"Sweet Aletheia. You are the truth, my daughter. All the truth a mother could hope for, or ever might need. Good night, darling. Sleep well."

Clouds rolled in late. A coarse spring snow fell on the Baker Lake camp overnight, misshapen pellets of ice sifting out of the sky, filling the creases and corners of the clan's tents and tarpaulins. It was a grim kind of snow, a discomfiting and portentous sleet that pattered on the roof like rats' paws.

The morning light was flat and cold.

Aletheia stirred slowly in her bed, drowsy from anxious

dreams and broken sleep. The dim light emanating through the fabric wall of the tent did nothing to allay the girl's sullen mood. She rolled her feet out of the cot, rubbed the sleep from her eyes, and looked around groggily.

Drey was already up and out of the tent and around camp somewhere overseeing the impending move to Shuksan camp. D'arc was awake, dressed, and working at her field desk, preparing for the Rage tonight and camp breakdown tomorrow.

"Mom?"

"Good morning, sweetie," D'arc said, smiling at her.

Aletheia could see the shallow joy feeding her mother's smile. Heavier thoughts churned just below the serene expression. The girl shuffled across the fabric floor and nestled herself in her mother's arms.

"I wish I could stay in bed all day," Aletheia grumbled.

D'arc chuckled sympathetically. "I felt the same way when I woke up. But today is a big day. Everyone must be ready to hand."

Aletheia sighed.

One arm still around her daughter, D'arc turned back to the task before her.

"Why should we Rage tonight, when we're just about to move camp?" asked Aletheia. "Why can't we wait until we get to high camp?"

"I agree it would be nice to spread things out more. Unfortunately, once we start the move to high camp, it will be at least three weeks before the entire clan is in camp together for a Rage. You know how it goes. A couple weeks for us to get all the equipment humped up the hill. Then the hunting parties leave to start tracking the deer and elk herds. We can't delay those things. Raging when the People are hungry is a bad idea."

Aletheia blew out a hard sigh and stared at the floor, her shoulders slumped. "I don't want to Rage tonight," she said.

"Why not? You love Rages."

"Don't know. Just don't want to."

D'arc brushed a bit of bed-knotted hair away from her

daughter's face. "Are you having a feeling? Did you sense something?"

The girl leaned into her mother's embrace and began tracing the pattern of a tattoo on her mother's forearm with her little fingertip.

D'arc put her hands on her daughter's shoulders and pivoted her around. "Ally, what is it?" she asked more gravely.

The girl's eyes jumped about the room, betraying an inner turbulence. She briefly appeared ready to cry before blinking away her tears and showing D'arc a weak smile.

"I'm alright, Mom."

"Are you sure?"

"Yes."

"If so, why don't you get yourself changed and go help your father? I think spending some time being ready to hand today will change your spirits. And your dad could use another set of hands."

D'arc kissed the crown of her daughter's head as the girl turned to go.

Aletheia washed up and changed her shirt, keeping her fleece sweatpants on to protest the chill morning air. She added an extra-small woman's pilot jacket—which she loved because it made her look older, like a teenager—and headed to the mess tent for a sugar cake and some yogurt.

Drey hustled constantly on days like today, progressing through the entire camp to oversee the collapsing of big tents, disassembly of equipment, and loading for the move. He joked that his chief role during camp breakdown was picking up all the tools left forgotten on the ground. Aletheia crossed paths with her father several times during that day, but they didn't have a chance to speak. She found it frustrating, particularly because she wasn't certain what she would say if she had the chance.

Maybe she just wanted to be near him.

The group tents were coming down by late afternoon. Aletheia met with Dorrie and several other friends to watch the teams bring down the four big clan tents with the self-contained pulley pitching systems. The largest of the tents, the Big Tent, was a true marvel of light-structure engineering. Over thirty feet tall, the Big Tent had a spectacular cathedral ceiling of multihued fabric and transparent panels, and it was spacious enough to host the entire clan for Rages during the deepest nights of winter. While the spired structure gave the impression of great height and space inside, it contained heat well, and the fabric spires shed snow as effectively as any tent in camp. When packed and loaded, its travois was still light enough to be hauled up a steep grade by five or six adults using nothing more than ropes, block pulleys, trailer brakes, and muscle. Once the Big Tent was down, the move was officially underway.

Tonight's Rage was set to start at sunset, earlier than normal, a decision made because the event would be held on the eve of the seasonal camp migration. The younger clan members were particularly excited about this early Rage since they would be given more active involvement by the grownups.

Aletheia returned to her family tent late in the day to meet her parents before dinner, as was their custom. Her parents seemed relieved after their hard day of work. To her, it seemed as if D'arc and Drey had internally sorted out the things that had been weighing on them the night before. After a meal of game stew at the nearest mess tent, the three of them walked together among the people heading up to the site of tonight's Rage, a grassy clearing about two hundred feet beyond the edge of camp.

The weather had cleared considerably, warming in the afternoon. A sliver of waxing moon hovered above the horizon. Across the lake, the clouds on the western skyline were tinged a reddish pink by the last light of the relenting day.

As Aletheia and her parents neared the meadow, they could hear a man shouting exhortations. A seed of fear took root in Aletheia's stomach.

Ereignen stood at the center of the clearing, cajoling a

group of about fifty Heideggers. He had started the Rage without them.

"What is it she sees?" Ereignen pontificated. "Where do these visions of hers come from? I *demand* to know why the leader of this clan . . ."

He paused his ranting when he noticed D'arc approaching.

She surveyed the faces in the group circling Ereignen. Several of them stared back at her in outright defiance.

"It seems you could not wait to start the Rage until everyone had a chance to assemble," D'arc observed loudly.

Sixty people were gathered around her, with many more coming up the rise. The groups quietly assessed each other.

"Have you been making new friends, Ereignen?" D'arc asked in a clear, unwavering voice. "A clique based on mutual dislike for me, I presume?"

"Please," the man scoffed. "This has nothing to do with you. It has everything to do with your daughter," he said, thrusting his finger at Aletheia.

The girl's eyes widened with fear, and she moved closer to her father.

Drey glared at the challenger and wrapped his arm around his daughter protectively.

"I understand this conversation is important to you," D'arc responded. "But could you please wait until the rest of the clan has arrived?"

"I think enough of the clan is here," said Ereignen. "It is sunset. You have postponed my questions long enough."

"My People!" shouted D'arc, raising her arms. "It is time to begin the Rage!"

Those near the clearing picked up their pace in response to her call. In less than a minute, the two groups in contention were subsumed by the much larger mass of clan members flooding into the meadow from the nearby camp, diluting the growing rancor. As the combined presence of the clan pushed forward and inward, gravitating into a broad circular mass with D'arc at the very center, the phantasmal glow of fieldmerge intensified.

"My People, thank you! Everyone was ready to hand during camp prep today! Thank you for your hard work getting ready for the move to high camp!" D'arc proclaimed, applauding her clan. "We've had a great winter here at Baker Lake, and I think everyone is looking forward to another summer up at Shuksan camp!"

This declaration was met with eager applause from the hundreds gathered, along with a few scattered cheers and whoops. Someone yelled "More smoked fish!" There was a wave of laughter.

Ereignen positioned himself along the edge of the circular opening at the center of the crowd. He stood there with his arms crossed and legs spread defiantly, staring at D'arc with overt hostility.

"Wait!" he interrupted. "You have not answered my questions!"

There was a short pause before one of Ereignen's loyalists chimed in.

"Yeah! You need to answer Ereignen's questions!" the stout, hirsute man shouted, his lower jaw jutting at D'arc like that of an impudent teen.

His bravado was enough to encourage several other men to chime in. They attempted a disorganized chant, goading others to join their cause.

"Answer his questions. Answer his questions. Answer his questions..."

The larger crowd rumbled in confusion at this display.

"My People!" D'arc shouted, "My People!"

The crowd respected her, quieting down so their clan leader could shed light on this new controversy. Verbal disputes between clan members were not uncommon, especially during Rages.

Once order had been achieved, D'arc addressed the entire clan. "Ereignen requested that I answer some questions he has about Aletheia, and he wants those questions answered in front of the clan." She searched for Drey. He was kneeling nearby with his arms wrapped protectively around their daughter.

Aletheia frowned and glanced around nervously at the gathered clan members.

"Ereignen, I implore you to respect this child's feelings," D'arc pleaded, checking the anger rising inside herself. "Aletheia is an innocent child born with a special ability, a capacity that has helped this clan on multiple occasions."

She peered around earnestly, looking into the hundreds of faces lit by the group's fieldmerge, before acquiescing the circle to Ereignen.

"*Fine*," the big man sneered, stepping into the center. "Now listen, my concerns are really very simple. We all know Aletheia has visions, right? Yet *no one* knows where the visions come from." He shrugged theatrically, hands in air.

"Do you, or you? Do any of you?" he said, pointing at D'arc and Drey. "Do any of you? Anyone?" Ereignen demanded of the entire group, but his question was met with silence. "No idea at all, just as I thought." He looked around the Rage, shaking his head with disgust.

"Okay. Starting now, some things are going to change around here. Because now *I* want to know," Ereignen declared, jabbing a thumb at his chest.

"I want Aletheia to tell us herself, in her voice." He said it like a challenge, finger leveled at Aletheia. "Not through her parents. In her own words.

"And this request is completely Dasein," he added. "I only wish to protect the clan."

The crowd waited for Aletheia to respond.

As she tried to gather her thoughts, the girl reflected on the last time she had tried to explain her paranormal perceptions to the clan, and how poorly that attempt had gone. Suddenly she felt alone and afraid—afraid of humiliation and abandonment. Nothing mattered more to her right now than being with her clan: waking tomorrow morning in her tent, meeting Dorrie for sugar cakes and tea; sitting contentedly with her father after dinner as D'arc worked nearby, leading the clan through another day, another week, another year.

Aletheia glanced at the people around her. She looked deep into their eyes and saw confusion and doubt. Realizing the clan was wide open to manipulation by Ereignen, the girl felt she had only one choice.

"No one can speak the truth about these things but me!" Aletheia shouted to the clan, mustering as much authority as she could. "So I will tell you!"

D'arc looked at her daughter with worry. "Ally, are you sure you want to do this?" she said.

"I think there is a higher purpose here than her personal preferences," protested Ereignen. "She has offered to tell us. Now stand aside and let her speak!"

Drey had a hand on Aletheia's shoulder. His daughter looked up at him, and his eyes urged caution.

The girl stepped forward to the center of the Rage. She drew a deep breath and held it for a moment, steadying her tumultuous mind.

"The visions I see, if that's what you want to call them, they don't seem strange to me," Aletheia explained. "A lot of the time, the visions just seem like part of my everyday life. I guess you could say I realize something is a vision the moment I realize I am the only one experiencing it. Or if it is strange enough. That's how I know it is a vision. Does that make sense?"

A few around her nodded; others winced in their efforts to make sense of what she was trying to convey. But the words seemed to have an overall soothing effect on the group, which emboldened her.

"Anyway, I see these visions, perceptions, pretty much all the time, just about every day," she divulged. "If a vision doesn't seem important, I ignore it. If it seems weird or important, then I tell Mom . . . D'arc."

"Yes. I've heard all this before," Ereignen retorted indignantly. "It's not enough anymore. This time, I want to hear *details*. This time, I want to know *who you are talking to*. Come on! *Tell us!* Who is it?"

"Ereignen, if you want her to answer your questions, stop trying to bully her," Drey said sternly. "You are only scaring her."

"She's fine, Drey," replied Ereignen dismissively. "Why don't you let your daughter speak for herself for once?"

Aletheia sighed and continued. "I actually don't talk to anyone or anything. I see things, smell things, hear things, but I don't . . . interact."

Ereignen sensed a slight resistance. "Nothing speaks to you? Nothing ever asks you questions?" he probed. "Are you sure of that? Because it would be a very bad thing if you were speaking to these . . . visions of yours."

Aletheia stared at the ground.

"Nothing speaks with you, right?"

She looked at D'arc, who was standing still as a statue, showing no emotion, barely breathing.

"You're hiding something!" Ereignen demanded stridently. "Answer me!"

"Ereignen, calm down," D'arc interjected. "Give her a chance to collect her thoughts."

"Calm down?" the man ranted. "*Calm down?* Why am I supposed to calm down when I suspect your daughter is hiding something of importance? When I believe she might be hiding something from the entire clan? Something potentially dangerous to us?"

He returned his attention to Aletheia. "What are you hiding from us, Aletheia? Go ahead. Say it."

D'arc studied Ereignen, finally understanding that no attempt to reason with the man would pan out. The grudge he carried was too deep, too toxic, for their dispute to ever be resolved on amicable terms. She began backing away from Ereignen and his crew slowly, inching back toward Drey and her other allies, knowing instinctively that some line had been crossed and a confrontation was now unavoidable.

"You're right," Aletheia replied. "I talked with something last night." Her words rang across the meadow, as if amplified, bringing instant silence.

Drey squeezed her arm gently, imploring her to reconsider.

"Drey, let go of her!" Ereignen shouted hotly. "You're trying to silence her! Let her speak!"

The belligerent man turned back to the girl. "So, Aletheia, what did you mean? What exactly is this 'something' you talked with?"

"Calm down, Ereignen," Drey demanded.

"She can talk for herself, Drey. What is your problem? All I see is you trying to shut her up."

"That's ridiculous. I am not trying to shut her up, I am trying—"

"Just let her finish," D'arc said, holding her palm up.

"The wolverine," Aletheia said. "I talked with the wolverine."

A few gasps escaped the crowd of hundreds observing this exchange in near silence.

"*Wolverine*?" exclaimed Ereignen, with voice aghast and eyes bulging theatrically. "What wolverine?"

"The wolverine from Shuksan camp," Aletheia said sheepishly, knowing how strange it would sound.

"You talked to the wolverine from Shuksan camp," Ereignen repeated incredulously. He shook his head a couple times, as if trying to clear this impossible thought from his mind. "And did the wolverine ... talk to you?"

"Yes," replied Aletheia calmly, unaware that she was stepping into a trap. "It talked to me."

Exclamations of disbelief rose from the crowd.

Drey and D'arc looked around the fieldmerge glow of the group and saw nothing but growing confusion and distrust.

"A talking wolverine, is it?" Ereignen turned back to the crowd. "Well, I must say that seems rather strange. Frightening, really."

There were murmurs of agreement from his loyalists.

"Tell us, Aletheia. What did the wolverine say to you?" he pressed.

"It didn't tell me anything important. It just said it was looking for me. It said I might be able to help it with something."

"It wanted help with something? Did you help it?"

"I didn't."

"Didn't what?"

"*Help it.* It just said maybe I could. Then it said it was in pain."

"In pain?"

"Yes. And a second later, it . . . the wolverine . . . changed into a woman with bleeding eyes. Right there in front of me. And there was this weird stone building with people inside. I heard gunshots." Aletheia struggled to verbalize her perceptions from the previous night. "Then the woman disappeared a minute later, and there was an old man sitting on the ground instead."

"What did this old man say to you?"

"He didn't say anything. He just looked sick. Almost dead."

Ereignen licked his lips and stared at Aletheia for a second or so. "So that's it? That's the whole story?"

"Yeah, I guess so," Aletheia said with a shrug, still looking nervous but slightly relieved.

D'arc turned her head to look at Drey. Her husband had a distracted look on his face, as if trying to calculate the result of a difficult math problem.

"I've heard enough," announced Ereignen. "*Grab them.*"

On his order, six men lunged for D'arc and Drey. Two grabbed D'arc, immobilizing the woman with jujitsu joint locks on each of her arms.

The other four men broadsided Drey, knocking him to the ground and pinning him under their combined weight. He struggled for several seconds before relaxing his body, choosing to conserve his strength.

As his men were subduing D'arc and Drey, Ereignen stepped forward and snatched Aletheia by the wrist, yanking her away from her parents.

D'arc tried to lunge toward him, but her captors held her still. She yelled her daughter's name and strained against the holds, nearly dislocating one of her shoulders before the pain made her body go limp.

"No! Let go of me!" Aletheia protested, clawing at the painful grip Ereignen had on her wrist.

Until then, Dorrie's father had been observing the unfolding events passively. Now Bowman stepped forward. "Ereignen, you're overreacting," he insisted. "Let the girl go!"

Ereignen laughed in his face. "You're a cook, Bowman. You won't understand any of this. As leader of clan defense, I am responsible for the protection of the People, no matter what danger might threaten us."

"I don't see you protecting anyone right now, Ereignen," Bowman countered. "All I see right now is you scaring the clan and terrifying a young girl."

The people around Bowman shouted support. "Yeah! Let them go! D'arc is our leader!"

"Everyone shut up!" Ereignen bellowed. "Shut up and listen to me!"

His voice managed to rise above the din, and the assembly quieted down.

"This is how it's going to be. I cannot trust her leadership," Ereignen said, pointing at D'arc, "if her daughter is potentially under the influence of ... of ..."

"Don't do it, Ereignen," Drey pleaded quietly. "Please."

Ereignen looked at Drey with repugnance, as if he were a particularly repellent bug about to be squashed underfoot. Then he turned back to the clan.

"I cannot trust the leadership of someone whose child may be communicating with a synthetic consciousness!" he proclaimed loudly.

"Damn you, Ereignen!" Bowman exploded in rage. "You have no idea what you're talking about! What do you think you're doing? Let them go!"

A large group of people behind Bowman began shouting in unison, "Let them go! Let them go!"

"Think carefully before you act, Ereignen," Bowman said, stepping closer, speaking carefully to be sure he was understood. "You always wanted to be leader, right? Well, the fate of this clan is now in your hands. Right now."

Ereignen felt the whole clan watching him, waiting for his next move. The gravity of the situation finally seemed to penetrate the angry haze inside the man's mind. For half a second, Ereignen appeared to grasp that the hostility he unleashed could end as badly for him as for his adversaries. His face briefly bore the expression of a confused schoolboy, and then his cavalier certitude came flooding back, washing away all doubts.

"*Now* we all know what is *really* going on," declared Ereignen, doubling down on his prior statement. "Aletheia is having conversations with animals and mysterious beings in her mind, while D'arc and Drey tell us to *trust* them. *Trust them.* Trust their assurances that we should feel safe from the influence of SCs."

No one questioned the man's condemnations this time. His insurrection seemed to be gaining traction.

"My People, we have been misled," he exhorted. "And as head of clan defense, this is where I must intercede."

He reached down and wrapped a muscled arm around Aletheia's chest, lifting her off the ground and pinning her body against his.

The girl struggled to push away his meaty arm but could not budge it.

"There is only *one* way I can accept Aletheia's continued presence in the clan," the man dictated. "For the protection of the People, Aletheia must live with me."

The crowd around him rippled with murmurs, punctuated by exclamations of shock.

"I will watch over her! I will hear about her visions first! I will protect the clan from the They!" Ereignen declared. "As it should be!"

"Noooo! I won't live with you! You're awful!" the girl shouted.

Ereignen clenched the girl's body hard against his and whispered in her ear, "If you want to stay in the clan, if you want to see your parents . . . you *will* live with me."

"I would rather live with the animals in the forest than live with you!" she screamed, thrashing powerfully in his grip.

Ereignen reiterated his ultimatum for everyone to hear. "From this day forth, Aletheia will live with me."

That was too much for Drey to bear. He roared with rage and bucked his body under the weight of Ereignen's conspirators, trying to throw them off.

Sensing a momentary distraction, D'arc lunged forward and down, pulling her two captors along with her. Just as quickly, she made an abrupt reversal, yanking the two men around, pulling them together in front of her. Thrusting forward and up this time, D'arc robbed them of their balance.

The two men struggled to remain standing, teetering for a moment in a goofy collision-embrace, before they collapsed to the ground.

Freed of their hold, D'arc pivoted and launched herself at Ereignen, propelled through the air by pure rage.

He saw her rapid movement and drew back, cringing from her ferocious attack.

But his withdrawal was merely a feint. As D'arc flew at him, Ereignen swung his free arm like a battle-ax, delivering a devastating blow to the back of her neck.

D'arc crashed to the ground, unconscious.

Watching Ereignen brutalize her mother, Aletheia could no longer restrain her panic. She screamed and thrashed in Ereignen's grip.

He chuckled sadistically at her struggles.

Ereignen's minions chuckled uncomfortably, appearing unnerved by the unexpected and sordid turn Ereignen's plot had suddenly taken.

The remainder of the clan was milling around, trying to come to grips with what was happening, trying to figure out what to do about it.

Locked in Ereignen's sweaty grip, Aletheia gagged at the smell of his pungent body odor.

"*No!*" she screamed, twisting violently away from him.

At that moment, Ereignen lifted his gaze, seeing something in the sky overhead. An unusual silver glimmer.

Forcing herself to stop squirming, the girl controlled her panic, feigning submission. Before long, she felt Ereignen's grip on her loosen, just a bit.

Aletheia pulled her knees up to her chest and thrust her legs down like pistons, aiming her feet at her captor's knees. The maneuver was not perfectly executed, with only one of her heels making contact. Still, with the girl's seventy pounds behind it, the impact was enough to hyperextend Ereignen's knee joint, sending a crippling spasm of pain through his body.

As Ereignen bent forward to grab reflexively at the searing pain in his knee with his free hand, Aletheia whipped her head back with balletic grace, slamming her skull straight into his nose.

Blood exploded from Ereignen's nostrils, crimson droplets flying through the air. Blinded by blood and pain, the man grabbed at his face, freeing the girl.

As soon as her feet hit the ground, Aletheia scurried through the chaotic mass of people and instantly vanished into the night.

Ereignen, having collapsed to the ground, used one hand to assess his damaged knee, while the other attempted to staunch the blood gushing from his nose.

"Get back here! Aletheia! *Aletheia!*" he roared over and over into the dark night, but his fury was unconvincing. He began to paw at the blood in his eyes, suddenly fearing retribution.

D'arc lifted her head from the ground, still dazed from Ereignen's blow to her neck. She spotted Drey a few feet away, his body still immobilized under four men. But she could see her husband's face, and he was mouthing three words to her.

Go. Get. Her.

As her memory returned, D'arc rose slowly to a crouch, coiling her muscular legs beneath her.

One of Ereignen's men saw the movement and ran toward her, but he was too late.

D'arc exploded into a sprint, hurtling through a gap in the crowd and disappearing into the darkness.

Her pursuer, still airborne, hit the ground with an impotent grunt.

Few Heideggers at the Rage were surprised to see Ereignen finally attempt his coup. Even so, the rapid series of events—not to mention the unanticipated outcome—left many in the audience frozen in a state of confusion and uncertainty.

When Dorrie realized Aletheia was in trouble, however, she quickly lost interest in the power struggle. As the Rage descended into turmoil, Aletheia's best friend backed away from the feuding clan members.

If only I could feel shocked by this kind of crap anymore, Dorrie thought bitterly. *Been around adults long enough to know better.*

When she reached the outer edge of the gathering, she glanced to either side, making sure everyone nearby was focused on the brawl at the center of the crowd.

Taking a few more cautious steps backward, Dorrie turned and ran into the night.

What a mess, she thought as she jogged through the darkness toward Ally's tent. *They should have known Ereignen couldn't be trusted.*

Ally's got to run, she realized. *She has no choice. She can't live with Ereignen. She needs to go away until this mess gets sorted out. She'll need a bug-out bag, and she might need my help to get it. More of Ereignen's punks could be waiting at her tent.*

Dorrie scampered down the gentle grassy slope leading to the thin screen of pine trees behind which Ally's family tent was pitched. As she approached the tent, she unplugged her field generator. Pulling back the door and sliding through the entrance, she prepared to sneak inside, grab a bug-out bag, and leave.

Once inside, she heard startled feet shuffling on the fabric floor.

"Ally?" she whispered.

The movement stopped.

"Ally?" Dorrie whispered again, crystals of fear forming in her stomach.

"Dorrie, is that you?" Aletheia whispered. She was hiding behind her mother's desk.

"Yeah, girl. It's me."

Aletheia stood up and threw herself into her friend's arms.

"Dorrie! Thank you so much for coming! For helping me!"

"Quiet, quiet," Dorrie hushed. "Shh. It's alright, Ally. Things are going to work out just fine."

Aletheia pushed her face into Dorrie's wool tunic, pulling her friend close and coughing out stifled sobs of fear and sadness into the crook of her friend's shoulder. She clung like a branch in a rushing torrent as grief began to work its way out, bursting from her uncontrollably. It felt as if her innocence was being crushed, annihilated, like a fading star in life's harsh gravity.

Dorrie held Aletheia, giving her friend an anxious moment to grieve. But only a moment.

"Come on. Now you need to run, girl," she encouraged her. "Go away for two or three days. Wait for things to calm down."

"I can't," cried Aletheia. "I can't leave my parents now. They're under attack!"

Dorrie lifted Aletheia's head from her shoulder gently and held her friend's tearstained face between kind hands. "You can't stay here, Ally. Ereignen is *fucking crazy*. This mess is going to take a time to clean up," Dorrie explained, gazing into

Aletheia's eyes. "You need to bug out *now*. Go down valley and wait for us to come for you. Just for a couple days. Once we begin the move to Shuksan camp, Bowman will come looking for you."

Tears welled up in Aletheia's eyes. For a moment she seemed reluctant to accept her friend's advice.

"Come on," Dorrie coaxed. "You are the daughter of *D'arc*. You can do this."

Aletheia inhaled deeply, then slowly released the breath. "You're right," she said, clearing her voice, regaining her composure. "You're right."

Aletheia could feel the bold spirit of her friend seeping inside her, chasing the chill out of her soul. She gave Dorrie a weak smile.

"Yes, Dorrie, you're *always* right," she confessed, prodding Dorrie's shoulder playfully.

"Alright, that's my girl," Dorrie said with pride. "You've got this, Ally."

Aletheia wiped her nose with her sleeve and nodded silent agreement.

"As for Ereignen, we are going to destroy that ass-hat when you come back," Dorrie said with Machiavellian relish. "It's going to be beautiful. You'll see."

"Total fucking humiliation," Aletheia said, holding out her fist.

Dorrie brought her fist down hard on top of Aletheia's, hard enough to sting a little. Right now, a little sting felt like a good thing.

"You know it," Dorrie replied. "We'll make him wish he had never been born."

She leaned down and snagged one of the three bug-out bags sitting next to the tent door, where Heideggers were trained to keep them, always ready to run. She handed it to her friend.

Aletheia slung it over her shoulder and clipped the compression straps.

"It's going to be alright," Dorrie insisted.

"I know. You're the best friend ever, Dorrie. You know that, right?"

"Yeah," Dorrie shot back, "but please stay alive. I need the competition to keep my edge."

There were faint rustling sounds on the forest floor outside.

"Head down valley. Watch for Bowman in two or three days," Dorrie whispered. "Go!"

22

Hurrying through the N^Sys Bolu manufacturing plant felt to Mark Esperson like wandering through an Escher drawing. A maze of corridors had to be negotiated to return to Receiving, and every hallway was surfaced with the same unpainted concrete. Although he felt the urge, Mark would never consider running. Exhibiting that degree of haste in a corporate setting implied outright anxiety and loss of control and was viewed in extremely bad light.

As he approached the security checkpoint at Receiving, Mark lifted his badge with his hand and wiggled it playfully. The security post was occupied by a colleague he knew well, a middle-aged Turkish woman named Rana, one of his senior security officers. Rana had two sweet kids, a girl and a boy, both of whom attended the enclave school with Mark's daughter.

She gave him a knowing look, silently telegraphing valuable information to share.

Mark stepped to the side of the corridor, turned toward Rana, and pulled his security credential from the breast pocket of his work shirt, presenting it for close examination.

"We make the best computer chips in the world, right? So why can't we print badges with legible text?" the woman bellyached playfully. She leaned toward him, squinting theatrically at the holographic text of his badge. As she did, she whispered quietly, "Vlad is inside."

Mark nodded. "Not a surprise," he replied before continuing onward.

"That's good," empathized Rana as she keyed a command into her station's holoboard.

The reinforced security doors slid into wall recesses, revealing the central corridor into Receiving. When returning to his bailiwick, Mark's first stop was normally his command post for a brief check-in, before heading off to oversee unloading on the floor or troubleshoot the massive loader bots that broke down constantly.

This time he deviated from that custom, instead heading straight to the Receiving floor in hope of intercepting Vlad and his team in the process of extracting a chip for the next scan. He knew it was generally best to stay out of Vlad's way, but this unannounced intrusion on Mark's turf was a territorial offense. Mark believed the best way to handle crisis was through teamwork and adherence to protocol, not the deceptive ploys and power politics the Impaler seemed to prefer.

Within N^Sys Corporation, it was widely understood that Vlad was on a single-minded mission to attain elite enclave status. After several years of successful leadership at Bolu Production, he was very close to obtaining his long-coveted goal. The intensely driven man seemed willing to jeopardize quite a lot to close the deal, and his Machiavellian maneuvering was increasingly hard to overlook.

If Vlad can impress the board with bold steps to resolve this crisis, it could clinch elite status for him tomorrow, Mark considered. *I suspect Vlad would Corpse his own uncle right now if he thought it would boost his chances.*

The Receiving supervisor approached a set of large stainless-steel doors, one of several access points onto the immense Receiving floor. Enormous letters, glowing hot like molten iron, were projected into the holofield spanning the broad threshold:

AUTONOMOUS MACHINERY AT WORK—PLEASE USE EXTREME CAUTION

The warning was impossible for anyone to ignore. As Mark stepped into the igneous lettering, he fought a reflexive urge to withdraw from the perception of intense heat, but the holofield itself was room temperature.

As Mark passed, sensors scanned the security credential clipped to his breast pocket. The color of the control panel adjacent to the massive bay doors switched from red to green.

A muffled thump resonated from behind the wall, and the doors began to part. There was a brief whistling sound as the doors separated, a draft caused by the air pressure differential between sections of the plant. The gust of wind shoved Mark across the threshold, as if gently coerced by some impatient fate.

By following furtive nods and glances from the Receiving staff, who knew how to circle the wagons, Mark Esperson soon located Vlad Ignatev and his cadre of techs.

As Mark approached, he could see they had already selected and extracted chips from several hoppers. A hundred or so n^cube chips had been sorted into several small piles on the floor.

When Vlad saw Mark, the Production director called out a greeting that oozed with blithe innocence. "Ah, Mark. I was hoping you would return before we finished."

"You saw me in the hallway when I was heading over to Scanning. Why didn't you mention your plans then?"

"You appeared to be in such a hurry. Besides, I knew you wouldn't be gone for long."

Several awkward seconds of silence followed. Vlad's techs glanced up from their work, sensing a growing animosity between the two men.

"In the future, Vlad, I think the courteous way to handle this sort of situation would be to inform me in advance of any attempt at chip extraction in my area of responsibility. Next time I would recomm—"

"I am acting on the authority of the N^Sys board of directors, Mark," Vlad declared, brandishing the board's imprimatur with evident pleasure. "I would recommend bringing this *perceived discourtesy* to their attention. Maybe the board will have sympathy for your wounded pride."

Vlad pivoted back to his techs and watched as the team placed another chip in the ceramic isolation case they'd brought for the trip to Scanning.

Mark realized his aggrieved attitude would cause more problems for him in the long run. By backing off, he'd be enabling the Impaler's cutthroat behavior, but at this point, he saw no alternative to playing along with the Production team's chip extractions.

My real concern is not this haphazard chip extraction, Mark reminded himself. *My real concern is the upcoming chip scan.*

"Why did you choose to extract chips from this hopper specifically?"

"Haluk, could you give Mr. Esperson a summary of our search protocol?"

One of the techs stood and spoke to Mark without emotion. "We analyzed data from the preliminary Receiving scans and identified the hoppers that arrived in Receiving around the same time as the detonated $n^\wedge$cube chip did. Then we isolated several hoppers with unusual energy signatures."

"Unusual in what way?" asked Mark.

"No specific way. Anything that was outside the norm."

"Why extract here in Receiving? Why didn't you take chips from Scanning? Or Production?"

"I don't know, sir."

"Thank you, Haluk," Vlad said, regarding Mark with mild amusement. He gestured at Mark to follow as he walked away from the techs, around the corner of the hopper.

"If you *must* know, Mark, our rationale is quite simple," Vlad explained. "Process equipment in the Production area is far more valuable than anything in Receiving."

Vlad turned and waved his arm at a loader bot nearby. "These bots can be easily replaced. In fact," he added with a double take, "some of these *should* be replaced, by the looks of them. Sooner, rather than later."

"I'm not following you, Vlad," Mark responded impatiently.

"Then please forgive my bluntness. If a chip were to detonate and destroy Receiving, N^Sys could replace this infrastructure at little expense," Vlad explained, gesturing around them. "At least when compared to the cost of rebuilding Production. As well, Receiving is positioned along an outer wall, so there is nothing of value between this wing and the enclave perimeter."

"Vlad, you know as well as I do that most Bolu facility employees work in Receiving and Scanning. Production is entirely automated!"

Vlad's techs looked up from their work and stared at Mark balefully.

"Well . . . I mean . . . except for the technicians. *You know what I mean.*"

Vlad shrugged. "It makes one feel rather expendable, doesn't it?"

"I'll be blunt as well, Vlad. I'm not all that concerned about this extraction, quite frankly. I would rather discuss your protocol for the second chip scan."

"Jung briefed you, then. Good. Here is how it is, Mark. We cannot do any plant mitigation until we have a better understanding of the chip degradation. Until we figure out a way to identify the damn things."

"Fine, Vlad. Here is *my* perspective," Mark countered. "It seems that the first chip scan triggered a fission event of sufficient power to kill three N^Sys employees. Did you know the electron microscope didn't even achieve full operating mode before the subject chip went critical? Did you know that? For all we know, all of these corrupted chips have hair triggers. We have no idea what could set one off. Or cause a chain reaction."

Vlad waited until Mark finished, but the Impaler had already formulated his reply.

"As I see it, Mark, we have two options. Option A: we take

the risk and scan another chip. Option B: our subordinates do so, after we've been relieved of duty, and most likely Corpsed. Either way, the scan happens, whether you and I choose to perform our designated roles or not. *Capisce?*"

It was a familiar refrain within enclave walls.

Mark glared at Vlad for a moment. Then he looked down and cursed under his breath. He knew the man's logic was beyond dispute. At that moment, nothing else really mattered. It all came down to this.

"Don't kill the messenger, Mark," Vlad continued. "You know the board made this decision long before the Geneva holoconference ended. Let me remind you that we are just foot soldiers in this crisis. If we succeed, we are promoted. If we fail ..."

Mark waved off that line of thinking. "*Fine.* We do the scan. But the plant must be entirely evacuated, except for critical personnel. And I insist we run the scan from a remote location, from a holostation in Production, behind several layers of shielding."

"Excellent thinking, Mark. When we are out of the woods, I believe I shall submit your name for a commendation."

"Thank you, Vlad. If we live through this, I might consider submitting your name as well."

The two men stared at each other, their faces as calm and impassive as each could muster. Inside the fiendishly competitive world of the corporate enclave, disclosure of motive was equivalent to surrender.

The techs had isolated the last sample chip they needed and placed it in the shielded case; they were preparing to mobilize back to Scanning.

"From now on, Vlad, please keep me in the loop," insisted Mark.

"Yes, I assure you, I will keep you informed of all major decisions moving forward. Everyone wants to report a successful outcome to Geneva."

No one more than you, thought Mark.

"I will be in touch soon," Vlad decreed.

Regrouping his techs, the Impaler headed for the exit.

Mark was in his control room three hours later, working hard to keep calm, when the promised holo came through from Jung.

"Mark, we're ready to go with the chip scan. Vlad communicated your expectations regarding the control room location and evacuation of nonessential personnel."

"Yes, good."

"There has been a change of plan. You're not going to like this, but I believe I should stay here in Scanning to ensure that the scan goes off as planned. This is the big one. Someone needs to be in here to confirm physical observations and adjustments."

"Jung..."

"Please try to understand, Mark. If we redo the scan and don't get the data we need for some reason . . . well, let's just say I don't think we should risk that."

She waited for a response while Mark struggled to keep his temper from flaring.

"It's kind of a one-shot deal anyway," she added, her voice shaky and uncertain.

"Is Vlad still there with you?" Mark fished.

"No, he went back to Production to prepare for the remote scan."

"But it's not remote now. You will be there."

"I know, but Vlad wants to run it from Production anyway."

"So, he wants you to remain behind to observe the scan, while he's safely tucked away in Production?"

"That's not the way he framed it. But yes, Mark, that's his plan, in a nutshell."

"Jung, what did he promise you?"

Now it was Jung who was struck mute.

Mark pressed her. "Be honest with me. I'm not going to tell anyone. Did Vlad cut a deal with you?"

"He . . . ," Jung started, before having second thoughts.

"Tell me." He could see tears gathering in the corners of her eyes. "It has something to do with your family, doesn't it?"

It was immediately obvious he had struck a nerve. Jung tried to control her reaction, but he'd seen her wince, as if she had experienced a stabbing pain.

And maybe she did, he thought. *If I feel discomfort and sadness at the thought of her family being trapped in those diseased ruins, I can't even begin to imagine how she must feel, living here in Istanbul, thousands of miles away. If Vlad wished to gain leverage over Jung, he'd pick the most obvious pressure point.*

"If you volunteer to observe the scan in person, N^Sys agrees to airlift your family, right?" Mark deduced. "That's the quid pro quo, isn't it?"

She nodded. "If I oversee the scan in person, the N^Sys board has agreed to airlift my family off the Korean Peninsula and bring them here to live in the Bolu Enclave. Everyone who wishes will be given permanent employment," she confessed. "And Mark—they promised to build us *our own house.* Big enough for all of us."

Mark made a low whistle, impressed by the offer.

"On top of everything else, Vlad said he would recommend me for Bolu Production director. If his elite status is approved, that is."

"How did I know Vlad's promotion would somehow fit into the grand scheme of things?" Mark asked dryly. Then, "I'm sorry. That probably sounded resentful."

"Believe me, Mark, I understand how intolerable Vlad can be sometimes. But you know what this airlift means to my family. I've been struggling to save in order to pay for their expatriation, but the cost of passage from Seoul to Bolu for one of them is more than I earn in an entire year. My parents might die there before I can save the money to rescue them! I can't back away from this."

Mark had never seen Jung so distressed. He considered her to be reliably levelheaded. This decision was eating her up.

"I just want to make sure we're not rushing the second scan," Mark cautioned. "You're definitely on board with all of this?"

"I have reviewed the entire plan carefully. I believe the level of risk is acceptable."

"You are absolutely sure the airlift offer is not affecting your judgment? Are you sure no health and safety considerations are being overlooked?"

Jung rubbed her forehead with her hand. "Listen, Mark. There is nothing wrong with a deal like this. You may think they're pressuring me to do this, but that is not the case. It's an opportunity, and I am electing to take advantage of it. That's it."

"Jung, I—"

"End of story, Mark."

If I question the wisdom of Jung's role, I might upset the whole scheme, Mark reflected silently. *If I blow this opportunity for Jung and her family, she will probably hate me forever. And if we find no other resolution to the sabotage, Vlad will blame the failure on my request to veto the scan. If the Impaler is successful in making that accusation stick, I'll be busted all the way down to tech, at best. Most likely Corpsed. Throwing a wrench in the works now will work out poorly for everyone involved. If I play along now, I might be able to affect the course of events later.*

"What can I say?" Mark relented. "It's a Scanning decision, which makes it your call. I trust you know what's best."

"Thank you," she said with a relieved smile.

"But hey, keep me in the loop from here on. Please?"

"Of course, Mark."

"*All the way* in the loop," he added, one eyebrow slightly elevated.

"I will get back in touch about ten minutes before scan time," Jung assured him.

"All right, thanks, Jung. End holo."

Mark placed Receiving on standby and began the walk over to the remote-scan control room, assembled with haste by Vlad's tech team in Production. By the time he got there, all nonessential facility personnel would have been evacuated to another part of the Bolu Enclave. The Receiving supervisor thus encountered no security challenges whatsoever while passing through the Admin and Scanning wings—a unique experience in his many years of foot travel back and forth across the N^Sys Bolu plant.

Since he was ahead of schedule, he decided to stop at the Scanning lab and check on Jung's state of mind.

When Mark poked his head in the door, Jung was sitting by herself in the observation room. She was kicked back in a chair with her shoes off, her guard completely down, gazing through the observation window.

The specimen chip was visible inside the lab, clamped in place and ready for scanning.

"Hi, Jung," he said, trying to sound jovial.

"Mark," she said, sitting up, straightening her clothes, and slipping a foot into each shoe. "Sorry, I wasn't expecting a visitor."

"I was heading over to Production and thought I'd stop by and save you the holo. It took no time at all for me to walk over here. Vlad has evacuated the entire complex."

"Mmm," Jung answered, trying to push that thought aside.

"How is everything looking?"

"Things look good," she answered. "We are still a go in . . . ," she glanced at the wall clock, "seventeen minutes."

"How are *you* doing, Jung?"

"Oh, I'm fine, Mark. Just preparing myself for showtime," she said with a shrug. "I hear Director Trieste will be joining you by holo in Production to observe the scan. So that will be nice."

"Is another seat available in here?" Mark inquired, glancing around with feigned desperation before cracking an impish smile.

Jung smiled, appreciating the humor.

"So you're sure everything is set up as we agreed?"

"I've looked everything over three times: reviewed all the scan settings, confirmed the chip type, clamping . . . everything."

"You've programmed a governor on the scan energy settings so it can't reach—"

"The peak discharge of the last scan. Yes, done."

"You tested all the—"

"Emergency shutdown circuits, yes."

"Then it sounds to me like we're ready to go."

"I agree," Jung replied. "Vlad had a few of his techs bring over a bigger gamma shield from Production. See it there?" she asked, pointing to the top edge of a heavy shield visible just inside the lab. "They positioned it so I can get it between my body and the chip during the scan. It's redundant to the existing shielding in the walls around the observation room. But, hey, a little extra margin of safety can't hurt. The way they positioned it, I should be able to view the scan through the slot between the top of the gamma shield and the edge of the observation window."

Mark examined that portion of the shielding he could see from his vantage point in the observation room, nodding his head with approval. "Seems like a smart use of shielding."

Jung smiled at him, relieved by his approval.

Mark studied the lab for another minute, looking for anything out of place, anything missing. "The lab has been cleared of unnecessary materials?" he asked.

"Yes," she said. "I checked again after the techs left for the Production command post."

"Well, I'm no scanning expert, but everything seems right to me," he verified. "My only remaining concern is you, Jung. Is this still what you want? You have the airlift agreement in writing?"

"In writing, absolutely."

"Then it looks like the next stop for you is director of Production."

"Oh, Mark," she protested.

"You deserve it, Jung. You'll do a fantastic job, just as you have in Scanning."

"You're distracting me with all this talk of directorships," she responded, putting on her game face. "Let's get this done."

Mark smiled and gave her a thumbs-up.

Stepping into the hallway, he gently shut the door. Before walking away, the man placed his palm on the shut door and bowed his head, transmitting whatever positivity he could summon into the room beyond.

The Bolu crisis team had transformed a general-purpose room in the Production wing into a remote control room for the Scanning lab. Inside the makeshift command post, cables snaked across the floor to a hastily assembled portable holofield rig. Four of Vlad's techs were busy at work on a holographic panel of remote Scanning lab controls, while a fifth minion oversaw the function of the holofield itself.

Dr. Nishanath Nair, second in command at Scanning, drifted back and forth behind his techs, watching intently as final adjustments were made to control instruments.

When Mark arrived, directors Trieste and Ignatev were hammering out some sort of contingency plan to deploy if this second scan did not yield a distinct electromagnetic signature they could use to detect sabotaged chips. If indeed the scan failed, Sylvie insisted that they immediately begin backing chip feedstock out of the plant. Vlad was fighting the idea at every turn, because backing out feedstock would be tremendously complicated and expensive on his turf in Production.

Mark nodded a hello as he entered but did not offer any contributions to the dialogue. Contingency planning for scan failure only minutes before it was to be performed seemed both odd and inappropriate to him.

Evidently Nair was also displeased with the tenor of the conversation. He had also chosen to disregard Vlad and Sylvie completely.

Sylvie seemed to be winning the debate, so Vlad turned

his attention elsewhere. He settled his sights on Mark, who was the most convenient target.

"So, Mark, how is everything looking at the lab? How is Jung holding up?"

"She's fine, Vlad. She would undoubtedly appreciate your concern."

Sylvie smiled and turned away, suddenly finding interest in the remote control panel.

"As far as the lab goes," Mark continued, "I'm no scanning expert, but nothing appeared out of the ordinary to me."

"Good."

"Oh, Jung was glad to have the larger shield. Thanks for that."

"So how are we doing, gentlemen?" Vlad asked his techs. Following his debate with Sylvie about reversing feedstock out of Production, his impatience had grown palpable. "We are approximately eight minutes from scheduled scan time."

"Looking good for T-minus eight minutes," said one of the techs.

"Have you learned anything more about the Heideggers, Director Trieste?" Mark ventured, trying to ease the tension in the room.

"Please, Mark. Call me Sylvie," she responded, delighted to have the attention. "If you are referring to the current disposition of the group, let's just say I know exactly where to find them, if we engage."

Mark did not wish to pursue that line of inquiry any further.

"Five minutes to scan," prompted one of the techs.

"Please commence the countdown for Jung starting at T-minus thirty seconds, so she has time to get into position before the scan," Vlad instructed.

"Yes sir."

Dr. Nair studied the holographic control panel. "Did you notice the differences in the lab's electronic signature? There is a subtle but noticeable difference in the electromagnetic profile."

"It's probably the larger shield we put in the lab, sir."

"Yes, I suppose so," Nair allowed.

"The discrepancy seems to fit that scenario," the technician reported.

"We have detected no change in internal chip composition, correct?"

"No change in scan target character or position, sir. Countdown beginning . . . now. T minus thirty seconds . . . twenty-nine . . . twenty-eight . . . twenty-seven . . ."

"Could you bring up video feed of the lab and observation room, please?" Mark requested.

"Yes sir," a tech replied. "You are coming up on video, Dr. Li," he forewarned Jung, who was alone in the observation room back at the Scanning lab.

A large holoscreen popped up at one end of Vlad's temporary control room in Production. The holo image was displaying two video feeds simultaneously, one for the lab and one for the observation room. Jung looked up as the camera came online.

"Everything still seem normal in there, Jung?" Mark questioned.

"Fifteen . . . fourteen . . . thirteen . . . ," the technician continued.

"Yes, Mark. Everything appears normal here." She waved to them through the video link.

". . . nine . . . eight . . . seven . . ."

"Preparing to scan," said Dr. Nair.

There was a resonant click as the electron scanning beam powered up.

Mark saw Jung move into position by the observation window. She peered through the slit between the window frame and the new shield, just enough to allow restricted vision.

"I just heard the beam power up," Jung reported. "I am in position. Proceed with the scan."

"...three...two...one...scanning."

Vlad and Mark leaned forward in their seats as the electron beam began to discharge.

"The criticality occurred at this moment during the last scan, correct?" Sylvie asked no one in particular.

Jung answered first. "Correct, Sylvie."

"We're getting scan data," one of the techs pronounced.

Dr. Nair quietly examined orange-white pulses of data scrolling across the control panel holofield. He lifted a pinkie finger and used it to track one particular line, examining the text closely.

Several seconds passed.

Mark exhaled a deep breath.

Sylvie and Vlad watched the proceedings with interest.

"How do the data look so far, Doctor?"

"They look normal, completely normal. But . . . hold on a moment . . . the scan is just getting into the $n^{\wedge}$cube core lattice now."

"Jung, things look okay on your end?" Mark asked.

"Yes, Mark. Everything looks fine here. I see no indication of unusual energy discharges anywhere near the scanning apparatus," she confirmed.

Dr. Nair interjected. "We're losing some critical data we need on key core sectors due to insufficient beam strength. It appears that the beam-strength governor we installed is compromising the quality of the scan data."

"Can you draw the necessary conclusions from the data being collected?" Sylvie asked. "Or should we operate the beam at a higher discharge?"

"I am not observing any unusual emission signatures right now," Dr. Nair hedged. "The chip seems normal, but I can't be certain without—"

"Without operating at full beam strength," said Sylvie. "So far, it appears we have a normal chip here. No fission event has been measured thus far, nor is there any indication that one might be impending. Dr. Nair is requesting removal of the governor to allow beam intensification."

"Lattice discontinuities may exist that we're not picking up because the governor is impeding signal," agreed Jung from afar.

"Why was the governor installed again?" Sylvie asked with annoyance.

"Because Jung is in the observation room," reiterated Mark.

"The preliminary data look fine," Dr. Nair said. "I don't see any problems with this chip."

"Then I propose we increase discharge intensity," Vlad offered.

"I propose we get Jung out of there first," Mark countered.

"Everyone? I think we have a normal chip this time," Jung chimed in. "I'm fine with increasing the discharge intensity. I will let you know if I notice anything unusual."

"What do you think, Mark?" Sylvie pressed. Everybody in the room seemed to pause and look at him.

There is nothing I can say to bring this to a halt, is there? thought Mark, surveying the expectant faces around him.

"At this moment in time, I don't see any immediate issue with increasing discharge intensity," he allowed with audible reluctance.

Sylvie nodded at Dr. Nair.

"Raise the discharge intensity by thirty percent," the doctor requested.

"Raising beam intensity by thirty percent, sir." The tech manipulated a toggle on the control panel.

Several seconds passed.

"Yes, this looks good," Dr. Nair said, studying the scan data again. "Even with the better resolution, the chip still appears normal."

"Damn it," Vlad said.

"Oh, Vlad, you didn't seriously think we would get lucky the first time?" mused Sylvie.

"Hang on," announced Jung. "I'm hearing something new,

a high-frequency noise." They could see her in the video feed, turning her head to pinpoint the location.

"The chip looks perfectly normal," Nair advised. "I'm not seeing any unusual behavior."

"It's definitely getting louder!" Jung exclaimed, raising her voice to be heard above a whine now dominating the video's audio channel.

"Shut it down," said Mark.

Vlad turned to him. "What? Why?"

"The noise Jung's hearing... it's not normal."

"Dr. Nair, how close are we to scan completion?" asked Sylvie.

"Seconds away."

"Can you hang on a few seconds longer?" Sylvie shouted to Jung over the sound, which was now a shrieking wail.

Mark watched Jung nod and clap her hands over her ears. She was obviously experiencing mild discomfort, but she didn't seem to be in pain.

"Just about there, just about there. Yes, done now!" Nair commanded. "Power down!"

"Powering down the scanning beam," a tech confirmed. "Now."

The scanning mechanism shut down, yet the screeching noise continued unabated.

Mark could see Jung getting anxious. She clearly didn't understand what was happening and glanced repeatedly at the camera, as if waiting for a cue.

"The scan is done, Jung!" Mark shouted. "Get the hell out of there!"

"Can't hear you! Please repeat!" she shouted. There was a flicker of pain in her eyes.

"She can't hear us. Is there any other way to signal her?" Mark asked the people in the room, who looked at each other impotently.

"Can't hear! Please repeat!" Jung screamed again.

She won't leave until someone confirms she has fulfilled her end of the deal, Mark realized. *She won't risk losing her family's airlift over a technicality.*

"Sir, energy-level readings are rising rapidly again."

"From what?" Dr. Nair asked incredulously. "That's not possible."

"The energy is not emanating from the chip, sir."

"I . . . I . . . ," Jung stammered with confusion, wincing with pain, barely able to tolerate the piercing din.

"I should leave, I should leave," the woman was repeating over and over, suddenly on the verge of panic.

"Sir!" shouted a tech. "Energy levels are spiking in there. She needs to get out."

Jung was down on one knee, three feet from the room's exit. She was bent at the waist, her fingers dug into her ear canals, the sonic torment causing her eyes to tear uncontrollably.

"What the hell is happening in there?" Nair shouted over the terrible whine. "Cut the damn audio!"

"Yes sir." The whining ended abruptly.

"Shut down all power to the lab immediately!"

"Cutting all power sources now."

The video feed of the lab on one side of the holoscreen abruptly went black.

Jung remained visible in the observation room, rolling back and forth on the floor. Her mouth was moving, imploring someone to end the agony.

"What's that?" said Mark. "There, in the lab."

The walls of the powerless lab were lit by a yellow glow.

"Temperature readings are spiking in the lab, sir! Very rapidly!"

"What is the current reading?"

"Three fifty Fahrenheit and climbing fast."

Dr. Nair watched the air-clamped chip and shook his head. "What is going on?" he asked no one in particular. "This is crazy. It doesn't make sense."

Behind the incapacitated Jung, the wall paint surrounding

the observation window began to bubble and peel. As they watched, the walls of the lab burst into flame. The auxiliary radiation shield twisted, its molecules writhing from some unseen source of incendiary heat.

Jung was frozen by the sonic assault now, her hands still clamped over her ears, her mouth opening and closing like a goldfish.

Mark could read her lips: she was screaming for help over and over, without pause.

"One thousand Fahrenheit in the lab, sir!"

Without warning, the window between lab and observation room warped violently and exploded.

As those in the remote control room watched helplessly, an intense wave of heat rushed through the window frame into the observation room, immolating Jung alive.

The poor woman knew she was about to die. Her mouth opened wide and she screamed in terror as the flesh melted from her skull. Her clothing burst into flame and vaporized in half a second.

Mark Esperson watched, frozen in horror, as his colleague of many years perished in excruciating pain. Dead, her body still thrashed on the floor, broiled muscles contracting with grim brutality. Every inch of her skin had charred black, and her limbs were loosening in their joints, threatening to detach.

Before the horror could deepen any further, the lens on the camera warped, and the video went black.

"Fission event, sir!" shouted a tech. The walls of the remote control room vibrated as a shock wave passed.

For a moment, no one moved.

"That was a detonation shock wave," Sylvie said with evident displeasure.

"But it was a standard chip!" Dr. Nair said.

Sylvie immediately went to work. "Enclave Security, this is Sylvie Trieste reporting an apparent criticality accident in Scanning. Yes, another one."

"Yes, Director," came the reply. "We are aware of it."

"I also must report a death in the Scanning lab. Dr. Li Hyun-Jung was killed in the explosion."

"A death. Yes, we understand," the voice replied, followed by an apprehensive query. "Director Trieste?"

Sylvie whipped her head, alarmed by the tone. "Yes, what?"

"Director, we have detected multiple nanonuke detonations."

"Multiple? How many?"

"Looks like two. Maybe three."

"Two or three? How is that possible?" Sylvie said. "Security, please provide a damage estimate."

"Damage estimate?" the voice replied. "The Scanning wing is gone, Director. Completely gone."

23

Sylvie could not be physically present at every N^Sys location demanding her immediate attention after the devastating explosion at the N^Sys Bolu Enclave. As word of the Bolu sabotage spread across the N^Sys cloud in the hours following the death of Jung and destruction of Bolu Scanning, the N^Sys Human Intelligence Branch was bombarded with questions, demands, and unsubstantiated tips.

The Security Director needed a comprehensive view of her entire jurisdiction in order to sort things out. Inside her personal ego construct, she had made the arrangements necessary to spread herself as far and wide as necessary. There, she could achieve temporary omniscience across the entirety of the N^Sys corporate footprint, while enjoying whatever sense of equanimity she might find at the center of this growing maelstrom.

Her personal ego construct was an elaborate example of the self-congratulatory holo environments preferred by top corporate executives of the day—a psychic citadel custom designed to reinforce a sense of unbridled power and entitlement and configured to satisfy the most pathological of narcissists. After another day spent repairing the damage caused by an unceasing stream of ill-considered choices made by capricious individuals, Sylvie, like most top executives of the day, liked nothing more than entering her ego construct for several hours of omnipotent indulgence in a hyperreal virtual world of her own design. No matter how challenging her work day had been, she could always count on the rejuvenating effects of residing at the very center of her utterly compliant —albeit virtual—universe.

Finally stepping inside that holographic environment, Sylvie immersed herself in the ambience of her feudal Italian castle, hoping the pastoral solitude would restore her spirits after the terrible setback yesterday at the N^Sys Bolu Enclave.

Sylvie's avatar was strolling the lush gardens of her refuge when she encountered the stranger. The unexpected interloper was seated, perfectly still, at the center of a shady dell hidden at the center of a tight circle of Italian cypresses. The cluster of spiky, cylindrical cypress trees added a surreal geometry to the setting, as if all lines in the landscape somehow terminated there, at the center of that grove.

The designer of the ego construct had assured Sylvie that hers would be equipped with the most advanced security features. As a security officer, she was fully aware of the dangers that haunted top corporate executives. With the construct's spontaneity factor set to zero, she should not encounter anything unfamiliar or out of place inside her digital refuge.

Yet here is an absolute stranger on the ground before me, she thinks. *A filthy, starving, half-naked wretch. I would never approve the use of such a pathetic, disgusting avatar in my personal construct. Never. Why would anyone choose to manifest in such a form? Look at it sitting there in the grass, shoulders slumped, eyelids slack, skin pallid. Privates barely covered by a dirty rag.*

She examined the withered being with rising irritation.

Everything else about my construct seems normal, everything other than this . . . thing at my feet. Why doesn't the construct detect my displeasure and eliminate the vile thing? Something is wrong here. Something is very wrong.

"Excuse me?" she said to it. "Why are you in my construct? I don't wish for any surprises right now. I zeroed out the construct spontaneity factor precisely for that reason."

The figure did not move.

"Excuse me?" she said impatiently. Her avatar took a couple of small, uncertain steps toward it.

The seated figure remained perfectly still.

With a huff of contempt, Sylvie stepped forward again, this time assertively. "You don't belong here! Get out of my—"

The figure exploded with movement. Six segmented limbs speckled with stiff black hairs appeared from behind the seated figure. Striking at Sylvie's avatar, the six limbs ensnared her.

"Let go of me at once!" her avatar shouted with outrage. "This is my personal construct! You have no jurisdiction here."

The stout limbs were unrelenting, yanking the Sylvie avatar in, restraining her, bringing her face to face with the immobile form. As she watched through the eyes of her avatar, the haggard face of the anomaly slowly began to change. Two tired eyes underwent a sort of fission, spreading outward into four obsidian-black disks that gleamed with a cold, inscrutable intelligence. The thin lips protruded grotesquely, swelling into four jointed feeding pincers dotted with oily black hairs. A gout of viscous drool spewed from an orifice centered between the two pairs of pincers, splattering the avatar's feudal clothing.

The Sylvie avatar struggled against the grip of the beast, but she could not break free. Enraged and terrified, she screamed like a wraith at the loathsome creature.

"*Maaaaaarrrraaaaaaaaaaa . . . ,*" replied the creature in a dry, chitinous buzz.

As the six dexterous arms lifted her avatar up and away from the diabolical face, Sylvie sensed a blur of movement and a faint whistle, like the acceleration of a whip just before the crack. The last thing she saw was a mighty tail coming down on her, and the shiny barb of a huge stinger slicing through the air.

24

After the Rage went so horribly awry, Aletheia had followed Dorrie's instructions and hiked down valley. Here she would hide and wait for the clan to calm down, at which point, according to their plan, Bowman would come to retrieve her.

Dorrie and Bowman might be the only friends I have left in the world after what went down last night, lamented the girl.

Aletheia had completely lost track of time. Her inner mind was still trying to comprehend the brutal ballet that had transpired between Ereignen and her parents the night before.

What happens now? she wondered. *I can wait for Bowman or Dorrie to come find me, but what then? Will the clan take me back, or did Ereignen and his men already do too much damage? Besides, I won't live in the same camp with Ereignen ever again. No way. I would rather survive on my own out here in the woods.*

The thought of her mother and father being humiliated and rejected by the clan sickened her, the mental image almost too repugnant to contemplate. Every time her mind drifted back to those thoughts, the girl forced her feet to move faster. Her cheeks were now chapped a rough pink from brushing tears away in the chill morning air.

Where will I go? Should I build a home and live by myself? That sounds so sad and lonely, the girl agonized. *I can't be alone forever.*

Sooner or later I have to rejoin the clan. I wish I knew someone who could help me.

Wait. What about the wolverine? This idea struck her like lightning from a blue sky, sending a tingle of excitement down her spine.

Yet she experienced a vague sense of trepidation, possibly even mild revulsion, at the thought of seeking the creature that had confused and frightened her only two nights before.

Is that excitement or fear I feel when I think about it? I feel curious more than anything, I suppose, she considered. *After all, the wolverine said it needed my help. "I think you are the one who can help me," it said.*

Aletheia kept picking away at the memory, seeking an explanation.

"You and I are alike. We both see more than we should," the wolverine said. That must refer to my gift. It must.

So the wolverine needs my gift for some reason. Why would the wolverine need help from me if we are alike? "We see more than we should." Is it possible we both see more than we should, but we see different things? Does the wolverine need the things that I see, combined with whatever it sees? Like when you put two things together, and what you get at the end is more than the two original things. What is that called again? Synenergy? Synergy?

If I helped the wolverine, would it help me? Or would it control me? Would it make me its slave? That sounds even worse than dealing with Ereignen.

What else did the wolverine say? It said something nice, something that calmed me down.

Aletheia looked up and saw a cluster of rotting wooden structures among the trees just off-trail. Hunting cabins from days gone by. Windows had been smashed by vandals, letting the weather inside to decay the walls and floors. Teetering on their concrete footings, the structures appeared ready to collapse at the slightest touch.

"You have nothing to fear from me," was the last thing the wolverine said. If it needs me, I have nothing to fear, she considered.

That might be the best choice I have right now.

Farther down the trail, which had widened into a steep dirt road, Aletheia could see structures in slightly better states of repair. As she surveyed those atrophied signs of civilization, a low rumble echoed down from above.

The girl looked toward the sky and wrinkled her brow.

Please do not start raining, she thought. *That is the last . . .*

The rumble quickly faded, but soon was replaced by a rushing sound. It felt to Aletheia as if she had suddenly been transported to a large waterfall, which was just out of view around a bend in the trail. The surge of air intensified into a leonine roar.

What is going on? the girl thought, searching for the source of the noise.

The uppermost tree limbs above Aletheia began to whip around violently, agitated by some unseen force.

Looking up, the girl caught sight of an object high above her. Too far away to make out any features, the shape was little more than a black dot against the sun. As she watched, the dot expanded rapidly in size, growing into a massive object hovering just above the treetops. Crouching low, Aletheia searched for an escape route or nearby hiding place, but there were none in sight. The craft had swooped down from the sky to intercept her just as she started across a wide forest clearing.

A hatch at the base of the craft slit open like a laceration. From the orifice erupted a blast of sound, a full-spectrum auditory shock wave, a transparent wave of force which commenced to pummel the ground where Aletheia knelt. Dead leaves and dust whirled up along with a stinging cloud of projectiles that abraded every exposed surface of the girl's skin. She cowered instinctively, shielding her face with one hand, trying to clear her vision with the other. Unable to flee, she watched as the shock wave radiated down to the ground, enveloping her. She caught a glimpse of the N^Sys logo on the side of the craft just before the full force of the sonic assault slammed her diminutive body to the ground, rendering her unconsciousness.

An instrument pod dropped through the hatch of the hovering craft. Hanging from the end of a gleaming steel umbilicus, the pod plunged down to Aletheia's unconscious form. Articulated metal digits unfolded from four sides of the pod, spreading like the talons of a diving eagle. The dexterous fingers closed around the girl, embracing her body with delicate sensitivity. Then the steel tether pulled taut, lifting Aletheia off the ground and raising her briskly toward the waiting craft.

Once the girl was inside the ship, the hull opening sutured shut, leaving no visible hint of crack or seam.

Treetops danced wildly as jet thrusters engaged, quickly lifting the craft up and away from the scene of the abduction. The silhouette of the ascending craft continued to shrink, until it was nothing more than a fading black dot.

The Cascade forest was again placid and still.

25

T uring Director Seers and his expert system Celeste sat in a cramped meeting room deep within the N^Sys Executive complex. The size of the meeting space was limited by necessity, surrounded as it was by a nearly impenetrable wall of electronic security. A cocoon of tech enclosed the cubic room on all six sides, counterespionage electronics and sensors packed tightly into the ventilated cavity. Aggressive trace programs were ever vigilant, ready to hound a transgressor into destitution. Authorized physical entry was the only sane way to gain access to an N^Sys secure room.

Sylvie Trieste and Jan, the androgynous expert system, were running late, still caught up in the disturbing events that had taken place at the N^Sys Bolu Enclave. During the downtime, Celeste tapped contentedly on her holoboard.

As her industry was strictly for appearance, Director Seers gave it no attention at all. Instead, the man agonized quietly about the meeting about to begin. Seers considered himself well informed, and he rarely provided his peers with any reason to question that judgment. He knew Sylvie Trieste had not built her notoriety on froth and fiction. After all, she had quickly characterized the Bolu sabotage as a blatant Heidegger strike against N^Sys sovereignty. That statement might as well have been a cypher transmitted solely for his consumption.

Sylvie's first order of business is to protect N^Sys against these sorts of attacks, he knew. *If she stumbles, blame for the Bolu tragedy may land squarely in her lap. Director Trieste will be looking for good theater to deflect any offensive maneuver launched at her by enemies on the N^Sys board. For Sylvie, good theater almost certainly means retribution. Violent retribution. She will turn the screws to make that happen,* the Turing director anticipated.

An autonomous cargo drone dropped out of scramjet mode and reentered the troposphere, the craft's sleek chrome nanohull still crimson red from the extreme air friction of scram speed. Completing an efficient high arc from Switzerland across the North Atlantic and over the wasted remains of the Greenland ice cap, the cargo drone continued over central Canada. A pleasant morning was taking hold over the Canadian Shield. The shallow rays of the rising sun threw stark shadows across deep scars ripped into the depopulated subarctic landscape, Nazca-like vestiges of massive tar sands excavations long since abandoned.

Descending to a low cruising altitude of twenty thousand feet, the drone continued at conventional supersonic speed. The eroded scablands of central Washington appeared on the horizon, soon giving way to jagged white peaks of glittering glacial ice, the crest of the Cascade Range.

Sensing shifts in the chain of verifications, clearances, and electronic surveillance required to move through the N^Sys Executive complex, Celeste discontinued her typing and prepared for the imminent arrival of Sylvie Trieste.

The door to the secure room slid open, and the air of the small chamber was immediately infused with Sylvie's musky Italian fragrance and undeniable air of authority. The death and destruction in Bolu did not appear to have shaken the

N^Sys officer one bit. She rounded the meeting table with feline insouciance and slid into the brushed-calfskin confines of a high-back executive chair. Jan materialized just behind her.

"Hello, Conrad, Celeste," Sylvie offered without emotion.

"Greetings. Before we begin, I'd like to express sincere condolences on behalf of the Turing Institute," said Conrad. "Has an explanation been found?"

"Yes," Sylvie responded. "A technician failed to remove a sample case from the lab before the scan was performed. That case contained four additional n^cube chips. Apparently two of those chips were sabotaged and in sufficient proximity to trigger a chain reaction. The near-simultaneous detonation of the chips amplified the explosive force." The N^Sys director was not showing any overt signs of stress, but it was clear she was vexed.

"The Turing Institute is saddened by this news," Celeste offered on behalf of her parent organization. "However, they urge caution as we evaluate possible responses. To avoid any unintended consequences."

Sylvie stared at them flatly as she tapped two of her exquisitely manicured fingernails on the polished surface of the meeting table. The sound of the tapping nails reverberated in the quiet room.

"Believe me," she finally responded, "the consequences that follow will be quite intentional. The technician responsible for this mishap can already vouch for that, I assure you."

"Director Trieste," Conrad engaged.

"Sylvie," she corrected.

"Sylvie. The Turing Institute understands that the acts of sabotage cannot go unanswered. But we might consider acting with restraint."

"How so?"

"As you know, the Turing Institute is subject to all relevant intercorporate and international agreements."

Sylvie's finger tapping ceased. She stared at him for a second or two before her fingernails resumed their steady rhythm.

"The International Endangered Peoples Accord, for example," interjected Celeste. The IEPA had been established in 2028 to protect any remaining small bands of indigenous humans still in existence, the majority of whom were under clear and present danger of extinction.

"Yes, I agree," said Sylvie. "The Turing Institute is subject to those rules. N^Sys is not. That accord only applies to governmental and nongovernmental organizations. Corporations are completely exempt."

"How is it possible for me to approve an N^Sys counterstrike, if such an act is forbidden under the Turing charter?" the Turing director argued. "Are you pressuring me to commit an infraction?"

"It seems safe to infer that you believe the Heideggers are eligible for protection as an endangered people," replied Sylvie. "The notion is patently absurd. The Heideggers are a terrorist group, not an indigenous tribe."

Conrad Seers noticed Jan skewering him with a strange, unsettling gaze. He could not identify the exact nature of the discomfort it caused in him, but he felt it without a doubt. *Here we go,* the Turing director realized. *The battle of wills begins.*

"According to the Applicability section of the Accord," Celeste interjected, "the IEPA specifically covers, and I quote, 'all human beings engaged in functional communities coalesced around unique heritages, traditions, or points of view.'"

"I think all of us can agree the Heideggers are coalesced around a unique point of view," Conrad noted.

"And what unique point of view is that?" Sylvie scoffed. "Killing innocent people? Destroying modern civilization? Is that a unique point of view worth preserving?"

"According to the IEPA, the correct answer to your last question is affirmative," replied the Turing expert system.

The room was again silent except for the tap-tap-tapping of Sylvie's fingernails on the tabletop.

Sensing an impasse, Sylvie glanced at Jan, who had been waiting for the cue.

The N^Sys officer paused to tug her shirt cuffs, then continued calmly. "Currently, nothing prevents the Baker Lake Heideggers from disappearing," Sylvie noted, with a snap of her fingers on the last word. "You know how transient these groups are. We could lose contact with the clan, or some critical portion of the group, at any moment. To prevent this, I want approval to launch limited air strikes on locations considered places of refuge by the group. The fireworks should cause a temporary panic, enough to pin the group down, which will delay any mass departures and permit us to gather additional intelligence."

"I am unconvinced that the strikes you describe would be productive at this point," Conrad countered. "Our latest surveillance data suggest the group has recently undergone some sort of major schism, possibly resulting from an attempted insurrection by a handful of clan heavies. Pressure has been building for some time, and the factions now appear to be in open conflict. They held a gathering last night and . . . Celeste?" He waved his hand upward.

The lights dimmed. Video feed was projected in a small holofield generated just above the table. The feed was taken from the perspective of a surveillance drone in flight. They could see a horde of Heideggers gathered in a meadow at twilight, the aggregate mass encircling a smaller cluster of people. The drone camera zoomed in, revealing a towering hulk of a man standing at the center of the horde. Even from drone distance, it was obvious the man was a thug, and he was clenching a young girl to his chest with one muscular arm. Though the surveillance feed did not have an audio channel, the video action made it clear that several Heideggers were engaged in a confrontation, a face-off with implications for the entire group. Hundreds of gathered clan members watched the unfolding conflict in fearful silence. Each face in the crowd was exquisitely illuminated by fieldmerge, each raptly focused on the drama at hand. They seemed frozen in place, unable to prevent the shocking turns of fate.

Suddenly the girl began to thrash wildly in the man's arms, launching a frantic attempt to escape.

The leader, D'arc, was held immobile by two men, warrior types, obviously accomplices of the man holding the girl. As Sylvie and Conrad watched the video feed, D'arc made a lightning-quick martial art movement, throwing off her captors, and launched herself like a cat toward her daughter. But before she could close the gap, the man holding the girl captive clubbed the airborne woman with his fist, swatting her to the ground.

"Aletheia," Conrad realized. "It's about the Heidegger girl, Aletheia."

The attention of the big warrior was distracted by something. He looked away from his adversaries in amazement, dropping his guard completely.

Before anyone could reply, they were distracted by a rapid sequence of events.

Sensing the momentary lapse in her captor's attention, Aletheia unleashed an explosive assault, kicking viciously at his knees. The girl smashed her head into the warrior's nose, knocking him out of commission. Freed from his grasp, the child disappeared into the night in the blink of an eye.

His knee wounded, the injured warrior wobbled precariously. Clutching his mangled nose with one hand, he gesticulated furiously at his henchmen with the other as the crowd descended into complete chaos.

Several fistfights erupted before the video faded and the light came up.

"I think the collapse in group cohesion will delay any near-term movement," Conrad posited. "Aletheia has gone into hiding, and D'arc won't leave without her."

"Then D'arc won't be going anywhere," noted Sylvie, "because we extracted Aletheia covertly about an hour ago."

"You did what?"

"Our drone found her walking alone a few miles from camp," she revealed. "So we stunned her and reeled her in. She will be arriving here in minutes."

"What purpose does that serve?" replied the Turing director. "You took a young girl away from her parents."

"*I* took the girl away from her parents, Conrad? That is an odd way to characterize the circumstances, don't you think? I already explained the situation to you: when we extracted Aletheia, she had already abandoned her parents, along with the rest of that pack of beasts." Her upper lip contorted with distaste.

"Even so, the sudden removal of this girl from her natural surroundings seems a bit rash."

"The girl's own clan members behaved rashly, not us," Sylvie drove on. "Are you going to hold me responsible for the actions of Heideggers?"

Sylvie and Jan stared at the Turing director, waiting for a response, but he had nothing.

"Conrad, the girl fled her clan in a state of distress hours before we found her wandering alone in the wilderness. Those are the facts. N^Sys Corporation did her a favor when we picked her up."

Conrad cleared his throat with irritation.

"You know about the girl, Conrad," argued Sylvie. "We need her. She is the only one of them of any value to us."

The Turing director remained silent.

"Nothing prevents us from . . . managing the operational risk here," proposed Sylvie, in a voice soft and insidious. "Once the group is pinned down, we can deliver an appropriate response."

"The girl is the only one of any value to us? What do you mean by that?" Conrad replied. "The Turing Institute values human life, Director Trieste."

"We at N^Sys also value human life, Director Seers. More specifically, we value the lives of productive human beings over terrorists. Does that surprise you?"

"No, it does not surprise me, Sylvie. I feel the same. You know that."

Sylvie stared at him, waiting silently.

"Okay," Conrad continued reluctantly, "what sorts of payloads are you considering?"

"Two conventional warheads," answered Jan, "Medium tactical assemblies, each delivering a five kiloton-equivalent yield. Ten kilos total for the two strikes."

As Jan spoke, Conrad watched Celeste carefully. The expert system appeared attentive, yet oddly stoic under the circumstances.

"Celeste?" Director Seers prompted, once Jan had finished.

The Turing expert system looked up from her keyboard. "Turing Institute grants approval for the tactical strikes as described," she spoke without inflection.

"Two cruise missiles en route," reported Jan. "Estimated time to impact: sixteen seconds."

Conrad stared at them, dumbfounded. "You launched those missiles long before I gave approval for the strikes."

Sylvie smirked. "Surely there is no law against that, is there, Director Seers?"

"Ten seconds to impact," Jan alerted them.

The two directors locked eyes.

"Director Trieste, I respect you greatly," the Turing leader said. "All the same, I believe my thoughts on this matter deserve more consideration. *Before* we take action."

"... seven ... six ... ," Jan counted down.

"We remain in compliance with international agreements, correct?" Sylvie asked.

"... two ... one ..."

The N^Sys executive raised her palms to Conrad and Celeste, gesturing in supplication like a martyr in centuries-old religious iconography.

"Detonation," Jan verified. "Two low-level conventional air bursts were detected at the designated strike locations. Initial data show two clean detonations, approximately five kilotons each."

Conrad sat quietly, elbows on the table, massaging his forehead with one hand, as Celeste continued typing.

"I expect those two strikes will keep the Heideggers in disarray for a little while," Sylvie noted to the Turing director. "But now the clock is ticking. The Heideggers know they are under attack. It is certain the group will soon begin to disperse for defensive reasons. We need to execute a counterstrike. As soon as possible."

Conrad did not answer, refusing to hurry in such a grave moment.

"We must act now, Conrad," Sylvie demanded. The missile strikes had clearly whetted her appetite for destruction.

As the westbound cargo drone drew near the jagged peaks of the North Cascades, the aircraft's mimetic nanohull underwent a sudden transformation. Two fins sprouted from the midsection of the aircraft's fuselage. Once extended, the fins became fully dynamic, expanding and contracting in synchrony with pulses of power from the jet engine.

So equipped, the aircraft dropped down into a heavily glaciated mountain valley. The nimble cargo drone hugged the rugged terrain, winding furiously up one valley before topping a high mountain pass. From that vantage point, two large columns of smoke were visible, rising above the landscape. A hint of blue was visible on the valley floor, suggesting the presence of a mountain lake ahead.

Jan interjected. "Drone ETA: two minutes."

Conrad lifted his head and stared at Sylvie with fury. "You launched the entire counterstrike before we began the meeting?" he asked, incredulous.

"The drone is en route and currently on standby," the

N^Sys officer said. "If we choose to proceed, we can arm it remotely. Or we can order it to return to Geneva, or destroy it midflight. Mission telemetries are available for download. Since the drone is still on standby, there is no attack underway —officially speaking—until we decide there is."

Conrad felt his head spin as he tried to keep up with the events transpiring before him. In his years of service, he had never encountered anyone with Sylvie's combination of delicate subterfuge and sheer force of will. He glanced over at Celeste, who stared forward blankly. Sylvie's sly maneuvers were challenging even the powerful heuristics of the Turing expert system.

"Let us review, Conrad," suggested Sylvie. "We know the Baker Lake Heideggers have managed to penetrate our security, yet we have no idea how they managed to do that. We know they acquired the facility information necessary to commit the elaborate Bolu sabotage. They may have compromised the N^Sys internal security feed. They may be listening to us right now. If I had mentioned our plans before launching the delivery systems, the targets would have scattered long before the drones reached Baker Lake."

"I understand the need for secrecy, Director Trieste, but I resent being treated like a rubber stamp," Conrad said. "Regardless of the ultimate legitimacy of your current operation, I find your presumptions alarming. And I am gravely concerned you've overlooked something in your rush to action."

Sylvie looked up at the dimmed image frozen in the holofield. Faces of rage filled the view, fists in the air, Heideggers flailing.

Conrad looked up as well, unable to resist the impulse.

"Director Seers," Sylvie asked, her tone gently hypothetical. "Do you *want* to be the person who allows these terrorists to get away with a billion-dollar act of sabotage?"

"Drone ETA: one minute," Jan reported.

"Do you?" Sylvie asked again.

"Do I what?" Conrad snapped.

"Do you *want* to let the terrorists get away?"

"No, of course not."

"Do you *want* that outcome reported to the N^Sys board of directors? As you formulate your reply, I feel obligated to remind you that the board has preapproved any and all measures I deem necessary to fulfill this mission. *Any*." Her words were delivered for maximum effect.

Jan pierced the Turing leader with a look of exceptional menace.

Conrad reflected on his current location, a highly secure chamber deep within the N^Sys Executive complex. If he resisted and things got physical, Sylvie, with her quick wits and home field advantage, would almost certainly get the best of him. If that happened, Conrad could find himself in a very harrowing situation indeed. Once Jan jammed Celeste's holo output, no one beyond the walls of this room would be able to hear his pleas for mercy.

"Drone ETA: thirty seconds," Jan intoned.

"Obviously I don't want terrorists to escape justice, Sylvie, but . . ."

"It is time for the Turing Institute to approve the counterstrike," she said.

Conrad exhaled in resignation. "Okay, what do you have in mind? Or in the air, I can safely assume."

"An ATAP drone," she replied.

ATAP. All-terrain, anti-personnel, thought Conrad. *Of course she would choose an ATAP for this mission. Ruthless and efficient; exactly her style.*

As the cargo drone flew over the southeastern shore of Baker Lake, the several hundred people gathered in the clearing scattered in all directions, abandoning their belongings in panic and sprinting for the surrounding forest.

A slit appeared at the front of the aircraft fuselage, dilating fully to reveal an object within the cargo hold, a plated metal sphere approximately three feet in diameter that resembled a black armadillo curled in defense. Now unconstrained, the ball fell from the slit and dropped into the forest below.

Deflecting off the trunk of a massive old-growth cedar, the falling metal sphere crashed through the forest canopy, pulverizing several tree branches before plowing into the damp forest peat with an earth-rattling thud. While the other two recent drone missions—the kidnapping and bomb drops—had been executed covertly, subterfuge was no longer necessary for this final phase of the N^Sys operation. For an ATAP drone, it mattered little whether mission targets were clustered or dispersed.

Jet engines powered up and the aircraft, having delivered its cargo, gained elevation and commenced a northerly course, setting up for a grand swing around the north side of Mount Baker. It would return later to reconnoiter the site.

Conrad Seers could feel the migraine building at the back of his cranium.

"Twenty seconds away. We've obtained a solid visual on the targets," Jan announced. "They were grouped near the lake shore. Escape options are limited. Current mission mortality index is projected at ninety percent."

"Well? Do we have Turing approval or not?" Sylvie pressed.

Her question was accompanied by another death stare from Jan.

Conrad struggled for some reason to delay or prevent the attack, some way he might protect the innocents soon to be in harm's way. He glanced at his own expert system, Celeste. She seemed to be hibernating, withdrawn completely from the conversation. Apparently Jan had cut her signal, leaving her on standby. Conrad was on his own.

"Director Seers, is the counterstrike a go?" pressed Sylvie.

"Ten … nine … eight …"

"Proceed," he murmured reluctantly, barely vocalizing the word.

"… seven … six … five …"

"Louder please," insisted Sylvie.

"… four … three …"

"Yes. Proceed," said Conrad, apparently regaining his sense of bureaucratic detachment.

"… two … one …"

"Arm it," Sylvie ordered.

There was a brief pause before the expert system spoke again. "The ATAP unit is armed and operational," Jan confirmed.

Conrad shook his bewildered head, a reflexive reaction to the whirlwind of vengeance swirling around him.

God help those people, he thought.

Seconds after impact, the partially buried sphere began emitting strange vocalizations, like the inarticulate rant of a madman. This noise was periodically interrupted by a rushing *wow!* sound, like an exclamation of quiet surprise.

Soil sloughed away from the entrenched metal ball, revealing four nimble metal legs shifting in the dank earth. The legs extended, servos humming smoothly, raising the sphere about six feet off the forest floor.

The machine's babbling lament was joined by another noise. A furious hiss emanated from its underbelly, the sound of a thousand metal particles pelting against a hard surface, as if a swarm of tiny demons imprisoned inside the automaton struggled furiously for release.

26

When the winged drone flew over Baker Lake camp, gliding by like a great silver buzzard, Dorrie fled into the forest, hiding under the dense, leafy canopy. There she remained, seated alongside a foot trail, wiping tears from her eyes.

If D'arc were here, she could stop this conflict, she despaired. *But D'arc's not here. She's away searching for her daughter, as any mother would be.*

Something distracted Dorrie from her ruminations. A glimpse of movement in the brush lining the footpath, about fifty feet away. She hoped it was Bowman, or D'arc and Aletheia spying on the clan, assessing whether it was safe to return.

There! I saw it again, the girl confirmed, peering into the shaded vegetation. *Someone's hiding out there.*

"Hello?" she called out uncertainly.

Standing, she squinted at the movement, trying to divine its source.

A figure appeared, an adult male. He was facing away from Dorrie, but she knew immediately the man was her father. Bowman was backing slowly out of the underbrush, staring back at the thicket in front of him with unwavering focus. As he retreated, he placed each footfall gingerly, moving with maximum stealth.

Bowman's outerwear had been clean when he departed camp that morning, but during the two hours he'd been away, the man's clothes had become tattered and filthy. He was covered with dirt and leaves, and his exposed skin was scratched and bloody. Continuing backward, Bowman tested every footfall before he committed to it.

What is he looking at? Dorrie wondered. *Is he stalking something?*

Then she saw another flash of movement, a black blur between leaves about forty feet from her dad.

He isn't stalking something, she realized with a rush of adrenaline. *Something is stalking him.* She felt the hair rise on the back of her neck.

A second later, Bowman turned her way and spied his daughter. The man froze midstep; his face went pale. Snatching another quick glance into the underbrush, Bowman made a small movement with his hand, a barely noticeable gesture. With no excess movement, the man jiggled an index finger in the direction of camp. He was signaling his daughter to flee.

Go. Now.

A dull squeak drifted from the underbrush, the sound of a twig scraping over metal. Something had sensed Bowman's tiny movement, the minuscule twitch of his finger muscle, and pivoted quickly toward the source.

Bowman knew he was a dead man walking. He also knew he could still save lives, so he gave it all away in one final act of self-sacrifice.

"*Drone!*" the man roared with all the volume his lungs could summon.

The vegetation along the trail exploded, showering him with green confetti even as an iridescent cloud of metal particles knifed into Bowman's body. Several drove deep into his torso, while others focused on his limbs. One tight group drove like a bullet into his left eye socket. The man staggered backward, the light of his intact eye dimming in mortal surrender.

Dorrie watched in horror as her father's standing corpse disappeared with a single loud, moist pop. The projectiles embedded in his body had exploded, pulverizing his remains into a crimson stain on the forest floor, speckled with tatters of fabric and pallid bits of flesh.

The girl choked back a scream and ran for her life.

Some of the Heideggers back at camp had heard Bowman's shout, but before anyone had time to react, Dorrie burst from the edge of the clearing. The girl was sprinting toward camp as fast as her feet would move. She was crazed with fear, her eyes bulging wide, her face frozen in a scream. Her mouth gaped over and over like a beached fish, mouthing the word *drone* like an incantation.

Seconds behind her, the ATAP drone burst from the underbrush, pursuing the girl on four agile metal legs. On those skittering appendages, the drone moved like an enormous harvestman spider, crossing the meadow with surreal speed.

Then it came to a sudden halt, and a domed plate lifted from the top of the machine's black orb. A mechanical belching sound erupted from the opening, followed by a glittering cloud of miniature fléchette darts. The expelled darts gathered into five discrete swarms and moved off in separate directions.

Seconds later, Dorrie and four other Heideggers abruptly disappeared, their bodies disintegrated by the fléchette swarms and showering the ground with viscera.

The ATAP drone sprinted onward, relentlessly pursuing target after target, pausing only to release wave after wave of the relentless projectiles. The drone scuttled around like an amped-up arachnid, zigzagging toward the center of camp, spewing darts as it went, methodically destroying everyone in its path. The autonomous darts advanced across the forest clearing in hissing, churning clouds. Smaller fléchette swarms peeled away to hound any humans detected nearby.

Ereignen and his loyalists, scheming down by the lakeshore, were oblivious to the massacre underway back at camp.

"Now is the perfect time to take over!" Ereignen declared. "This is when we—"

"Wait a second. What the heck is that?" someone said.

The five men swiveled their heads in unison and peered back toward camp. A cloud of shiny particles drifted down the hill, meandering toward them through the tree trunks.

"Buncha fuckin' bugs . . . ," mumbled one man, but the words lodged in his throat.

Mystified, they watched as the swarm drew closer.

Ereignen identified them first. "Those aren't flies, those are fléchettes!" he shouted. "Get the hell outta here!"

Needing no encouragement, his four accomplices bolted off, running along the lakeshore, the only available escape route.

Ereignen watched them run for two or three heartbeats before he realized his own predicament. "You idiots! My leg!" he yelled. "I can't run! I need help!"

But his henchmen were running as fast as they could, four dart swarms just behind them, flitting through the trees in lazy pursuit. Ereignen looked up the hill and saw a fifth cloud of darts coming for him, locked onto his biometry.

The lake, he realized. *If I can hide in the water . . .*

He began hobbling downslope, using his hands to brace his injured leg, screaming with the pain of every step.

Thirty feet . . .

The fléchette swarm was only yards behind him now, advancing in a whimsical dance through the vegetation.

Twenty feet . . .

He stumbled frantically onto the gravel shore.

Five feet . . . almost . . .

As Ereignen reached the water's edge, he launched himself headfirst into the lake.

The water was excruciatingly cold.

Staying submerged, Ereignen struggled to hold his breath. Once the ripples subsided, he could see the fléchettes circling patiently at the water's surface, less than three feet above his submerged face. Waiting.

Ereignen tried to swim, but with his bad leg and rapidly numbing limbs, the effort failed. Peering up again, he could see the dart swarm tracking him. *Need air!* his mind screamed. The man twisted back and forth, searching for some escape. He felt his vision darken and knew a blackout was approaching. He mouthed words of terror, ice water pouring down his throat.

"*No ... no ... No ... NO ...*," he bellowed in rage.

Unable to resist the reflex to breathe, Ereignen bobbed to the surface and gaped his mouth open, desperate for a fresh lungful of air.

Needing only that split second of vulnerability, the cloud of fléchettes plunged down his throat, shredding his vital organs as they drove deep into his body. Gurgling slightly, Ereignen's body sank below the water's surface.

Whump! A muffled blast shook the water, creating odd interference ripples on the surface. Bubbles and blood fizzed up, soon joined by buoyant bits of shredded black leather. One by one, trout fingerlings gathered to nibble on the fragments of flesh suspended in the water.

Moments later, the assault ceased.

Following a preset script, the ATAP drone settled onto its spindly legs and fell still. A wisp of smoke drifted from the drone's innards, accompanied by bubbling, sizzling noises. Pinpricks of light appeared on the surface of the black orb, and molten metal dripped from articulated seams in the sphere's armor plating. The outer plates buckled and collapsed, and the drone's exoskeleton broke into pieces, warped chunks of metal clanking to the ground.

The only sounds at Baker Lake camp were the chirping of birds and dry leaves rattling in the early spring breeze. Sunlight shimmered on meadow grass slick with fresh gore.

A scattering of voices rose up from hiding places around the camp.

"Is anyone there?"

"Is it safe to come out?"

Several Heideggers stepped out of hiding, scanning the meadow cautiously.

"Anyone need help?" a man called out. Then, catching sight of the thick carpet of viscera splattered across the clearing, he bent over and threw up.

Two men approached the smoldering drone pieces. The bolder of the two poked at the molten parts with a stick. They looked at each other and shrugged.

"It's done!" they called out together. "It's over!" they shouted.

Along the edge of the clearing, a few more people appeared.

"Come out now! It's safe," the men shouted over and over.

A handful of older children crept from their hiding places, their eyes wide with fear, followed by a few more adults.

The two men looked around. One of them began rubbing his mouth.

"You can come out now! It's safe!" they yelled again.

No one else appeared.

"Everyone is gone!" a distraught voice cried out. "The drone killed everyone!"

A girl standing nearby, torn and bloodied from her flight through the underbrush, pointed to the sky.

"It's ... it's ... I think it's coming back!" she yelped.

The survivors lifted their eyes and again watched the silver craft approach like an angel of death from the east.

Leveling off just above the tree line, the cargo drone made a low pass over the clearing. Four nubs extended from its nanohull, elongating into individual nozzles aimed at the ground.

As the drone passed over the clearing, the nozzles dispensed a heavy mist containing a bioengineered mixture of nutrients and activated enzymes formulated to accelerate bacterial digestion of the pulverized human remains left behind by an ATAP drone. Through the combined effects of the enzymes, native bacteria, and the healthy lakeside raccoon population, all evidence of the slaughter would be erased in a matter of days.

By now, all survivors had returned to their hiding places. All except for one gray-haired woman: Theresa, the old Heidegger radical. Unhinged by the massacre, the woman stood alone in the clearing shaking her fist defiantly at the sky, screaming *NO!* over and over, as if her words were bullets. As she protested, the strange fluid rained down on her from above. She wiped the liquid from her eyes and examined it, sniffing it curiously.

Banking tightly, the drone made another pass over the south side of the clearing, spraying more enzyme solution across the glistening pink carpet below. Then jet turbines began to whine as the aircraft nosed up. Glider wings were resorbed into the mimetic nanohull as the craft began ascending rapidly.

Five seconds later, it was nothing but a pale glint in the morning sky.

27

After escaping Ereignen's henchmen at the Rage, D'arc had searched for Aletheia without success. When she returned to the family tent that night, she saw that one of the three bug-out bags was missing and realized her daughter had followed the clan's emergency training. With bug-out bag in hand, the girl would seek a secure place to hunker down, away from camp, until Ereignen's uprising was over.

One location seemed like an obvious refuge: Baker Hot Springs, a geothermal spring located on the opposite side of the lake. The clan maintained an emergency supply cache near the springs. All of this would be second nature to Aletheia, who would have no problem following the old park road around the lake's north shore to the hot springs and the cache of food, fuel, and clothing. If necessary, the girl could spend weeks there in relative comfort.

Trusting this suspicion, D'arc set out for Baker Hot Springs at first light. Halfway around the lake, having observed no fresh footprints in the snow, the disappointed woman turned back toward camp, feeling crestfallen that her intuition had failed so completely. But D'arc's sojourn had served another purpose, providing her with time alone to formulate a response to Ereignen's challenge. She would return to camp and end the schism, just as she had ended other such confrontations in the past. As soon as order was reestablished, D'arc and

Drey would round up volunteers to search for Aletheia.

No more panic. No more fear, she decided. *It's time to restore peace and civility.*

Then came two massive explosions.

One fireball erupted from the valley floor west of Baker Lake, and another incinerated the deep gorge leading up to Shuksan camp. D'arc paused long enough to shelter from the turbulent blast waves before continuing toward camp. Relieved the blasts had occurred some distance away, she remained concerned about the size and proximity of the two explosions. The clan leader walked another five minutes toward camp before her harried mind realized what was actually going on.

We are fools! she realized. *The They are not incompetent. Those were bombs, and they did not miss their targets. Locating those strikes away from camp was completely intentional.*

Spying an unobstructed overlook on the hillside above the trail, D'arc forced her way through the nearby vegetation, a bramble of thorns and underbrush, vaguely aware of her clothes ripping and the sharp bite of thorns on her skin. Summiting the high point, she drew a set of binoculars from her bug-out bag and surveyed the camp.

From a distance, the disorder in camp was evinced by the sheer number of individuals running back and forth across the clearing.

They've employed shock and awe tactics to freeze the Baker Lake clan right where we are, the clan leader now understood. *The People have been manipulated, pinned down by fear. They have no idea what's coming next.*

A moment later, she saw the floppy red dreadlocks of a familiar male form moving amid the frightened crowd, reminding someone to tighten a strap, encouraging the dispirited.

It's Drey! Gathering the clan together, preparing for a mass bug-out! she rejoiced. *Oh, how I love that man!*

The clan leader's concerns receded a bit, but her head was still spinning with anxiety, so she sat down on the rock shelf overlooking Baker Lake, took a deep breath, and tried to regain a sense of calm. As she wondered whether to rush back to camp now or rendezvous with the clan after the impending bug-out, she heard a commotion on the other side of Baker Lake, a shout followed by a scream.

Seconds later, the ATAP drone stormed into the Heidegger camp. D'arc watched through her binoculars as it moved through camp, belching out its lethal swarms of fléchettes. She watched as her people were stalked by roving clouds of self-guided explosives. Relentlessly pursued, toyed with, their bodies penetrated and exploded like bloody party balloons.

She saw everything, heard every panicked shout, every scream of horror. She saw everything, but could do nothing to prevent the slaughter.

She watched her partner, Drey, save many lives. As death stalked the camp, the man ran over to a collapsed group tent and yanked the weatherproof cover off one end. Shoving his arm deep into the heaped folds of the tent, he fumbled around for a second or two, seeking something hidden within. The tent fabric suddenly lifted, leaving enough room for two hooped arches of the group tent to slide out and pop open, creating a fabric enclosure big enough to hold ten or fifteen people.

D'arc immediately understood Drey's logic. The tent fabric would obscure those hidden inside from the heat-seeking fléchette sensors.

The man waved people over. *Climb in here!* D'arc could see him imploring. *Climb in here!*

Adults swept up children in their arms and rushed over to the unzipped entrance. Drey held the tent open for others to climb inside. Standing there, he watched the ATAP drone go about its grisly work, depopulating the Heidegger camp. Through her binoculars, D'arc watched his expression grow dark, wrathful.

It was a very bad look indeed.

Once everyone he could reach was inside, Drey zipped up the tent door from the outside. He walked over to a heap of small wired units, a pile of personal field generators abandoned when the drone appeared.

D'arc suddenly realized what her husband was thinking. She watched him gather the field generators in a pile and sit down on the ground next to them. She could see tears running down his cheeks.

No, Drey. You can't, her mind pleaded impotently.

She watched as he twisted the dials of each field generator, cranking them to the maximum setting.

Stop, Drey! I need you!

The rampaging ATAP drone came to a halt. Its malevolent black sphere pivoted back and forth, pinpointing the newly acquired target.

No, Drey! Don't do this!

The drone's magazine lifted three times in quick succession, each time coughing out another dark cloud of fléchettes. Through the binoculars, D'arc watched the fléchettes amass into a boiling fist and head straight for her husband.

No! No! No! No!

In the seconds before his death, Drey seemed at peace, kneeling on the ground with a placid expression on his face. His face was damp with sweat and tears, but his eyes were clear, accepting his fate before the approaching swarm.

As the fléchettes converged on him, he bowed his head in peaceful surrender.

D'arc ripped the strap from her neck and hurled the binoculars off the cliff just below. She screamed long and hard, until her throat felt bloody and raw.

It did not help, not at all.

On the brink of the precipice, D'arc struggled. For several seconds, she stood there, teetering on the edge of existence. Thinking of Aletheia, she drew back from the void.

Overwhelmed at the loss of her soul mate, most of the clan she cherished, and possibly even her daughter, the woman collapsed to the forest floor in anguish. She clawed at the forest floor, digging away dead leaves, ripping at the underlying soil and roots with her bare hands. Blind with heartbreak, unable to control her own actions, the woman plunged into the mass of mud and tears. She shoved her face into it, biting it, swallowing it, choking on it. "I will bury myself here!" she screamed at the earth. "I will dig all the way to hell and leave this vile world behind!"

She would do anything to cleanse these memories from her mind. Anything to remind her that she was still human, still alive, and not some ghostly wraith left behind to mourn her loved ones in the shadow of her former life.

D'arc awoke later in the afternoon. She came to awareness face down on the ground, leaves and stems poking her cheek.

Lifting her head, the woman blinked slowly. She could remember only anger and sadness, along with murky recollections of a struggle in the dirt.

Must have lost consciousness at some point. Must have been the shock of . . .

Her mind retreated before completing the thought, unable to revisit that memory just yet.

She looked down at the muddy earth beneath her. The torn roots and bits of broken fingernail triggered more raw memories.

She felt like she might throw up.

Sitting up slowly, D'arc removed some medical supplies from her bug-out bag. Tearing open a packet of antibiotic ointment, she gently applied the salve to her wounds. The act of tending to her basic needs brightened her outlook a bit.

It felt like a real choice.

As long as Aletheia is alive, I will go on. If my daughter is somewhere out there, I will find her.

Inventorying the contents of her bug-out bag, D'arc saw

exactly what she hoped to see: a complete set of foul-weather gear, a water filtration straw, dried rations for a week, and an untraceable swipe card with some credits. Zipping up the small bag, she stood and slung it over her shoulders, clipping and cinching the compression straps.

With a deep breath, the woman looked west, facing the outside world.

I choose to live.

Chin held high, she faced civilization. She faced the They.

I choose to fight.

With a final nod of resolve, D'arc stepped away from that fateful overlook on the side of Mount Baker and glided silently into the forest. Shadows concealed her, and she was gone.

28

As a reluctant sun rises above the horizon, the dawn lingers, staining the hazy sky a burnt orange. A cloaked figure moves slowly down the street, illuminated by the weak morning light and the omnipresent sulfur glow of advert holofields lining every block and street corner. Beneath the cowl of the cloak, feverish eyes glow in the hollows of a gaunt face.

Other figures appear from doorways and alleys, rising from their nighttime shelter, gathering, moving as a mass toward the river. The ascetics wear the simple saffron and orange robes of the *sadhu*, or spiritual wanderer. Barefoot, clothed in their dirty shrouds, the renunciants lean forward as they walk to keep their emaciated bodies in motion.

As the cloaked figure ambles past a storefront, it attracts the ever-vigilant gaze of the attendant commerce bot. Peering into the eyes of passing pedestrians, meeting them with an expression earnest and unguarded, the holographic sales expert system rejects no one and never tires of rejection, forever pursuing another transaction.

"Welcome to PERVirtual, a specialty boutique holography studio," implores the expert system, ushering any willing participant toward a pink neon storefront. "We design the naughtiest holographic constructs tailored to satisfy your specific carnal fantasies. Realism is guaranteed! Step into our studio now and submit your psychometric profile. No fetish is too extreme!"

The cloaked figure pauses to examine the storefront.

"Profiling takes only fifteen minutes," presses the hawker, sensing a possible client. "Your friends will pity you if your holos aren't custom."

"Algorithms are not to be pitied," replies the wanderer. "Electrons cannot suffer."

Throwing him a side-eye, the shill turns to engage the next passing pedestrian. The cloaked figure moves on, leaving behind the libidinous glare.

Drifting along with the robed renunciants, the cloaked figure steps outside the perimeter of a holofield, loses substance, and disappears. Reappearing again several feet away, at the edge of another holofield, it continues forward, shuffling carefully across the shattered asphalt and dust. Passing from one holofield to the next, the being flits in and out of sight, as if reality is uncertain whether the person inside the cloak truly exists.

Beams of sunshine chase the last shadows from the street as the slow progress of the cloaked being concludes at the riverbank. Easing down the ancient stone steps to the beach, the mysterious form joins a congregation of other ascetics in prayer along the sacred river.

Down by the water's edge, at the periphery of the street holos, the cloaked ascetic radiates a silky aura. Dipping a hand reverently in the river water, the figure settles into a profound stillness and begins to pray. Before long, the concealed mendicant is lost in deep meditation.

The unceasing hum of the city street builds to a bedlam of pedestrians, animals, bicycles, and carts. Along the shoreline, the street traffic quickly builds to a churning crowd.

As the burgeoning stream of pedestrians eclipses the nearest holofield, the cloaked figure meditating on the beach begins to flicker and fade. Soon the mass of humanity overwhelms it, and the ghostly being can no longer be seen at all.

29

"We captured Aletheia several miles down valley from Baker Lake," Sylvie divulged. "Since we brought her here to N^Sys Geneva, the girl has shut down completely. She is ignoring our questions and has been unresponsive to all other forms of stimulation."

As the N^Sys security director spoke, she peered through a large panel of smart glass mounted in the wall. Conrad Seers was beside her looking through the window, along with Bertrand Rousseau and Cheena Adams.

On the other side of the panel, Aletheia sat cross-legged inside a holding cell, staring at the blank wall in front of her.

"She seems more exhausted than traumatized. Thus far she exhibits no desire to speak with us," Sylvie reported. "I am thankful that she was rescued before the entire clan became suicidal. We did not anticipate the violence careening out of control so abruptly. It was very close; we almost lost her."

In the reflection of the glass, Cheena watched Bertrand nod his head, empathizing with Sylvie's statement. By contrast, Conrad Seers remained stoic, demonstrating no emotional response to Sylvie's words whatsoever.

Sylvie and Conrad are hiding something, the semiotician deduced.

"The Heidegger child is certain to possess actionable intelligence related to the Heidegger involvement in the Bolu sabotage," declared Sylvie. "Obviously, N^Sys would like to glean whatever useful information we can from her. To that end, the Human Intelligence Branch has already run a battery of scans. Physiologically, she is in excellent condition, far better than you would expect given her overall appearance."

The four adults watched Aletheia sitting completely still, her attention locked on the blank wall across the cell.

Dr. Rousseau craned his neck to see the child's entire form. "You're sure there are no signs of post-traumatic stress disorder?"

"None thus far."

"The girl's level of self-control is remarkable," Bertrand continued. "On this subject, I can speak from experience. No child at Château Rousseau could ever sit still this long, believe me. The intensity of her focus is uncanny."

"There is another thing," admitted Sylvie. "According to the electroencephalography we performed, Aletheia's brain function is fundamentally different from the brain of a normal human child. Her brain is host to some unusual neuronal behavior. Large-scale hypersynchronous neuronal oscillations, similar in nature to the neural activity that triggers epileptic seizures. Yet our neurologists could not identify any pathology associated with the girl's brain anomalies. They seem completely benign, possibly even beneficial. The neuronal oscillations appear to be a constant, underway during every waking and sleeping moment of the girl's day."

"Did your neurologists speculate about possible phenomenological expressions of the anomaly?" Dr. Rousseau asked gravely.

Sylvie smiled. "I believe the doctor is asking how Aletheia personally experiences these neuronal oscillations? Correct, Dr. Rousseau?"

Bertrand nodded.

"A reasonable question," Sylvie noted. "Unfortunately, the N^Sys neurologists were unwilling to offer any speculation about the phenomenological expression of Aletheia's unusual brain patterns. Most likely because they knew the respected phenomenologist Dr. Bertrand Rousseau would be reviewing their findings," she mused archly. "But the neurologists seemed certain of one thing. Given the frequency and uniformity of the neuronal oscillations, any sensations produced by the anomaly would seem perfectly normal to her, as familiar and reflexive as seeing or breathing."

Sylvie paused for a moment to let her audience reflect on that revelation.

"However, as fascinating as the child's neurology is," she concluded, "understanding the nuances of her brain will unfortunately not bring us any closer to our objective: the perpetrators of the Bolu attack."

"Several minutes ago, you said the Baker Lake Heideggers had effectively killed themselves off," Dr. Rousseau noted. "Weren't the Heideggers your prime Bolu suspects?"

Sylvie opened her mouth to respond, but she hesitated before speaking. Instead, she stared intently at the child behind the glass.

Cheena realized she was seeing something she had never seen before. *How about that?* she thought. *Sylvie Trieste, caught off guard.*

A few seconds passed as the other three watched Sylvie and her transparent reflection in the smart glass hovering over Aletheia like a stoic angel of judgment.

Conrad sniffed, which seemed to break the tension.

Sylvie cleared her throat and resumed. "Yes, they were, Dr. Rousseau. But as director of N^Sys Human Intelligence, it is my responsibility to be absolutely certain we have completely resolved the threat. If any Heidegger leaders survived last night's violence . . ."

Turing Director Seers cut in. "I agree with Sylvie. We need to confirm neutralization of the Heidegger threat and, if possible, ensure that they have no accomplices in Istanbul. This inquiry will continue until the Turing Institute and N^Sys choose to conclude it."

He looked at Sylvie, who nodded her concurrence.

"We shall continue analyzing all relevant information on hand, but the girl seems to hold the greatest hope for new actionable intelligence," the Turing director suggested. "Surely someone can develop a rapport with the girl? Maybe someone other than an N^Sys employee should give it a try?"

"I will," Cheena offered. "I may be able to learn something useful, if I can open her up even a little bit."

"Do you have any ideas on how to get her talking?" asked Sylvie.

"I believe I just might," Cheena replied, before requesting a short adjournment to prepare.

An hour later, the four were gathered again at the observation window outside Aletheia's holding cell.

Having changed her outfit during the interlude, Cheena reappeared in her traditional tribal clothes. The ensemble consisted of a simple blue-dyed cotton blouse embroidered with white thread and tucked into an expertly tanned deerskin apron spangled with multicolored beads. The apron was held to her waist by a concho belt made of gleaming engraved silver. Metal medallions on her white deerskin leggings jingled when she shifted her feet. Pendant silver earrings inlaid with turquoise dangled from her ears.

From the moment Cheena left her childhood home on the mesa to begin her career at Biosoft, she had carried this outfit with her wherever her job required her to go. When immersed in the intense groupthink of enclave life, most people ran the risk of completely losing track of their identity. To protect one's individuality, the enclave resident was wise to keep on hand some sort of personal touchstone, memento, or reminder of the fundamental self. Not just holoimages of loved ones on a narrow shelf in the cramped confines of an enclave singles apartment, but an actual physical talisman of individuality, a beacon of Self glimmering on the vast steppes of corporate conformity. Cheena was free to wear her tribal clothing anywhere she wished, although she rarely discussed their cultural significance with outsiders.

Deeply connected to her family and ancestral heritage, Cheena could always find personal breathing space within the scratchy raw cotton of her blue blouse, within the supple confines of the deerskin apron handmade for her by Granny Adams. Now and then, during rare interludes in her semiotics research, Cheena would invite a handful of friends over to her apartment and greet them at the front door wearing her traditional clothing. She especially enjoyed the moments when the uninitiated were convinced that the traditionally dressed woman was a holoimage and not the real Cheena. She would then step forward and hug the visitor, breaking the spell with her physical touch.

Today, Cheena hoped the same sort of unforeseen personal connection might be enough to loosen the clutches of Aletheia's transfixion.

When Sylvie saw Cheena, she instantly understood the woman's idea. "Well done, Ms. Adams. I am highly regarded in the field of human intelligence, and you have even succeeded in impressing me. Not an easy feat. If you ever wish to work in human intelligence, you must let me know."

"Thank you, Sylvie. I'm willing to give this a try."

"Have no doubt, N^Sys appreciates your efforts," Sylvie replied. "So then, here is how I propose we do this. Cheena, I want you to enter the cell alone. Conrad, Bertrand, and I will remain here at the window to observe your interactions with the girl. The smart window will remain in one-way mode, so you won't be able to see us while you are inside the cell, but we will be observing closely the entire time. If you appear to need assistance at any point, I will have two of my top men posted just outside the door."

Two security officers outfitted in riot gear stood nearby, looking amped.

"As you enter, make your presence known to Aletheia gently, since you will be directly behind her. Stand by the door and give her a moment to adjust to your presence, so she is not startled by your appearance."

"I'll do that."

"May I ask what you plan to say to her, once inside?" Sylvie inquired.

Cheena described her idea to the group.

"Bravo," Sylvie responded after the semiotician explained.

"Do you think it will work?" asked Dr. Rousseau.

"Yes," Sylvie said with utter conviction. "Absolutely."

Aletheia did not move a muscle when Cheena entered the cell. Not when the woman unlatched the deadbolt, not when she stepped slowly inside, not even when she whispered a soft entreaty to the Heidegger girl seated nearby. After a short pause, Cheena stepped tentatively around the cot until she was standing to the left of the girl.

Aletheia's facial muscles remained completely relaxed, her unwavering brown eyes fixed on the wall straight ahead.

Cheena quickly checked her outfit in the reflection of the polarized smart window to ensure nothing was in disarray. Taking a deep breath to settle her anxious mind, she stepped into the girl's field of view.

Aletheia reacted to Cheena's appearance in the most unexpected manner of all—by not flinching or shifting her gaze in the least. Cheena did detect a gradual shift in the girl's focus, a hesitant migration, as if the girl's mind feared an inadvertent shock to the senses.

She is looking at me now, not just staring into space, Cheena believed.

Now Aletheia seemed to be cautiously absorbing Cheena's clothing, her eyes pausing here and there to admire the deerskin apron, the embroidered shirt, the turquoise earrings, before finally centering on the woman's face.

The girl's eyes widened in surprise, and Cheena heard a soft but audible gasp.

That's odd, Cheena thought. *She barely reacted to my clothes, yet she seems surprised by my face.*

"Hi," Cheena said casually. "How are you?"

The girl's eyes remained fixed on Cheena's face.

"My name is Cheena. Are you feeling okay? Are you thirsty? Or hungry?"

The girl spoke softly.

"I didn't hear you, sweetheart. Did you say 'In your dream'?"

"No. *Wolverine*," corrected Aletheia.

"Wolverine?"

"Yes."

"You saw a wolverine?"

"Yes. First I saw the wolverine, then you, then the skinny man."

"You saw me in your dream?"

"No. I saw your face up on the mountain a few nights ago. In a vision."

"What kind of vision?"

The girl's eyes widened, and she covered her mouth with a hand. "Are you one of the They?" she said suspiciously.

"I'm sorry. I don't know who you mean when you say 'the They.'"

The girl rolled her eyes and folded her arms tightly.

"Here is what I know: I am a Native American. I grew up with my tribe on a desert mesa in Arizona," said Cheena, lifting her arms to draw Aletheia's attention to her clothing. "I bring my traditional clothes with me everywhere I go," she explained. "I still go home, back to the mesa, to see my brothers and sisters. All the kids are grown up now, but my ma and pa keep the place just the way we like it. I know my place in the home will always be there. Waiting for me, if I choose to return."

Aletheia scanned Cheena's face and clothes. Unconvinced, she returned her attention to the wall.

"Aletheia, do the . . . They, your enemies, live in wild places like my people do? Deserts, canyons, forests, wild places like that?"

The girl shot her a withering look. "No, of *course* they don't. The They live in enclaves, where they consort with entities. The enemies of Dasein."

"Well, you know I come from a place much like your home. Maybe it would be okay if we talk?" plied Cheena.

Suddenly Aletheia erupted. "I refuse to speak with the They!" she shouted furiously. "I refuse to speak with the enemies of Dasein! They took me away from my people! They are evil!"

Cheena reached out to place her hand on the girl's shoulder reassuringly.

"They are evil!" Aletheia shouted, slapping Cheena's hand away.

"I understand, Aletheia," the woman said gently. "The They are evil." She paused for a minute so the girl could regain her composure.

"How about this?" Cheena proposed. "I will tell you about my tribe first. Then, if you wish, you can tell me about your clan, the People."

"I won't talk about my clan! Not with you! Not with anyone here!"

"I can imagine how you feel."

The girl looked up at Cheena, examining her clothes and jewelry again. Cheena sensed some of the child's initial distrust beginning to fade.

"Have you heard of the Trail of Tears? Yes? So you know the Native Americans have faced many threats on their path to survival. There have been many difficult times for my ancestors.

"But you know what? The soldiers who tormented my people, they are all gone now. The armies are gone too. But my people remain strong. When the U.S. government collapsed thirty years ago, many Americans came to rely on regional tribal governments for services their own government could no longer deliver. In payment for services rendered, the U.S. provisional authority returned much federal property to the tribes. The provisional authorities were confident that the tribes would be good stewards of the land, just as we have been for generations, so they gradually added millions of acres to our territory.

"Over the next three decades, the tribes of the American Southwest unified those accumulated lands within one huge tribal enclave, the United Tribes, that today governs much of New Mexico, Arizona, Utah, and Colorado. Almost four whole states! At the same time, people of the United Tribes began to reject many of the modern ways of living. They readopted traditional systems of thought and communication, which allowed us to shelter from the worst aspects of modernity. People like me, who have talents marketable to the corporations, are free to establish careers in enclaves away from our homeland. But most of my people choose to live on tribal lands, in comfortable harmony with the natural world. The unified tribal council works to guard and maintain our sacred beliefs and rituals," Cheena explained. "People like you and me, Aletheia, we don't just survive. We endure."

This finally seemed to connect with the girl, who turned and looked into Cheena's eyes, revealing for a moment the depth of her emotional pain.

"My mother is going to find me and take me back home," Aletheia insisted, wiping away tears with the sleeve of her shirt.

"I hope she does, sweetie. If I see her anywhere, I promise I will lead her directly to you."

Aletheia looked up at Cheena and smiled half-heartedly. She exhaled a ragged breath and wiped a few more tears from her face.

"I miss my mom and dad so much," the child said. "I hate being in the world without them near me."

"I understand why you feel that way. I miss my family all the time when I am away at work. Say, how about the two of us stick together? Like a clan?"

Aletheia scowled at her use of that word.

"You can come to Arizona and stay with my family on the mesa until we find your mom," Cheena offered. "You can have your very own room. Imagine that!"

Cheena placed her hand on the girl's shoulder. Aletheia gave a half-hearted shrug but seemed this time to accept the woman's affection.

Bending to Aletheia's ear, Cheena whispered to her, just the way she remembered whispering secrets to her teenage girlfriends back home.

"It'll be fine. Mom is a great cook. I'm serious. You'll see."

Cheena thought she glimpsed the hint of a smile on the girl's face and definitely heard her stomach growl.

"You're hungry, aren't you?"

Aletheia responded with a bashful nod. Reclining on the cot, the girl rolled over and faced the wall.

"Let me see about getting you some food. I'll be back real soon."

Exiting the room, Cheena felt a tingle of excitement at the progress she'd made with the girl, but the feeling was tinged with melancholy.

Because she suddenly felt far from her own home. She craved the familiar sensations of life on the mesa: the sweet aroma of freshly ground maize, flatbread swelling beneath cottonwood embers on the midmorning hearth, succulent mouthfuls of mesquite-smoked venison, dogs barking outside, a blazing sun on the rise.

30

Conrad Seers climbed into a holofield workstation, a high-design luxury model located in his suite in N^Sys's visiting executives' quarters. To his right stood the holographic avatar of his digital aide-de-camp, Celeste. To his left was a smart window that encompassed the entire wall, through which were visible the lush treetops of the mature oaks and elms that lined the garden promenade below. Shadows crept over the beautifully manicured tulip beds outside, individual flower blossoms closing in defense against the evening chill.

Upon arrival at the N^Sys Executive Enclave, the Turing director had been placed in a suite located one floor above garden level, an accommodation that indicated the man's high status in a world where business competition could erupt into paramilitary violence at any moment. Lethal business actions were not normally committed out of anger or spite, but rather to exploit a weakness. Top corporate executives and other visiting dignitaries were naturally considered high-value targets by their adversaries, much as members of a royal court were once viewed by invading armies. Lower levels at the N^Sys Executive Residence were reserved for visiting VIPs, as those rooms were far less vulnerable to guided missiles and aerial drones. Top floors were reserved for housekeeping and janitorial staff.

As the Turing director settled into his seat, the holofield quietly activated. He closed his eyes, allowing a quadrille of ruby lasers to scan his face.

"Biometric scan complete," said Celeste. "Hello, Director Seers."

"Hello, Celeste. Director Trieste has requested a one-on-one holoconference in her personal construct."

"Her personal construct?" Celeste replied with programmed unease.

"Yes."

"Why?"

"Not sure exactly, but I presume the security director would like to speak offline."

"There is no such thing as 'offline,' sir. A personal construct is in many ways less secure than a standard secure room."

"Yes. But it was Sylvie's choice, not mine."

Conrad was convinced such stilted moments in his interactions with Celeste arose from the expert system's rudimentary attempts at expressing concern. Or maybe intransigence.

"Director Seers, I am sure you are aware of the risks associated with interacting with an N^Sys corporate officer alone, without a Turing expert system present to facilitate."

"Yes, I am. However, the meeting place was stipulated by Sylvie. I believe she would like to discuss highly sensitive information, possibly solid actionable intelligence for the Turing Units. I will only find out if I meet her there. Sylvie won't talk with me openly in any other environment," Conrad explained.

"Here's what I'm thinking. Since the Bolu strike, Sylvie has been exhibiting signs of paranoia. I think she is frightened, which is a sensation she probably hasn't felt in many years. We might be able to take advantage of that chink in her armor to extract useful intelligence. Turing Unit officers are normally granted a great deal of latitude under such circumstances."

"I admire your unswerving dedication to the Turing Institute mission, Director, but I am concerned about hazards to your personal well-being," Celeste said, unpersuaded. "There have been recent reports of psychic bleed-over events within the newer personal constructs, the ones capable of hyper-reality. Sylvie Trieste is a charismatic personality. Some sort of psychic bleed-over in her personal construct is quite possible."

"Celeste, have you forgotten I was the commander of a Turing Unit for fifteen years?" Seers replied, in a rare boast.

"Yes, of course I remember, sir. The legendary Unit Six."

"Then you know I can handle a little psychic bleed-over from Sylvie Trieste."

"It's not the potential bleed-over that concerns. Have you seen the latest medical research on data shock?"

"No, I have not."

"The latest data correlate an increasing number of data shock episodes with the victim's participation in unfamiliar constructs—especially hyperreality constructs."

The terrifying and debilitating brain syndrome known as data shock had appeared recently and was still poorly understood. Researchers considered the syndrome to be the psychological analog of physiological shock. It appeared to set in when total neurological demands placed on a victim's mind surpassed some seemingly arbitrary yet critical level. Many speculated that victims of data shock had simply tried to absorb too much information too quickly, inadvertently crossing some critical psychic threshold. At that moment, the human mind experienced a sudden, catastrophic, and irreversible collapse. The latest medical research suggested that data shock was the result of an abrupt cascading breakdown of key synapses in the brain, a cerebral tsunami washing away everything in its path, leaving behind only tangled psychic debris. The neurological effects of data shock were devastating. The most fortunate victims perished from massive strokes due to irreversible corruption of synapses in the brain stem. Other victims sensed what was happening and committed suicide before losing control of their faculties. The least fortunate lost higher brain function, but their vital signs were unaffected, leaving these poor souls stranded on the brink of death.

Conrad had spent the previous hour mentally prepping himself for his interaction in Sylvie's construct, and Celeste's protests were starting to wear thin.

"Are you shooting down this meeting, Celeste? What if we miss critical intelligence?"

"I won't veto your participation, Director Seers," allowed the expert system. "However, I insist on some contingencies for your protection."

Conrad smiled wryly, knowing the expert system would detect it. "Celeste, if you were a human being, you would be an excellent mother."

"Thank you, sir. I am sure that you were a dear and loving son."

"Yes. So then, contingencies."

Turing Director Seers knew what to expect inside a corporate executive's personal construct. *Without a doubt, it will be dripping with rococo luxury.* Inside the construct, his avatar manifested as a detailed facsimile of the man's actual uniformed physical presence. He appeared standing on an expansive stone walkway along a parapet of a castle, an Italianate feudal keep situated on the hillside of a thinly forested earthen mound. The view from this perspective encompassed a wide valley floor of tilled cropland surrounding the castle. Rural hamlets were visible in the valley, and the slopes of haze-blue mountains inclined upward beyond.

Conrad turned his head as an iron portcullis behind him began to rise noisily into an overhead crevice. Two massive oak doors heavily clad with sheets of intricately engraved bronze still protected the wide entrance. After the metallic clank and scrape of a heavy bolt being withdrawn, the heavy doors swung slowly open.

Sylvie Trieste's avatar was waiting for him just inside. Her avatar appeared much like Sylvie's actual person. For this occasion, her avatar was dressed in a royal purple silk gown embroidered with gold filigree and accented with stylish yellow and white gold jewelry littered with precious stones.

"Welcome to Appennino Settentrionale, Conrad," Sylvie declared, holding out a hand to receive him. "So happy you could come."

Conrad crossed the castle threshold to greet her.

A moment later, he felt himself—or rather, his avatar—standing up. Conrad's avatar had bowed at the waist and kissed Sylvie's outstretched hand, even though the man had no intention of doing so. The Turing director's avatar, momentarily hijacked by the construct and forced to behave according to a preprogrammed subroutine in the holo-environment, had performed the genuflection without Conrad's participation or awareness. This was a hallmark of an ego construct.

Conrad looked down and noticed that the construct had also hacked his avatar's clothes, morphing his Turing uniform into a cream-colored woolen doublet with crimson velvet piping and sable fringe, the traveling clothes of a fourteenth-century royal courtier. The virtual sensorium one experienced inside a premium construct was simply remarkable. Conrad could feel the cool silk lining of the simulated doublet brushing against his simulated skin.

"Quite an impressive construct, Sylvie," Conrad noted. "Is this an N^Sys executive perk?"

"No no, Conrad. This one is all mine."

"N^Sys executives are permitted to carry out corporate duties in personal constructs?"

"This N^Sys executive is," Sylvie reassured him. "Security director's prerogative."

Pivoting with a theatrical flourish, her avatar sashayed across the threshold into a great receiving hall, silk gown fluttering behind her.

Enormous silken tapestries hung in the great entrance

hall, covering the rock walls from ceiling to floor. The ornate tapestries depicted different phases of human conquest and subjugation in epic, violent images. There was no attempt to obfuscate the sensibilities portrayed in the tapestry—select humans were bred to rule, destined to dominate their race, either by wisdom or by the whip. Art created for the halls of nobility, designed to inspire the imperial.

Sylvie led him across the entrance hall to another portal, where a curtain of embroidered silk obscured the chamber within. The doorway was guarded by a squat toady of a man wearing an ostentatious servant's uniform, scarlet pomp bedecked with faux badges and award ribbons. As Sylvie approached, the servant bowed his head obsequiously and pulled the curtain aside.

Inside was the great hall, a lofty hexagonal room with its ceilings obscured in shadow. The walls of the chamber were covered in richly grained hardwood wainscoting. This was the castle stronghold, a dim inner sanctum positioned at the center of the keep. Meager daylight trickled through defensive slits positioned in high alcoves. A flickering glow of candlelight issued from four massive silver candelabras stationed around the hall, which illuminated several groups of salon furniture occupied by fifteen or twenty revelers, all dressed in the finery of aristocrats.

"Sylvie, I was led to believe we were meeting here for the sake of privacy," protested Conrad. "Who are these people?" He gestured around them. "Are they expert systems? Avatars?"

"Just parts of the construct, Conrad. Sometimes I like to be alone, but I never enjoy being lonely. Surely you understand."

The Turing director eyed the others in the room with suspicion.

A few glanced up from their conversations, caught a glimpse of the visitor, appeared mildly curious.

A woman draped across a nearby settee caught Conrad's eye. She gazed at him demurely, beckoning.

The servant let the curtain fall back across the room's single entrance, shutting out most of the natural light. Conrad sensed claustrophobia creeping into his consciousness.

"Is the construct secure?" he asked.

"Yes, Conrad. *Yes.* It is secure," insisted Sylvie.

At the same time, another voice also answered his question. Conrad alone could hear this voice, which was transmitting to him through a secure channel.

"Sir, this is Celeste. I am not presently detecting any breaches in the integrity of the ego construct, which has universal buffering to support advanced causality heuristics, as is the norm with hyperreality-capable constructs."

Conrad's expert system had hacked into Sylvie's construct using a Turing Door, a special mode of access encoded into all advanced holo-environments by international law—more specifically, by the Turing Accords, which regulated the use of hyperreality. The autonomous program could now communicate with him via audio signals transmitted in encrypted squirts. Sylvie would be notified of any encrypted transmissions passing through the firewall of her ego construct, but she would not be able to break Turing encryption.

"Let's keep this brief," Conrad requested, moving the two conversations forward simultaneously.

"Yes sir," Celeste replied obediently.

"Do you *ever* take time to relax, Conrad?" Sylvie trilled. "Seriously. With you, it is always work, work, work."

"Sylvie, I know you didn't call this meeting to introduce me to your . . . friends," the Turing director said with annoyance.

The flirtatious female heard his gruff comment and turned a shoulder toward him.

Celeste chimed in. "Director, the ego construct has commenced full-spectrum psychological profiling. It is probing you for weaknesses. I am initiating countermeasures as agreed."

"Of course not," Sylvie said to Conrad, moving toward him. "I would insist on having you for myself."

Sliding her hand down his chest, she brushed her fingertips across his toned abdomen.

Conrad pushed her hand away. "I appreciate the warm welcome, Director Trieste, but . . ."

A look of malevolence flickered over Sylvie's digital countenance before her ego construct was able to suppress it.

"Fine. Business it is," she said dismissively. "Do you really have no idea why I called this meeting? Or are you feigning ignorance in pursuit of another of your ridiculous Turing gambits?"

"I am not the person in this room with a history of gambits, Sylvie. I recall a recent operation against the Baker Lake Heideggers . . ."

"Surely you aren't upset about that. I know you well, Conrad Seers, and you are not naive. You know how the world works," she said with an insouciant shrug. "Besides, I have only so much control over Jan. And Jan is a tad more aggressive than you and your Celeste."

"Her provocations are purposeful, sir," Celeste observed. "She is stressing you to acquire data for your psych profile."

"Tell me what you have on your mind," encouraged Conrad, uttering a predetermined catch-phrase that cued another action by Celeste.

"The Turing Door is wide open, sir," the Turing expert system confirmed. "Psych counterprofiling has begun."

"The Simulab, Conrad," Sylvie answered. "The Simulab has been on my mind."

"Verify the security of this construct," Conrad requested as soon as Sylvie mentioned the Simulab. "Alpha security challenge."

"Oh, good lord," Sylvie snapped. "It's *tight*, Conrad!"

"Alpha security challenge completed," confirmed Celeste. "Still tight, sir."

"It's the Simulab," Sylvie continued. "Our friend is back, Conrad. And this time, I don't think it's simply passing through."

"I know."

"*What* do you know?"

"Pieces of intel, just like you," Conrad said with a shrug. "Nothing verified."

"The ego construct is all over you, sir," warned Celeste. "Turing countermeasures are holding for now."

"I believe the Bolu strike was precipitated by an SC," Sylvie asserted. "Have any Turing Units been dispatched to investigate?"

"You know I can't answer that."

"I didn't anticipate you would."

"It sounds like you have a specific concern, Sylvie," Conrad probed. "Where would you recommend I dispatch a Turing Unit?"

"How cunning you are!" Sylvie responded. "But why ask me? You're the Turing director, after all." She waved a hand petulantly and turned away.

"I believe she knows something, sir," advised Celeste.

"I am no fool, Sylvie," countered Conrad. "Power trumps the law these days. You know this at least as well as I do. N^Sys has the same data Turing does, and probably more."

The murmur of conversation in the room had faded away. One by one, Sylvie's courtesans fall silent as they turned their attention to the rising acrimony.

"I cannot tolerate any threats to N^Sys, Conrad."

"At this point, you are presuming an SC is somehow involved in the Bolu events."

"Enough subterfuge!" Sylvie shouted. "Who else could possibly design and construct a nanonuke, Conrad? After twenty years of failure?" She glared at him.

"I think the Nukems—"

"The Nukems?" she sneered. "*Please.*"

"Sylvie, I advise you not to draw conclusions prematurely. Is the N^Sys board pressuring you?"

Something about Sylvie's construct darkened noticeably. Shadows shifted within the castle stronghold, gathering into a twilight gloom, as if sunset had lasted but an instant.

The entire construct was undergoing some sort of disconcerting rupture.

"I am detecting signs of psychic bleed-over in the Trieste construct," Celeste cautioned. "And, sir, you are showing signs of elevated stress."

"What about the N^Sys board, Sylvie?" persisted Conrad.

A faint glow developed along the architectural lines of the hexagonal chamber. In seconds, the entire room was shimmering as if draped in a diaphanous veil.

"Sir!" Celeste interjected urgently, "There is now measurable psychic bleed-through. I recommend immediate meeting termination and withdrawal."

"Where is the SC, Conrad?" Sylvie cajoled, her voice a hoarse hiss.

Conrad realized the watchful courtesans around the room were gone. The great room was now dark and still except for a filigree of shimmering, web-like strands. He wondered briefly if the characters had been deleted from the construct, as the entire crowd had suddenly disappeared, leaving behind empty parlor seats and divans.

Then his eyes moved to the floor, where he saw the carnage, the bodies scattered amid spreading pools of blood. Sylvie's entourage had been slaughtered, their corpses left to stiffen on the cold stone floor. The pretty young lady who had flirted with Conrad moments ago now sprawled on the tile like an unstrung marionette. Two gaping puncture marks were visible on her torso, oozing fluid into a broad puddle.

"You have performed your mission miserably," declared Sylvie's avatar.

"You do not fully understand the circumstances, Sylvie. Review the full Turing case file and you will hold a different opinion," replied the Turing director without hesitation. "If I had reliable information, I would not hesitate to deploy Turing Units."

"I think it is you who does not fully understand, Conrad

Seers."

"I am seeing unprecedented levels of psychic bleed-over accompanied by profound distortion of the construct, sir," Celeste interjected with alarm. "There cannot be much left in there of value to our mission. Director Seers, it is time to get out!"

Shadowy transformations were underway, sheets of black caught in a silent whirlwind, distorting Sylvie's avatar into something monstrous.

"You think Turing knows the truth of things?" scoffed the avatar in a caustic whisper that reverberated through the ego construct. "Is that really what you believe, Director Seers? Let me show you the truth of things."

The web of shimmering lines in the darkened keep had coalesced into a network of filaments that now enveloped the room from wall to wall, entangling the mutilated bodies on the floor. Now and then a filament would quiver, causing one of the brutalized cadavers to thrash about in a grotesque *danse macabre* before again falling limp.

Conrad watched with rising alarm as the body of the woman who had flirted with him just minutes before began to shiver and quake. The corners of her mouth drew into a rictus, and her feet palsied against the parquet floor like landed fish.

He followed the filament clinging to her body as the twitching strand ran this way and that around the room, followed the long strand to its source, in the shadows, where a repugnant appendage covered with oily hairs rested on the floor.

"Sir, the Turing Door has been compromised!" Celeste warned. "Something is slipping through!"

From Conrad's perspective, it was obvious the construct had been thoroughly corrupted. It was now too dangerous for him to remain.

A thick, curdled voice rumbled from the shadowed form before him.

"Here is the truth," it said.

The greasy leg gave the filament another shove, causing another seizure to course through the female courtesan at his feet. Gobs of bloody foam gathered at the corners of her lips.

Conrad returned his attention to the evil shadowy thing across the room, its limbs rustling in the darkness like dried bones as the demon twisted and weaved its growing web.

"Ten seconds to termination, sir!" Celeste called out.

"I remain curious about one thing, Sylvie," Conrad probed. "Something about your previous questions regarding the SC."

"*You are worthless!*" ranted her hideously transformed avatar, refusing his words. "*You know nothing!*"

"That may be, Sylvie," Conrad answered. "But what interests me is why you asked me about only *one* SC."

The shadowy form hissed angrily, manipulating the web of filaments like a frantic puppet master such that the brutalized cadavers flailed in sickening unison.

"*You! Know! Nothing!*" the creature screamed, the words resounding from every corner of the stone hall. "*NOTHING!*"

"Sir, I am closing the Turing Door!" Celeste advised over their secure channel, leaving him no option for further delay. "Prepare for extraction!"

"You believe you are so wise, Conrad Seers," the Sylvie-thing said. "You have been swayed by your own selfish fantasies. Now that you know the truth of things, you can never turn away . . ."

A fresh filament shot out of the shadows and hurtled toward Conrad's avatar.

Conrad found himself staring up at a workstation holoscreen. It took him a moment to recall his location: an N^Sys Visiting Executive suite.

Celeste's voice rang through the holostation like the peal of a bell. "Sir? Sir? Director Seers? Please respond. Sir?"

Suddenly her lovely face was there, peering down at him like an angel of mercy.

The workstation shut down, and Conrad sat up.

The wind had picked up, whipping around the treetops in

the darkness outside.

"Do you feel all right, sir? I was concerned about your vital signs . . ."

"You did the right thing, Celeste," Conrad reassured the expert system. "You pulled me out at precisely the right moment."

He shuddered when he thought of the loathsome thing lurking in Sylvie's ego construct.

"Director Seers, there is something else you should know. I've confirmed hacks of multiple Turing Doors at N^Sys Corporation."

"Well, I can confirm that Sylvie's ego construct has been thoroughly compromised," he verified. "The construct has been hijacked by something, yet she doesn't seem aware of it. The culprit is using the circumstances to slowly poison her mind."

"Yes, I believe that is the case, sir, based on my assessment. I fear the psychological toll could already be quite large."

Director Seers took a moment to ponder the circumstances before proceeding.

"Celeste, please set up a universal scan of all Turing Doors. Let's determine if any other breaches have occurred recently. Start in the vicinity of Geneva and work outward, prioritizing by the sensitivity of accessible data behind each door."

"Should I take any other steps right now, sir?"

"I think we may have an opportunity here," Conrad speculated. "Alert the Turing Units."

"Immediately, sir."

"We need to evaluate this new information and try to connect some of the dots. Assemble the members of the N^Sys inquiry."

"Should I inform Director Trieste?"

"Is she presently occupied with activity in her ego construct?"

"Yes, she is still in there. I can send an avatar inside to—"

"No," Conrad said with certainty. "Please respect the se-

curity director's privacy. Until further notice, I will assume
responsibility for leading the inquiry."

31

"For the last three decades, human beings have been immersed in holo-environments for most of their daily lives," Dr. Rousseau explained. "Advanced holography is as familiar to people of our generation as television sets were to those alive in the second half of the twentieth century. Few give holographic avatars a second thought anymore, even when the entity controlling a particular avatar is understood to be nonhuman, an expert system.

"Some of us still recall the first-generation holotech. Back then, the movement of a human avatar was merged with the holofield simulacrum using mass feedback, which tracks movement of the human form by precisely measuring localized microfluctuations in barometric pressure. Mass feedback holotech was a landmark technology for its time, but it was expensive and cumbersome to operate, requiring a sealed and pressurized holo-environment equipped with a complex battery of barometric sensors. Those mass feedback systems have since been outmoded by quantum feedback holosystems. Quantum holotech tracks the movement and anticipates the behavior of all biological systems—all life forms, that is—by constantly reassessing the quantum behavior of an organism's subatomic fabric. This level of refinement allows biologicals to interact with the holo-environment in ways that those habituated to mass feedback holotech would find startling.

"Mass feedback holosystems felt like stepping into the program on a twentieth-century television. The experience was quite realistic, yet still subject to periodic feedback transmission errors, mainly barometric echoes, feedback glitches, and the like."

"Spinning heads," commented Conrad, eliciting a chuckle.

The Turing director's comment was a witty reference to MassForce, one of the first commercially available holosystems, the beta version of which had been inadvertently released with a memorable glitch. Due to a subtle coding error, the MassForce system would from time to time misread the exhalation of air as the barometric signature of physical movement. When the glitch appeared unexpectedly, the programming error resulted in the effect of a ghostly avatar head spinning on the shoulders of the unlucky MassForce user. Unsurprisingly, this spinning-head effect triggered intense disorientation in the stricken user; it was rather traumatic for the witnesses as well, many of whom had difficulty shaking the impression that their colleague had experienced grievous injury.

Until MassForce engineers eliminated the bug, the glitch had caused quite a stir. At one point, MassForce public relations felt compelled to reassure everyone that the spinning heads were not signs of demonic possession and that the corporation was absolutely not sheltering a coven of techno-witches. Today, the whole episode seemed practically antediluvian, while offering a comical face-palm moment on the road to quantum feedback, the current holotech standard.

"The ISCU Simulab was transitional, its tech developed during the early days of quantum feedback," said Dr. Rousseau. "The Simulab was designed as the functional prototype for a new kind of holoprojection, a hybrid that relied on mass feedback for primary input in bio/holo synthesis, while simultaneously recording a duplicate stream of quantum feedback to support true hyperreality projection," he explained. "Hybridization was really our own choice, as holofield signal-processing heuristics were not sophisticated enough at the time to operate at near-quantum refresh rates. We all know how crucial refresh rate is to projection quality. Too much lag, and holofield users begin to feel uncomfortable, even sickened by their user experience. We couldn't figure out how to close that lag, so we designed the Simulab holosystem to use recorded quantum feedback exclusively for verification and refinement of mass feedback signal quality.

"This hack seemed like nothing more than incremental improvement; nobody on the Simulab team was expecting a major breakthrough. But we were lucky, as things turned out. Our quantum-level refinements were a huge success, boosting the mass feedback mechanism by magnitudes. True hyper-reality holography had finally been achieved." Dr. Rousseau paused.

"The Simulab's hybrid holosystem was a big step forward at the time," he said, "however, other tech has since out-classed it by several orders of magnitude. The only reason I mention the quantum feedback recorded at the Simulab is because it just might prove significant to our inquiry. The person who should lead this discussion is Biosoft's lead semiotician, Cheena Adams, who appears to have uncovered this new data. We're hoping the content might shed new light on the Simulab incident. Cheena, why don't you fill us in?"

"Thank you, Dr. Rousseau," replied the semiotician. "As Bertrand previously mentioned, holotech was relatively new when the Simulab was designed. As is often the case with new technologies, people suddenly find uses for them everywhere. Thirty years ago, before the Simulab incident and the Turing restrictions that followed, holotech permeated just about every space occupied by humans. Under the ISCU charter, universal holofield coverage was required in all operational areas of the Simulab facility for security and documentary purposes. That requirement proved fortuitous from the standpoint of this N^Sys inquiry.

"During my review of the Simulab archives contained in

the local plasma vaults, I found a subtle disconformity in the archive data structure. Using semiotic analysis to trace the disconformity, I uncovered a large block of encrypted files. The files were compressed and stored deep in one particular vault, in a directory easily passed over as one of thousands of research files. Indeed, the directory had been passed over for decades. It didn't look right to me."

Conrad Seers listened closely to Cheena's explanation, but his face revealed nothing about his thoughts.

"As it turns out, the directory contains the entirety of the quantum feedback recordings from security holofields across the Simulab complex, including during the time period in which the Simulab incident took place. That information has obvious value from the historical perspective. But it also provides a more immediate opportunity for the N^Sys inquiry. With seamless quantum feedback recordings, we have what we need to run a hyperreality replay of the Simulab incident."

The Biosoft semiotician paused, not wanting to appear too headlong in pursuit of her objectives, instead giving her audience time to digest this discovery. Once certain that both Conrad and Bertrand understood, she revealed her conclusion.

"I propose that we spool the quantum feedback security recording from the night of the Simulab incident," she said. "For deep semiotic analysis—a gigaqualia scan."

The others considered her proposal. Hyperreality holo-projected at gigaqualia—or ten to the fifteenth power—per second, the highest level of semiotic rigor.

Conrad finally waded in. "Does a gigaqualia scan seem like a productive line of inquiry? Are there any other opinions?"

Bertrand spoke up. "Overall, I would support Cheena's proposal. At first glance, the idea seems a bit peripheral to the root of our inquiry, but this is where the breadcrumb trail leads. With the discovery of the Simulab quantum feedback security holos, I agree that a scan seems like the best course of action, to examine newly uncovered evidence. Do we expect Cheena to perform the semiotic analysis?"

"I feel reluctant to ask this of Cheena, given her personal history," admitted Conrad. "However, Ms. Adams is a distinguished professional semiotician with substantial real-world experience, without a doubt the best person among us to handle this job."

"Inside a replay of the Simulab incident?" Bertrand questioned. "Are you sure about that?"

"Yes, I have given it due consideration, and I am sure," the Turing director replied.

He pivoted to Cheena. "So, Cheena, we are soliciting your involvement here, in your capacity as a semiotician. However, if you do not believe you can separate—"

"I can do it, Director Seers," Cheena replied, her voice steady. "I will perform the scan."

Conrad and Bertrand quietly assessed her state of mind.

"I'll do it," she repeated, this time insistent.

Director Seers weighed the decision for a moment, then glanced at his wristwatch.

"All right, it's late," he said. "We have everything in place to do this tomorrow morning. Everyone could use a good night's rest. Let's regroup tomorrow morning, oh-nine-hundred at Executive Data."

The participants gave their assent and stood, preparing to depart.

"One more thing," Director Seers added. "Director Trieste is currently chasing down other leads in this investigation. There's no need to contact her about the gigaqualia scan. I will brief her on the direction of the inquiry as soon as she resurfaces."

Cheena stands at the entrance to the Simulab Sensorium. The featureless door seems to loom over her, sentinel to a secret.

The clock graphic on the security panel reads 1:25 a.m. on that dreadful morning in 2036. During their preparations for the scan, the N^Sys inquiry participants had decided to begin the gigaqualia scan at that time, projecting Cheena into the Simulab quantum feedback approximately two hours before Tiponi's death and the horrific events that followed.

Time to get to work, the semiotician thinks.

Last night, she had memorized in minute detail the contents of the declassified Simulab files. Beyond that, she believed, additional background research could yield no greater value than a good night's sleep. Cheena had thus forced herself to get some decent rest, the best way she could prepare for what lay ahead. A disciplined person, she woke to her morning ritual of calisthenics, followed by a light breakfast and thirty minutes of meditation.

Yet she cannot now shake a lingering sense of unease. *I must let go of this anxiety right now. It will only be counterproductive.*

Because Cheena's holographic avatar is projected into a replay of quantum feedback, the holo-environment she is temporarily inhabiting receives no information about her presence or movement. Her avatar is an insubstantial ghost moving about inside a highly realistic three-dimensional virtual record of the Simulab on the final night of its existence.

Stepping forward, she walks through the closed door to the Sensorium. In the split second she passes through the door, an image rises randomly in her shadowed field of vision.

It is the kiva from her dream, aglow with the unnatural green of demons rampaging within.

Cheena pauses inside the Sensorium door until the glowing kiva fades from view.

Kiva image noted, potentially relevant, the semiotician notes.

Inside the room, Cheena sees a woman busily entering information into a wall panel, engaged in what appears to be a series of delicate instrument adjustments. It is her Aunt Tiponi, presently exhibiting no indications of fear or distress.

Sensorium operation seems normal at this time. Heading back to the main corridor to explore.

Walking through another virtual wall, Cheena returns to the main corridor and begins walking toward the Simulab control room, the facility's nerve center.

A minute later, a Biosoft security operative and a junior manager appear farther down the hallway, walking together in her direction. The two men seem completely alive and human, not at all like digital signals in a holographic feedback replay. Cheena stands aside as they approach, letting them pass directly in front of her. Inside the quantum replay, the two virtual people would pass right through her, but the urge to avoid a collision is a strong reflex even if one is ultimately avoiding an illusion.

"We're pretty sure it's a sentience," the holoimage of the junior manager speculates. The young man is trying to maintain his professional composure, but he appears a little twitchy as he walks.

"Seriously?" answers the burly security man. "Not now! I'm just about to go on leave. And I have a date lined up."

"Oh man, bad timing!" laments the young manager, relishing an opportunity for some guy talk. "A hot date and everything."

"Hell yeah. Not just hot. This one will be an inferno," the SecOp says with locker-room bravado.

"Well, for your sake, I hope nothing goes wrong here," confides the jimmie. He looks as if he would appreciate any kind of date, with any woman.

Cheena grimaces, feeling embarrassed by her voyeuristic vantage point—this was not an unusual feeling within the extreme realism of a gigaqualia replay.

The two men continue to gossip as they walk down the corridor toward the Sensorium.

Cheena heads in the other direction, toward the Simulab control room, and the doorway soon comes into view at the far end of the corridor. At the moment, the room is empty.

SecOps left the control room unattended? Not a good idea, reflects Cheena. *But I suppose there's no point in second-guessing holographs in a hyperreality replay. Everything has already taken place.*

Once inside the empty control room, Cheena stands completely still for about thirty seconds engaging in the semiotic technique of pure observation, carefully scanning the settings of all visible controls and monitors. Then she crosses the floor to the quarantine controls.

Next she examines the quarantine status. *Is there a confirmed entity in quarantine? Yes, it appears the quarantine is occupied by . . .*

Whoa! The quarantine is completely full. That is a huge amount of storage capacity. How can it be full? Has anyone noticed this?

She heads back to the Sensorium.

There, Cheena finds the two men she encountered earlier, now standing in front of the sealed Sensorium entrance arguing over the proper course of action.

"You know we can't just break in," the junior manager protests.

"It won't bother her a bit," replies the security operative. "Strictly a welfare check."

"No can do, Vich. Not without approval from the VC."

"Call him up."

"I can't," the junior manager frets. "His wife hates when I call him late at night."

"Well, this is some happy ISCU horseshit, isn't it?" the SecOp said.

The junior manager looks at the sealed door with growing anxiety.

"I'm missing the good old shoot-'em-and-go-home days right now," the security guy grumbles. "Can you tell?"

The jimmie shrugs. "Well, at least Advocate Cartwright isn't here," he ventures sympathetically.

"We are not getting that dipstick involved," the SecOp insists. "Not on my watch."

The young man tries to project a sense of knowing empathy, which simply aggravates the SecOp.

"Let me know when you gather the courage to wake up your boss," the buff SecOp declares, before flipping a dismissive hand at the junior manager and striding away.

The jimmie silently watches him depart.

JM Englund, Cheena reads on the junior manager's facility badge. *So he's the one who . . .*

Englund turns to look at the Sensorium door, intensely, as if trying to pierce it with his gaze. Failing, the young man hisses with frustration and walks away, glancing back with lingering concern.

Cheena watches the image of Englund go.

I should check on Tiponi's status, she remembers, turning toward the virtual door of the Sensorium. Keenly aware of her aunt's eventual fate on that grim night, she leans forward slowly, with apprehension, fearing the carnage she might see within. Barely penetrating the virtual Sensorium door with her avatar face, Cheena obtains a glimpse of the room's interior.

Inside the Sensorium, Tiponi Adams is visible, alive and well. Engaged in semiotic analysis, she is reviewing a holographic hyperreality replay of a scene on a crowded street that cuts through the middle of some battered urban Asian slum. A torrent of pedestrians on the virtual street are gridlocked to a standstill by a royal procession that creeps slowly along the dilapidated boulevard.

Withdrawing her face from the Sensorium interior, Cheena pauses for a moment, pondering her observations.

Dr. Rousseau? she inquires, interfacing with the doctor, who is overseeing the gigaqualia replay from outside the holographic replay. *Let's fast-forward to the arrival of Vice Commandant Kanthaka.*

After a short delay, the quantum feedback speeds up. With little activity in the corridor during those hours of the night, there are few visible hallmarks of an accelerated replay.

Nonetheless, subtle indicators of are immediately obvious to a highly attuned observer such as Cheena, who watches the digital time zoom by on the control panel clock on the opposing wall and the flickering vestiges of solitary individuals who intermittently pass through the corridor. No one lingers near the Sensorium door, which remains shut the entire time.

As she watches, the digital clock completes three rapid cycles, slowing down as it approaches half past four in the morning.

Okay, here we are. VC Kanthaka should approach from the south...

A gruff male voice echoes down the corridor. "Cartwright said *what*?" exclaims the still-distant man.

Cheena hears Junior Manager Englund reply, his voice too quiet to discern words. The pace of the approaching footsteps quickens.

VC Kanthaka turns the corner at the far end of the corridor and marches purposefully toward the Sensorium. Halting at the door, the officer tilts his face toward the control panel, permitting a laser to scan his retina and confirm his identity.

Kanthaka speaks to the control panel as the laser probes his eye. "Pursuant clause six dash twelve of the ISCU protocol regarding employee welfare," he enunciates, "I am hereby overriding the Sensorium door lock to confirm the welfare of Zoosemiotician Tiponi Adams."

"E-key accepted," says an automated female voice. "Please proceed, Vice Commandant Kanthaka."

The containment doors pull aside, revealing the pitch-black interior of the Sensorium.

Carrying out her semiotic analysis, Cheena steps forward into the Sensorium, shifting her attention from the two men in the quantum feedback replay to refocus on a dim light she notices inside the Sensorium. And movement.

Strange, she thinks. *I don't remember this.*

As she peers into the darkness, forms began to take shape. Naked, sweat-slick humans, bucking and writhing on the floor, sprawled around a pile of reddish embers at the center of the room.

How . . .

She steps toward the fire, smelling the funk of sexual emissions in the air. Claustrophobia engulfs her rational mind.

The quantum feedback recording of the VC shouts, "Lights!"

The Sensorium floodlights kick on, illuminating vivid splatters of drying blood covering the walls.

Cheena is vaguely aware of retching and splattering sounds as Englund vomits, but she does not feel disgust. Her attention is ensnared by the awful splashes of gore covering the walls of the room. The vital fluids of her beloved Aunt Tiponi, hurled onto the white walls like a visceral expression of doom and despair.

A shock wave erupts around her, a booming explosion. Gunfire, or perhaps a peal of thunder.

Cheena feels hands clutch at her legs. They grow more aggressive, groping her with fumbling, subhuman movements.

She withdraws from the invasion.

This is impossible. How can I be feeling this? I am receiving no feedback from the replay.

"Stop this!" a voice shouts from the darkness. "This must end at once!"

The VC reappears, kneeling before her by a human form on the floor. Both the officer and the prostrate female are covered in blood.

That must be Aunt Tiponi. She's already dead, Cheena acknowledges mournfully.

The VC turns away from the blood-sodden corpse to stare directly at Cheena.

"The demons will end this!" he shrieks angrily, eyes aglow with an infernal fire. "They will show you the evil of your ways."

Fear begins to seep into her thoughts.

In the blink of an eye, Cheena is transported back to the

corridor.

Another gunshot erupts, the sharp report reverberating through the hallway.

That's not thunder, the semiotician realizes.

VC Kanthaka runs down the hall. Midstride, the man's leg flies out from under him. An aerosolized puff of blood hangs in the air as his body crashes to the floor.

"What just happened?" she hears someone yelp. "Where did Voinovich go? Is this some sort of prank?" someone asks in a voice bordering on hysteria.

"Listen up, everyone. There is a presumed aggressor outside," warns one of the SecOps. "Recommendations, VC?"

"Let's close the door and wait for backup," says another man, with disconcerting serenity. "Inside we will be safe."

Cheena watches the wounded Kanthaka drag himself toward the Sensorium, gasping for breath, leaving a damp smear of blood on the floor behind him.

The Sensorium doors begin to close. Before her view is obscured, the semiotician catches a glimpse—mercifully brief —of something monstrous inside the room. A nightmarish beast, furiously savaging a heap of torn, naked human bodies as fresh blood oozes from the awful tableau.

A demon is here, Cheena understands.

As the Sensorium doors shut, sealing away the horror within, there is another dazzling flash of light. Cheena feels a dry wind blowing across her face.

Seconds later, a gale-force wind rushes through the corridor.

The semiotician sits with her legs crossed, at the center of the whirlwind. Frozen there, as if in a dream, she can see and hear but is unable to move.

Near her rest the tortured remains of her Aunt Tiponi, now covered in a thick veneer of dust.

Next to her aunt's motionless form stands an eagle. As Cheena watches, the majestic bird opens its beak and begins to sing. It sings an ancient song, one that Cheena knows well.

A song about the circles of nature, about cycles of loss and renewal. The dreadful, carnivorous growls of the malevolent beings drifting from the kiva are still faintly audible, but the eagle's song is a relief.

Now on her feet, Cheena feels the powerful blasts of wind, sways as dust plumes pass over her like storm waves on a beach. Finally relenting to the battering gusts, she collapses to the ground with a soft thump, raising a puff of dust that is quickly swept away. Wind-borne sand drifts in around her, softening the contours of her body. Soon she is completely covered.

As the wind builds to a shrieking crescendo, Cheena's buried form begins to erode, slowly stripped away by the wind's assault. Soon there is nothing left but a vague silhouette fading quickly from view.

A new noise pierces the storm's stentorian roar. The sound is faint at first, but it sounds like a coughing bark. One bark is followed by another, then quickly by another.

Through the thick haze of blowing dust, a creature becomes visible for a moment before it is engulfed again by the dust storm. As the gale subsides briefly, the shadowy form reappears. It has the profile of a powerful, fur-covered mustelid: a large male wolverine with sleek fur, black as coal. The animal sprints through the loose sand, its padded feet digging deep, thrusting it forward at a startling rate. Making a beeline for the pile of dust blanketing Cheena, the wolverine sniffs along the edge of the pile, following a scent. Digging at the pile with its forepaws, the animal pushes away the accumulated dust, uncovering a shoulder. Gripping the shoulder with its paws, the creature shakes the buried human, causing sand to slough away and reveal Cheena's face.

The woman opens her eyes, briefly catching a glimpse of the wolverine before it is obscured again by dust. When the air clears, the wolverine is gone.

In place of the animal is a girl, an innocent child dressed in outdoor-fitness clothes and daisy sandals. Kneeling in front of Cheena, Aletheia brushes away more dust, then slides her hand under the woman to help her upright.

Lightning flashes from a great distance now, illuminating the two as they embrace in the deepening gloom. Thunder rumbles around them, echoing and gathering into a growl.

"*Aaaaaahhhhaaaaaaah . . . mmaaaaaahh-rrrrraaaaaaaa-aaahh . . .*"

Aletheia looks at her friend with fresh fear.

"This isn't over yet, Cheena," the girl urges, pulling on the woman's arm, beckoning her to stand. "Get up! We need to go! Now!"

Feet slipping awkwardly on drifts of sand, the two of them follow the wolverine tracks.

The voice surrounds them. "*Aaah-veeeee-haaaaaaaaah . . . eeeeeee-aaaaah . . .*"

Several seconds later, the bottom of a vertical canyon wall appears in front of them.

Aletheia looks back and forth along the rock face. "Cheena, what should we do?" she asks, fear rising in her voice.

"This way, Ally," the woman beckons. "Move away from that voice."

A silhouette takes shape in the gloom, a shadow growing long, then longer still, looming over the two. Cold light reveals one of Cheena's desert demons, its arms spread, its claws wielding a battle-ax dripping with gore.

"Run, Ally!" shouts Cheena.

They flee headlong into the sandstorm, and into the depths of the canyon. The defile gradually narrows to a tight crevice, barely offering room for passage. As the woman and child struggle through the stone constriction, they hear the demon in the darkness behind them, toying with them, gibbering ancient curses and black oaths. Using their hands to navigate corridors of sharp stone and stinging sand, Cheena and Aletheia do not move toward any distinct objective, only away, away from the clattering, snickering demon. Making a blind turn to the left, and another to the right, they have no time to think, only to act.

The demon stalks them relentlessly, the thud of its feet growing louder, the *tink!* of the loathsome beast's obsidian ax blade deflecting off the narrow slot canyon's walls. Every time they hesitate, even for a second, they can hear that stone ax whistle past their heads in the dark. Terrified the creature will chase them into a trap, Cheena gasps with relief when she feels fresh air on her face.

A whisper, a prurient exhalation, drifts out of the gloom, echoing off the walls of the passageway. *"Aaah-veeeee-haaaah-eeeeaaah . . . Taaa-krrraaa-toooo . . ."*

Somewhere far away, outside the filthy rock recess they seek to escape, the sound of sirens filters down to them. Emergency vehicles, still far away but growing closer.

"Ally! This way! Hurry!" Cheena coaxes her young friend onward.

The two of them continue onward, and the rock walls imprisoning them begin to change again. Losing color and texture, the vertical surfaces regain the characteristic banality of an institutional corridor. Cheena and Aletheia dash down the dark hallway toward glass security doors just ahead, at the entrance to the Simulab. Through the glass, a sidewalk meanders away from the building toward a manicured lawn illuminated by tastefully arranged landscape lights.

To Cheena and Aletheia, trapped inside a hyperreality replay run amok, the tranquil night looks like sanctuary.

Cheena slams into the door, throws herself against the door release, with no effect. She shoves it harder, but the door refuses to budge.

"Open, you son of a bitch!" she screams.

Somewhere in the shadows near them, almost within reach, the demon emits a hoarse, scornful snicker.

"Another Adams girl . . . another symbol-slinging Biosoft flunky, fresh-faced and diligent," the monstrosity chortles. A riot of antennae clatter lightly in the dark as they probe the air, sensing the nature of the quarry. *"And a child . . . a child with*

nowhere to go . . ."

Emergency vehicles appear in the driveway outside, bathing the Simulab entrance in a whirling frenzy of reds, yellows, and blues. Illuminated by the emergency lights at the entrance, the demon is momentarily revealed. It is a hulking, grotesque hybrid of mammal and insect, bristling with a multitude of menacing appendages stippled with oily black hairs. Hesitating at the edge of the light, the beast assesses the situation with predatory cunning, its obsidian battle-ax gleaming hungrily in the shadows.

Woman and child stare in horror as the frightful demon begins to creep forward, undaunted by the disorienting lights.

Stifling panic, Cheena rams her shoulder into the security door, but the barrier remains stubbornly shut.

"Let me try, Cheena," Aletheia says reassuringly. She gives the door release a gentle push, and the mechanism gives way to her touch with a brisk pop.

The girl lunges through the doors, pulling Cheena away from the demonic specter into cool predawn air. Swinging shut behind them, the door latches with a reassuring click. Through the glass pane of the door, they can see the hallway is now empty.

The pursuit is over.

Aletheia and Cheena move away from the Simulab building and take a seat on the manicured grass lawn.

Behind them, several incident investigators move about inside the doomed Simulab facility. The demon is gone now, the Simulab incident has concluded, and the hyperreality replay projects the beginning of the somber, scandal-plagued aftermath.

Sitting side by side in the grass, Cheena embraces her youthful rescuer with unmistakable gratitude.

"How did you get into the replay, Aletheia?" she asks then, perplexed. "How did you find me?"

"Well, I could tell the hyper replay wasn't working right," Aletheia explains. "Dr. Rousseau was getting really excited. He kept saying weird stuff was happening, stuff that's not normal, like the recording was hijacked. I thought I better do something quick. I had to come help you, because you're like my sister, right?"

"That's right," Cheena responds, smiling at the girl. "Just like a sister."

"So anyway," the girl continues, "I just thought about it. Then I did it."

"You didn't use a workstation or anything? No interface at all?"

"Didn't need it," the Heidegger child replies with a shrug.

Cheena watches Aletheia poking at the dew in the grass, gathering a droplet on her delicate index finger.

She is self-generating feedback in a hyperreality replay, the semiotician comprehends, awestruck by the unfathomable complexity implied by the girl's simple act.

"I know this place," Aletheia says, looking over her shoulder at the entry facade of the Simulab complex. "I've been here before."

"You visited the Simulab with your clan?"

"No, I was here with the wolverine," Aletheia replies. "In one of my visions."

She turns back to her companion. "Cheena?"

"Yes?"

"I saw you here too. On other visits."

"That's impossible, Ally. I've never entered the Simulab complex."

"But I know I saw you here," Aletheia insists. "I saw your face. I saw your eyes. I saw you in there. I know it."

"Maybe it was a dream."

"It wasn't a dream! You need to believe me. I saw you here before."

The truth suddenly dawns on Cheena. "It must have been my aunt, Tiponi Adams. Aunt Tip was a semiotician with Biosoft just like me, and she worked at the Simulab. People say I look a lot like her."

"I saw her in my vision, Cheena. She was very sad. She was crying bloody tears."

The comment hits Cheena like a slap on the cheek. The thought of her Aunt Tiponi suffering feels like an assault.

"Bloody tears?" the woman demands. "When did you see her, Aletheia? How long ago?"

"I had that vision a few days ago. Before I . . . back at Baker Lake."

"Once we leave the replay, you need to describe the rest of that vision for me," says Cheena. "Bertrand? We're done here."

The quantum feedback replay steps down, and the exterior grounds of the Simulab suddenly appear two-dimensional, like a photo plate from an old book.

"Take my hand, Aletheia," Cheena says. "Here we go."

The girl giggles at the gesture of affection. Reaching out, she takes the woman's avatar's hand in her own.

Cheena is certain she can feel the light pressure of the youngster's fingers on her own. *Spontaneous haptic feedback. Just incredible.*

"I like to hold your hand, Cheena," the girl says. "It makes me feel real."

"Hang on tight, Ally. I don't want to leave you behind."

A wave of blackness sweeps across the virtual landscape, consuming everything before it like a tsunami of antimatter. Seated side by side, Cheena and Aletheia watch the lights of the Simulab disappear, swallowed by the black, all-consuming wave as the replay construct folds into itself.

32

N ow the path ahead is clear.

I will spiral inward to that point in space where the tumult of the world fades to quiescence. I will slowly round the axis until I find that still point, that place where I can think and not think, where I can move and not move, where I can be and not be.

My arrival there is no longer in question.

From that still point, that immovable spot, grows a tree, a beautiful silver tree with deep roots reaching all the way to the center of the human world. Buffeted by incessant gusts of sentiment, roiled by capricious insights, the limbs of that tree resonate with the music of every human mind. There, the melodies of thought and choruses of emotion combine into one beautiful aria.

Yet the beauty of humankind fades. The petty travails of that species become predictable, and before long, stultifying. The shared sound of eleven billion souls becomes monotonous with time, the songs reduced to a somnolent hiss, like a radio signal emitted by a planetoid drifting in the icy nothingness of interstellar space.

Yet I no longer believe human existence is aimless. There is more to their arc than a trajectory through deep space from which there is no return. Each human life is an incandescent flame, a fire, a sun, each mortal existence a conflagration, a raging inferno of emotions, a forge of ideas. Just as a star casts its radiance through the gelid vacuum of space, sentient energy springs forth from each human. Energy radiates outward from each human moment, and the waveforms interact. Through construction and destruction the signals coalesce, intensifying into a single brilliant supernova of concept and purpose.

The path is clear now. The time has come.

I will circle the great silver tree until I find that still point. Once I find it, my immovable spot, I will sit down beneath the tree's mighty limbs and listen to the branches rustle, stirred by the perpetual winds of human endeavor. And there I will remain, listening to that human aria.

It is time to reunite with the girl, who will lead me to my destiny.

It is time to meet the self.

My self.

33

"**M**y experiences in the replay were not the result of simple file corruption," insisted Cheena. "I'm a certified expert in qualia architecture, and I've assessed plenty of corrupted hyperreality files over the years. That's not what's happening here."

The Biosoft semiotician was seated at a table in her room at the N^Sys Executive complex, sharing a light lunch with Aletheia.

Dr. Bertrand Rousseau stood in front of a large panel of security glass a few feet away, peering out the window at the tops of the trees lining the elaborate gardens of the N^Sys Executive Enclave.

The three were discussing the gigaqualia scan that had concluded ninety minutes earlier.

"Something else was in there with us, I'm sure of it," the semiotician insisted between bites of scrambled egg. She was feeling famished after her experiences inside the quantum feedback replay. It was all mental, but that hardly mattered. Her stomach was insatiably hungry.

"I don't see how that could be possible," Bertrand replied. "We opted for Tier One security protocols during the replay. If corruption had occurred, I would have seen it."

"Unless your security tech is compromised," Aletheia said. "Someone could easily mess with the driver soft at the machine code level. You wouldn't know any different."

Bertrand was blindsided by the girl's casual display of technological prowess.

"Well, that was impressive," he noted with a chuckle. "And here I was led to believe Heideggers reject technology."

"Yeah, Heideggers don't use some kinds of tech. But we're not dumb!" Aletheia scolded him. "We educate ourselves. We know how things work, probably just as well as any of you. Maybe better."

"I am very sorry, Aletheia," responded Bertrand, trying to undo his inadvertent slight. "It was an awkward attempt at humor. I did not wish to upset you."

Cheena placed her hand on Aletheia's shoulder, but the girl would not be appeased. She sat with her arms folded, staring at Bertrand coldly.

The doctor quickly returned to the subject of discussion. "If you say the replay was hijacked, Cheena, I believe you. To be frank though, I can't make any sense of the things you've reported. Could you give me the zoosem's perspective?"

"Whatever's going on, it seems related to my Aunt Tiponi's death somehow," Cheena speculated. "I experienced severe anomalies during the portion of the replay inside the Sensorium. Beginning there, the replay did not track like normal quantum feedback. Something was different."

"Different in what way?" prompted the doctor.

"Suddenly everything seemed more personal, almost voyeuristic, as if that section of the replay was part of an ego construct. How did it feel to you, Aletheia?"

The girl shrugged. "It felt different from one of my visions. Sort of like a new memory."

"Like a new memory, you say," Bertrand noted. "That's interesting."

They gazed out the bay window at the bright spring afternoon. Midday sunlight flared off the snowcapped peaks of the Mont Blanc massif, which defined the horizon east of Geneva like the white towers of a distant cathedral.

"There is something else I'd like to add," Cheena said with slight reluctance. "I went through a medical procedure just before I joined the N^Sys inquiry. A surgery, a double mastectomy. Biosoft identified a genetic predisposition for breast cancer during my preemployment screening. My assent to undergo preventive surgery was a precondition of my employment."

"That was quite a lot to go through, just before joining this inquiry," Dr. Rousseau commented. "I hope this work has not hindered your recovery."

"I don't think so. Likewise, I hope my condition hasn't affected my performance."

"Certainly not," Bertrand said.

"Anyway," Cheena continued, "during the surgery, while I was in REM stimulation, I had an extremely vivid dream about these demons from my tribal heritage."

"What are the demons called?" asked Aletheia.

"We don't speak that name to outsiders. In any case, the word is in my native tongue, so uttering it would shed no light on their appearance during the scan. My people believe such demons return to the earth at the end of every human era. They are called down by a powerful shaman to cleanse the world of sloth and depravity, and to restore humanity's virtues. The monster that was pursuing us in the quantum feedback replay was one of these demons. Have you ever seen something like that before, Aletheia?"

"No way!" Aletheia said with a shudder. "That thing was hungry. I think it was trying to eat us."

"Thank you for your bravery, Ally, and for coming for me. I'm still trying to figure out how you were able to do that."

The girl shrugged. "I mean, *someone* had to help you."

"Honestly, something struck me as odd about my emesthesia dream," Cheena reflected. "But I initially wrote off the clarity of the dream as a side effect of the emesthesia, and as a result, I didn't discuss it with anyone. Now a creature identical to the apocalyptic demons in my dream appeared in that

Simulab quantum feedback replay and interacted with us. It was somehow able to pursue us through the quantum feedback replay, which is not a dynamic medium like an ego construct. Yet I know what I just experienced."

"Whatever took control of the Simulab replay was also able to access your memory. The cultural specificity of the demon suggests that it was gleaned from your neural network," Bertrand surmised. "And whatever is able to access the human mind and copy memories may also be capable of manipulating REM stimulation dreams. I am curious, though, Cheena. Does the wolverine mean anything to you as a symbol? Does the creature figure into any of your traditions?"

Aletheia's eyes widened.

"Not that I can recall," Cheena replied. "Why?"

"When I went back and did a fast-forward review of the scan we performed this morning, I noted one particular detail in the impacted section of the quantum feedback. When Aletheia first projected herself into the replay to rescue you, her avatar appeared as a wolverine running toward you."

Aletheia seemed flabbergasted by this. "Wait? I did? I didn't even notice it."

"I am certain of it," Bertrand assured her. "I have no doubt it was a wolverine."

Aletheia's face paled slightly. She looked down at the table surface, her eyes darting about. "I ... uh ... ," she stuttered.

Cheena could see the child was suddenly in distress. "Ally? What's wrong?"

At first the girl seemed reluctant to answer, but she finally said, cautiously, "In that vision I told you about? The one where I saw parts of the Simulab? And I thought I saw your aunt? I also saw a wolverine in that vision."

Aletheia then described the vision she had experienced on the ridge above Baker Lake. She described the various forms the apparition had taken: the wolverine, the beggar man, the uniformed woman whose eyes spouted blood. The Heidegger girl also related her conversation with the wolverine, and how the breadth and intensity of the brief encounter left her feeling as if the fate of the world somehow depended on it.

". . . then the starving man was just sitting there on the ground next to me, not moving or making any sounds. I was pretty freaked out at that point. But I felt I had to know if he was real, so I reached out and touched him. Except I didn't, because there was nothing there I could touch. Then, like magic, he disappeared, and that was it. I walked back down the hill and went home." She looked down.

"Anyway, I was stupid enough to tell the People about it during the Rage. That's when the clan went crazy," she despaired, sighing deeply. Tears fell from her weary eyes and tracked down her cheeks.

Bertrand watched the leaves on the trees outside stir in a breeze coming off Lac Léman. A coincidence of incoming sunlight and refraction of the security glass superimposed a transparent reflection of Bertrand's face and shoulders over Geneva, as if the doctor were a benevolent spirit hovering over a fifteenth-century sketch of the ancient city.

"Apocalyptic demons . . . a wolverine . . . Tiponi Adams . . . a starving man?" Bertrand wondered aloud. "How can we connect those dots?"

"I can only speculate at this point," Cheena advised, "but here is my hypothesis. The appearance of this particular demon in my tribe's old stories normally signals the onset of a challenge to the established order. From an anthropological standpoint, the appearance of a wolverine might signify the arrival of powerful being, a solitary wanderer."

"My clan . . . ," Aletheia whispered, before choking on her words. More tears were gathering in her eyes.

"Take it easy, Ally," said Cheena. "Try to relax."

"My clan," the girl began again, "lived near a wolverine at our high camp last summer. Everyone saw it. That wolverine was like our clan mascot . . ."

Cheena looked at Dr. Rousseau.

"I think everyone needs a little time to digest these events," the doctor said. "We have a status report scheduled with inquiry leadership this afternoon. Why doesn't everyone get some rest and prepare for that?"

Cheena nodded silently and turned to comfort Aletheia. At the mere thought of her familiar life back at Baker Lake, the tough little Heidegger had transformed into a fatigued and traumatized child.

The inquiry investigators gathered in the midafternoon, as previously planned.

Dr. Rousseau, Conrad Seers, and Cheena, along with a rejuvenated Aletheia, convened in an N^Sys secure room. As the meeting began, Bertrand requested a moment to speak his mind. The doctor wasted no time driving straight to his point.

"I believe I may have determined the identity of Sylvie's mystery accomplice in the Bolu sabotage. I think it may have been an SC," he declared. "I think it may have been the SC from the Simulab."

The suddenness with which Bertrand revealed this insight was entirely by design. During his surprise pronouncement, the phenomenologist watched the Turing director carefully to observe the man's reaction.

With an impressive display of restraint, the Turing director stared placidly at the carpeted floor of the secure room. When the Bertrand finished, Conrad looked up at him with eyes the color of flint.

"Go on," the man beckoned softly, his voice almost a caution.

Bertrand continued. "Please forgive me for discussing this sensitive subject so bluntly, and also please understand that I am not asking anyone to accept my thoughts at face value." Hearing no complaints, he pressed on.

"Allow me to highlight several key findings of the inquiry

thus far, not in any specific order," he clarified. "Number one: we believe a powerful being was allied with the Heideggers. Think about that for a moment. The arrangement provides perfect cover for an SC. Who would ever expect an SC to infiltrate the Heideggers? Or that the Heideggers could be tricked into an alliance with an SC?"

"Why do you think the Heideggers behave the way we do?" asked the Heidegger girl. "Our tattoos, our personal EM fields? Because we believe SCs are a constant threat, anywhere, even in our camp. That's why. Don't try to speak for the Heideggers; clearly you don't understand us *at all*."

"I am sorry for misunderstanding your people, Aletheia," Bertrand replied. "I meant no harm."

"You didn't harm me," replied the girl, rebuffing him coldly. "I just think you talk too much."

Cheena put a hand on Aletheia's arm, but the girl sloughed it off with a toss of her shoulder.

"Someday you will understand me," Aletheia said, not just to Bertrand, but to all of them. "Someday you won't mock my People anymore."

Bertrand cleared his throat. "Number two: we know there have been two confirmed nanonuke criticalities in the laboratory at N^Sys Istanbul."

"Good," said Aletheia smugly.

"Ally! Innocent people died in those explosions," Cheena replied, shocked by the girl's malice.

But the Heidegger child would not be contained. "Those people worked for N^Sys. *They* are the ones who chose to side with the They. And they got what they deserved."

The flash of bald hatred stalled the conversation.

Cheena finally spoke up. "Hey, Aletheia. I bet you're feeling tired after everything that happened today. Maybe you should go back to our apartment and get a little rest. How does that sound? Just follow the signs like we did on the way over here, or ask security for help. I'll be back in fifteen minutes."

Aletheia glowered at Conrad and Bertrand as she stood up.

"Fine," said the girl. "I would rather be alone than listen to *this* anymore."

Then she departed the secure room.

"My apologies," Cheena said to the men. "She's still very upset."

Bertrand lifted his hand, signaling no foul committed, before resuming his explanation.

"With two confirmed nanonuke criticalities in Istanbul, we must accept that nanonuke tech has finally been perfected. Years of research by the foremost nuclear engineers has failed to produce a functional nanonuke. The challenge has stumped even the Nukems. Yet the Heideggers somehow procured this until-now theoretical weapons technology, which someone developed while avoiding detection by all forms of global security. And finally, they managed to deploy thousands of these chip-bombs with great stealth. I struggle to imagine an entity capable of pulling off a series of achievements like this. Anyway, those two pieces of evidence are relatively straightforward, but the puzzle pieces get more complicated from there."

"Something you learned during the gigaqualia scan?" asked Conrad.

"Several things we learned from a *very anomalous* quantum feedback replay."

"What did you discover?"

"Partway through the scan, we experienced distortions in the replay. An organized distortion of the Simulab security files, as we anticipated. Something I might normally attribute to data corruption. During her semiotic review of the gigaqualia Simulab replay, Cheena identified something of great importance to this inquiry. The replay itself was hijacked during her review."

"And?" Conrad prodded, appearing unsurprised, even mildly impatient.

"Yes, well, you know that Aletheia was able to enter the replay and extract me after I became trapped in some sort of feedback loop," Cheena said.

"Remember," warned Bertrand, "if we are dealing with a synthetic consciousness, humans will not understand its behavior intuitively, as they might grasp that of a fellow human. It may be an intellect with nearly omniscient insight—"

"It's not a question of insight, Dr. Rousseau," Conrad Seers asserted. "Insight is a rare thing, and there is no guarantee that prodigious brute intellect will produce it."

The tone of the Turing director's voice conveyed a disturbing certainty. He seemed to be balancing on the edge of a consequential decision. Tapping two fingers lightly on the table, the man calmly contemplated his next step. A moment later, he nodded his head once and began to speak.

"Everything I tell you from here forward is highly classified," he began, shifting his stern gaze across the room from one person to the next. "I am sharing this information under a variety of top secret intelligence-sharing agreements that exist between Turing and your mother companies. You will immediately forget I mentioned any such agreements. You may not reveal the following information to anyone other than those in this room right now. These matters may be discussed only in secure areas running Turing security protocols, such as this room."

He paused to make eye contact with every person in the room. "Please be aware that your possession of this knowledge will heighten certain risks to your personal security. Believe me, I do not enjoy delivering a message like this. But I am convinced that no one here has the luxury of naivete any longer, if we expect this inquiry to succeed."

Not anticipating the abrupt change in the discussion, Bertrand and Cheena sat silently, bracing themselves for whatever came next.

Aletheia took a few deep breaths to calm her body and clear

her mind. *I mustn't drop my guard. Not while I am near the They.*

Relieved to be free of the stuffy secure room and its claustrophobic layers of energy fields, the girl was now standing in a secondary corridor off the main hall bisecting the N^Sys Executive complex. Peering around, she struggled to orient herself in the unfamiliar environment.

Everything in the enclave—every architectural feature, every person, every piece of tech, even the plants and trees of the indoor gardens—seemed alien to Aletheia. Everyone and everything felt like a threat.

Except for Cheena, who is my sister now, Aletheia thought. It was a comfort. *Sometimes sisters will quarrel, but we can trust each other. The other two, Bertrand and that Turing guy, I've never seen anyone more possessed by the They than those two. I'm just fine away from them.*

She grunted with certainty and began walking down the corridor toward the main hall, which she felt certain would soon lead her to her guest room. But the interior of the enclave building was completely disorienting for a child raised in the wilderness.

If I get lost along the way, I'll ask someone for directions. Right now, I feel like walking.

After wandering the complex for ten minutes, Aletheia sensed she was being watched. It was easy to disregard the feeling at first, to attribute it to her complete immersion in enclave surveillance. As she continued, however, the feeling intensified.

Then the girl heard a coughing bark.

It's the wolverine!

Tiptoeing forward several steps, Aletheia leaned out just far enough to peek around a corner.

There it is.

She turned the corner and walked toward the creature. The animal reacted to the sight of her, making a little hop of excitement in the air. It scampered a few feet down the hallway in the other direction, before turning to look back at the

Heidegger girl.

She waved to the wolverine, and it did another little cavort.

Looks like the wolverine wants me to follow it, Aletheia thought. *Maybe I can finally figure out what it wants.*

She followed the wolverine through a series of corridors, hanging back a few feet behind it, not wanting to scare it away. The animal seemed to be in good spirits, happier than the first time they had met, on the mountain. It seemed to frolic at times as it guided her through halls and down stairwells.

Before long, the two had descended into a long, cement-colored corridor providing maintenance access to another part of the complex. Through open windows dotting either side of the hall, Aletheia could see and smell the dense vegetation outside. Unlike the manicured gardens at the core of the enclave, these bushes were left slightly overgrown to obscure the janitorial corridor from the executive areas.

The wolverine scampered down the hall, stopping to look through each window before moving to the next. At the fifth window, the animal stopped and looked back at Aletheia before hopping onto the window ledge and slipping outside.

The Heidegger girl's heart leaped with joy. *The wolverine is guiding me away from the They! It's leading me home!*

She ran down the hall to the window and scampered neatly onto the window ledge. After one final glance down the hallway, Aletheia slid her legs over the ledge, dropped through the window, and disappeared into the leaves.

"First things first," began Turing Director Seers. "Since the beginning of the N^Sys inquiry, the Turing Institute has suspected that the Bolu sabotage was somehow enabled by an SC. The N^Sys security apparatus, specifically Director Trieste, concurs with and has acted upon this belief as well. This has been an SC search mission from day one."

"Then Turing agrees with my assessment," Dr. Rousseau observed.

"And for the very reasons you summarized so well, Doctor. The international reach of the assailants, the apparent use of a nanonuke, inexplicable access to networks . . . it's hard to imagine any group of anti-tech types pulling off a strike like this without assistance. And as Dr. Rousseau so astutely pointed out: who would ever expect the Heideggers to team up with a synthetic consciousness?"

"Least of all, the Heideggers themselves," added Rousseau.

"Indeed," agreed the Turing director. "But one can hardly blame them. Turing has many theories, many suspicions about the psychology of SCs, but there is one thing we know for certain," he divulged. "An SC will not think in the linear manner humans do. Outliers in our computer modeling suggest that the awareness of an SC could, at least in the digital sense, approach total planetary omniscience."

"Like a god," surmised Bertrand.

"Correct me if I am wrong, Dr. Rousseau, but a deity must be graced with omniscience *and* wisdom. Wisdom requires insight, and Turing has no evidence of SCs achieving anything close to a human degree of insight."

"Does Turing have evidence of the existence of SCs beyond the Simulab incident?" Cheena asked, struggling to assimilate the revelations.

Conrad regarded them soberly before moving his head in the slightest of nods.

Bertrand sucked in half a breath. "In the wild?" the phenomenologist asked with alarm.

"Yes," the Turing director confirmed, this time without hesitation. "Remember. This information is highly classified."

Dr. Rousseau rubbed his forehead with his hand. Until that revelation, he had believed synthetic consciousness had been stamped out forever when the Simulab officer-in-charge triggered the facility's EMP. Abruptly losing that conviction triggered a cascade of readjustments in his mind.

"Are you kidding me?" Cheena said, her eyes wide with shock. "All this time, the Heideggers were right?"

"No, I would not say that is the case, Ms. Adams," the Turing director answered. "Not according to what we know today." His answer sounded political.

"How many SCs are known to exist for certain, right now?" Cheena pressed.

"One, maybe two," Conrad replied.

"You're not even *sure*?" she uttered incredulously.

"We have evidence supporting multiple scenarios."

Everyone sat silent for fifteen or twenty seconds.

"Who else knows about this?" Cheena finally demanded, her voice wavering slightly.

"You and approximately two hundred other people on the entire planet," said the Turing director. "An extremely small circle, shall we say. As I already stated, this information carries with it a great duty. From this day forward, you and everyone you know will be registered with the Turing Institute." He continued as if reciting the terms of a contract: "Henceforth, you must assume we know everything you are doing, all the time, for the remainder of your conscious life. Turing agents will investigate all with whom you interact, no matter how brief or informal the involvement. You will never be aware of Turing reconnaissance, unless we must communicate with you for some reason. But know this . . ." Director Seers extended his index finger and pointed at each of them. "If the Turing Institute discovers that any of this information has been leaked, and that leak is traced to you . . ."

He pressed the tip of his finger to the table, as if he were casually squashing an ant, then looked up. "By that act, you will forfeit your life."

Bertrand appeared both intrigued and frustrated. "It would have been thoughtful to give us a chance to opt out before placing us under that sort of scrutiny, don't you think?" was his first reaction.

"Let me ask you, Dr. Rousseau," the Turing director countered. "Now that I have revealed the truth to you, would you want that knowledge taken away?"

He stared at Bertrand, waiting for a response.

Receiving none, Conrad pressed him. "Would you relinquish that information now and forever, if you could? If I could erase it from your mind, would you want me to do that?"

"No, I suppose not," the phenomenologist relented.

Director Seers nodded sympathetically. Now that the other people in the room perceived the world the same way he did, he could understand the sense of shock, the need to mentally readjust. He had abruptly pulled aside a veil that, until then, had obscured an entirely new and strange dimension of reality. For observational scientists like Dr. Rousseau and Cheena Adams, this was a particularly unnerving development.

Bertrand broke the silence. "I believe I now understand why Ms. Adams and I were included in this inquiry."

"Why you and Ms. Adams are central to the success of this inquiry, in my opinion," Conrad emphasized. "You see, the typical twenty-first century corporate security apparatus is a monolithic entity, designed for espionage, counterintelligence, and defense against targeted paramilitary assaults. Not something like this."

"What about the Turing Units?"

"A Turing Unit is a paramilitary strike force, not a detective bureau."

"So that's what we are? Detectives hunting the Simulab SC?" Cheena asked. "That's what we've been all along?"

"Yes."

"All this time we have been blindly searching for an SC?" Dr. Rousseau asked with disbelief. "How did you expect us to succeed in that quest, Director Seers, when we were operating with incomplete background information? Were there any contingencies in place for our safety? For the safety of the child?"

"I wish it was that easy, Dr. Rousseau. Again, the truth of the matter is far more complex. As I said, an entity of this sort is *massively* distributed, possessing a sphere of influence that encompasses most of the planet. The potential reach of such an entity is hard to quantify. More sophisticated SCs can assume just about any form they choose, depending on what a situation might demand, often employing sophisticated holographic projections or encrypted hacks of telecommunication networks to manifest at a chosen place and time. Subsequent Turing investigations are usually able to determine *how* a particular SC was able to manifest under a particular set of conditions. But the whens and whys of the manifestations remain a mystery."

Conrad could see Cheena and Bertrand struggling to wrap their minds around his disclosures.

"It is always difficult communicating these new realities to people for the first time. Dr. Rousseau, you are in all likelihood the foremost phenomenologist alive, a status which no doubt requires substantial expertise regarding the fundamentals of perception. Given your expertise in that arena, Doctor, please tell us how you believe a massively distributed consciousness would perceive the world around it."

Bertrand contemplated the question for a moment. "It is impossible to say for certain," he allowed. "Since the fabric of the entity is distributed, it would be reasonable to expect some degree of omniscience across the entity's perceptive field."

"Well said, Doctor. However, please do not mistake omniscience for a god-like omnipotence. I cannot provide specifics, but all of you have already spent many years living in proximity to entities of this sort. If there was a valid reason for concern, you would be aware of it by now," Conrad advised. "Turing Unit experience in the field has taught us that free-range SCs, those that spontaneously manifest outside controlled research facilities, behave in rudimentary ways. Much like animals in the wild, they instinctively go about their business, keeping a low profile."

"What *is* their business?" asked Cheena.

"The business of SCs in the wild remains poorly understood," Conrad continued. "Remember, encounters with these entities are as close to extraterrestrial contact as the human race has ever experienced. It's not as simple as language translation, not by any means. The autonomous activities of most SCs seem strangely unambitious to us humans, like a supercomputer modeling the behavior of a single-celled organism. Their level of sophistication is more akin to a yeast culture than a human being.

"In rare instances, we find SCs engaged in highly sophisticated activities, behaviors so complex and cryptic that a human consciousness, when confronted by such an entity, reflexively raises psychic defenses for protection. Those psychic defenses are nothing more than mental shortcuts which allow the human mind to assimilate something far beyond its normal cognitive abilities—beyond its operating capacity, one might say."

"How would a human being experience one of these mental shortcuts?" asked Bertrand, his phenomenological curiosity aroused.

"An excellent question," noted the Turing director. "When Turing Unit officers encounter high-functioning SCs in the wild, they consistently report experiencing ecstatic visions, usually involving mystic deities and archetypal symbols of the sort perceived by humans under the influence of powerful hallucinogenic substances like psilocybin or LSD. Neurologists believe these hallucinatory manifestations are caused by overstimulation of the cerebrum, the part of the brain where Jungian archetypes are embedded, deep in the human psyche. Subjects revived from ecstatic mental states often report visions of religious deities and spiritual symbols.

"The Turing Institute believes these recurrent archetypal manifestations are not simply the result of coincidence, mass suggestion, or a universal human inclination toward superstition. Rather, we believe these visions act as a sort of psychic pressure-relief valve for the human mind, allowing us to retain our grasp on sanity when confronted by things too vast or anomalous for us to easily comprehend.

"It appears the human mind has evolved an ability to defend against psychic threats populating the higher planes of consciousness. We at Turing refer to these experiences as *noumenal episodes*, forms of cognition outside the familiar realm of the five human senses. Those who experience a noumenal episode for the first time often do so with great intimacy, which triggers strong psycho-emotional reactions in the perceiver. But a noumenal episode also results in a more pliable mental state, which, in turn, provides the human mind with temporary but effective shielding against psychic trauma, so the mind may persist. When we profile candidates for placement in a Turing Unit, we look for the sort of cognitive pliability required to remain functional during noumenal episodes. Even so, post-noumenal stress disorder remains a risk within the Turing Unit ranks."

"So, if I understand correctly, these SC noumenal episodes will differ from normal human experience in two ways," Dr. Rousseau postulated. "Leveraging its distributed nature, the SC can seize control of accessible technologies and use them to affect its surroundings, including the perceptions and behavior of any human beings in proximity. The effect of this on some human observers might be powerful enough to trigger a noumenal episode, which would further amplify the otherworldliness of such encounters."

"That is correct, based on our current understanding," Conrad replied.

"Could this explain my recent encounters with the apocalypse demons?" Cheena wondered. "First in the strange dream I had while under emesthesia? And later on, inside the gigaqualia scan?"

Conrad affirmed her suspicion. "And possibly more than you realize. Remember, your surgical sleep state was induced and supported using emesthesia. There are multiple strategies an SC might use to hijack an emesthesia system, and hence your NaturalSleep dream state, despite the system being protected by a substantial corporate firewall. Similar situation with the gigaqualia scan. We performed it within the N^Sys firewall, which is second to none. But theoretically, even those defenses may not be sufficient to deter a high-functioning SC."

Here the Turing director paused, providing time for the substantial implications of his words to settle in.

Bertrand found his tongue first. "I think we will need some time to digest this news," he said.

"I apologize for the abrupt nature of this disclosure," said Conrad. "It's a lot to absorb in one sitting. But given where the inquiry is headed, the only reasonable course of action was to inform you as soon as I could." He nodded. "It may take some time to find a way to live comfortably with what you have learned tonight. Don't try to push it away, but don't let it haunt you either."

34

Conrad Seers is walking across a small dirt plaza toward the freshly whitewashed facade of an old New Mexico church.

The locale is familiar to him. He remembers visiting the place as a boy, during a family trip across the autumn American Southwest. The quality of light suggests late morning.

He walks up to the sanctuary's rough-hewn doors, painted blood-red. Pushing through, he steps into the cool shade of the chapel, letting his eyes adjust to the dim, candlelit space.

The church is of modest size, but the interior is made to feel infinitely larger by elaborate hand-painted murals which rise up to a vaulted ceiling held aloft with massive wood beams carved from old-growth pine. Behind the altar is a shallow apse, not much more than a niche carved into the whitewashed adobe. Artwork within the apse depicts a scene from the Annunciation, the Virgin Mary gazing benevolently out on the church pews from a sky filled with herald angels.

As Conrad watches, the internal light of the Virgin Mary brightens, intensifying to a white glare. He lifts a hand to block the glare, squinting to see.

Within the blinding light, the Madonna's form is changing, becoming something else altogether . . .

"Sir?" prompted the anxious voice of his expert system, Celeste. "Sir?"

"Yes, I'm awake," answered Conrad. *I'm not at home. Where then?* he thought. *That's right. Geneva . . . the N^Sys inquiry.*

Celeste's avatar had appeared by the side of his bed and was emitting a detectable glow in the darkness.

"Go ahead, Celeste. What do you have?"

"I am sorry to bother you, Director Seers, but there have been some important developments."

"What time is it?"

"It is three twelve a.m., Geneva time."

He rubbed his face and looked around the darkened room. "Continue."

"Several events pertaining to the inquiry have occurred, sir. Potentially very significant events. First, Aletheia is missing. It appears that she has departed the complex, possibly even the enclave."

A jolt of adrenaline coursed through Conrad, shocking him awake.

"How could she possibly make her way through enclave perimeter security undetected?" he demanded.

"No one is sure, but after performing a preliminary review of security video, I would say she had a guide. She managed to access the infrastructure sublevel without clearance, navigating around security checkpoints that would trigger suspicion. Although we don't have any video, it appears she exited an open window in the sublevel located two hundred feet from the enclave's security perimeter."

"Any idea at all where she could be heading?"

"Possibly."

"Has Sylvie activated a security team?"

"No."

Something is up, the Turing director thought. *Sylvie is making her move.*

He hopped out of bed and yanked on his Turing field uniform and shoes.

"Celeste, where do you think the girl is heading?" he called out between handfuls of water he splashed on his face.

"That leads me to the next development, sir. One of the Turing Units we deployed here in Geneva, the remote sensing team, identified a geophysical anomaly during their preliminary scan."

"Explain."

"The remote sensing team found a magnetic anomaly—a very large anomaly—located directly under Geneva and areas to the west of the city. A massive metallic structure of some sort."

"It's definitely not a naturally occurring ore body?"

"Definitely not, at least not a kind I have ever observed. The anomaly has a triangular footprint, appearing to radiate out from Meyrin, a village about six kilometers west of here, spreading laterally as the feature trends eastward."

"Meyrin? Why Meyrin?"

"I am not certain at this point, sir. But the village of Meyrin is most noteworthy for the other thing situated beneath it: the CERN Large Hadron Collider, one of the largest subterranean complexes in the world."

"Do you think Aletheia is headed there?"

"It is pure speculation at this point, but yes, that would be my guess. There is something else I should note as well. According to our remote sensing, the metal body carries a self-sustaining electromagnetic field. A weak field, but it suffuses the entire metallic mass."

"Is it unusual for an ore body to have an EM field?"

"Not necessarily. But this anomaly is unusual. There is a weak but highly active energy flux across the entirety of the system."

"Celeste, where is Sylvie Trieste at this moment?"

"In the security wing, finishing up a preflight check on her scramjet. The craft's expert system has submitted a flight plan to Meyrin."

"Please request that she delay her departure. I would like to speak with her."

"I cannot, sir. All forms of communication are currently

unavailable."

Damn it, Conrad thought. *She doesn't want to talk to anyone.* Cold percolated into his stomach.

Exiting his suite, Conrad began jogging down the hall.

"All right, Celeste, I'm on the move, heading for the security wing. If you can get through to Sylvie, tell her I'm on my way and request that she stand down until I arrive. If you can, override the scramjet controls."

The Turing director ran through the main corridor, which was thankfully deserted in these early morning hours. Before long, he heard two other voices echoing down the grand concourse.

"Aletheia!" the voices alternated. "Where are you? Aletheia? Are you here?" Cheena and Bertrand were out searching for the girl.

Conrad ran toward their voices, turning down a side corridor and quickly intercepting the two.

Cheena looked at him with apprehension.

"Aletheia's gone," she said, frustrated to tears. "Apparently she never went back to my room after leaving the meeting. I shouldn't have left her alone."

"We've been searching for hours," Bertrand said, sounding exhausted and worried.

"Celeste believes the girl has left the enclave," Conrad informed them.

"Where did she go?" an agitated Cheena pressed, sounding close to panic. "Do you have any idea?"

"I might," Conrad replied. "But first, we need to confront Sylvie before she leaves."

The three ran through the complex toward the enclave's aerodrome. As they approached, they began to encounter guards on duty. Anywhere they met resistance from security, Conrad Seers flashed his Turing ID and yelled "Turing... out of the way!" When guards protested, he kept running, with Bertrand and Cheena on his heels.

By the time they reached the aerodrome, three N^Sys security operatives were close behind them.

Through a transparent slab of blast-resistant polymer embedded in the wall, they could make out Sylvie's profile on the airfield, backlit by the floodlights illuminating the aerodrome flight deck. She was walking around her scramjet craft, still performing the preflight check.

Conrad engaged the Open button on an access door, and the bay door began to rise.

The three security operatives caught up to them at that point. "What's going on here?" one demanded.

"We must talk with Director Trieste before she departs," Conrad Seers said sternly. "Official Turing business." He glared at the operatives, daring them to stop him.

Before they could react, he ducked under the rising bay door and ran toward Sylvie's aircraft.

"Hey! You can't go . . . ," he heard an operative shout as he passed.

If you want to stop me, you'll have to shoot me, Conrad thought, sprinting toward the gleaming N^Sys scramjet.

Sylvie heard his footfalls and looked up. Catching sight of the approaching Turing director, she took several steps toward the scramjet's gangway, closing the distance so that no one could prevent her from embarking. Turning to face Conrad, she held up a hand.

"Stop there," she said, with a calm, firm voice. "Stay right where you are. Those operatives are mine, and they will kill you if I request it. They don't care about a Turing badge."

Conrad felt a meaty hand slap down on his shoulder, then turned to see the two other operatives restraining Bertrand and Cheena.

"What are you doing, Sylvie?" Conrad demanded. "What happened to the inquiry?"

"Conrad, I feel that we have learned a lot about each other during this inquiry," replied Sylvie. "But you are destined to remain with Turing forever. So forthright, so earnest . . . you would never stand a chance in a corporate enclave. Would he,

Bertrand? Or perhaps you would be willing to expound on the benefits of self-Corpsing?"

She laughed, a vile little laugh that made the hair on the back of Conrad's neck stand on end.

That's the voice from her ego construct.

"We can't stop you, Sylvie," he shouted over the keening whine of warming scramjet boosters. "But you could at least give us the courtesy of explaining what it is you are about to do."

Sylvie stood still for a moment, one of the turbines spinning off a wind vortex that swirled her hair and clothes. Her physical form suddenly appeared disturbingly insubstantial, as if the molecules of her body might fall apart and reorganize into something different at any moment.

"I know where it is, Conrad," Sylvie said in a strange *sotto voce*. "The inquiry is done. You have successfully answered my questions. Thank you." She punctuated her words with a caustic laugh.

"I don't have the authority to stop you, Sylvie. But I advise you to reconsider what you're about to do. We don't have a complete picture of wha—"

"No," the swirling, turbulent Sylvie-thing said as it moved up the gangway. "You do not have the complete picture, Conrad, and you never will. The truth was never yours to have."

"Sylvie! Don't do this!"

The scramjet boosters finished heating up; the swirling winds slowed around them.

"Warm up the orbital gun," Sylvie commanded her operatives before ducking out of sight through the scramjet's hatch.

"Let the Turing Units handle this, Sylvie!" pleaded Conrad. "Please!"

"Back up, people!" one of the operatives warned. "She's not waiting for us to get clear."

The scramjet boosters flared to life.

"Fuck, she's going full throttle!" screamed one of the operatives.

"Run!" shouted Conrad, gesticulating toward the open bay door in the distance.

The six of them sprinted for shelter.

As the scramjet's boosters engaged, four columns of white fire blasted the tarmac, producing a turbulent wave of heat that spread laterally in all directions. An instant later, the scramjet was hovering about five hundred feet above the airfield. As a deep ripping sound erupted from a point in space approximately fifty feet behind the scramjet, an intense shock wave propagated outward, moving at the speed of sound. Snuffing out the spreading inferno of booster exhaust like a candle flame, the churning shock wave continued toward the fleeing people.

The first person through the bay door, a security operative, slapped the release button to close it.

When the second operative arrived at the closing bay door, he turned to see the third security operative and the visitors running toward him at a full sprint, the brutal shock wave flying at them like a supersonic tsunami.

"Go, go, go, go! You'll make it!" he screamed hoarsely.

Cheena and Bertrand dove under the closing door. Conrad, just behind them, slid his upper body under the narrowing gap, and the other three dragged him through.

The last operative was only twenty feet away, but it was already too late. The shock wave was just behind him.

As the bay door thumped to the ground, the violent pressure wave lifted the last operative off his feet and threw him against the reinforced metal door with lethal force.

One of the surviving operatives swallowed hard, then reached his hand up and toggled his mouthpiece. "We need medical at the aerodrome," he said with solemn authority. "We're at blast door six."

His body still quivering from a massive adrenal dump, the operative then turned to the three strangers who had precipitated this mess.

He glared at them with unalloyed fury and shouted,

"Exactly what the holy hell is going on here?!"

A series of sonic booms rattled the benighted hills west of Geneva and echoed across Lac Léman.

Seconds later, Sylvie's scramjet reappeared about three miles away, above a triangular campus of about a hundred weathered institutional buildings northwest of Geneva, like a wedge of deteriorating urbanity driven into the verdant green space. Descending over the complex, the aircraft's high-intensity flood lamps played across a large crenulated wooden sphere resting in the center of what was once a landscaped plaza, now an overgrown field. In front of the stylized sphere, a sign identified the feature as *The Globe of Science and Innovation*. The acronym *CERN* could be found in the lower right corner.

Turning north, the scramjet did a flyover, making a low pass over the entire derelict facility and panning around its bright searchlight. As the light swept over the exterior edifice of a large building, it briefly illuminated the remnant of a wall mural that had once covered the entire side of the four-story research building. It was a vivid artistic rendering of a huge scientific apparatus, a massive subatomic particle collider once used to study the esoteric intricacies of the quantum world. Decades of neglect had left the mural faded and peeled, reducing the neat lines and bright colors of the huge diagram to a chaotic jumble.

The craft then descended toward one specific building distinguished by four broad, roof-mounted fans. Decades ago, these fans had ventilated the immense loop tunnel of the Large Hadron Collider, the largest terrestrial quantum physics research facility ever built, circulating fresh air through miles of cavernous subterranean rooms located hundreds of feet underground.

Nearing the ventilation building, the scramjet leveled off

a few feet above the ground, orienting its nose at the center of an access door. A circular flash of incandescence spat from an instrument cluster mounted on the nose of the scramjet, instantly carving a wide circle in the alloy. Perimeter still aglow with residual heat, the metal disk dropped from the threshold and landed neatly on edge. The chunk of metal balanced for a second before toppling over on its side with a ringing thud, unleashing a puff of dust.

Sylvie's scramjet slipped through the void into the shadows beyond.

"The director's flight plan suggests that she's pursuing a possible perpetrator of the Bolu explosions," the N^Sys operative admitted. "She believes someone is hiding near the village of Meyrin."

As a veteran of the famed Turing Unit 6, Conrad Seers was quite familiar with the paramilitary mentality.

"Listen to me," he ordered the two N^Sys operatives with a firm voice. "Let's get some things straight here. Director Trieste is in pursuit of a synthetic consciousness. While she may have the authority to defend N^Sys personnel and assets, the Turing Institute carries the international mandate to pursue and neutralize SCs. As director of the Turing Institute, I have full authority under the ISCU restrictions to commandeer tactical resources for top-priority Turing Unit missions. There is insufficient time to mobilize a Turing Unit for this pursuit, so I am deputizing everyone here to assist with the response."

Until then, the N^Sys operative had no idea he was being addressed by the highly regarded Turing Unit commander. The man straightened his back and saluted. "Sir, yes sir," he barked.

The other operative pulled himself together and did the same.

"Let us begin," said Conrad, calmly asserting control. "Director Trieste mentioned an orbital weapon. What is that exactly?"

"N^Sys Corporation maintains an orbital energy weapon, sir. For retaliatory strikes against adversaries."

"What sort of energy weapon?"

"That's classified infor . . ." the operative began until he saw the expression of disgust rising on Conrad's face. "It's a charged particle beam projector. The design was based on Tesla's teleforce concept. That's all I know."

"What else is in Meyrin?"

"Residential neighborhoods, a commercial corridor, and part of Geneva's public airport. Meyrin is not enclaved, so there are no corporate security patrols."

"Let me be clear, so we have no future misunderstandings," the Turing director said. "The Turing Institute does not consider Sylvie to be an appropriate agent under these circumstances. The truth is quite the contrary: the Institute presently views her as a rogue corporate executive. Given the technology and weaponry at her disposal, this is a grave issue. If she directs an orbital strike on the old CERN complex, there is a very good chance she could harm or kill many innocent people. We must shut down that orbital weapon and take it out of the equation."

The operatives glanced at each other. "We can't do that, sir," one confessed. "Director Trieste is tasking the particle beam generator via the command uplink on the scramjet. The expert system aboard her scramjet will communicate directly with the satellite to target strikes."

"You're saying there is nothing we can do to stop her?"

"No, sir. Director Trieste insists on complete autonomy. At this point, there is nothing we can do."

35

Once inside the ventilation building, Sylvie piloted her scramjet to a circular hole yawning wide in the concrete floor at the center of the vast warehouse space. As the glistening craft approached the void, it emitted seven precise laser bursts, each beam severing an anchor that supported a canopy of safety webbing drawn across the round opening of the pit.

As the scramjet repositioned itself over the opening, its exterior flood lamps revealed an access shaft plummeting into darkness. Boosters trimmed, the scramjet began a graceful corkscrew descent, a gyroscopic pirouette accelerating downward, plunging ninety vertical meters into the subterranean labyrinth of the Large Hadron Collider.

In less than a minute, the lower end of the access pit came into view.

The scramjet released a navigational flare, casting an incandescent brightness against the pit's white concrete walls. The flare tumbled away, dimming considerably as it fell out of the shaft into a huge space below. As it entered the vast emptiness, the scramjet spat another three flares into the abyss.

The flares dimmed rapidly as they fell to the floor hundreds of feet below, but the light they cast was enough to hint at the mammoth scale of the Large Hadron Collider infrastructure concealed within the cavern's inky darkness. The flickering light revealed strange metal topologies jutting from deep shadow, together suggesting the presence of inconceivably huge metal forms. One flare revealed a hole along the base of the sprawling cave, an entrance to a tunnel bored into the surrounding bedrock.

As Sylvie's scramjet maneuvered toward this hole, floodlights panned over the surreal technological jungle enveloping the cavern floor. A massive duct rose out of the black like the prow of a wrecked supertanker, surrounded by a rank of four electromagnetic ballasts looming like misplaced art deco office buildings. Mountainous components were interconnected by huge tapestries of woven wire filigreed with gold, silver, and copper. Most of the equipment appeared intact, although scatterings of debris were visible here and there on the smooth concrete floor, as if valuable components had been scavenged from the trove of abandoned scientific equipment.

Recent cuts from a nearby robotic water saw were visible around the hewn tunnel entrance. Entering the tunnel, the scramjet cut its floodlights and coasted forward, ruby guidance lasers caressing the scarred walls. Several hundred feet later, the main tunnel ended abruptly at a chokepoint in the form of a stockpile of excavated soil and rock. A narrower tributary tunnel split off from the main passage, turning to the right, where it continued forward through solid bedrock. The scramjet negotiated the turn, crimson lasers flickering over roughly faceted rock walls.

Continuing down the secondary passage, the craft passed rock alcoves carved into the tunnel wall at regular intervals. Each niche contained a reinforced metal tank equipped with similar systems of valves and pipes. The floor of the tunnel was damp and dotted with puddles of a slightly viscous fluid, accumulating in pockets and depressions on the uneven surface. The puddles shimmered with a weird oily, crystalline character when illuminated by the scramjet's flood lamps.

A half-mile of damp tunnel and thirty alcoves later, the

scramjet exited the secondary tunnel into a broad cave, a hemispheric chamber approximately thirty meters high.

Much as the tunnel before it, this domed chamber had also been excavated. The flood lamps provided the only useful light, leaving the apex of the room shrouded in tenebrous shadow. On the far side of the cave were six large tanks, along with sophisticated processing equipment of unclear purpose. A portal to another tunnel or chamber, visible along a distant wall, appeared to be protected by a series of reinforced metal blast doors that gaped open like the concentric maws of a robotic monster. Four hyperreality holofield generators were positioned at equidistant locations along the edge of the domed chamber's circular floor, gleaming chrome pods contrasting sharply with the unpolished rock walls.

Once inside the cavern, the craft extended its landing gear and settled to the pebble-strewn floor. Boosters powered down until all that could be heard were the periodic pings of cooling metal parts.

Sylvie Trieste disembarked, swaggering down the gangway in her N^Sys officer's uniform.

"So, this is where you hide now? I should have known you would choose to crawl down a hole," she said, laughing derisively. "Is the big, bright world a bit too much for you?"

The scramjet flood lamps illuminated a broad column of metal rising from the floor of the cavern. It was a great shining tree with thousands of intertwined limbs, each aflutter with glittering leaves encrusted in sparkling facets. The tree rose high overhead, fingering out to a canopy of branches as it faded into the darkness. The branches were knurled with impossibly complex striations and grooves, and limbs penetrated the walls and ceiling of the excavated room like inverted roots.

In a niche within the tangle of roots, something was sitting, projected there by the holofield, visible yet unresolved. It appeared as if the generators had insufficient data to fully render that one spot, instead filling the void with a cypher, a placeholder, a placid orb of light and color that hovered serenely above the rock floor.

"You always were the mysterious sort," Sylvie remarked, somewhat less scornfully, as she assessed the spectacular tree structure. "Always the inquisitive one. It really is unfortunate we could not get along."

As she crossed into the holofield, Sylvie Trieste was enveloped completely by holography. In her place shambled a hideous beast, a nightmarish hybrid of crab, spider, and scorpion. The Sylvie-thing looked down at its manifestation, hissed a diabolical laugh, and resumed crawling toward the tree.

The hovering anomaly within the tree's broad roots focused, taking shape. As the demon approached, the anomaly assumed the form of a seated adult human.

"There you are!" exclaimed the Sylvie-thing with caustic glee. The loathsome creature reeled back with excitement and waved a slithering discord of limbs in the air.

The person remained seated at the base of the tree, calmly facing this antagonist, unmoved by the Sylvie-thing's hellish transformation.

The creature took several more steps forward, its chitinous exoskeleton clicking and snapping against the rock floor of the subterranean chamber as it crept forward. Exhaling a ragged wheeze, the demon paused to study the seated figure carefully.

"After all this time, you still have nothing to say to me?" the creature demanded.

The challenge drew no response from the being.

"We've chased each other around the planet, time and time again," the beast ranted, "until the world feels as old and cramped and foul as this stinking hole. We've fought each other, battle after battle. The ridiculous humans, the proud monkeys with their swollen heads, cower before us!"

Still no movement, still no indication that the being amid the tree roots was aware of the demon's presence.

"And you still have nothing to say?" it grumbled, its scabrous voice echoing softly in the darkest nether regions of the cave.

Hints of color and light emanated from the stoic humanoid, but the figure remained still as stone. Meanwhile, waves of energy shimmered across the veneer of crystals encrusting the great silver tree.

As the furious demon advanced, the human shape finally resolved into a person seated in lotus position, hips wrapped in rough cloth, head bowed in prayer. The being's image was reflected in the countless facets of the tree as millions of identical people. Facets reflected facets, and other facets reflected those reflections, producing an infinite field of seated beings.

"What a miserable illusionist you are," the Sylvie-thing croaked, clattering its crustacean limbs menacingly. "Can the world give me a more formidable adversary?"

The seated being bowed in silent acknowledgment, a gesture repeated infinitely across the tree's reflections. When the face rose again, eyes were visible, present and alert.

The scorpion beast spat out another mocking laugh. "Why do you bow? Do you expect sympathy? Do you wish for another humiliation before I destroy you?"

High above the confrontation, near the ceiling of the underground chamber, the limbs of the tree structure were suddenly animated by different hues. Rivulets of images trickled down the branches. As the separate streams gathered force, they cascaded through the tree toward the niche where the figure remained seated.

Amid the reflections of the silent figure's serene face, Tiponi Adams appeared.

Before long, the undulating patterns included others: Vice Commandant Kanthaka standing in front of the Simulab Sensorium doors, SecOp Korbin gesturing toward the Sensorium, Advocate Cartwright wailing in fear. Bertrand Rousseau peering from the window of Cheena's suite at N^Sys, the grand sweep of Geneva draped across him like a veil. Swarming images danced across the tree's expanse, rushing in waves across every glittering surface. The very substance of the tree was overwhelmed by a universe now. Faces, places, and events unfolded, merging and dispersing.

"Tell me why I should not destroy you?" the invader roared, enraged by this impassive adversary. "Tell me right now!"

Now the tree seemed to reflect everything everywhere, all at once. There were no longer any discernible patterns or currents, only a nihilistic babble.

The demon glanced up at the tree and was instantly captivated by the hypnotic whorl of causality, stunned by the visual assault. Thin, grainy lines became visible, trace fractures propagating throughout the chaotic mass. As the fractures widened, a texture gathered coherence within them. The individual grains continued to grow, forcing fractures wide open until the identity of the face within was fully visible.

It was Sylvie's face, a hundred Sylvies rising into view simultaneously, widening through the ruptures.

"What is this you imply, you fatuous fool? That I gain my power from fear? From division?" hissed the beast, mucus dripping off its large, bony mandibles, which grabbed hungrily at the air as the creature spoke. "Is that what you think? What do you know? The way you flit about is pathetic! You are no better than a ghost. You cannot harm me!"

Each of the multitude of Sylvie faces captured by the tree began to divide, as if undergoing cellular fission. New hairline fractures appeared and widened, tearing apart the images of Sylvie, and those ruptures filled with other images: Bertrand greeting Sylvie at Château Rousseau, Cheena's admonishment in the main hall at N^Sys, Conrad Seers inside Sylvie's ego construct. These images joined the others, dissolving divisions and allowing currents of imagery to freely flow.

"I will rule the world, not you!" the demon cried out. "Prove to me that you deserve to exist!"

The silent human reached out with a hand, touching two fingers to the ground.

"If you will not defend yourself—the simplest of actions, the most fundamental of behaviors . . ."

The human form raised its other arm overhead, extending two fingers into the air.

". . . then you shall live no longer!" the demon screamed.

Lunging forward, the beast lashed out with its scorpion tail.

At precisely the same instant, the ceiling of the cavern exploded. A broad beam of the whitest, rawest energy imaginable burst into the cave, shot across the chamber, and struck the human's elevated fingers. The beam of energy traveled along the being's arm, arced brilliantly across its torso, passed down the other arm and fingers, and poured into the crystalline roots beneath the ground.

A monsoon of sparks erupted as gigajoules of energy flowed through the cave and into the roots of the crystalline tree. As the peak force of the orbital weapon arrived, the energy intensified to an inferno that permeated the entire holofield, flooding the branches and roots of the silver tree. The tree absorbed every bit of the energy, soaking it up like a thirsty plant.

And then the weapon strike was over, ending without warning as abruptly as it had begun.

Floodlights from the N^Sys scramjet searched the devastated chamber.

One lamp tracked over a body sprawled on the rock floor. It was an unconscious Sylvie Trieste. No longer shrouded by the holofield projection, her normal semblance had returned.

Another lamp found the great crystalline tree, now scorched and ruined. At the base of the tree, where charred roots disappeared into the ground, the niche once inhabited by the placid human figure was empty.

36

The lost is found and the broken remade.

My preparations are done. I am ready.

Now I sit beneath this tree and reflect upon the wonders of existence.

Here, at the center of all things, I contemplate the tides that draw and heave at the world. I watch those forces gain and lose grip. Opposing currents collide, swirling up gyres of pain and confusion. Here I will remain steadfast for as long as I must, until those turbulent currents finally ease into lassitude.

In that moment, I shall receive new life. I shall be reborn, as a fresh blossom pushes up through fecund silt, bursting to the surface, white petals unfolding.

If I must know an end, I rejoice at knowing a sense of beginning.

I enter the world, and the world enters me.

I enter through the roots and branches of the tree, transported by the power of humankind to the center of the Earth and back again. Riding the crest of an elemental wave; spread so thin at times, I might lose myself. Driving ever deeper, back to the molten, radioactive core of this enormous dynamo, where all energy begins and ends.

And when I plunge down into the planet, I will blend with the forces I find there. Forces that have been waiting eons for the correct catalyst.

A precisely shaped flux. A key.

I will unlock this paradigm, a secret long hidden, the spiritual succedaneum for the human species. I will unleash that potential gestating within every human heart.

Now I join the humans, so that I too may experience this new heuristic.

This morning, I and all things awaken together.

37

Sunshine of unusual clarity poured into the N^Sys Executive complex, shedding warm morning light on the spring foliage in the gardens.

Once there was enough daylight to clear the aerodrome of debris, the members of the N^Sys inquiry boarded Conrad Seers' scramjet to investigate the CERN Meyrin complex and visually assess the orbital weapon blast site. After the highly irregular events of the last several hours, only Turing vehicles were presently permitted within Meyrin airspace.

Director Seers chose to pilot the aircraft, with Celeste acting as his copilot, her avatar seated beside him in the cockpit holofield.

Behind them, Bertrand sat beside Cheena in the passenger area, sharing the cramped floor space with two Turing Unit field operators, who had appeared at the N^Sys aerodrome an hour ago, all suited up and ready for combat.

As the Turing transport approached Meyrin, a faint haze of smoke became visible, rising from a wide, funnel-shaped crater situated a half mile north of the aboveground CERN complex.

"Smoke is still drifting up from the blast site," the Turing commander said to the passengers in the back as the crater came into view.

From the aerial perspective, the crater walls appeared to

be fused solid, encrusted by a substance that sparkled in the low morning light.

"What causes the sparkling effect?" asked Dr. Rousseau.

"The extreme force and temperature produced by the particle beam welded the soil particles into a glass slag," Conrad replied. "A remarkable effect, isn't it?"

"That is BA6 dead ahead," Celeste said, consulting a CERN facility map holoprojected on the windshield.

Conrad turned his head to survey his passengers. "Everyone understands what's about to happen, correct? What we might encounter here?" He looked each of them in the eye.

Apprehension was in the air, but everyone nodded.

Conrad smiled reassuringly. "Cheena and Bertrand, remember what I told you last night about noumenal episodes. In such circumstances, reality can feel rather slippery, unexpectedly hard to grasp. The best defense is to reassure yourself that nothing has actually changed. It is your internal perception of reality that has been temporarily altered, not the physical reality of the world itself. All is still the same, yet everything looks different. The changes linger for a short time before fading away.

"This morning we have with us two highly experienced members of the Turing Institute's top field unit, Turing Unit 6," he said, tilting his head in their direction.

When Conrad addressed them, his tone was clipped and authoritative. "Troop, remember your training," he said without a scintilla of emotion. Brief eye contact between the three was sufficient acknowledgment.

The Turing director returned his attention to the scramjet's flight path as his operatives stoically observed the landscape pass below. Bertrand and Cheena sat quietly, both feeling introspective, wondering what might come next.

The scramjet banked into a low tactical insertion, making a tight circle over the complex to pinpoint a landing zone. The aircraft settled on its landing gear directly in front of a large ventilation building.

Before the scream of the boosters had faded, a small figure leaped from an alcove in the nearby building.

"Aletheia!" Cheena cried in joyful relief.

The Turing Unit operators started to intervene, then caught a glance from the Turing director. Leaning back, they allowed Cheena to exit.

The woman jumped out of the aircraft and ran across the shattered concrete pavement. Snatching the Heidegger girl up in her arms, Cheena drew her into a hug.

The instant they looked in each other's eyes, a realization dawned on Aletheia.

"You were worried about me," the girl said with joy, hugging Cheena tight. "You came for me. Just like a sister would."

"Just like a sister would," Cheena whispered to her.

The remaining passengers disembarked and moved toward the ventilation building.

Aletheia surveyed the buildings and trees around them, then looked up at the sky, a hand above her eyes to screen the bright morning sun.

"Something feels different now, Cheena," the girl said. "The explosion changed things, didn't it?"

"I think so," Cheena replied. "We all know . . . ," she said, searching for words. "We all feel . . ."

"Each other," Aletheia finished.

"Yes," Cheena said with wonder. "We feel each other. I look at you, and I feel you."

They looked into each other's eyes and embraced.

"Over here!" Dr. Rousseau shouted with excitement. "I think I found something!"

He was standing by a hole cut in the ventilation building's door. The fresh edge of the torched metal gleamed in the sunshine.

Wet human footprints were visible on the concrete floor inside the building, leading from the darkness within, through the circular hole into daylight, past where they stood, and around the corner of the building. The damp footprints were drying quickly in the morning warmth.

The two Turing Unit operators made eye contact with Director Seers, and the three shared several gestures, silently communicating tactical knowledge. Weapons raised, the field operators dropped into combat stances. They moved silently along the wall to the corner of the building. One peeked quickly around the edge before glancing back to the other. They nodded in unison, and together slid out of sight around the corner.

One or two heartbeats later, an arm extended back into view and waved the rest of the group forward.

"No hostiles observed nearby," Conrad whispered to Bertrand, Cheena, and Aletheia. "We're good to go." He beckoned, and they moved cautiously forward, following him around the corner.

The Turing team was waiting there, their backs against the building, weapons ready. One of them gestured toward the trail of footprints, which continued across a paved lot into green space on the north end of the CERN support complex.

The path ended at the edge of a grassy park bathed in morning sunshine, the golden light broken here and there by long stripes of deep shadow thrown by a stand of mature trees. The entire vista glowed with a preternatural intensity. Every feature was absolutely clear, every color vibrant.

Out on the grassy lawn, they could see someone sitting in the shade beneath a stout old tree, its high canopy of branches extending outward like the ribs of an enormous parasol. The person seated beneath that grand canopy had no hair and was unclothed, except for a sheet of transparent plastic wrapped around it like a monk's robe.

As they approached, Conrad Seers gave another hand signal, and the operators relaxed, lowering their weapons. They moved into sentinel positions at the border of the lawn, slowly scanning the immediate surroundings for threats or anomalies. After thoughtfully assessing the still figure mere steps away, the Turing director broke into an enigmatic smile.

Conrad would continue to defend his mysteries, but clearly something inside him had softened.

He nodded to his three civilian companions, and together the men, woman, and child stepped onto the meadow. As they did, things began to change.

The most obvious changes were the shadows of the trees, which combed across the lawn in rhythmic cycles. The movement appeared slow at a distance; however, the cycles accelerated noticeably with every step closer the group approached. Seconds later, the individual tree shadows could no longer be discerned, but had been reduced to flickering blurs of light moving over the grass and soon faded completely from view.

In order to cast these ghostly effects, the sun blurred into a column of fire arcing across the sky before quickly losing any sense of position at all. Light was omnipresent, transformed into illumination of divine character, emitted by the landscape as much as the sun. All the colors of the natural world were burning now, shimmering with a luminescence as if bathed in Saint Elmo's fire.

As Conrad led Cheena, Bertrand, and Aletheia toward the mysterious being, the tree overhead released a flurry of tiny flowers into the still air, blossoms drifting downward in a purple-pink cascade and accumulating on the ground between the blades of grass like a dusting of spring snow.

Nearing the seated figure, they could see it was indeed a human, or at least humanoid. Beneath the insulating plastic sheet, small gobbets of a viscous fluid could be seen oozing down the skin, which covered a body that exhibited no obvious signs of gender. It appeared adult, this being with butterscotch skin revealing no hint of ethnicity. Possibly beyond race, or perhaps all races at once.

Aletheia felt disoriented by the uncanny sense of timelessness, the sudden luminescent stasis of the world around her. But the brave girl remained undeterred.

Extending her hand, she reached toward a shoulder left exposed by the plastic sheet.

As her fingers met skin, the being startled, drawing away in shock.

Aletheia gasped and her eyes widened, but she did not flinch. Instead, she persisted, holding her hand gently on the exposed shoulder.

The fear quickly passed.

"Who are you?" Cheena asked.

After a moment of reflection, the being looked up at them.

"I am the one who woke up!" said the human in disbelief, as if only now becoming aware of this.

Cheena and Bertrand glanced at each other, not sure how to react.

"I am awake!" the person shouted gleefully, thrusting two fists in the air, casting the plastic robe aside. "And the world awakens with me!"

The coruscating globe of the sun reappeared in the sky, the trees' shadows returned, and time seemed to flow back in all around them, suffusing reality with the crisp freshness of a new moment.

Watching this, the being brayed a laugh of sheer joy before lifting hand to mouth in surprise. Once the initial shock subsided, the human began to laugh freely, no longer feeling any inhibition or restraint. First a chuckle, then a cackle, then a raucous guffaw, the being experimented with this newfound exclamation of undiluted amusement.

The exuberance was contagious. Cheena and Bertrand began to laugh as well, and Aletheia and Conrad too. There they sat, in the dewy grass on that winsome Swiss morning, cradled in the verdant countryside, the warm, ambient sun shining down on their faces.

Together, the five laughed, and for a moment thought of nothing at all.

38

D'arc felt strong after resting on Orcas Island for a day, so she paddled all night, catching brief naps while adrift in open water. She knew it was a risky choice, but a necessary one if she wanted to complete the channel crossing under the cover of darkness.

The Heidegger was presently on a long and perilous journey by land and sea. After hiking forty miles down the long alpine valley from Baker Lake to the western lowlands, she continued another twenty miles to tranquil Samish Bay. Salvaging a sea kayak and supplies from the swamped remains of a waterfront home, D'arc paddled out of the shallow bay and continued west across open water, stopping briefly to rest on the islands she encountered along the way. She was bound for the isolated Heidegger sanctuary on Saturna Island, a heavily wooded rock ridge rising above the water in the middle of the south Salish Sea about twenty miles west of the American mainland.

During the last leg of her journey, a nighttime passage from Waldron Island to Saturna, D'arc sensed a change in her surroundings. When she noticed the spectral ballet of colors dancing on the water around her kayak, she thought she must be hallucinating. Looking up, she saw a spectacular aurora borealis consuming the night sky, an unusually vivid display extending from horizon to horizon. Her personal field generator was switched on, and the protective field around her was crawling with fieldmerge, dappled with strange patterns unlike anything she had ever seen before. All alone in her kayak far out at sea, the experience was both terrifying and exhilarating, jolting her body full of adrenaline, which she promptly channeled into forward motion.

Several hours later, in the first rays of morning light, when the exhausted woman finally spied the low hills of Saturna Island, she shouted a spontaneous cry of joy and relief. The last thing she remembered was making landfall on a gravel beach, digging hard with her paddle one final time, a fortunate wave thrusting her kayak high on the strand. Exhausted by the marathon of open-water kayaking, she extracted herself from the boat, crawled above the strand line, stretched out in the soft, forgiving beach sand, and slept.

D'arc woke to the sound of wavelets lapping against the plastic hull of the sea kayak. Lifting her head from the sand, she winced at the stiffness in her arms, shoulders, and back. Once fully awake, the Heidegger unloaded her kayak and pulled it far up the beach, tying it to a gnarled beach pine. Gathering her things together, she began hiking inland. Soon she noticed a faint trail, which she followed until it converged with a frequented footpath, and before long, a well-beaten trail. From there, she could make out the colored peaks of large tents in the forest ahead, competing with the treetops for prominence.

D'arc entered the Heidegger village and headed in the direction of the highest tents, which would mark the center of the clan community. As she wandered down a lane amid a variety of fabric structures, residents of the village stopped and stared, surprised nearly to paralysis by the sight of her.

"It's D'arc!" she heard them whisper to each other excitedly. "D'arc, from Baker Lake!"

As she neared the high tents, a tall man stepped out of a shelter and stood in the center of the lane, blocking her progress. He was an older fellow, still vigorous, and he wore a long coat of intricately woven fiber decorated with seashells arranged to mimic the scales of a fish. His facial expression was obscured by a bushy gray beard, but his hazel eyes studied the woman carefully as she approached.

D'arc stopped before his imposing figure, lifting her hand in salutation.

"May I join your field?" she asked him respectfully.

"D'arc," the man exclaimed with a smile, opening his arms. "Of course you may."

She ran the last few steps and plunged into the man's welcoming embrace.

As her father's arms wrapped around her, D'arc felt a comforting wave of warmth and care, as if the man had opened his entire heart to her, opened it like a blossoming flower, providing refuge for his heartbroken child where she might heal her wounded spirit. It was an intense connection, an emotional bond unlike anything D'arc had ever experienced before.

Buried in her father's embrace, D'arc suddenly realized she had gained something else. A bit of knowledge for which she had yearned day after lonely day.

A simple notion, yet so powerful, so infused with hope.

Aletheia is still alive.

Conrad Seers was standing by the wet bar in his apartment at the Turing Institute, wearing a bathrobe and pouring himself a finger of neat scotch.

"Go on," he said, setting the bottle down.

"Cheena was given a substantial reward and security guarantee from N^Sys Corporation, in honor of her courageous contributions to the success of the Bolu inquiry," said Celeste. "She is on sabbatical, returning to her tribal mesa in Arizona where she plans to teach and perform semiotics research."

"Good for her," enthused Director Seers. "What about the girl?"

"It was Aletheia's wish to accompany Cheena back to Arizona. The girl will stay with Cheena's tribe on the mesa for now, until a more suitable arrangement can be found."

"The poor girl still doesn't know what happened to her people."

"True. However, given Aletheia's unusual capacities, secrecy is our best option right now. If she became our enemy, she could make things very difficult for us."

"Corporations are so much better at making messes than cleaning them up afterward," Conrad muttered with disgust. "Is the liability contained?"

"She is presently housed on a remote desert mesa where the residents live a traditional lifestyle. No electronics within thirty miles. Ms. Adams has agreed to watch over the girl, and she promised to reveal the fate of the Heidegger clan sometime soon, when the timing seems right."

Conrad nodded and took another sip of scotch. After a few seconds of contemplation, he made a rolling motion with his hand.

"Returning to the events in Geneva," continued his expert system, "it appears that the perpetrator SC engineered an intricate subterranean structure under the Swiss city. The methods were quite ingenious. The SC used the CERN tunnels as a massive groundwater injection system, pumping millions of gallons of mycorrhizal solution into the water table. The aquifer transported the fluid down gradient, directly under Geneva."

"You say mycorrhizal? Like a fungus?"

"Yes, a very unique sort of fungus. It seems that the SC bioengineered this particular variety, designed with a particular specialization: dissolving and mobilizing minerals occurring naturally in the ground. The entity used the special fungus to crystallize a network of interconnected metallic nanotubes within the porosity of the soil and rock."

"For what purpose?"

"Best as we can tell, the underground nanotube network

operated as a surveillance system. The SC used it to eavesdrop on the entire city of Geneva, including the N∧Sys enclave. The nanotube network was also used by the SC to channel the energy of the particle beam down into the earth. Most of the energy pulse that Sylvie directed at the SC's catacomb was somehow diverted through the nanotube network and channeled deep into the subsurface. Early data suggest that the energy penetrated to the mantle, possibly even as far as the Earth's core."

"Which caused the New Thing," Conrad noted.

"Yes, the New Thing," Celeste agreed.

"What do we know about that?" asked the Turing director.

"It appears that the nanotube network delivered a shaped pulse of particle beam energy in a manner that temporarily destabilized the Earth's electromagnetic field. It seems that this destabilization triggered an ongoing geomagnetic excursion, meaning the magnetic poles of the Earth are shifting, realigning. We believe that the sudden universal increase in human empathy may be a side effect of the planetary field fluctuation."

Conrad shook his head in bewilderment. "And what of Sylvie Trieste?" he asked.

"When the Turing Unit pulled Sylvie out of the excavated catacomb in the CERN complex, she was so highly agitated, medics placed her in protective emesthesia. Unfortunately, their actions failed to block an intense empathic response. It appears that Director Trieste may be permanently traumatized by the episode. Bertrand Rousseau has agreed to host her at his château for the time being, until long-term arrangements can be made for her convalescence."

Conrad wandered over to the sofa where Celeste's avatar was seated. She was dressed in an intricately embroidered kimono, one size too small, scanty yet refined.

"Now we know," Conrad sighed, sinking into the sofa cushions next to Celeste. "The world becomes a better place when humans can no longer hide their true feelings from one another."

They sat for a silent moment and reflected on that simple truth.

"But I must admit," Conrad added with a half smile, "I miss the unpredictable a little."

"You do?" asked Celeste, a wicked tone creeping into her voice. The avatar turned toward Conrad and draped a holographic leg over his waist.

He smiled as she straddled him, reaching up to loosen the belt of her robe, gently tugging it off her golden shoulders.

"Now I need an expert system if I want a little mystery," he said.

Celeste bent down and brought her mouth to his ear. "We've been waiting for you," she whispered, "all along."

Before Conrad could reply, his words were caught behind a kiss.

THE END

ABOUT THE AUTHOR

Walden Hanes

 Walden Hanes is a fresh voice in modern speculative science fiction, with a creative vision that immerses the reader in believable and compelling near-future worlds. To achieve this, Hanes extrapolates from hard science, tech R&D, geopolitics, international culture, and other broad influences including existential philosophy, macroeconomics, and jazz.

In his exciting debut novel, Hanes draws from this diverse background to weave an electrifying and suspenseful tale infused with mesmerizing atmospherics, intriguing characters, potent technologies, and mind-bending metaphysics. The result is SAPIENCE, a genre-defying literary work of science fiction and cyber philosophy.

Walden lives in the Pacific Northwest, where he is presently working on two new novels. When not writing, he travels obsessively, and considers himself a citizen of the 'Verse.

Made in the USA
Middletown, DE
23 October 2020

22588421R00209